BABY GRAND

BY DINA SANTORELLI

D1377970

Stonesong Custom

Designed by Peter Romeo, Wooly Head Design
Cover design by Natanya Wheeler
Produced by Stonesong www.stonesong.com

BABY GRAND

BY DINA SANTORELLI

To Fay,
All best!
Dina Santorelli :)

1

Baby Charlotte clung to the skirt of the sofa. She yanked the dense pleats this way and that with her tiny fist as if testing their construction, their ability to withstand duress. Satisfied, she extended her left hand up to the top of the seat cushion, her fat fingers clawing at the white piping along the perimeter, but after several attempts, including a last-ditch swat, she relented and laid down her arm. Quickly, as if not to lose momentum, she reached up with her right hand and grabbed a good chunk of upholstered fabric in the middle of the seat, and, while working her other hand up to steady herself, planted her feet and pulled on the material so hard that she let out a little grunt.

Stunned, Charlotte stood against the sofa front, her arms stiff and locked into place, her hold so tight that the pink skin around her knuckles had become blotchy. She peered at the tops of the cushions, the silk decorative pillows, the things she rarely saw from her usual ground-level vantage point. Then she let go, holding her hands in the air dramatically, as if she were performing a death-defying circus act, and stood on her own, wobbling, for a full second before toppling back down onto her diapered bottom, a puff of baby powder released upon impact. She giggled.

From a few yards away, Rosalia giggled too. She had been watching the determined ten-month-old for days as she attempted to stand on her own. It seemed like only yesterday that those blonde curls were zigzagging their way across the floor in a hurry. The only crawling Charlotte did now was straight toward the walls or sofas or coffee tables—any vertical surface, really—so that she could begin her climbing regimen. That morning at breakfast, Rosalia caught Charlotte, who was eating Cheerios in her high chair, studying the back-and-forth of her legs as she wandered about the kitchen. Rosalia tried to move a little slower for her rapt spectator, conscious of every step and muscle flex. It took her twice as long to unload the dishwasher and clean the countertop, but she enjoyed the attention—it had been a long time since anyone took such interest in her legs.

Now Charlotte had decided to try a new tack: she placed her palms on the floor under her shoulders as if she were going to do a push-up and straightened her legs. With this approach, her butt arched up into the air and wiggled, but her little knees gave out, and she tumbled to the hardwood floor again.

"*Hmpf*," Rosalia groaned, eyeing the unforgiving surface of the strip flooring.

As beautiful as genuine hardwood was, Rosalia always had been fearful that the baby would hurt herself with every move across the floorboards. She had been only too happy to see several area rugs being brought into the house, which not only warmed up the worn, aged look of the historically decorated living and dining rooms but offered Charlotte more comfortable spots to crawl and play.

Charlotte had found something interesting in the far corner of the room—the latest issue of *Time* magazine—and, taking a break from standing, crawled her way over to it. Rosalia left the kitchen to be sure that Charlotte would not be getting into any trouble, that there were no electrical wires or loose, small objects lying around, and took the opportunity to walk upon the sumptuous threading of the Persian area rug in the living room with her bare feet. Mrs. Grand frowned upon the staff taking their shoes off when indoors, even late at night or on the weekends, but neither the governor nor his wife were home, so Rosalia took the opportunity to stretch her tired arches. The hand-sewn rug felt good on her soles, and she bunched the pile fibers between her crooked toes. Rosalia smiled as Charlotte leaned backward and kicked her feet toward the ceiling and appeared to be reading the magazine, which was upside-down, over her head.

The arrival of little Charlotte to the Grand household had been a blessing to Rosalia and had reignited a fire in her belly. Her own two children, who were grown and living downstate in Queens while attending college, didn't seem much interested in babies—having them or acting like them, not even for the sake of their aging and lonely mother—so Rosalia was more than thrilled when Mrs. Grand told her that she was *with child*, as she put it; she'd said it as an afterthought during Rosalia's year-end evaluation two Christmases ago. Rosalia suspected that Mrs. Grand had become pregnant mostly to please the press and her husband's constituents, and after the baby was born, the governor's wife seemed to want nothing more than to get back to her social calendar, which was a dream come true for the lonely housekeeper, who would become Charlotte's primary caretaker.

Those first few weeks after Charlotte had been brought home, Rosalia had begun spending some nights at the mansion, rocking the baby to sleep and singing her the songs that Rosalia's own mother used to sing to give her good dreams. Rosalia had met every feeding and diaper change with enthusiasm and would sometimes just let Charlotte sleep in her arms during the day so that she could feel the warmth of her body against her breast. In the past ten months, Baby Charlotte had grown into a beautiful, inquisitive, and headstrong child.

Having spotted Rosalia, Charlotte scooted across the wood floor toward her, but made a pit stop at the center of the area rug in the main dining room, where her favorite doll, Miss Beatrice, whom Charlotte called MaBa, had been abandoned earlier.

Rosalia returned to the kitchen to continue unpacking groceries. She sensed that she was running late, and she was right. It was nearly ten o'clock, time for Charlotte's morning nap. Rosalia tried to keep Charlotte on a strict schedule, so that she could do most of her chores in the morning and leave the afternoon free for playtime.

There was a tug on her polyester skirt. Charlotte was trying to pull herself up, but she was slipping on the marble floor.

"*Ay, Carlota!*" Rosalia said, bending down to scoop up the child. She ran her hand through Charlotte's tiny blond curls, and the child mimicked her motions by wrapping her little hand around Rosalia's long gray hair.

"Time for a nap, my angel," Rosalia said, kissing Charlotte's forehead. "We play later."

The nursery, tucked away on the top floor of the mansion away from the publicly viewed rooms, was a pale shade of yellow, and the furnishings were made of delicately hand-carved brazilwood, which also complemented a small bookshelf and an old-fashioned rocker. It was a pretty little space, decorated by some local designers who got their pictures in the area newspapers for their handiwork. The afternoon sun shone through the large window on the southern wall, and a cool, gentle breeze caused the sheer drapes to billow, giving the room a fresh scent.

Rosalia placed Charlotte on her back in the crib, covered her with the checkered blanket that she had knitted, wound the mobile above her head, and placed a gentle kiss on her forehead. "*Te amo, Cara,*" she whispered.

As Rosalia was leaving, she heard tiny protests from Charlotte, who remained lying on her back and peering at her through the crib bars, the blanket still neatly placed up to her neck. The child hadn't moved, but her eyes had followed Rosalia across the room, and her usually happy face had turned into a slight pout. Rosalia blew a kiss toward the crib as Charlotte's eyes blinked with drowsiness, and she turned and left.

Downstairs, Rosalia entered the kitchen and turned on the baby monitor. She could hear Charlotte still making some weak sounds of disapproval. Rosalia took some boxes of crackers off the table to put into the pantry, which was well stocked with foods of all ethnicities and types, including a variety of cookies, the governor's not-so-secret guilty pleasure. Sometimes Rosalia would come to work in the morning and find cookie crumbs hastily brushed into the corners of the pantry floor and brand-new boxes of candy-topped chocolate-chip cookies, purchased the day before, half-eaten and stowed under full boxes. More than once, the governor had chastised Rosalia in front of Mrs. Grand for buying the bargain brand cookies, but when she wasn't looking someone inevitably would scribble things like *Mini Oreos* and *Chewy Chips Ahoy* at the bottom of her shopping lists. Rosalia never tattled, and she suspected that was one of the reasons she managed to stick around for six years, well into the governor's second term, while her coworkers seemed to come and go.

Rosalia glanced at the baby monitor, which was now silent, the red indicator light showing an uninterrupted glow. She smiled and grabbed some more groceries to put away.

After the kitchen counter was cleared, Rosalia ran her palm over the smooth granite, feeling for crumbs, and spotted Miss Beatrice lying facedown near the dishwasher. She picked up the doll and examined it. The threading was beginning to unravel under the left arm; she'd have to fix that. Rosalia brought the doll to her face and brushed it against her cheek. She could smell Charlotte's shampoo on the fabric, and there were traces of baby powder in the seams. She tucked the doll under her arm and walked back up the staircase.

The nursery was quiet. She tiptoed over to the far wall and placed Miss Beatrice on the top bookshelf with all of Charlotte's other doll friends who leaned lazily on one another with the familiarity of old pals. Then Rosalia had a thought: She picked Miss Beatrice up again, brushed her off, and matted down her hair as she walked toward Charlotte's crib. She smiled as she brought Miss Beatrice up over the bars to place next to the sleeping child.

But the crib was empty.

2

J amie wiped the sweat from her palms onto the sides of her skirt, pushing down so hard that the linen hem moved forward and covered her knees. She had done it so many times that she imagined making grooves on her thighs in the way pacers wore holes in carpeting.

She had been sitting in the lobby for nearly fifteen minutes, watching flamboyantly dressed men and very skinny women in short skirts hurry in and out of elevators chatting amicably; some held breakfast or stacks of papers in their hands, others zipped through with cell phones pasted to their ears, and, as if by consensus, all passed by with nary a glance at her. She sat a little straighter, imagining that invisible string pulling her up toward the ceiling, like her yoga instructor once had suggested, and tried to look calm and bored like when she rode the subways and wanted to thwart the would-be pickpockets hunting tourists. To pass the time, she tried to guess which of the four elevator doors would open next.

A repairman was fixing a burnt-out recessed lightbulb high above Jamie's head, causing threadlike dust to hang and tumble in the air. She swished herself to the left on the long, leather bench to avoid being hit, but it was too late. Using her suit sleeve, she brushed off the top of her black binder, in which her entire professional career was neatly presented on 8½" x 11" paper—her hot-off-the-printer resume, letters of recommendation, names and addresses in case she needed references, and clips of freelance articles she'd written, in reverse chronological order. And tucked under the front inside flap was a disk, carefully labeled with a Sharpie and containing digital files of everything she had on paper. She reached in to make sure it was still there and hadn't fallen out in transit. It was. *Relax, you're ready*, she told herself.

The receptionist, a pretty, young blonde, was deftly handling the phones, signing for packages, and greeting workers. She glanced at Jamie and said, "Ms. Wiles knows you're here and will be right with you."

"Thanks," Jamie smiled as a rolling rack jam-packed with clothing came speeding through the reception area led by two harried young women.

"Ms. Carter?"

Jamie looked up to see a tall, slender woman wearing a suit with a very short skirt. Her hair was auburn and tied back in a neat bun, and her eyeglasses were small and stylish.

"Yes." Jamie stood up and shook the editor's hand.

"I'm sorry to keep you waiting. A morning meeting ran long. Would you like some coffee?"

"No, thank you," Jamie said.

She followed Ms. Wiles through the glass doors and was struck by the expanse of the publishing company's editorial offices. There must have been two hundred cubicles all lined in a neat, little maze, with heads bobbing in and out of view and voices that were loud but not understandable.

A petite girl with a ring where her left eyebrow was supposed to be ran up to Ms. Wiles as soon as they turned the first corner. "Lauren, we just got the photos for the taffeta story, and I think you need to take a look at them."

"I'll be there in a few minutes," Ms. Wiles said and continued walking.

"Lauren!" a man yelled, sticking his head out of a cubicle about ten feet away. "We need you!"

"Five minutes!" Ms. Wiles thundered, holding up the five fingers of her right hand for emphasis. She turned to Jamie and rolled her eyes as she guided her to a room on the left, where there was a conference table and two people sitting at the far end.

"I need this office," Ms. Wiles said to the man and woman, who scrambled to get their things and leave. Once they did, Ms. Wiles closed the door.

"Are Tuesdays always this crazy?" Jamie asked.

"Every day is this crazy," Ms. Wiles said, taking a seat at the head of the table.

The door opened, and before a young man in a Led Zeppelin T-shirt could say anything, Ms. Wiles said, "Five minutes, please."

The door closed again.

"So," Ms. Wiles said, "what brings you to Gerbury Communications?"

"Well," Jamie said, her stomach twinging, "I'm looking for full-time work. Freelancing's great, but it's not reliable."

"*Hmmm*," Ms. Wiles nodded. Jamie could feel the editor studying her, trying to make quick judgments about her work ethic, about her ability to fit into the magazine's hectic setting, all in the ten seconds she'd known her. "Is that your portfolio?"

"Yes." Jamie pushed her black binder across the table.

"Let's see what you got . . ." Ms. Wiles looked over Jamie's resume. "*Hmmm*, you worked at *USA Baby*?"

"Yes, I was an associate editor for about a year."

"Do you know Karen Jennings?"

Jamie shook her head. "No, I don't think so."

"Oh, I think she left before you got there. Why did you leave?"

"I was laid off."

"*Hmmm* . . ." Ms. Wiles continued flipping through the pages of Jamie's portfolio. "Have you ever written about fashion before?"

"Well, yes, I did, but for children."

"No, I mean, ready-to-wear, couture, that kind of thing."

"No, not really,"—*c'mon, Jamie, sell yourself*—"but as you'll see from my clips, I have a very diverse portfolio as a freelance writer. I've covered everything from swimming to nursing to—"

"Yes, I see, you've been keeping busy."

Keeping busy. Like she had been knitting a sweater.

"Well, I tried to . . ."

"The thing is, though, Jenny . . ."

"Jamie."

"Oh, I'm sorry, Jamie. . . . The thing is that we really need someone who knows the markets. We don't have the time to train anyone."

"I'm a fast learner," Jamie said, trying not to sound—although she knew she did—too eager.

"I'm sure you are, honey, and these pieces look wonderful, but I'm afraid we're looking for someone already familiar with this territory. Fashion can be murder."

"So can screaming toddlers."

"You haven't met our models."

Jamie forced a smile.

Ms. Wiles stood up. "You know . . ." She handed Jamie her portfolio, "Our division also has a parenting book. It's for the trade, not the consumer market. If you like, I can give your name to the editor there."

"That would be great. That's very nice of you."

"Oh, it's nothing, really." Ms. Wiles extended her hand. "Well, it was nice meeting you."

Jamie shook it. "You too, and good luck with everything," she said, motioning to the office door.

"Yes, I'll need it." Ms. Wiles opened the conference room door, and five anxious-looking people holding paperwork were standing behind it led by the guy in the Led Zeppelin T-shirt. "Good luck to you too. I'm sure you'll find something that suits you."

3

etective Sergeant Mark Nurberg peered out the missing infant's nursery window, which was three stories up from ground level. He had never been to the governor's mansion before. The view was breathtaking. Perched on a hill above the Hudson, the stately home was surrounded by lush and delicately landscaped greenery, all with a historic air: The weeping elm in the back of the house had been planted by Governor Charles Whitman to commemorate the birth of his son, and the sugar maple to the left was planted by President Harry Truman and Governor Averell Harriman in observance of Arbor Day on April 25, 1958.

Nurberg turned his attention inside, where two forensics officers were finishing up and the governor's housekeeper was sitting still in a rocking chair. The team already had been through this room several times and found nothing. It was as if the child had just vanished.

Since joining Albany PD's Children and Family Services Unit two years ago, Nurberg had seen his share of domestic-violence incidents, juvenile delinquencies, sex-offender violations, and other crimes where children were both victims and offenders. The CFSU team was relatively small, consisting of six detectives, two domestic-violence advocates, two detective sergeants and one detective lieutenant. Until today, there hadn't been a missing-persons case involving a child—let alone a toddler—or a crime this high profile.

Rosalia sat still in the rocking chair with her feet close together and Miss Beatrice in her hands; she absently played with the doll's hair. Nurberg walked over to her.

"Ma'am?"

Rosalia sat up straight and wiped her eyes. Her cheeks were flushed and puffy, and strands of her long, gray hair were wet and tucked behind her ears.

"Ma'am, my name is Detective Sergeant Mark Nurberg of the Children and Family Services Unit of the Albany Police Department." He bent down onto one knee next to Rosalia. "I know this is difficult, but can you tell me what happened?"

Rosalia took a deep breath. "I . . . I already told the other *policía*." She wiped again under her eyes, where the eyeliner and mascara were falling and leaving black circles.

"Yes," Nurberg said gently, "but I need you to tell me again, if that's all right?"

Rosalia nodded and told him what she had told the other officers and what she had gone over and over in her mind for the past two hours: She had placed Charlotte in her crib for a nap, like she always had, gone downstairs to put groceries away, and when she had returned, the child was gone.

"How long were you away, from the time you first put down the child to when you returned?" Nurberg asked.

"Not long," she said. "Maybe ten minutes or fifteen?"

"Okay. What happened next?"

"I . . . I . . . started screaming, and . . . Henry come running up."

"Who's Henry?" Nurberg asked. He knew the answer—in fact, he knew most of these answers—but wanted to hear it from the housekeeper.

"He drives the car for Governor Grand."

"Is that when you called the police?"

Rosalia shook her head. "Henry . . . he called the police."

"You didn't call?"

The skin around Rosalia's eyes tightened. "I . . . I . . ." She buried her head into Miss Beatrice, her cries muffled by the yarn of the doll's hair.

Nurberg stood up and looked down at the crumpled housekeeper, trying hard to resist the urge to put his hand on her shoulder. "Do you remember anything out of the ordinary? Anything that was different this time that can help us?"

Rosalia shook her head again.

"Where is Henry now, ma'am?"

"I don't know." Rosalia was talking to the floor, her eyes fixed on the doll in her hands.

"Ma'am, why don't you come with me downstairs? Have you had something to eat?"

"No, I want to stay here," she said.

"We'll need to cordon off this room in a little while. You can stay until then, but then you'll have to leave, all right?"

Rosalia nodded.

"Do the other officers know how to reach you if we need to speak with you again?"

"Yes."

"All right, then." Nurberg turned to leave when Rosalia grabbed his hand.

"Please, Detective . . . please find my baby." Her voice cracked. "She must be so scared. Who will calm her? Who will tuck her in? Who will know . . ."

"Mrs. Garcia," Nurberg said. The housekeeper's hand was trembling, and he placed his other hand over hers. There was a sweet sincerity in her eyes, a rare quality in Nurberg's line of work where glassy stares and averted eyes were the norm. "I'll do everything I can, ma'am. I promise."

As Nurberg exited the nursery, the word *promise* echoed in his ears. His thoughts flashed to his boss, Det. Lt. Grohl, in the way that a child thinks of a parent whenever he or she has done something wrong. Nurberg had a nasty habit, as Grohl liked to say, of making promises he couldn't keep. Last month, he had pledged to a young, distraught newlywed whose husband had disappeared after a drunken rampage that he would bring him back safely. The man was found dead hours later inside the valet booth of the parking lot behind the downtown Hampton Inn, apparently having gotten inside by breaking the glass and then using the shards to slit his wrists. "You're not Superman," Grohl had scolded. "Not all problems are fixable or cases solvable. If you make promises, then they have expectations and false hope. You have to remember that and just do the best you can." Since then, Nurberg had been tempering his assurances to the much more attainable *I'll do everything I can.* But in his attempt to shield the public from disappointment, he felt as though he was letting himself down.

"Excuse me, Detective Nurberg?" Det. Matrick stood on the top step of the mansion staircase. "The governor and Mrs. Grand are downstairs."

"Thank you," Nurberg nodded. "I'll be right there."

The governor and his wife had been across town, at the first of several personal appearances scheduled for Phillip Grand that day, when they received the call from Henry, who contacted them immediately after calling 911. Under normal circumstances, Henry would have accompanied the governor on these types of local outings, but he told police he had stayed behind because of a late-morning dental appointment—which, although it checked out, already was causing some speculation among the detectives. Gossip was also spreading fast about Mrs. Grand, who had answered Henry's call, since the governor was in the midst of a speech, and she had ostensibly allowed him to finish as well as field several questions from the press before breaking the news to him of their daughter's disappearance.

As his colleague descended, Nurberg lingered on the landing, his eyes resting on *The Marriage of Pocahontas*, a nineteenth-century oil on canvas by Henry Brueckner that hung at the base of the staircase within the realm of the public viewing areas. Although the mansion didn't have an official art collection, it was filled with striking paintings and sculptures throughout on loan from some of the state's museums. This particular one was donated by Governor Rockefeller and depicted Pocahontas' marriage to John Rolfe in Virginia in 1614 in a scene that was grand and romanticized, considering the actual setting for such a wedding probably would have been small and commonplace. And Pocahontas, who, as the story goes, saved adventurer John Smith from death at the hands of her father, appeared rather demure on the canvas, falling in line with traditional gender roles and perhaps obscuring the facts of history that described an energetic and courageous young woman whom generations had come to know through school books. Nurberg could not think of a better painting to hang inside the household of Governor and Mrs. Phillip Grand.

4

The traffic light turned green, and the crowd surged into the crosswalk. Jamie held her portfolio tight to her chest to keep it from being bumped by the other pedestrians and kept her hand locked on the strap of her pocketbook, the way her mom used to. Frank's Deli had been Jamie's favorite place to eat when she'd had a bad day at *USA Baby*, and she could already taste their homemade egg salad, a Brooklyn recipe that was reminiscent of the kind her grandmother used to make. She tried not to think about the interview at Gerbury, but it was impossible. That was the third interview this month. With so many writers out of work, it was going to be difficult to find something, even with her years of experience. And as magazines continued to fold, and content, particularly the long-form, objective kind that Jamie had been trained for, continued to become devalued with the rise of blogging and e-zines, she was never going to be able to pay her rent. She already owed her brother five hundred dollars from last month.

A taxi driver inched his way into the flow of pedestrians, trying to turn onto Sixth Avenue, the nose of his cab jutting forward not quite so gently and causing a few people to glare and give him the finger, but the driver remained impervious. Jamie stopped to let him go by, annoying the people who had been walking behind her, who huffed and puffed their way around her as if she were an obstructive buoy in a strong river current. As the taxi sped down Sixth, she was reminded of something her mother once told her when she had gotten her learner's permit:

"Driving is easy—go when it's green, stop when it's red. The real trick is learning to live your life that way." It was a maxim, as the taxi driver probably could attest, that Jamie could never quite master.

There was a bottleneck of people at the curb—customers exiting the deli, men and women waiting in line at the magazine kiosk, walkers trying to get by in every direction. As Jamie jostled her way through the patterns of people, the cover of *O, The Oprah Magazine*, hanging from the window of the kiosk, caught her eye:

SINK OR SWIM: THE TIME IS NOW TO LIVE THE LIFE YOU DESERVE.

Another headline below it, in purple, screamed out:

NEVER LOOK BACK: 10 SUREFIRE STEPS TO MOVE FORWARD.

The cover photo showed Oprah wearing a floral print dress with her feet up in the air on a children's swing and looking as happy as could be—the kind of carefree that, Jamie knew, came but once in a stream of digital photos featuring mostly closed eyes, awkward expressions, and misbehaving props, the kind of carefree that, she also knew, was probably one in a million in the real world. Still, she got in line, paid the four bucks for the magazine, and found a spot against the deli's dirty front window to flip through its pages as the nearby subway entrance emitted a harsh puff of warm air and a train rumbled somewhere below. Bob had always teased Jamie for buying *O*. He said it was a waste of money and time and that Oprah had made a living out of duping people into believing that what she said mattered; that alone made Jamie feel that it was the best four dollars she'd ever spent.

She looked north, across the street, where Bryant Park was filled with people. It was a beautiful day in Manhattan. The local weathermen had all predicted an unseasonably sunny and warm April day, and after a dreary morning of keyboard punching and sales meetings, modestly successful professionals were flocking to that tiny, renovated grass area, the only immediate and economically sound choice for weary fingers and brains.

The idea of sitting inside the deli and eating as fast as she could, only to dash onto the subway and catch the earliest Long Island Rail Road train home—Jamie's typical MO—suddenly lost its appeal. It was one thing if there were a destination that demanded hurrying off to—schoolchildren to escort off an afternoon bus, dinner to make for a returning husband, or even a rush-hour crowd to beat—but Jamie had none of those things awaiting her and nothing else planned for the day. For the first time in a long time, she was feeling untethered, which was a strange and unusual feeling for a thirty-two-year-old woman who had spent practically all her life as someone's *girl*—a mother's daughter, a brother's sister, a husband's wife. She looked again at the magazine in her hands:

NEVER LOOK BACK.

Across the street, a hot-dog vendor catered to a long line of patrons, and, on a whim, Jamie got on the back of the line, deciding to forgo the egg salad and the comforts of routine. "One with mustard and sauerkraut and a water, please," she said when it was her turn in line. The vendor never looked up as his hands flipped metal covers open and shut and his hands slid the dog into its bun. Years from now, Jamie imagined that she would remember this hot dog as emblematic of the beginning of a new life path, how she had chosen the hot dog of tomorrow rather than the egg salad of yesterday. She paid him and made her way toward Bryant Park.

It was hard to believe that Bryant Park, with its lovely gardens and European-flavored promenades, had seen its share of ill repute over the years. Back in the days of disco and graffiti-ridden subway cars, the park was an eyesore, a mainstay of muggers and drug lords, and was avoided by savvy New Yorkers. However, since that time, it had been transformed into a Manhattan oasis of lush greenery, while still retaining its "city park" feel with a spattering of historical monuments and urban amenities. In 1994, Bryant Park became the locale for Fashion Week, the semiannual fete in which clothing designers premiered their latest collections in invitation-only runway shows, but Jamie was glad when the event moved uptown to Lincoln Center a few years ago—the sudden intrusion of celebrity, hidden beneath a series of large white tents, made the park look to her as if it had sprung a glitzy fungal infection.

Jamie searched the grass for a chair, but the quest was formidable. Not quite 2:00 p.m., the lunchtime masses had descended upon this tiny patch of green hidden within Manhattan's vast concrete and steel landscape. Men, clad in business suits just ten minutes prior, were now stretched out on the grass—jackets off, ties loosened, and shoes and socks placed neatly beside them. Women of all shapes and sizes were baring midriffs and painted toes.

Jamie navigated the grounds, asking sheepishly, "Is this seat taken?," but to no avail. Manhattanites could be territorial about their seating, hurling unwanted jackets, pocketbooks, and brown paper bags on chairs that, if not in use now, must be available to hold their elevated feet at a moment's notice. *Oprah would never approve*, she thought with a smile.

A couple was sitting at a table near the park's entrance, where there was an extra, empty chair beside them, but the gentleman pulled the seat closer to him when he noticed Jamie and leaned his forearm across its top. In the distance she spotted a bench that appeared vacant just off the grass. She quickly made her way across the park, balancing her lunch on the magazine on top of her portfolio. When she got there, she realized that one of the legs was broken, making the bench wobbly, which explained its availability. She decided to sit down anyway, careful not to lean back too much and to keep most of her weight on her left side.

It wasn't until her bottom had touched the cool metal of the seat that she realized how nice it was to sit down. When the full-time employment in Manhattan had stopped, so had the walking, since driving was pretty much the only way to get around in the suburbs, and she found that the tiniest aerobic exercise exhausted her. She unfolded the aluminum foil from around her hot dog and unscrewed the cap from her water, careful to place her pocketbook on the foil, so it would not go flying into the breeze, and keeping her arm looped through its straps while she ate.

The bright afternoon sun blazed down upon the park, and she put her sunglasses on and scanned the evolving crowd, which seemed to change minute by minute like the ebb and flow of a tide. In the center of the grass was a woman sitting alone and sipping what looked like an iced cappuccino, judging by the insignia of her tall paper cup. She was tanned from head to toe with skin tones that contrasted with her white suit, consisting of a halter top and miniskirt, and she had that relaxed, LA look about her—one of her white sandals had been tossed carelessly onto the grass, while the other dangled from the big toe of her left foot. To Jamie's left, a man was lying in the grass with his arms and legs stretched out as if he were making an angel in snow. People stepped over him in their search to find a vacant chair, but he didn't budge, seemingly unaware that anyone was around. Further west, near the Sixth Avenue entrance, a dark-haired, broad-shouldered man in a black suit leaned on the veterans' monument. Everything was still on—his suit jacket over a white-collared shirt, which was unbuttoned at the top revealing a large gold cross—and he was wearing dark sunglasses with his arms crossed over his chest, a far cry from the untroubled mood of the crowd. Jamie took another bite of her hot dog and watched several sheepish-looking men approach the woman in white and hover around her like bees while she stretched her arms in the air like she'd just awoken from a nap, her shifting halter top revealing a silver belly ring.

Jamie looked down at her own double-breasted suit that she had plucked from the can-wear-one-more-time-before-dry-cleaning rack in her closet. She imagined her body language wasn't enticing anyone to just wander over and chat. *Did she even remember how to do that?* She looked again at the man in black. Jamie probably looked as unapproachable as he did.

"Excuse me," someone said, making Jamie instinctively tighten her grip on her pocketbook. "Do you have the time?"

In front of her was a short, balding man in a tracksuit wearing the kind of eyeglasses that strapped around one's entire head. He was still jogging, in place, looking a bit tense, waiting for Jamie to answer. She pulled out her phone.

"Yes, it's just about two o'clock," she said.

"Thank you." The man jogged there for a few seconds longer than he should have, according to Jamie's standards, before nodding and heading off toward Sixth Avenue.

Jamie kept her eye on him, hoping he wouldn't turn back around, since he looked a bit creepy. She marveled at how in a park packed with people, the guy had chosen to approach her, kind of like how she always managed to be the one to come home with all the mosquito bites after a summer outing while everyone else got away scot-free; the whole bit her mother used to give her about being so sweet did little to stem the itching, although she had to admit that it did make her feel better. She wondered if it was her sweetness that prompted jogger-guy to stop by, or whether it was more likely that Jamie looked as if she had nothing better to do than dig in her bag for her phone. Jogger-guy hurried up the park entrance steps and out onto Sixth Avenue, passing right by the man in black who still stood by the veterans' monument with his arms folded. *Had he not moved all this time,* Jamie wondered.

Her phone vibrated in her hands. It was a text from her brother Edward.

HOW DID IT GO?

Jamie smiled at the four little words, which reminded her that, despite her feelings of isolation, or freedom, she did have someone she was still tethered to. She texted back:

SHITTY.

She waited a moment. The phone vibrated again.

THEIR LOSS.

She smiled and wrote:

DAMN STRAIGHT!

She was watching the men wave and walk away from the blonde sun goddess in the grass when another text arrived:

WHEN ARE YOU HEADING BACK?

Jamie wrote:

WHAT R U WRITING A BOOK? :)

Within seconds came the reply:

NO, BUT U SHOULD B.

Jamie sighed. Edward never gave up. He had been encouraging her to write fiction since she won a short-story contest in the fifth grade—a story that she got to read on a local radio station. And as much as she pooh-poohed the idea to friends and colleagues, becoming a creative writer had been a longtime dream of Jamie's, a dream she had set aside when she took a job at a local newspaper just out of college, a dream that she kept aside while married to Bob. Somewhere, lurking in the deep recesses of her brain, and her hard drive, three enthusiastically started but abandoned novels lay dying.

Another text arrived:

DINNER TONITE. MY TREAT. B/C U R UNEMPLOYED & BROKE . . .

And then another text:

AND DIVORCED & LONELY . . .

Jamie smiled and started to text back when her phone vibrated again:

& UGLY 2 . . .

Jamie laughed out loud. She typed:

SOUNDS GOOD & I'M HAVING DESSERT!

She put her phone away and turned her attention back to the blonde who was now packing up her things and presumably returning to work. Lunchtime was coming to a close, as more and more chairs lay abandoned and New Yorkers prepared to suck it up for just a few more hours until the five o'clock whistle. Jamie, of course, had nowhere to go. At least, not until dinnertime.

A little girl about four or five years old popped into view, hopping along in front of a woman who was beseeching her to "slow down" and "stay with mommy." Her young face was radiant, with her long, dark hair pulled back into a ponytail and a slight sunburn on her cheeks and the bridge of her nose. When she slowed down so that her mother could catch up and take her hand, she surveyed the park with fascination and caught Jamie watching her; she responded with a smile and a wave, which Jamie returned.

From the corner of her eye, Jamie saw the man in black wave too and wondered if he mistakenly had gotten the impression that she had been waving to him, and not the little girl, but then he settled back against the veterans' monument as before, hands crossed in front of him, left leg bent. *He must have seen someone he knew*, she thought. Only there was something different about him now, and it took her a moment to realize what it was—he was smiling. It was hard to see, because his face looked as impassive as before, but the corners of his mouth were turned up; Jamie was sure of it, because the shadows on his face had changed. Then he began to move methodically, almost robotically, unfolding his arms, brushing down his suit sleeves, which had bunched up in the crooks of his elbows, and bending his right leg up from the knee, and then his left, as if he were about to go for a jog right now in his black tailored suit. When he brought his left hand up toward his sunglasses, Jamie was rapt, as if in the audience of an open-air theater, eager to see the elusive man behind the shades, the man who seemed to exist unnoticed by the mass of people leaving the park, as unnoticed as the stone monument behind him. And as he lifted the sunglasses off the bridge of his nose, her entire body froze.

He was staring at her.

Jamie nearly toppled over on her wobbly bench. Her flight response kicked in, and she had the sudden urge to run, to just get up and go, the kind of thing adults tell children to do when they're in trouble, but instead she stayed put, telling herself that she had to be mistaken. She looked to the right and left of her, but no one was there, and her mind filled with questions: *Had he been staring at her all this time? Does he think he knows her? Does he know that she had been looking at him too? Was she overreacting?* Then the man in black moved again, this time at an angle to the monument, his body turned so that he was facing her. In a flash, his right hand was in the air, waving, a broad, purposeful wave, the kind you see at a rock concert.

Now the alarm bells were sounding, since Jamie had ignored the original distress notification, but, again, instead of hightailing it out of the park, she did the complete opposite—she sat perfectly still as if she were a small animal finding itself face-to-face with a predator in the forest.

What are you doing, she asked herself. *Get the hell out of here.*

She yawned and, as nonchalantly as possible, stood up from her chair, pretending she hadn't noticed him at all, that she had just decided it was time to go, although her hand trembled fiercely as she placed her bottled water into her paper bag. The park still had a good amount of people, but it suddenly seemed so empty, like the man in black could just reach out and touch her even though they were a half a block's length apart.

Jamie picked up her portfolio and magazine and tossed the rest of her lunch into a nearby trash can. Then, without hesitation, she walked east, away from him, with purpose, like she had somewhere to be. She walked as fast as she could without looking like she was trying to.

The boundaries of the park were crowded, and she was walking against the tide. She looked at the magazine cover in her hands:

NEVER LOOK BACK.

But now she couldn't help it. As she crossed through the park's south exit, Jamie glanced at the spot where the man in black had stood. But no one was there. She lifted her sunglasses up and looked once again over the tops of the heads around her. She looked in the grass, by her chair. He was nowhere.

As she flipped her sunglasses back down, someone grabbed her shoulder and jerked her body forward. Before she realized it, someone was kissing her hard—too hard. She couldn't breathe. She couldn't move, and she felt the lunchtime crowd surging around her:

"Hey, asshole, get out of the way!"

"Jesus Christ, get a room, buddy."

She felt bodies brushing past her and the strength of the man holding her, and she tried to pull away, but something sharp was digging into her side, and her arms were pinned against her portfolio, which was trapped against his large chest as he squeezed her against him. She squirmed and tried to reach up, but her arms felt like they were caught in a vise and only her fingers could move, and when they did, they felt the coldness of the large gold cross hanging from his neck.

"Don't make a fucking sound or I'll kill you," the man in black breathed into her mouth.

Jamie's eyes welled with fearful tears that no one saw through her dark sunglasses.

5

"Keep walking," the man said, holding Jamie tight against him and pressing the sharp object into her right side. His left hand reached into her pocket, took out her phone and placed it into his own jacket pocket. He grabbed her portfolio and carried it at his side, like a businessman, as the magazine fell to the ground.

Jamie felt her legs giving out beneath her as they hurried down Fortieth Street. She stumbled, but the man held her so tightly that she was forced to move her feet in step with his. She wanted to scream. She thought of all the people who would say at her funeral, "Why didn't she yell for help? There were hundreds of people around her." But she couldn't cough out a word. She could barely breathe and felt what she knew was warm blood, dribbling down her right side, as the sharp object dug deeper into her.

The man crossed diagonally against oncoming traffic to the south side of Fortieth. As Jamie walked, her eyes, behind her sunglasses, beseeched every passerby. She tried to mouth the words, *Help me*, but everyone was busy: Taking photos of buildings, of each other. Texting. Chatting. Laughing. No one looked at her.

As they approached Fifth Avenue, a black limousine stuck out noticeably at the intersection, causing irritated pedestrians to walk around it. As they got within a few yards of it, the back door opened.

"Get in," the man said to her.

Jamie's knees buckled.

"Do you want to die here?" he said through a feigned smile, holding her up and pressing the knife deeper into her side.

Before she could react, she was pushed onto the floor of the limousine, the door was shut, and the limousine sped off into traffic.

Inside, the stench of cigarette smoke was asphyxiating, as Jamie was thrown back and forth while the car made a series of hard turns. It took her eyes a few moments to adjust to the darkness of the car, and she realized that she and the man weren't alone. There were others.

She looked up at the new faces. Two men. One wearing a suit, the other wearing jeans and a white T-shirt.

"This is the one you picked?" asked the bald man in the suit sitting just behind the driver.

"Shut the fuck up and put her out," said the man who had grabbed her, who was sitting in the backseat on the passenger side. He and the bald man seized her shoulders.

"Get off me. What do you want?" Jamie screamed, feeling lightheaded from the cigarette fumes. She slapped at the dark, smoky air, the edge of her sunglasses getting caught on her sleeve and falling to the floor as the car windows were systematically rolled up, closing out any last traces of blue sky.

As they wrestled her down, Jamie's eyes went to the man in the jeans, who reached down to pick up her sunglasses, neatly folded them, and placed them onto his lap. She realized that he wasn't a man at all, but a kid, maybe about sixteen or seventeen years old.

"You're just gonna fuckin' sit there?" the bald man asked him.

"Leave him alone," the man in black said, pulling Jamie's arms behind her back while trying to secure her kicking legs.

"Take it easy, sweetheart," said the bald guy. He took a handkerchief out of his pocket. "This won't hurt a bit."

Jamie spat at him, which elicited a loud chuckle from the driver. The bald man slapped her. "Are you fuckin' kidding me?" he said, grabbing her neck.

"Hey," roared the man in black. "Knock it off."

The bald man hesitated and then pushed the handkerchief, which was wet, over Jamie's mouth. The smell was horrible, and she started gagging.

"No more spitting for you, Dimples," the bald guy said, holding his hand over her mouth.

Suddenly, Jamie found it more and more difficult to kick her legs, feeling as if she had fallen into a pool of water and was fighting the resistance. Her breathing was becoming labored, her mind hazy. She fought back her drooping eyelids, but her eyesight was getting blurry. As they hauled her off the floor and onto the seat, Jamie's eyes briefly focused on the sunlight that was filtering through the backseat window, how it glittered off the river, and she repeated over and over to herself, *We're heading north. We're heading north.*

6

The wind whipped through Reynaldo's hair, uncovering the gray roots that lay below the thick, black waves. He stood motionless, hidden behind the intricate mass of interlacing steelwork, nearly choking from the exhaust that swelled from the growing number of commuting vehicles crossing the Albany County Bridge.

He took a long drag from his cigarette and watched the exhaled smoke swirl into nothingness as the lights of the neighborhoods came to life across the river. He looked at his watch. It was time for him to go.

Reynaldo gazed down the 157 feet from the bridge's center to the water's surface. The outline of the Hudson River, which only minutes ago had been vivid and rhythmic, now appeared imperceptible as the daylight waned, having been unsettled by faraway motoring as well as other unseen tuggings of the universe. He flicked his cigarette out toward the water and stepped onto the narrow ledge.

He closed his eyes and pushed one leg forward and held it there, quivering, challenging both the elements and his own misgivings. After a few moments, he found his center. He thought of Pedro and Ricardo. He thought of his *mamá*, God rest her soul, and the wobbling stopped. With resolve, he jumped. Backward.

Reynaldo's knees buckled as they landed hard on the bridge's walkway behind him, his face scraping against the jutting metal of his bicycle, which had been lying on its side. Somehow, he had misjudged the height of the ledge this time. Dazed, Reynaldo stood up and brushed himself off. He glanced at the steel columns flanking him and at the oncoming traffic. As usual, no one had noticed him.

Lighting another cigarette, Reynaldo hopped onto his bike and pedaled north, wiping the blood from his face up and into his hair. He looked at his watch. He had to get back to work.

7

The main ballroom of the mansion had an unusual, almost inappropriate brightness. The heavy drapes had been tied back, the windows opened, and a subtle chill suffused the air as Nurberg descended the grand staircase from the upper floors. Most of the mansion's staff already had been questioned and sent home, so there was an eerie stillness to the large space, and the shifts in wind caused the drapes to sway in a soft dance at the very corners of the room, forcing Nurberg's trained eye to dart from one end to the other.

As the years had passed, the governor's mansion had evolved from a simple two-story house into the picturesque Queen Anne–styled building it was today. In the early '70s, the mansion, and its surrounding grounds, had even earned a place on the National Register of Historic Places. In May of last year, First Lady Grand unveiled the first installation of solar panels, which, the subsequent press release claimed, was a significant step toward reducing the mansion's energy consumption and pollution, serving as a role model for the rest of the state. Eager to show off her svelte post-baby body, the First Lady scheduled a press conference, and Nurberg remembered that it had been held prematurely, about a week before the work had been completed at the Rockefeller Pool House. As Katherine Grand showed reporters how the new panels were already providing energy for the mansion's upkeep and cutting greenhouse-gas emissions by 50 percent, the workers' hammering in the background drowned out practically every word.

That was the last time Nurberg had seen the First Lady in person until he entered the mansion's small, private dining nook in the kitchen adjacent to the main ballroom. Mrs. Grand was sitting at one of the pine chairs, her legs neatly crossed, her eyes fixed upon her husband, who was seated at the booth side of the table. The governor's graying head was plopped into his hands, and his tall frame sagged forward. On any given day, the governor, who was six foot four, towered over his wife, who was no slouch herself at five foot seven, but today Mrs. Grand was the one whose physical presence commanded Nurberg's attention—bizarre considering she seemed even thinner than last year, the bones of her wrist sticking out as she carried a steaming cup of tea to her pursed lips.

"That incompetent housekeeper! I told you to fire her, didn't I," she said, after taking a long, slow sip.

Governor Grand raised his head. "Rosalia? That's absurd. She loves Charlotte."

"I never trusted her." Mrs. Grand placed the cup of tea in its saucer. "Always with her Spanish, voodoo nursery rhymes."

Nurberg stepped forward before the governor could respond.

"Governor Grand. First Lady Grand." He showed his badge. "I'm Detective Sergeant Mark Nurberg of the Albany Police Department's Children and Family Services Unit. I'll be handling your daughter's case."

Governor Grand stood and extended his hand. "Good to meet you, Detective. We got here as quickly as we could." Nurberg resisted shooting the First Lady a look.

"Detective." Katherine Grand, who remained seated, gave Nurberg a single nod of a greeting, while taking another sip of tea.

"Have you found anything yet?" the governor asked.

"Well, our team did a preliminary sweep of the entire mansion and the grounds, particularly in the nursery, but it showed nothing. I'd like to run down any security cameras around the perimeter during the hours the alleged abduction took place."

"Alleged?" the governor asked.

"Well, we have to consider all possible scenarios, Governor,"

Nurberg explained. "We searched under the beds, in the closets and basements, just in case the child crawled out of her crib and simply managed to get herself stuck somewhere or was injured and couldn't cry for help."

"Interesting how the housekeeper hadn't thought of that," Mrs. Grand said, to no one in particular, while staring out the kitchen window.

"Katherine, please," said the governor. "Go on, Detective."

Nurberg continued. "Or sometimes, the child will just crawl away and fall asleep. Hours later, she'll wake up happy and innocent and come out of the hiding spot, without ever knowing all the havoc she caused."

"How often does that happen, Detective?" asked the First Lady, whose attention Nurberg finally seemed to have.

"Does what happen, ma'am?"

"That a reported kidnapping results in a happy child lost somewhere in the house."

Nurberg's eyes met the First Lady's for the first time. They were a sharp and piercing blue.

"Not very often, ma'am. But it is a possibility."

"Indeed." Mrs. Grand returned to her tea.

"What can we do?" the governor asked Nurberg.

"I'm assuming the first officers on the scene questioned you both along with everyone else in the home."

"Yes," the governor said. "I don't know how much help I was. Katherine and I were at the Kliger Nursing Home on the other side of town when all this happened." The governor massaged his temples with his right hand. "I just can't believe this . . . I've cleared my schedule for the next few days. I'm available for anything you need."

"There are some reporters skulking around outside, Detective," Mrs. Grand said, motioning with her chin toward the kitchen window.

"They may have followed the police cars here, ma'am." Nurberg walked over to the window and gazed out.

"Can't you control them?" the First Lady asked.

Nurberg couldn't help but smirk. Mrs. Grand, a seasoned PR

strategist before she married the governor and began her life of charity events and proclamation dinners, had a reputation for turning any event, no matter how small, into a media frenzy. She had press conferences for each of her three trimesters; for the decorating of the nursery; for the naming of the child, who was named after the First Lady's paternal grandmother—a descendent, she claimed, of Mary Boleyn, mistress to Henry VIII—and, of course, for the actual birth, baptism, and first tooth of Charlotte Grand.

"We'll do our best," Nurberg said. "In fact, it would be a good idea if we kept this quiet for as long as possible. The last thing we want is a media circus, which would just hinder our ability to conduct a thorough investigation." He paused. "Do either of you have any ideas as to what could have happened here?"

The First Lady placed her teacup down. "I'm not sure what you mean, Detective."

"Well," Nurburg said, "any thoughts on who might have taken the baby or why?"

"No, not at all," the governor said. "Everyone loves Charlotte. She has brought so much joy to everyone's life. Right, Katherine?"

Mrs. Grand's nod was short and tight. If Nurberg hadn't been looking for it, he would have missed it altogether.

"Any enemies, Governor?" Nurberg asked.

Governor Grand threw up his hands. "Take your pick, Detective. The political climate is hostile these days, particularly for Republican government officials. Anyone who is anti-gun, pro-abortion, or anti–death penalty seems to have, at one time or another, picketed in front of my door, called me names, and made my political life hell, as if my principles were of any less value or substance than theirs."

"Recently, though, sir, any threats or people with a particular ax to grind?" Nurberg asked.

The governor thought for a moment. "No," he said. "No one comes to mind."

"And you, ma'am?" Nurberg turned toward the First Lady, who was staring out the window. "Ma'am?"

Mrs. Grand took her napkin and patted her lips, wiping off the last traces of lipstick she was wearing. She placed the napkin down and shook her head. "Why don't you ask me what you really want to ask me, detective?" she said.

"And what is that, ma'am?" Nurberg kept a steady eye on Katherine.

"If I had anything to do with the disappearance of my child."

"Now, Katherine, please . . ." The governor walked toward the sink and poured a glass of filtered water.

Nurberg said nothing as the First Lady sat back in her chair, pushing her tongue against her bottom front teeth. When she did, her eyes squinted.

"Sure," Mrs. Grand said. "I could see it the moment you looked at me; because I'm not sitting here weeping and distraught means that I don't love my daughter, that I'm to blame. Well, Detective, I'm disappointed. You think like a police-academy graduate. Would you rather I be like those mothers who cry and scream and go on television and beg for the return of their child? The ones for whom there is public outcry, national AMBER Alerts. The ones sought after by the morning network programs for exclusive interviews, and for whom the local press has a field day, thrilled to have something else to cover besides ribbon cuttings and teen graffiti." Mrs. Grand stood and put her teacup in the sink, her eyes now wild and incredulous. "Neighborhood watches are formed. Law enforcement canvasses the neighborhood, led by the grieving mother who is draped in blankets crocheted by neighbors. Quiches are baked, lakes and ponds dredged, manpower is doubled, supportive family and friends arrive in droves . . . Only, in the end, to find out that it was that helpless, pitiful mother who . . ."

Mrs. Grand caught herself. Then she continued in a calmer, more controlled tone. "So you'll understand and forgive me, sir, if I don't feel the need to waste my time and put on a dog and pony show to satisfy your delusions about what grief actually looks like."

"You still haven't answered my question, ma'am," Nurberg said. He knew he was pushing it, risking both the governor's enmity and dismissal from the case, but he also knew it was important for him to stand his ground early and often with Mrs. Grand, who had a long and dubious history with the Albany PD. If she wanted a pissing contest, then that was what he'd give her, as long as it would help him, in the end, to find Charlotte Grand.

The First Lady gave a flippant laugh. "Very good, detective. The answer is no. I can't think of anyone who would want to see my daughter harmed." She paused. "Including myself. And now if there's nothing else, may I go?"

"Just doing my job," Nurberg said. It was true. Sort of. "I will contact you if I need anything more."

"I'm sure you will," spat Mrs. Grand, who grabbed her pocketbook and strode out of the kitchen.

The governor and Nurberg watched her leave. She left in such a huff that some idle paperwork had flown off the nearby counter onto the floor. The governor bent down to pick it up. "We're all on edge, Detective, as you can imagine," he said.

"Yes, sir, I understand."

The governor neatly stacked the papers where they had been, and then the most important political figure in the state of New York stood facing the corner like a child sent into a time-out. "The house seems so quiet," he said finally, when he turned around. "Don't you think?"

Nurberg, of course, couldn't say, having never been to the mansion before. And although the assorted murmurs of detectives and uniformed officers were creating an undercurrent of noise, right now the governor was simply a man standing in his home missing the sounds of his infant daughter.

The words came out before Nurberg could stop them. "Governor Grand, I promise you, we will find Charlotte and bring her home."

8

The lit ash of Gino Cataldi's cigarette burned brightly in the small, dank cell of the Stanton Correctional Facility. Early that morning, officers had removed all of his personal belongings, allowing him only his underclothing and a pair of state-issued sandals, made of paper. The morning edition of the *Daily Telegraph* was strewn next to him on the threadbare mattress, and as he thumbed through the pages, black smudges appeared on the pads of his wrinkled, yellow fingers. He took a long drag of the cigarette that he had bummed off the night-duty guard in exchange for a tip in the seventh race at Belmont, and as he did, deep crevices formed around his mouth like concentric circles of a tree. A passing guard made a discourteous comment about the gloriousness of the weather, and although there were no windows in Gino's cell, he could smell the fresh air on the guard's clothing.

In two days, six hours, and twelve minutes, Gino Cataldi would be the sixth man put to death in New York State in six years. And leading up to that moment, there would be a guard stationed in front of his cell round the clock, watching his every move.

New York State, considered blue through and through, had surprised all the political pundits—and Gino as well—six years ago with the election and then reelection of Governor Phillip Grand, a junior state assemblyman and staunchly conservative Republican. Capitalizing on the continued illegal-immigration and terrorism fears after 9/11, Grand quietly had assembled a coalition of hardworking, blue-collar constituents, the very same ones that President Barack Obama had once claimed clung to their guns and religion, and managed to eke out a victory against his popular Democratic rival.

This was good news for the rural counties of upstate New York that crowded the Canadian border and were known as *Little Siberia* because of their harsh winters and because prisons were a big part of the local economies, viewed with the same allegiance as the area's factories or farms. Prior to Governor Grand's election, declining inmate populations threatened the livelihood of many otherwise unskilled New Yorkers who had worked in those facilities for decades; during that time, Gino had heard lots of talk among the guards of downsizing and forced retirements, eliciting a general bad mood among prison staffers. As promised during his campaign stumping, Grand, once elected, increased state funding to local municipalities to beef up their law-enforcement agencies, particularly in the northern and western sections of New York, and within six years' time there was no more talk about closing prisons—inmate populations tripled. Ever since, Gino noticed a few changes at the prison, including vending machines in the west cafeteria, new computer terminals in the rec room, and a hint of lavender on his prison uniform. For his part, Governor Grand canvassed the state claiming that because of his efforts, the streets were safer, crime syndicates had been dissolved, and drug warlords were dethroned. He was hailed as the Rudy Giuliani of upstate New York.

Grand also made reinstitution of the death penalty a central theme of his campaign, and it was his first priority once sworn into office. Gino knew that with the simultaneous increase in arrests and, therefore, inmate populations, the governor conveniently had a pick of the litter in terms of the cases in which to urge execution. The state of Texas, of course, puts to death more people than any jurisdiction, but in less than ten years' time, New York, the former political kingdom of Democratic softies like Governors Hugh Carey and Mario Cuomo, was becoming a capital-punishment contender. Although Gino heard the dissenters picketing in droves outside the correctional facility—armed with statistics that showed only a small percentage of police chiefs believed that the death penalty significantly reduced homicides and arguing that the death-row inmates' cases had been compromised by unreliable evidence, as well as dubious defense attorneys and psychiatric testimony—all five of the executions under Grand's administration had gone off without a hitch.

Over the years, Gino had kept a very close eye on the political comings and goings of Phillip Grand. Every morning of his fifteen-year stay at Stanton, he scoured the local newspapers and, later, googled Grand's name at the prison library to view the national and international news coverage of the up-and-coming statesman. After his failed appeal five years ago for the 1992 murders of three witnesses in the trial of Bobby DeLuca—horrific deaths to which Gino never conceded guilt— the governor leapt at the opportunity to pursue a capital-punishment sentence when Gino bludgeoned a fellow inmate to death with a pair of solid steel barbells in the prison weight room. After Gino's well-paid lawyers exhausted all possible legal avenues, the date was finally set for April 12, 2012.

Gino lay back upon the flat mattress of his small cell and extinguished his cigarette on the crumbling brick wall. His thoughts turned to the philosophers and poli-sci students who, at that very moment, probably were arguing whether the death penalty was an effective deterrent to crime or a violation of the US Constitution. He remembered reading that Carol Rosenstern, witness number fourteen in the case against Bobby DeLuca, had been the head of the SUNY Cortland chapter of the National Coalition to Abolish the Death Penalty. He would have gladly debated the moralities of capital punishment with her before he cut out her tongue with a steak knife.

"Just think," snickered Hank, the sentry outside Gino's cell. "In two days' time, this will all be over."

Gino smiled and said nothing.

9

"Rise and shine, Dimples."

Jamie felt hard slaps on the sides of her face and opened her eyes. She was lying on the floor of the limousine. The doors were open on both sides, and a strong, fresh breeze swept through the car interior like a wind tunnel. Horizontal sunlight streamed across her, although it did nothing to cure her shivering. Her body ached, and the bald guy was hitting her.

"Give it a rest, Leo," said the man who'd grabbed her. "She's awake." He looked at Jamie. "C'mon, honey, let's go."

Jamie emerged from the parked car on all fours. Her head was cloudy, and her cheeks stung. The red haze of dusk coated her surroundings so much that it was difficult for her to see exactly where she was. She pushed herself up and saw the bald guy, Leo, standing behind the car next to the driver, his arm around the shoulder of the kid in the jeans.

With the sun behind her, Jamie faced east as her head cleared and her brain made sense of the puzzle pieces coming in through her senses: Trees. Crickets. A wood-burning stove. They were in the woods. Somewhere upstate, she guessed. In front of her was a beautiful three-level log cabin, but other than that there was nothing else within view except for natural landscape as far as the eye could see. The sounds of running water hummed in the background, and Jamie thought she could see low mountains behind the cabin, which appeared to be on a hill. If there was anywhere to run, Jamie couldn't find it. She swatted her left forearm, squashing a mosquito, which left a small trace of blood.

The man in black was standing on the deck of the cabin, flipping through mail, his elbow leaning on one of those rural mailboxes whose little door was hanging open like a tongue. The name on the mailbox, written in big, gold capital letters, was "Bailino."

"Don," the driver called, walking toward him.

Don Bailino.

"Whatcha lookin' at, Dimples?" asked Leo, standing in her line of sight.

Jamie looked away, but Leo followed her gaze.

"Peekaboo," he said, popping again into view.

Leo was shorter than Jamie had first surmised in the limo. He probably only had a few inches on her, but he had considerable bulk. His eyes were deeply set into his round face, which had a line of pockmarks along the cheekbones, and he had plucked his eyebrows so thin that his features appeared bloated and exaggerated. He was about to say something else, but stopped when Don Bailino came toward them.

"Okay, here we are," Bailino said to Jamie. "You're here because of me, and I can just as easily get rid of you. As far as you're concerned, you do as I say, and things will go a lot smoother. Understand?"

Jamie nodded obediently, dizzied by the closeness of Don Bailino, whose size and presence was just as foreboding as she had remembered. A tiny voice inside beseeched her to run, anywhere, told her that if she entered that house he would never let her out. And although she believed it, she didn't move.

The sun vanished under the horizon, taking with it the last vestiges of light and heat, and Jamie's shiver became a tremble. Bailino took off his suit jacket and placed it over her shoulders.

"Okay then, let's go." He took her hand in his, a large, calloused knob, and led her toward the house like a parent bringing a reluctant child to her first day of school. As they walked, the three other men followed behind.

The inside of the log cabin was even grander than the outside. The entrance led into a generously proportioned space that was anchored on the right by a state-of-the-art open kitchen featuring stainless-steel appliances and a wide, two-tiered kitchen island flanked on one side by four bar stools. A stack of dirty dishes was piled in the sink as well as on the table of a breakfast nook situated in the rear. Across from the kitchen, a leather sofa and loveseat faced a stone fireplace that also served a small, but stately dining room. On the back wall, large glass sliding patio doors, which seemed to divide the house in half, were closed. To Jamie's immediate left were a bedroom and bath, the only enclosed rooms on the floor. The smell of wood, which had been so strong when they first entered the home, was now mixed with the stench of cabbage and nacho cheese—and urine.

Bailino stopped and looked around. Then he led Jamie through the kitchen and made a sharp right and pulled her down a set of stairs that led into a basement. Although the lights were off, twilight trickled into the small windows that were high on the wall, revealing more bedrooms and a laundry room with appliances that still had the sticker prices on them. At the far end was a rec room with a pool table and dartboard, a plasma television on the wall, and a large sectional. Under any other circumstances, the home would have been the perfect vacation home. *Or hideaway*, Jamie thought.

Bailino led the group toward a room on the far right, one that was closed off from the rest of the open space and looked as if it didn't belong. There were panels of Sheetrock and insulation material lying against the walls, and a hammer and nails were scattered along the floor. The door was closed, and as they got closer, Jamie could hear a string of muffled noises coming from inside. She braced herself. Even muted, the sounds were oddly familiar, and just as Bailino opened the door, she realized what it was. A baby was crying.

10

Bob sat in the usual evening rush-hour crawl on the Long Island Expressway, hoping, pointlessly, that traffic might let up. He opened his car window, clicked to the '90s station on his satellite radio, and adjusted himself in the still-crisp leather seat of his new PT Cruiser. He looked at his watch.

"Shit," he muttered.

Bob flipped down his visor and looked at himself in the small mirror. Even he had to admit, he looked damn good. He moved his face from side to side, then up and down, and reached into the glove compartment and pulled out a small bag. He took out a tweezer and plucked a stray hair above the bridge of his nose.

"Gotcha, you devil," he said, flicking the hair out the window.

Something caught his attention on the road up ahead: a glimpse of blinking red lights around the bend. *Thank God, an accident,* he thought, again looking at his watch. Once he passed it, he put his foot on the gas pedal, merged into the left lane and sped east.

His cell phone rang.

"Hello," he said into his headset without checking the caller ID.

"Hey, Bob, it's Edward."

Bob felt a gnawing in the pit of his stomach. "Edward? Um . . ."

"Listen," Edward continued without waiting. "I was just wondering if Jamie was with you."

"Jamie?"

"I didn't think she would be, but we haven't heard from her since this afternoon, and she's not picking up her cell."

"No," Bob said. "I haven't seen her since yesterday. Since . . ."

"Yeah, I know, but I thought maybe there was additional paperwork or something that maybe . . . I don't know. It was just a thought."

"Sorry," Bob said. "I'm sure she'll turn up. Cell's probably dead. You know Jamie."

"Yes," Edward said. "I do."

The call clicked off without a good-bye, but Bob pressed the *call end* button on his cell anyway. This wasn't the first time he'd gotten a call from Edward looking for Jamie, and, despite his hopes, he was sure it wouldn't be the last. The previous day had gone as smoothly as possible, considering . . . Divorce is never easy, but he and Jamie had worked out an amicable agreement. He got the condo, she got the car, and they'd split everything else down the middle. It was a generous divvy, as far as he was concerned, since his salary as a lawyer far exceeded Jamie's as a freelance writer. Since Jamie didn't want alimony—which was fine by him, let her mooch off Edward—the whole thing had taken only a couple of hours.

Traffic was slowing down again, and Bob put his foot on the brake. *Fuck.* His thoughts turned to Brenda—tall, slender, not-interested-in-anything-serious Brenda—who was making dinner and who-knew-what-else for him that moment. Bob leaned back on the headrest. It had been a long time since he could daydream about sex after a long day at work and there actually be a chance of having some. A flashy Camaro zipped past him in the middle lane, driven by a kid with his arm hanging out the window. Faced with a wall of brake lights up ahead, the Camaro scooted in front of him, switched to the shoulder, and, with a roar of its engine, zoomed past the crawling cars until it reentered traffic about a quarter mile down.

There was a time when Bob would have done the same thing, thrown caution to the wind—risking a ticket for reckless driving, points on his license, absurd Nassau County penalty fees—all for just that feeling of derring-do and the indignation, or jealousy, of the other drivers. And, for a moment, Bob gripped the steering wheel, but, at age thirty-five, he had learned that the highway wasn't the place for aggression or admiration. What's the sense in riling up a bunch of strangers? He had learned to make his mark in the places that mattered: The classroom. The boardroom. The courtroom. The bedroom.

He winced when thinking of that last one, but then sat a little taller in his seat. Today was a new day, he thought, and he felt different. Freer. The guilt was gone. The constant, never-ending, suffocating guilt, the clouds that once followed him, had dissipated. He smiled. It was good to be single again.

11

"What happened to you?" Pedro asked.

"I fell."

Reynaldo wheeled his bicycle into the service-station office, parked it in the back room, and then took his place behind the counter. He ignored his brother's stare, although he felt oddly exposed—as if the blood on his face revealed a personal, secret aspect of his life that was now visible for others to see and read. He preferred being a closed book.

"*Hermano*, you should buy yourself a real car—and I don't mean that old can of sardines you call an Escort." Pedro took the pencil out from behind his ear and scribbled some notes onto a clipboard. "No wonder you don't go out with girls. Where would you put them?"

"I can think of a few places," said Ricardo, who was lying on the cushioned wooden bench. A newspaper covered his head.

"*Sí*, they can ride on the handlebars." Pedro sat on the counter, rocking back and forth, mimicking the motion of a bicycle. "*Pero* you won't be able to date any *burritos grande*."

"*¡Qué lástima!*" chuckled Ricardo.

Reynaldo paid no attention to his brothers and opened the cash register to examine the credit-card receipts that had accrued while he was gone. The day's take was on the low side, but, overall, the garage was still doing considerable business despite the downturn in the economy. People were looking to hang onto their cars now more than ever instead of buying something new. That, coupled with the reputation Santiago's Garage had for honest labor in an industry filled with greed and deceit, generated enough income to let his father retire to Florida at age sixty last year and to keep his brothers from having to grow up at all.

Across the small office, Ricardo was reaching for a container of power-steering fluid and threatening to douse Pedro, who had left the counter and was whacking him with the rolled up newspaper.

"*¿Dònde* Nada, Ricardo?" Reynaldo shouted over the squeals.

"*No sé*," Ricardo yelled as he pushed his brother onto the floor and pretended to pour the fluid on him.

"*Está tarde.*"

Ricardo stepped behind the counter. "*Son las cuatro y media.*"

"*Sí*, I want to close up soon."

"She'll be here. Don't worry, *jefe.*"

The front door opened, jingling a small bell, and a tall, broad-shouldered woman wearing a long black dress entered the office. "*Buenas tardes*, Rey."

"Good afternoon, Mrs. Lapinski."

"Please, I told you. Call me, Racquel, Rey."

"*Sí, sí.* Racquel. You have an appointment?" Reynaldo furrowed his brow. He searched the list on the wall, but Mrs. Lapinski was not on the schedule.

"No, I was hoping you could squeeze me in for an oil change." Mrs. Lapinski threw her keys onto the counter and pulled her hair back behind her ears. "My goodness, that's a nasty scrape you've got there." She reached over to touch it, but Reynaldo backed away.

"I'm all right, *gracias.*"

"He fell," Ricardo whispered. He and Pedro stood at the counter, shaking their heads and tsk-tsking.

"Oh," Mrs. Lapinski said. "Poor bambino."

Reynaldo punched the keyboard. "Mrs. Lapin . . . er, Racquel. It says here you just got the oil changed on the twenty-third."

"You must log a lot of miles, yes?" Ricardo said.

Reynaldo shot Ricardo a hard look.

"I've been traveling. I sell cosmetics." Mrs. Lapinski told him, returning her attention to Reynaldo. "Do you think you can do me in an hour? I have to get back on the road."

"Uh, I don't know, *señora*. We were about to close and . . ."

"Please?" She reached down and lifted her skirt up to scratch an itch on her lower thigh. "*Por favor?*"

"Okay," Reynaldo said, glancing at Ricardo, who was making kissy-faces behind Mrs. Lapinski's back. "I'll work on it myself."

"I'd have it no other way." Mrs. Lapinski sat down on the leather bench, satisfied. She inched up the bottom of her skirt to cross her legs and picked up the newspaper.

The front door jingled again, and Nada walked in carrying coffee. Reynaldo pointed to the clock.

"I know, I know. It's your brother's fault. He kept me up half the night. I fell asleep in my car listening to the radio on my break."

"You loved it." Ricardo reached for Nada across the counter.

"*Basta*, Ricky! Get to work, please." Reynaldo grabbed Mrs. Lapinski's keys and pushed Pedro into the garage ahead of him as Nada took his place behind the counter. "Nada, please offer Mrs. Lapinski some coffee."

"I know *that* . . ." Nada rolled her eyes.

Reynaldo made his way to the front of the service station, followed by Pedro. "You know, Rey, you don't look good." The two got into Mrs. Lapinski's car.

"No?" Reynaldo started the engine.

"Why don't you go get something to eat when you're done? Take Nada with you."

"Nada?"

"*Sí*, you both have to eat. She's a girl. You're a boy. It might do you some good."

Reynaldo pulled the car into the garage. "You think Ricardo would like that?"

"He wouldn't mind."

"*¿De verdad? Gracias, pero no.*"

As Reynaldo opened the car door, Pedro grabbed his arm. "Okay. Actually, Maria is supposed to be coming by this evening, and Ricardo was hoping you could . . . I don't know, send Nada on an errand or something?"

"Ah, I see." Reynaldo took Pedro's hand off his arm. "Listen, little *hermano*, don't worry about me. I'm fine. And tell Ricardo to fix his own women problems."

Reynaldo got out and returned to the office, brushing past Ricardo, who ran over to Pedro.

"So?" Ricardo asked, sticking his head inside the passenger's-side window.

"He said no," Pedro said.

"*Ay*, no!" Ricardo put his head into his hands.

"He said to fix your own problems."

"*Ay*, no! Why doesn't he want to go with Nada? She doesn't have much to say. He won't have to talk."

"I'll go with Nada," Pedro said, smiling.

Ricardo put his brother into a playful choke hold and wrestled him out of Mrs. Lapinski's car and onto the hood until Reynaldo yelled at them from the office.

"*¡Sí, jefe!*" Ricardo called out, releasing Pedro with a final shove.

"Why can Rey go and not me, eh?" Pedro rubbed his neck.

"*Porque*," Ricardo said. "Just *porque*."

Reynaldo returned to the garage with a pair of gloves.

"Rey?" Ricardo clasped his hands together as if in prayer.

"No," Reynaldo said. He pushed a few buttons on the wall, and Mrs. Lapinski's car elevated.

"You don't know what I was going to say."

"You always say the same thing." Reynaldo pulled the oil-recycling container out from behind a garbage pail and swung it under the car.

"What? I do not."

"*Sí*, you do. You ask me to clean up your messes." Reynaldo pulled open a drawer and rummaged through a pile of tools. Exasperated, he threw up his hands. "Where is the oil-filter wrench?"

"Right here." Ricardo held out his hand; the wrench dangled from his middle finger. Reynaldo grabbed it, stepped under the car, and went to work on the drain plug.

Pedro looked concerned. "Rey, are you okay?"

"I think that bump on the head shook up his brains." Ricardo said, returning to the office.

Pedro stepped closer, leaning his arm across the bottom of the car. "Really, Rey, is something wrong?"

Reynaldo shook his head. "No, I'm all right. Just tired, I guess," he said as a long, smooth line of black oil poured between them.

12

Bailino pushed open the newly painted door, and powerful wails pierced through Jamie's body. Inside the narrow, windowless room, lit only by a small floor lamp in the far corner, a tiny, naked body was sprawled upon a table, kicking her feet wearily into the air. Her pale, almost white skin was covered with large red blotches, mostly on her cheeks and legs, and her puffy eyes were small slits of blue and white that were hidden behind long strands of wet, curly blonde hair.

Jamie stopped at the sight of the child, but felt a large push on the small of her back and stumbled forward. Her sudden movement into the room startled the little girl, who turned in Jamie's direction and fixed her eyes upon her. For a moment, the crying stopped.

"MaBa, MaBa," the little girl said to Jamie in between large heaves that shook her entire body.

"What?" Jamie asked. Her own voice seemed inaudible to her.

The little girl's swollen lips quivered, and it wasn't until Jamie got a little closer that she realized that the child was shivering. There were goose bumps across her arms and legs, and her tiny hands were blue.

"Ma . . . Ba . . ." the child said again, her breath slowing and her eyes drooping as she used her hands to prop herself up, teetering on the table from side to side as if exhausted.

Jamie lurched forward, scooping up the little girl, who looked around the room as if she were seeing it for the first time. Her eyes blinked, and two long tears dropped to her cheeks. Jamie ran her hands along the sides of her arms to help soothe the goose bumps. The red patches felt warm to the touch as her palms grazed over them, and the child lay limp in her arms. Every few seconds, her body shook and then would relax again, and she leaned her head on Jamie's shoulder, her right hand reaching up to grab at her hair.

There was movement at the far side of the room, and Jamie discovered a man that she hadn't seen before standing in the darkness. The other men crowded the doorway behind her and appeared as shadows formed by the sunlight coming in from the windows of the outer rooms. She took off the jacket that Bailino had placed on her shoulders, wrapped it around the little girl almost like a swaddle, her dangling feet now tucked in, and buried her head into the little girl's neck, breathing onto it in an effort to keep her warm. Snot dripped onto Jamie's shirt from the child's nose, but her breathing had become even. Without realizing it, Jamie rocked back and forth on the balls of her feet.

"Why the fuck is the kid naked, Tony?"

Leo's acerbic tongue cut through the silence.

"She started cryin', and I didn't know what the fuck to do," Tony said.

The baby picked her head up dizzily at the sound of the talking voices, but then rubbed her runny nose on Jamie's shirt and lay back down on the wet spot.

"So you take off her clothes?" Leo mocked.

"I thought maybe she needed a diaper, but I couldn't figure out how to get the fuckin' thing on, and what's-her-face was no help."

"Where is she?" Bailino asked. Jamie could feel Bailino standing behind her and that he was very close.

"In the closet," the man said. "She told me to go fuck myself."

"So," Leo said. "Did you, Tony? Fuck yourself?" The driver snickered.

"She locked herself in the utility closet. I shoved a chair under the knob and figured she ain't goin' anywhere, so I let her stay in there and thought I'd try to get the kid to stop cryin'."

"She's not crying now, is she?" Bailino asked.

Jamie could feel the eyes of all the men on her.

"Who's this?" Tony asked, eyeing Jamie.

Bailino ignored the question and left the room. After a few long seconds, Leo spoke.

"Nice ass, huh?"

"Shut the fuck up, Leo," whispered the driver.

"I'm just sayin' the girl has a nice ass, Benny, that's all. I'm dreamin' in my mind of how that ass would look in front of my cock."

"That's all you'll be doing is dreamin'," said Tony.

"Who the fuck asked you?"

There was a knock, and for a brief moment Jamie felt her body straighten at the hope that she would be rescued, that the limousine had been followed, and that she and this unknown little girl would make it out of this thing. But as she heard the knock again, Jamie saw through the open door that the sound was coming from Bailino, who was tapping on another door across the basement floor.

"C'mon, open up." Bailino had removed the chair that had been wedged under the knob and was talking in a soft voice into the wood of the door.

The men in the dark room gathered around the doorframe to watch. As Leo moved closer, the cuff link of his suit sleeve scraped Jamie's arm; she leaned in the other direction.

Bailino put his hands on his hips and spoke once again to the closet door, his voice growing tetchy. "Let's go, open the door," he said.

Nothing.

Bailino reached into his pocket and took out a set of keys. He stuck one into the keyhole, and as he whipped open the door, a vacuum-cleaner accessory boomeranged out of the closet, nearly hitting him in the head.

"Stay the fuck away from me," hissed a female voice from the closet.

Bailino charged inside as violent shrieks reverberated through the house, causing the baby to jolt awake in Jamie's arms and to scream again.

"Shut that fuckin' kid up," Leo said.

Jamie pressed the child's head to her shoulder so that her right ear was covered and then cupped her left hand over the baby's other ear.

She kissed her warm cheeks and rocked her again as she watched in horror as Bailino came out from the closet dragging a woman along by the hair and holding a rake in his other hand.

The woman's voice became a shrill, constant scream as Bailino yanked her across the floor, her long legs sprawled out under her, unable to find traction. As she raised her head to bite Bailino's legs, Jamie noticed her face: She was a bit older than her long blonde hair implied—her features were weathered, and there were deep grooves across her forehead—but she had pretty, petite features, or Jamie imagined she once did. Her tanned arms grabbed at the air, and all the while Bailino said nothing and walked across the room as if he were pushing a lawn mower leisurely across a front yard. He threw her to the ground, and as she crawled toward the stairs, Bailino raised the rake up into the air and heaved it down upon her head.

Jamie gave a small, muffled yelp as blood spattered across the room. She could feel urine dribbling onto her underwear and down her leg. With that one blow, the tall, lean woman remained motionless on the floor, but Bailino continued to strike until her skull cracked open and her face was no longer recognizable.

Satisfied, Bailino motioned to the men. "Come with me." He stopped the tall, quiet kid with his hand. "Joey, watch her, yeah?" Bailino said, pointing to Jamie. The young man nodded and returned to his place outside the doorway.

"You're leaving Joey with her?" Leo asked, pulling the blonde woman's body to the corner of the room by her arms, while Tony threw a large blanket on the ground. Not a word of instruction passed between any of the men, who performed as if having done this routine many times before. The driver, Benny, rolled the woman on top of the blanket as Leo and Tony held the corners to keep them from bunching up. Then the woman who had fought for her life just moments before lay compliant and quiet as they tossed the ends of the blanket over her and wrapped her with twine. Bailino stood supervising, lost in thought, and then as if remembering Leo's question, glanced at Jamie.

"She's not going anywhere," Bailino said. A small smile curved up his lips, the same smile that Jamie had seen at Bryant Park, as the four men hoisted the woman's body up and across the room toward the front staircase.

Bailino had spoken with a certainty and self-assurance that reminded Jamie of Bob, who liked to offer his opinion on what Jamie was capable and not capable of doing. She remembered how every fiber in her being would want to prove him wrong, to vault over his wall of denial and defy his expectations. But as she stood there in the dark room with the sleeping child in her arms, she knew in her heart that Bailino was right: She wasn't going anywhere.

13

The low whirr of the ceiling fan always filled Reynaldo with sadness. The metal blades sliced through the dusky air with cruel efficiency, frightening the dust out from its hiding spots and into the darker sections of the empty living room, and blowing the top of Reynaldo's curly graying bangs away from his forehead. From the worn couch, Reynaldo stared up, his hands folded behind his head, watching the blades go round and round. How many times had he lay in this very spot in the past forty-two years, he wondered. When he was a boy, his little legs were too short to reach the third cushion of the couch, but now his feet dangled off its side. He straightened his legs and pointed his toes as far as he could, scraping the edge of the wall unit with the top of his big toe. Yes, he had gotten bigger. But had he grown?

From here, Reynaldo could survey all areas of the main floor of his home—the dining room, kitchen, front door, staircase—while watching television, if he chose to. Right now, the set was off; the screen was coated in a thin layer of dust in which Ricardo had etched the word *jode* with his finger the last time he had come over, which was Christmas. In the early days, there had always been something going on in the house— people coming and going with trays of food; his brothers sneaking this way and that, pulling one girl or another; his mother having coffee with the neighborhood women; his father snoring on the recliner. Reynaldo was ten years old when his grandmother fell ill and came to live with them, and he gave up his bedroom so that she had a place to sleep, making him a hero among his family members, his mother in particular. But for Reynaldo it was a dream come true to be able to sleep in his favorite place, on this couch, and even after his grandmother passed away, he never went back to his bed.

Now, the room once filled with so much laughter and movement was quiet. He looked at the kitchen sink, filled with dishes, and imagined his mother standing before it, yelling at his brothers in Spanish and forcing a washcloth into a tall glass and twisting it.

"Rey, you don't want to go outside and play?" she'd ask when she saw him lying there, knowing full well that he didn't.

"No, *mamá*, I want to stay here," his eight-, ten-, seventeen-year-old self would say every time.

"All right, but be careful you don't get stuck to that couch for good!" she'd say with a laugh, never realizing that one day her prophecy would come true. Reynaldo had been stuck for so long, the years blowing past him, and he wondered where all the time had gone. Still, at the same time, lying there, wasting time idly—away from the responsibilities of his life, his brothers, the garage—he'd never felt freer.

His cell phone rang. Reynaldo looked at the number and picked up.

"Aunt Ro?" Reynaldo was concerned. Aunt Rosalia never called this late in the day, particularly from one of the mansion's land lines.

"Rey? Rey, are you there?"

"Yes, *Tía*. Are you okay?" Her voice, usually filled with a singsongy lightness, sounded troubled and afraid.

"Rey, can you come and pick me up tonight at the governor's? Something has happened."

"What?" Reynaldo asked, pulling on his shoes and grabbing his keys. "Are you all right?"

"Yes . . . No . . . Please come, *Reyito*."

"I'll be there in fifteen minutes," Reynaldo said and hurried out the door.

14

"Wait here," Joey said, leading Jamie and the baby, still asleep in her arms, into the upstairs master bedroom. Even though he was in his late teens, there was a boyishness about Joey: His hair was long, and his facial features were soft, with an expression of textbook adolescent apathy, as if everything bored him. Even as Bailino was doing the unthinkable in the basement, Joey exhibited zero response, and Jamie wondered whether it was because he was a veteran of such brutality or if he had simply zoned out listening to his iPod. One of his earphone wires dangled from his ears, and a thumping bass line dotted the silence as he gently ushered Jamie into the bedroom and then walked past her and out the door. Jamie heard the dead bolt click and noticed that there was no knob on the bedroom door—a key was needed from either side to open it.

She stepped toward the floor-to-ceiling windows on the right side of the room. It was difficult to see in the night, but she still could make out the hazy outlines of the mountains in the distance, a blackness before them that was murky and still. The moon, nearly full, was coming up just over the tree line of the western horizon and appeared large and red, and Jamie heard the familiar chorus of crickets through the thick glass of the windows. Other than that, she didn't recognize anything.

The master bedroom of the log cabin was a luxurious space decorated with an upscale country motif and anchored by a king-size bed off to one side and a large, wrought-iron chandelier hanging in the center. Everything looked new—no scuff marks disturbing the gloss of the wood-strip flooring, no dust gathering in the corners of the room, the heaps of luxurious bed linens arranged just so. Two small rooms connected to the bedroom: The first, to the left, was a bathroom. Jamie could see some of the bulbs of the vanity and the pedestal sink. The other room was to her right, with the door slightly ajar. Jamie peeked in. The room, probably once a walk-in closet, had been converted into a makeshift nursery: The walls were white and bare, and there was a strong new-carpet smell; a wooden crib stood in the center. A ripped-open pack of diapers was laying on the floor, along with several unopened containers of formula, plastic baby bottles, rubber nipples, packages of baby wipes, rattles, toys, blankets, clothes, and socks—all with the price tags still on them.

Jamie rubbed the blonde curls of the baby's head. She could feel the little heart beating against her chest, which gave Jamie an odd sense of comfort. The crib had no bumper or bedding of any kind—just a mattress covered by a thin white sheet. It looked like a prison cell. Jamie took a deep breath and laid the child in the crib on top of Bailino's jacket. The child stirred, but remained asleep. Jamie grabbed a few wipes and held them between the palms of her hands to warm them, then took a diaper and placed it under the little girl and cleaned her with the wipes as best she could without waking her. She closed the diaper and, unable to find a trash can, tossed the wipes on the floor. Carefully, she pulled the jacket out from under the baby and hung it on the crib post. The little girl shivered, and Jamie held up one of the onesies she'd seen lying on the floor. It seemed small. She checked the label: *newborn*. There was no way it would fit. She tossed it back and grabbed a pair of size *1T* flannel footie pajamas with a picture of Pooh Bear on the front; she slid the little girl's arms and feet into the clothing and zipped her up. Then she picked up the blanket from the floor and placed it over the child.

Jamie looked down at the little girl sleeping peacefully. Her raspy wheezing had subsided into a quiet, rhythmic breathing pattern. She pulled up on the side of the crib so that it was as tall as the other and the child wouldn't fall out, but a price tag prevented the hook from catching. Pushing it out of the way, Jamie set the latch, hearing a soft *click*.

There, she thought. Safe. For now.

She reached for the large price tag, rubbing her fingers along the sides of the plastic, wondering if it posed a threat to the child. There was a paper receipt stapled to it that was stamped in black ink with the word *FLOOR MODEL*. At the bottom, the receipt read, in small print, "Babies'R'Us, 221 Wade Road, Latham, NY . . ."

Latham? Where was that? Jamie wondered. She kept reading. ". . . 12110 (518) 783-0632."

Area code 518. She knew that. Her best friend from high school had moved to Ballston Spa, New York, when she was eighteen years old, and his new phone number had the same area code. It was near Albany, about three or four hours from Manhattan. She looked at the little girl asleep in the crib. *Is that where they were?*

There was a faint noise behind her, and Jamie was startled by Don Bailino, who was leaning against the doorframe.

"You have a way with children," he said, glancing at the sleeping baby. "Jamie."

Jamie's body stiffened at the sound of her name.

Bailino shifted the weight on his feet. "That is your name, isn't it? Jamie?" he asked, studying her.

She looked at the baby, who was still asleep. She didn't know whether to lie or to tell the truth, or to say anything at all. Her thoughts raced to the blonde woman who had screamed and fought her way to an early death. She pressed her lips together to keep from saying the wrong thing.

"Jamie Carter, 520 Franklin Street, Massapequa, New York 11758." Bailino pulled Jamie's portfolio out from behind him and flipped it open to the first page. "Graduate of Hofstra University, BA in Journalism. 3.52 GPA."

Jamie listened in horror to the recitation of her carefully crafted resume.

"Worked for two years at the *Massapequa Tribune*, three at *Home*

Furnishings World as home editor, a year at *USA Baby* as an associate editor, currently freelancing . . . Interests: Travel, Women's Issues, Children." Bailino closed the portfolio and placed it on a bureau behind him in the master bedroom. "References furnished upon request." He walked toward her.

Jamie backed away. In this small room, Bailino was an even more imposing figure. He was not a very young man, probably around fifty, judging by the deep lines on his forehead and around his eyes and the graying hair just above his ears, but his formidable body was that of a considerably younger man. The large cross that hung from his neck was turned backward, and his white sleeves were rolled up to the elbows; there was fresh dirt in the crevices and around the threaded edges. The scent of his cologne was strong, as if he'd just put some on, and filled the room like poisonous gas. His eyes were fixed upon her the same way that they'd been in Bryant Park, and that cold, menacing look made Jamie shudder. She bumped into the crib, jerking it a little, but the child remained undisturbed. She was out cold.

Pressed against the wall, Jamie shook her head no, putting her arms in front of her to push against Bailino's body as he closed in on her, but he was like a tank. She tried to speak, but her voice came out as a whimper.

"*Shhhh,*" he whispered before his large mouth closed in on hers. She clenched her lips and teeth together, but his hand grabbed the sides of her jaw and pulled it down, forcing her mouth open, and his other hand wrapped around her head and pushed it forward.

She shoved her face away and gasped for breath, watching the sleeping baby as Bailino landed powerful kisses on her neck and shoulders, sucking on her skin, pulling it in between his teeth and stretching it until she felt like it was going to rip off.

"Nooo . . ." she wheezed, wincing from the pain, the tiny bites feeling like slices of a razorblade.

Bailino released his grip, but before Jamie could react, he slammed his body against hers to hold it in place as his hands quickly undid the button and zipper of his khakis. His pants and underwear slid to the ground, and as he kicked them to the side, he grabbed her hand and placed it on his hairy groin.

"Noooo," Jamie said again, trying to pull away.

"Touch me," he rumbled, his voice a heavy whisper.

"I . . . I can't." Tears streamed down her face, stinging the area around her mouth, where Bailino's five o'clock shadow had left her skin raw.

He grabbed her hand and, cupping it with his, placed it on his penis, which felt like a missile in her hand. He held it there and squeezed, a small gasp escaping from his mouth, which he threw again onto Jamie's, his saliva covering her lips and cheeks. Pinning her shoulder back with his free hand, he moved his lips down to her chin, his tongue following the crevice of her cleft, and then, methodically, to her neck, the area between her breasts, and down to her stomach and below her waist. Jamie picked her feet up off the floor, hoping gravity would help overcome his hold, and it did: She slid until suddenly Bailino crouched down and threw her over his shoulder with ease.

"Please," she cried, as she picked her head up and saw the baby through the bars of the crib get further away as he carried her out and into the bedroom.

The large muscles of Bailino's biceps worked like the well-oiled gears of a tractor as he flopped Jamie onto the bed and charged forward. Before she could catch her breath, he was on top of her, ripping her shirt open, pulling her bra straps down from her shoulders, and burying his face between and under her breasts. Piece by piece, the layers of the white luxurious bedding fell to the floor as Jamie groped for something to hang onto, feeling as if she were grabbing handfuls of fluffy snow while dangling from atop a cliff. Bailino's large hands groped at her body, squeezing her nipples, and Jamie slapped at his hands, pulling at the coarse patches of hair along the fingers in a futile effort to pull them away. She reached outward for something, anything, to use as a weapon.

She managed to turn over and wrap her fingers around the top of the headboard, but Bailino heaved her arm back, sending a searing pain through her shoulder, and then flipped her onto her back again and landed on top of her. While Jamie struggled to regain her breath,

Bailino flicked her hands aside, pushed her skirt up and tore at her underwear, which was still wet with urine; Jamie felt a surge of pain as Bailino pressed open her legs and jammed into her, slamming her head into the delicate iron scrollwork of the headboard. She called out, but Bailino covered her mouth with his hand, and her nostrils flared as she sucked air through her nose. The weight of his body was overpowering, and she grew lightheaded as she tried in vain to push him off. Bailino pounded against her, banging her again and again into the headboard, causing the hanging pictures above to bounce in the same rhythm. As the intensity grew, a low growl emanated from Bailino's lips, and their eyes met as they bobbed up and down in synchrony, faster and faster, until suddenly everything stopped.

Bailino dropped his hand from Jamie's mouth, and the air went rushing inside, filling her hungry lungs with oxygen. His body, laced with sweat, lay on top of hers, and the two of them remained still, heaving, breaths slowing. The crown of Jamie's head ached, a pain that shot down to her eyes and sinuses, and the sores along her neck and shoulders prickled against the pillowcase. The open air felt cold and abrasive to the scratches on her face, and there was an intense throbbing between her legs, where Bailino was still in her, but all she could think about was having to look into his eyes, having to face him in the stillness of the room, in the wake of what had just happened and might happen again.

But she didn't have to. Bailino slipped off and plopped onto the mattress beside her, his arm reaching around, his hand slipping under the band of her shredded underwear. His body began rising and falling in soft, steady pulses, and Jamie sighed with relief, savoring the moment she had to think, to figure out a game plan that would somehow get her out of there—and the baby too. But instead her eyes blinked with fatigue and, slowly and unwillingly, she passed out next to the man who raped her.

15

Phillip Grand studied his wife from across the bedroom as she tapped at her keyboard, the glow of the monitor hardening her already sharp features and drawing all the pigment from her tanned, taut skin. But even in this harsh light, Phillip thought Katherine was striking, a modern-day embodiment of the word *handsome*—a type of beauty that was no longer appreciated in a media-obsessed culture that put undernourished, frail women on a pedestal. To him, Katherine was pleasing and dignified, and what stood out to Phillip now were her heavily lashed, curious eyes, which, as he had often noted, were identical to those of their daughter Charlotte.

Charlotte . . .

Phillip focused on his wife's fingers, long and skinny, moving swiftly, their pads meeting the concave keys with ease, a byproduct of some thirty years of practice since tenth-grade typing class.

"Honey, why don't you come to bed?" he asked. "You need to rest."

Mrs. Grand either didn't hear the request or ignored it.

Phillip lay back on the bed and thought through the day's events—the blur of policemen going in and out of the mansion and the intense questioning of his staff, a small band of ambitious twenty- and thirtysomethings he once considered loyal, but all of whom now seemed distrustful and aloof. All day long, the possibility that he had a traitor in his camp, the thought that someone, out there, had his little girl, and the worry that the media would get wind of Charlotte's disappearance, weighed on him. Detective Nurberg seemed to think, and Phillip was inclined to agree, that the media would only muddle the investigation at this point. Although, despite the consensus among his Republican colleagues that the liberal media was out to get them, the press in general had been kind to Phillip Grand over the years. Was it naïve of him to think that more searching eyes might be better than a few?

Phillip rubbed his temples. He couldn't think anymore. His head ached, and he was exhausted. It probably didn't help that he hadn't had anything to eat besides a half package of Oreo cookies. And he didn't remember seeing his wife eat at all.

The typing stopped.

Katherine was dialing the bedroom phone. He looked at his watch.

"Who are you calling at this hour?"

She held up her hand to silence him.

"Ellie . . . Ellie . . . It's Katherine," Katherine said into the handset. "Yes, I know. I had a question about the Tanner project. . . . Yes . . . No, I'm fine . . . Well, I guess we can speak in the morning . . . If that's easier for *you*. Well then . . ." She hung up and continued typing.

The governor shook his head. The police had placed emergency wiretaps on the mansion's landlines, and he knew it would seem odd—suspicious—for his wife to be placing business calls at 1:13 a.m. He was about to say something, but then thought better of it and leaned his head back against his pillow.

Drive and ambition were not only a passion for Katherine Grand, but a necessity, a coping mechanism that got her through difficult times; they were two of the qualities that had attracted Phillip to her. Having grown up with maternal role models who spent their days idly, complaining about the color of wallpaper or the inconvenience of a cool spring, Phillip thought Katherine was a breath of fresh air—she had no intention of becoming a trophy wife, just as he had no intention of having one. He remembered the day she came storming through the door of his office when he was running for state assemblyman in the 131st District. Dressed in one of those broad-shouldered, pinstriped power suits popular in the 1980s, she had put her briefcase on his desk and told him that she was going to be his campaign director. He already had one. She was confident, forthright. "You need me," she'd said. "I can get you elected." She opened up her briefcase and handed him an envelope containing incriminating photos of the Democratic incumbent whose seat Grand was contesting.

Phillip immediately showed his distaste. "I'm sorry, but I don't need to win that way," he remembered telling her, even though he was trailing in the polls by seven points with the election six weeks away. "I'm afraid you're barking up the wrong candidate." She smiled and left his office. The next day, compromising photos of Assemblyman Mitchell Tuttle and a student intern appeared in the *Albany Times*. Six weeks later, squeaky-clean Phillip Grand—war veteran, philanthropist—won the assemblyman seat in a landslide. The following day, Phillip hired Katherine as his media spokesperson. Two years later, he married her.

Phillip got up from the bed and stood behind his wife. He put his hands on her shoulders.

"Phillip, you're annoying me."

"Come to bed," the governor said.

Katherine stopped typing. "I can't," she said.

"You need to sleep."

"I *can't* sleep." Katherine stood up and walked to the window. A family of moths hovered just beneath the recessed lighting of the overhanging eaves, flapping their tiny wings in confusion. Arthur, the night guard, was sitting in a chair just outside the security post at the main gate talking to a policeman.

"We'll find her," Phillip said. He walked over to his wife and spun her around so that she was facing him.

"This is my fault," Katherine said.

"What?"

"It is. I'm Charlotte's mother." Her face seemed softer away from the white light of the computer screen, the crevices returning around her eyes and mouth, the freckles visible again on her nose. "If I had been here, this wouldn't have happened."

Phillip reached in and hugged his wife. She stood there hard, resisting, as she always did for the first few moments, but her body weakened. "I don't think there's anything that you could have done," he said, "that I could have . . ."

"The press is going to have a field day with this," she muttered into his shoulder.

As much as Phillip was a media darling, Katherine Grand hadn't been so lucky. She and the press had had a loathe/hate relationship from the start—they accused her of spoon-feeding them fluff, and she charged them with demanding nothing but dirt. Over the past ten months, in particular, Katherine had taken a lot of hits in the media for being an unfit mother—a "Mommie Grandest"—to quote one local blogger who went so far as to run a press photo of Faye Dunaway as Joan Crawford beside a headshot of Katherine Grand.

"The press doesn't know anything," Phillip said, as Katherine released herself from his grasp and sat down. She unbuttoned her jacket, hung it on the back of a chair, and slid her feet out of her pumps, rubbing the ball of her right foot.

"You don't really believe that, do you?" Phillip sat on the floor next to his wife.

"Believe what?" Katherine asked. He could already feel her distancing herself from the vulnerability of just a few minutes before.

"That this is your fault."

"Do you?" she asked.

Phillip wiped the smudged mascara flaking on her bottom eyelid with his thumb.

"No," he said. "I believe it's mine."

"Oh, Phillip," Katherine said, with a wave of her hand. She stood up and walked back to her desk. "There you go again, taking responsibility for things that don't concern you."

"How can you say that?" Phillip's voice grew loud. "How do you know that? Katherine, you are an accomplished, amazing woman, but it's not your name they've got etched onto picket signs. It's not your face they've got drawn on a doll-sized body hanging from a noose, parading it around."

"Phillip, that was two years ago."

"I don't care!" Phillip stood up and began to pace in front of the king-size bed. "I've kept that haunting image in my mind for two years, *two years*, wondering how anyone, *anyone*, even if they're diametrically opposed to something I feel strongly about, would feel compelled to do that."

It took a lot to rattle Phillip Grand. He was repeating words twice, Katherine thought, a telltale sign that he was serious. She turned from her computer.

"There are schmucks in the world, Phillip. C'mon. You know it deep down. It amazes me that after forty-seven years on this earth, it still surprises you when bad people do bad things."

"It doesn't surprise me, Katherine. I've seen my share of people doing horrible things."

"Oh, here we go again." She rolled her eyes. "The war."

"I love how you dismiss that. You always have. As if what happened over there was a figment of my imagination. To this day, every day, there are casualties there. Kids, *kids*, fighting for people they don't know and will never meet. For God's sake, you gave a speech at last month's Wounded Warrior Project luncheon."

"I don't dismiss it, Phillip," Katherine said calmly, unscrewing her post earrings and placing them in a crystal bowl on her dresser, "but I also don't dwell on it."

"Well, maybe you would if you'd been there."

"Oh, that's just great." Katherine took out a pair of flannel pajamas. "I love how people who have fought in military conflicts don't think much of anyone who hasn't."

"It's not that we don't think much of you," Phillip said with a sneer. "It's that we don't have the luxury to wonder and theorize like you do."

But Katherine wasn't listening. "It's just like parents."

"What?" The two of them somehow had slipped into a familiar argument. Phillip couldn't remember what had set them off.

"Parents—*breeders*—they think you're not really an adult until you have children. It doesn't matter what you accomplish, if you work your way through college, part-time, and start a company from scratch, if you're not getting up in the middle of the night to breast-feed, then you're *less than*." Katherine had now disrobed, except for a pair of panty hose that she peeled off leg by leg, revealing a pair of black bikini-cut underwear, and Phillip watched her fight her way into her pajamas, first the sleeves, then the pant legs, muttering to herself the whole time. The only words he caught were "egotistical" and "flabby whores." She went to the bathroom and shut the door. The water faucet was running, and Phillip imagined Katherine's face covered in suds and her mouth a big gaping hole that continued to open and close.

Phillip lay back down on the bed. He hated fighting with Katherine. He hated fighting with anyone, really, and this was accomplishing nothing, but Katherine's last words about parenting were ringing in his ears. He had pushed for a child—a litter, actually—practically from their wedding night, but Katherine wouldn't hear of it. He wore her down over time, and she agreed to "one child—that's it." Charlotte had been born just before Phillip and Katherine's fifteenth wedding anniversary, and no sooner had he seen those tiny fingers and toes than he had begun hinting for another. Phillip knew the loneliness of the only child. He remembered how, even as a preschooler, he had tried to use his money to bribe his classmates to play with him, how he'd ask for a brother or sister every Christmas, but instead had opened box after box of toy trains and cars. Charlotte needed a sibling.

It wasn't until that very moment that Phillip realized that, deep down, he *did* think that everyone should have kids, that it was a natural rite of passage for adults. Did that make him a horrible person? "Egotistical"? He thought again about the Phillip Grand doll hanging from the noose, which had left such an indelible mark on him. He hadn't even seen it in person, but on the evening news, which was covering a pro-choice rally at a local Planned Parenthood clinic after his State of the State address in 2009. "The governor is telling us what we can and can't do with our bodies," the young woman, named Laurie, told the news reporter. "He says it's murder." Then, with a sly grin, she looked into the camera and pointed to the doll. "Murder like this, governor?"

Katherine opened the bathroom door. Her face was scrubbed and shiny, and her hair had been combed back around her ears. She stood before the bed.

"I'm . . ."

"It's okay," Phillip said. "I'm sorry too."

Katherine gave a quick nod, turned off the bedroom light, and climbed into bed next to her husband. Phillip turned toward her and put his hand on her waist. "We'll find her, Katherine. We will."

Katherine stared up at the ceiling and then turned onto her side, away from her husband. The vibration of Phillip's cell phone on the nightstand startled them both.

"Is it Nurberg?" Katherine flipped around, flinging off the covers. Phillip had given the detective his personal cell number.

Phillip looked down at the caller ID. It wasn't Nurberg. The telephone number was familiar, though he couldn't place it, and there was no photo accompanying it, which meant that his phone didn't recognize it.

"I don't think so," he said.

"Who else would be calling your private line at this hour?" Katherine asked, and then she bolted upright. "Oh my God!"

"I don't know. Just relax." Phillip's hand was shaking.

"I'm running downstairs to get Detective Matrick. They're not calling the landline. Oh my God! They're not calling the landline! They're calling your personal cell phone. We're not ready. We can't trace it. Can we?"

"Wait."

Katherine didn't wait. She grabbed her robe and ran out the bedroom door.

The phone kept ringing. There were only three people who had this telephone number: Katherine, Rosalia, and, now, Detective Nurberg. Katherine had insisted that she be able to reach Phillip at any time and bought him this cell phone last Christmas, and Phillip had given the number to Rosalia just in case she had to reach him in an emergency. Even his mother called him on his business cell.

Ring . . . ring . . .

Phillip looked toward the bedroom door. He couldn't chance letting it go to voice mail. *I know this number,* he thought, and pressed *call accept,* but it was too late. He heard a dial tone.

Damn! He called his voice mail, but there were no new messages yet. Someone must be leaving a message. *Right now.* Phillip's palms were sweating, as Katherine and Det. Matrick ran into the bedroom.

"Did you get it?" Katherine asked.

"I didn't. . . . Not in . . ."

"For God's sake, Phillip, what are you waiting for?"

Suddenly, his phone dinged, signaling a phone message.

The three of them stared at one another.

Phillip dialed his voice mail as Katherine sat on the bed, and the officer placed a call to Detective Nurberg. Katherine reached over and pressed *speaker* on Phillip's phone: *"One new message."*

Phillip pressed *one* and braced himself as an automated message began to play:

"This message is for (pause) Phillip Grand . . . We have important news about your Visa credit card ending in 2543. Please call us at 800-832-2093."

"Jesus!" Katherine said. "Fucking telemarketers. It's goddamn two o'clock in the morning. How did they get that number? I told you not to give it to anyone."

"I have no idea," Phillip said.

Det. Matrick flipped his phone closed. "No worries, Mrs. Grand. You did the right thing. It was just a false alarm. I've made Detective Nurberg aware of the situation, and he said he will be here first thing tomorrow morning."

"Thank you," Katherine said as the detective left the bedroom and shut the door.

She rehung her robe on the poster of the bed, climbed onto the mattress, and pulled the blankets up to her neck. "Fucking telemarketers," she grumbled as she turned onto her side.

Phillip sat on the bed with the phone in his hand. Something was bothering him. That telephone number. He knew it. He had an uncanny memory for numbers. In grade school, he had dazzled his fourth-grade teacher by memorizing his multiplication tables up to twenty, and when he was in the military, he had won a bet from another private by reciting the serial numbers of all the men in his unit. He looked at his call log and was studying the telephone number when his phone vibrated again.

Katherine turned toward her husband.

"It's the same number," he said.

Katherine turned back. "Answer it or decline the call already, Phillip." She pulled the blankets up higher.

The governor pressed his index finger on the *call accept* button and brought the phone to his ear.

"Hello?" he whispered, as the familiar voice spoke. The governor listened to every word and then pressed the *end call* button and put the cell phone down on the bed next to him.

"So?" Katherine asked without turning over.

The governor blinked. "Fucking telemarketer," he said and wiped his brow.

16

Blackness engulfed the master bedroom where Jamie's eyes blinked nervously, the only body parts she allowed to move at all; the rest of her remained still under the immobile, hairy arm of Don Bailino. The static silence of the room would have been overwhelming had she not been consumed with the violent, intense battles taking place within her mind: *Why was she here? Whose baby was it? How long would it take Edward to realize she was missing? Would Bailino rape her again? Why didn't she fight harder? Who was the blonde girl? Why didn't she fight harder?* She used the calming techniques that she'd practiced during the adult ed yoga class she'd taken last summer to assuage the disjointed discourse in her mind, and, for hours, while the monster slept beside her, she mentally segmented the events of the previous day, putting them into neat columns. But it all came down to one inevitable conclusion: Bailino was going to kill her.

That was clear to her. She knew names, faces, and had witnessed the brutal death of another human being—the thought of which once again jolted her nervous system into panic, but Jamie willed her body to relax. She could feel the clouds of her mind rearrange, and her breathing became so light she feared she might even stop breathing at all. She ached for the familiarity of her apartment: the nighttime ticking of the wall clock, the one her brother had given her for Christmas so she would never be late; the beeping of her next-door neighbor's car alarm as he left the house at 11:15 p.m. for his night shift at the twenty-four-hour McDonald's in town; the way her pillowcase smelled when she first rested her head on it.

Bailino's warm breath crept up the nape of her neck and blew a steady stream of stale, used air down her back. Was he awake? She didn't know, and her thoughts flashed six months back to the night of October 15, the last night of her marriage: It had been nearly as dark as it was now, the LED lights of her alarm clock tingeing the lacquered nightstand red as she lay in her usual corner of the king-size bed. Bob lay on the other side, a few feet of springs separating them, but miles of distance. She could tell that Bob was awake. She'd learned the patterns of his breathing while he slept, and as she stared off into the nothingness, she'd heard him say it, clear as day: "I'm leaving you." How still she lay there that night, as she was lying now, conscious of that stillness, of making no reaction. Jamie remembered the wave of relief that swept over her with those three little words, followed by the grip of disappointment that she hadn't said them first.

Bailino lifted his head and nuzzled his chin sleepily against her side, and Jamie held her breath until he settled back down again. A little voice inside told her she had this coming: How many times had she daydreamed about a tall, dark stranger swooping in and carrying her away from her life? Or about Bob being hit by a car and killed at the scene, rendering her free—all because she was too much of a chicken to walk out the door? Why was she always looking for someone or something to save her?

A horrendous thought jolted Jamie back to the present: She needed to use the bathroom. The urge came out of nowhere, and there was no way she could hold it long. Bailino's arm felt like a weight on her side, but she rolled left. Instantly, his right hand grabbed her waist. He *was* awake.

"Where are you going?"

"The bathroom," she whispered.

Bailino thought for a moment. "Okay, go, but hurry." He released his grip, and Jamie rose to a sitting position. The dizziness was immediate; she caught herself from falling backward. She couldn't get up.

"Well?" he asked.

Jamie fumbled with her clothing, which hung from her like ripped streamers after a lively party, and managed to get herself up and off the bed. Even in the dark, Jamie could feel Bailino's steady eyes on her, and she became self-conscious about her nakedness, something she wasn't totally comfortable with on any given day, let alone that day. She stepped in the direction of the bathroom, stifling a moan as a twinge of pain shot through her upper thighs as she separated her legs. She took what felt like baby steps across the dark bedroom and finally passed through the doorframe. The coolness of the ceramic floor tile soothed the soles of her feet, and she closed the door before Bailino told her not to and then ran her hand along the wall near the molding to find the light switch. She flicked it on.

The fluorescent brightness shocked her tired pupils, and she closed her eyes until they adjusted, putting her hands against the wall for support. She locked the door and then waited, but there were no protests from the other side. She shuffled across the room to the toilet and, in a small moment of utter joy, relieved her bladder, her eyes scanning the large bathroom, decorated in a warm, yellow color palette, and resting on a small window that was above the Jacuzzi bathtub. Was it big enough for her to climb through? Possibly, but unlikely, she thought, and even if she tried, she was two flights up from the ground. There were small heating and air-conditioning ducts next to the tub, but they were hardly large enough for one leg. The truth was, the only reason Bailino would probably let her go to the bathroom on her own was because he was confident that there was nowhere she could go, and Jamie felt the anxiousness return to her insides. She thought she heard footsteps outside the bathroom door, and she sat still and listened, watching the doorknob, but nothing happened. She knew he wouldn't let her stay in there for long.

She reached for the toilet paper, pausing a moment in surprise to see that the ends of the paper had been carefully creased on both sides into a neat point. She flushed and reached across the shiny porcelain pedestal sink to wash her hands, splattering water on the smooth curves of the gleaming chrome faucets. The hand soap gave off a milk-and-honey fragrance. The entire bathroom had a springy freshness about it, as if it had been scrubbed with daisies. While she washed her hands, out of habit Jamie glanced into the vanity mirror and gasped at the horror of her own reflection: A large, red bump burst through the skin just above her hairline. Her tousled, matted hair looked glued to the sides of her face, which had large, blood-speckled scrapes along them. Her coloring, normally fair, was ashen, and her eyes were red and puffy, sagging at the corners in sadness. Or was it shame? She looked away and pressed her back up against the cool tiled wall, finding comfort in the geometrical order of the tiled walls and floors surrounding her, as if she were in a protective cage. If only she could stay in there. She again looked into the mirror, at her unrecognizable self, and reached her hand out, her finger tracing the sides of her reflected face and leaving smudge marks on the glass. NEVER LOOK BACK the headline had read on *O* magazine. Jamie grabbed the corner of the mirror and pulled, and the door to the medicine cabinet opened with a click.

The cabinet shelves were rather empty, containing only three items: a half-used bottle of Old Spice aftershave, an electric razor, and a clear, plastic makeup bag, which Jamie picked up. Inside she found some hair clips, makeup in an array of childish fluorescent colors, body lotions, and a nail clipper. She took out the nail clipper and studied it, running her index finger along the sharp edge. She folded out the attached nail file and held it up to the vanity light. *How much damage could it inflict?* she wondered. Could it kill him? Could it kill her? Could she kill anybody? She pressed the edge of the nail file into the soft skin of her left wrist when loud, muted wails broke the silence.

The baby!

Jamie replaced the nail file in the makeup bag, returned it into medicine cabinet, and threw open the bathroom door.

The light from the bathroom shone into the dark bedroom, revealing a pile of bed linens but an otherwise empty bed, and Jamie ran over to the door of the nursery, again suppressing the pain she felt between her thighs. Bailino stood in the small room, facing her, the screaming baby held out in front of him by her armpits, her legs kicking down.

"The baby's crying," he said, pushing the child out toward her like a newborn's weary father.

Jamie reached for the little girl, who, upon seeing her, screeched louder and extended her hands. When released into Jamie's arms, she clutched her neck and rested her head on Jamie's shoulder.

"Feed her, and get her back to sleep," Bailino said, leaving the room. "Then come back to bed."

17

Rosalia was standing just outside the front gates of the governor's mansion when Reynaldo pulled up. For such a large, stately home, the mansion, with its wide, lavish grounds, was set so far back from the iron gatework of its perimeter that you could almost miss it while driving down Eagle Street, especially in the dark. The front gate was still open, and his aunt was chatting with Arthur, the night guard, and another man, whom Reynaldo recognized to be a policeman as he drove closer. The entire first floor of the mansion was dark, with only a few lights on upstairs. Reynaldo heard his aunt utter a soft good-bye, and she hurried into the passenger seat of Reynaldo's car, which he had cleared of paperwork and soda cans. She held up her hand when she saw that Reynaldo wanted to talk and said, "Drive." Without hesitation, he obeyed.

As he drove, Reynaldo glanced at his aunt, who was looking straight ahead. Sitting like that, quiet and introspective, she looked even more like his mother than he remembered, and a feeling of tremendous loss came over him, but it was Rosalia who began to cry.

"Aunt Ro, what is it?" Reynaldo asked. He extended his arm across to her.

"The baby . . ."

"Baby? What baby?" Reynaldo asked. "You mean Charlotte?"

"Yes," Rosalia sobbed. "They took *Carlota*."

"Who took her? Where?"

"I don't know," Rosalia said. "The *policía* were here today asking me questions. It's my fault."

"*Qué?!*" Reynaldo pulled over to the side of the road, and the car jerked to a stop. He faced his aunt. "What is your fault? Why are the police here?"

"I put Charlotte down for her nap, and when I went to check on her, she was gone."

"What do you mean 'gone'?"

"*Ay*, Rey, she wasn't there anymore. She . . . disappeared." Rosalia reached into her pocketbook, pulled out a tissue and blew her nose. She looked so tired, Reynaldo thought.

"Could she have climbed out?"

"No, no . . . I would have heard. I heard nothing. I look at the baby monitor all the time. You know how I am . . ."

He did. Charlotte Grand couldn't have asked for a more dutiful or loving caretaker than his aunt, the woman who had been a second mother to him and his brothers after their mother died. Reynaldo reached across the car and put his arm around Rosalia, and as she leaned onto his shoulder, he stroked her wiry, gray hair. He could smell her perfume, the same brand his *mamá* had worn; the familiar fragrance conjured up happy memories of large family gatherings, crowded rooms filled with cigarette smoke and laughter, always laughter. Rosalia had taken it upon herself to keep the family together when her sister died. Once a month, for as long as Reynaldo could remember, she cooked a giant meal for the whole family—a tradition set by his mother when he was a little boy. Over the years, fewer people attended—many of the older relatives died, his cousins moved downstate, and his father retired last year, leaving only him and his brothers, and these days Pedro and Ricardo would use any excuse to avoid having to visit with Aunt Ro, who didn't have cable television. But Reynaldo showed up every time. He remembered asking her once as a child, "*Tía*, don't you get tired of cooking and cleaning and looking after everyone?" And she had told him, "Some people are meant to care for others, Reyito."

"Where could she be?" Rosalia asked. "She is an innocent child."

"We will find her, *Tía*. What did you tell the police?"

"I told them the truth. What I told you."

Reynaldo thought for a moment. "I'm going to take you home with me," he said. "I don't want you to be alone."

"No, no . . ." She put her used tissue into her purse. "I need to stay in my house. I gave them my telephone number. They said they would call if they needed to reach me. I want to follow directions."

"What about your cell phone?"

"They took it."

"Who? The *policía*? Why?"

"I don't know, Rey. But what do I need it for anyway now? I have nowhere to go." Rosalia choked up on those last words, as if the thought of being alone and unneeded was too much for her to bear, and Reynaldo felt a pang of guilt for reveling in those two very things earlier that evening.

"Then I will stay by you," he said.

"Oh, Reyito," she said, patting his cheek. "You are a good boy. I will make you some *jamón quesadillas* in the morning. Your favorite."

"Okay." He knew it was fruitless to argue and that cooking would help keep his aunt's mind busy. He pulled back onto the street and drove toward her house, the city seeming very big to him all of a sudden—unprotected, vulnerable—particularly with no cars on the road. The beams of the car's headlights were like flashlights searching in the shadows, looking for Baby Charlotte with every turn. It had only been a month ago that Reynaldo had seen the little girl last, her blonde curls springing up and down as the governor bounced her on his knee while sitting on the mansion's wraparound porch, her smile bright and sincere, her laughter carried across the grounds by the evening breeze, and his heart sank at the thought of a world without Charlotte Grand.

18

It wasn't unusual for Detective Nurberg to be at the station before sunrise, but 4:30 a.m. was a new record even for him. After spending most of the night tossing and turning, unable to get out of his mind the heartbreaking image of the Grands' nanny Rosalia—her distress, the pleas to find her charge—and the strange, melodramatic performance of Mrs. Grand, Nurberg found himself meticulously running through the procedures he'd conducted, as if on a loop, to make sure he hadn't left anything out. Every mansion staff member, including kitchen workers, drivers, tour guides, and security guards, had been interviewed. All video of those coming and going had been checked again and again, as were the grounds, which weren't too expansive, but because they were so close to the street traffic, it was easy for someone to slip into a parked vehicle—although nothing had been captured on video and the entire area was under continuous surveillance.

Nurberg entered his small office and threw the folder containing the mansion's visitor manifest on his desk. All twenty-five pages had been laid out on his bed only hours earlier, and he could probably recite each name from memory. No one seemed strange or out of the ordinary. No police records. No red flags. There had been quite a few tour groups at the mansion yesterday, including elementary school children who had been bused in from outlying areas, and it was possible that someone had slipped in as a teacher or school aide and had gotten upstairs undetected. It was mansion policy for visitors to have ID with them upon arrival, but, even in these days of shoe removals and full-body scans at airports, it was rarely checked; so other than a roster of visitors who were *supposed to be* at the mansion, there really was no way of knowing exactly who *had* been there that day. Truth be told, there had never been an incident at the Executive Mansion for the two years he'd been on the Albany force or as far back as he could remember for that matter, so he could see why security may have been a bit lax. But even so, was it possible for someone to have gotten out of the building undetected with a baby who, unless she was drugged or worse, presumably would be crying?

Nurberg sat back in his creaky swivel chair. He dreaded having to face the Grands this morning with the news of no progress on the investigation. Besides the interviews and videotapes, his men had checked every air duct, stairwell, and alcove on the premises, but Charlotte hadn't turned up, nor had evidence of any wrongdoing. Nurberg was used to having a clear perpetrator in the cases he'd handled: a drunk dad, a frustrated mom, a jealous sibling. This was killing him.

There was a brief commotion outside his office door, where several detectives walked in the entrance chatting idly with Missy Giles, his domestic-violence advocate. The abduction of Baby Grand, as she was known among the locals, had the officers working overtime, and Nurberg's boss, Det. Lt. Grohl, had pulled men from the force's other divisions to lend a hand, so there were no less than twenty detectives working a case that had absolutely no leads. When the group saw Nurberg, they stopped and seemed to collectively catch their breath until Nurberg shook his head no, and then they continued across the station floor.

Behind them, Grohl walked in, and before Nurberg could hide and pretend to be on the phone, his boss called him into his office.

"Well, Ice?" Grohl asked, setting his car keys and the newspaper on his desk.

"I filed my report last night, sir."

"Yeah, yeah, I read it. Nothing."

Nurberg groaned. Grohl was more anxious than usual. It wasn't every day that the governor's daughter disappeared, and he wasn't one for the spotlight. "Anything happen last night?"

"Well," Nurberg said. "Matrick called me from the Grands when there was a suspicious phone call."

Grohl's eyes opened wide.

"But it was a false alarm," Nurberg added. "Telemarketer on a personal line that only two people know the number for."

"Well, obviously more than two people if you include the telemarketer. Did you run the number?"

"Detective Matrick gave me the number left on the automated voice-mail message. It checked out. It was for a twenty-four-hour customer-service center for Citibank, which is the bank behind Governor Grand's MasterCard. Seems legit."

Grohl nodded. "Anything else?"

Nurberg shook his head.

"Damn." Grohl leaned back in his chair. "This isn't good."

"I'm doing everything I can, sir."

"Well, keep on it. There's gotta be something we're missing." Grohl pushed a pencil across his desk. "How about the First Lady? What's your take on Mrs. Grand?"

Nurberg tempered his response. Katherine Grand was the odds-on favorite in the station pool for being behind this. "What's her motive, sir?"

"That she's a bitch and a half?" Grohl said.

"I don't know. It doesn't make sense," Nurberg said. "She's a smart woman with her political sights set way beyond Albany. Say what you want about her, but I can't imagine her doing anything that would put that career path in jeopardy."

"Doesn't a baby put that career in jeopardy?"

"Not when your husband's voting base is the traditional family. In terms of political career advancement, Charlotte may have been the best thing to happen to Katherine Grand. And I think she knows it."

"Okay, I'll buy that." Grohl picked up the newspaper on his desk. "Well, here's one good thing. Glad to see that the press hasn't gotten wind of things yet." The front-page headline of the *Albany Times* read

"Bridge to Nowhere" and showed the halted construction of the new Bay Park Bridge.

"Yeah, a few reporters were skulking around asking questions," Nurberg said, "but they seemed to buy that we were performing drills at the mansion over the next few days."

"Good. The more time we have without the media on our backs, the better."

"I agree."

"Well, all right," Grohl said, picking up his phone. "Keep me posted, Nurberg."

"I will," Nurberg said, taking the hint. He left Grohl's office and returned to his own. There was a steaming hot cup of black coffee on his desk; next to it, on a small paper plate, was a frosted brownie. He glanced up and saw Missy Giles talking to a few officers near the front of the main office. She saw him and smiled. He smiled back and, for an instant, forgot all about the beleaguered investigation into the disappearance of Baby Grand.

19

The glow outside the bedroom windows was bright and cleansing, but did nothing to alleviate the filthy feeling that gnawed at Jamie's insides. Just several minutes earlier as she pretended to sleep, Bailino had stepped into the bathroom and shut the door. The shower water had been turned on, and she could hear him humming.

Although Charlotte had gone back to sleep while Jamie fed her a bottle of formula, she stalled as long as she could in the nursery, terrified of returning to Bailino's bed. But there was no way around it—she *had* to go back. What choice did she have? It was only when she heard him shuffle to the bathroom that she slipped under the covers, praying that he would leave her be. When Bailino returned, there was a pause before he climbed into bed, and then he fluffed his pillow, kicked out the flat sheet until it was tucked under his feet, and before falling asleep, slid his hand between Jamie's legs. And that was where it remained.

Jamie had been awake ever since. She spent hours thinking about Edward, trying to create a time frame in her mind as to when her brother would realize that something was wrong, that she was missing and start looking for her and then how long it would take to find her. It was only now, in the blinding light of day, that the truth hit her hard: *No one knows where you are.*

This was the first time that Jamie could remember ever being truly alone. It seemed as if her entire life, there had always been somebody—her mother, her brother, even Bob—running around beneath her with a net while she was walking the high wire of her life. She attended the same college as Edward—now that she thought about it, she never even entertained going anywhere else other than Hofstra, which was so close to home. Talk about a safety school. And it was the recommendation—a strong one made over the phone—of her journalism professor that had secured Jamie's first job at a local newspaper. And it was her mother who had picked the venue for her wedding reception. Jamie began thinking about every major milestone of her life, and suddenly it seemed as if she had little to do with any of them, and a hopelessness descended upon her as she lay in the unfamiliar bed. Plus, her last totally spontaneous decision, made on her own—to eat in Bryant Park rather than inside Frank's Deli yesterday—was the thing that had landed her in this mess.

A soft coo came from the nursery, and Jamie got out of bed and, still feeling woozy and sore, hurried across the bedroom. The baby was sleeping soundly in a corner of the crib, making sweet little gibberish sounds as she exhaled. Her little chubby legs were bare, having kicked off the blanket Jamie had placed on them during the night, and her little socks had fallen off too. As she lay there, peaceful, in the bright daylight, there was an unmistakable familiarity about the little girl, and Jamie wondered if she'd seen her before. She dismissed the idea, thinking that perhaps she was being reminded of Peter and Sara, since she practically lived with Edward and Tricia when the kids were born. *You have no connection to this child*, Jamie chided herself, although she knew that was untrue. A bond had formed the moment she saw her lying helpless on the basement table, and in her heart Jamie knew that any thoughts she had of escape were going to include the little girl. But just how do you sneak a baby out of a second-story room without anyone noticing?

With her eye on the bathroom, Jamie hurried over to the bedroom door, but was confounded by the strange mechanism there in place of a doorknob. A small light in the corner of the device glowed red. She needed a key.

She pulled open the top drawer of the nightstand, expecting, for some reason, to find a copy of the Bible inside, but instead found only loose change and some toiletries. She surveyed the wide room, whose edges seemed to crystallize in the daylight, and wondered if there was anything she could use to get out of there or as a weapon. At the far left were a dresser and chest of drawers and over to the right, a baby grand piano she hadn't noticed last night. She tiptoed past the bathroom door and opened a drawer or two of the dresser, finding nothing but clothing, but was so afraid Bailino would open the bathroom door and catch her snooping that she abandoned her plan and went back to the other side of the room, near the windows.

Jamie pressed her face against the large panes of glass, which looked out onto the vibrant blue of the sky where healthy cumulus clouds were drifting eastward. At this early hour, the sun cast long shadows of the area's surrounding tall trees, forming long black bars across the lawn. A shovel lay idly on the ground near a small shed.

The water turned off in the shower, and within seconds the lock of the bathroom door was unhinged, and Bailino's head emerged from the bathroom, wet, water beading on his skin.

"Could you bring me those clothes on the nightstand, please?" he asked her.

Jamie hesitated and then handed him several articles of clothing, without meeting his eyes. She turned around and returned to her spot near the windows.

Bailino reemerged from the bathroom dressed in a black V-neck T-shirt and a pair of gray khakis. His bare feet were making dewy footprints on the hardwood floor. He sat on the bed and rubbed the towel on his head, which made his short hair stick straight up in untidy spikes.

"Did you sleep okay?" he asked.

Jamie said nothing. She imagined he knew she was up most of the night.

"I asked if you slept all right." Bailino turned toward her.

"Okay, I guess," she said, looking at the baby.

"She sleepin'?" Bailino asked.

Jamie nodded.

"I asked you a question," he said, his voice becoming disagreeable. Her eyes searched for answers in the dark, glossy knots of the hardwood flooring. Jamie knew she had to find a way to stand her ground without inflaming Bailino, while giving herself enough time to sort through her options, if she had any.

"Please look at me when I talk to you." Bailino got up and tossed the wet towel into the bathroom and walked toward her.

She met his eyes this time and kept her feet planted even though every inch of her body wanted to run and hide. He stopped just in front of her, his eyelashes wet and clumped together in sections, an after-shower glow to his skin that offset the darkness of his deep-set eyes. She could smell the Old Spice aftershave she'd seen in the medicine cabinet. "Yes, she is still sleeping," Jamie said bravely, just as Bailino reached his hand underneath the bottom of her shirt and grabbed the front of her bra.

"What's this?" he asked.

"My bra," she said. The feeling of his wet hand on her chest no longer felt foreign, and Jamie mourned the death of the girl she had been just the day before.

Bailino reached behind her and deftly unhooked the bra with two fingers, causing it to hang beneath Jamie's torn blouse. "You don't need this when you're in here with me. I don't want to see it on you anymore in this room. Understand?"

Jamie nodded.

"Understand?"

"Yes," she answered.

"Now take it off," he ordered.

Jamie reached her left arm into her right sleeve and brought the strap of her bra down over her hand and then pulled the bra out from her left sleeve. She placed it on the nightstand.

Bailino sat on the bed. He unraveled a pair of black socks and crossed his legs. "I see you found Gina's play makeup bag in the bathroom. You like nail files?" He reached into the drawer of the nightstand and pulled out a small clipper, which he used to trim the nail of his big toe.

"I was looking for a Band-Aid, something for my head."

"Stop looking around so much." Bailino pulled his sock up toward his knee. "You'll be better off."

"Are you going to kill me?" The words came out before Jamie could stop them, and Bailino stared, before letting out a laugh. "You're a no-nonsense kind of girl, huh?"

"Not really. But I just want to know. Makes it easier . . . to know what you're up against."

"Some people would say it's better not to know."

"My mom used to say that."

"Used to?"

Jamie thought of her mother lying in bed, wasting away to a third of her size, day after day, never letting the doctors tell her or anyone how much time she had left. *You don't always need a doctor, or people, to tell you what's going to happen, sweetie,* she'd told her. *Some things you just know.* And maybe her mother did know, and maybe she was saving Edward and her from waiting around for the inevitable, but not knowing also left them unprepared for when her mother didn't wake up three weeks before Jamie's wedding. Not knowing led Jamie to convince herself that the diagnosis could be wrong, that her mother could beat the odds, that being in the dark could stop something from happening. It didn't.

"I never understood that," Jamie said. She let out a slow breath and, suddenly feeling vulnerable, crossed her arms to hide her exposed breasts.

Bailino nodded. "Well, I don't know how to answer your question exactly," he said, running his fingers along the waistband of his slacks, "although I tend to want to know things myself." He studied her. "Do you have a boyfriend?"

Jamie shook her head.

"I asked you . . ."

"No," she said.

Bailino smiled. "I don't believe you."

"I don't. I was married for eight years. He left me. I don't have a boyfriend."

"Edward?"

"Edward?" Jamie's thoughts drifted and then remembered that

Bailino had her cell phone. He must have been doing some snooping of his own.

"He was your husband?" Bailino asked.

"Edward's my brother." There was no use lying, she thought.

"Oh." Bailino seemed satisfied and disappeared into the bathroom. "Why?" he yelled.

"Why what?" She could hear him moving around and the soft clink of metal to porcelain.

"Why did your husband leave you?"

"I don't know," she said. "I guess he didn't love me anymore."

"Did you love him?"

"No." It surprised Jamie how quickly, and adamantly, she said the word.

There was a pause. "Did you ever love him?"

"No," she said again, without hesitation, although she had never admitted that to anyone. Not even Edward.

"Then why did you marry him?"

"I don't know. I guess sometimes you get caught up in something and don't know how to get out of it."

"That's very true." Bailino emerged from the bathroom. His wet hair was parted just off center and combed back on both sides. Jamie detected traces of baby powder in the creases of his neck, from which the hanging gold cross gleamed atop a coat of coarse black chest hairs, as if showcased upon a velvet-lined jewel box. "You want to shower?"

Jamie hesitated. She wanted nothing more than to take a hot shower, to wash the previous day completely away, but in her *own* bathroom.

"You'll find towels in the linen closet and an extra bathrobe behind the door," he said, as if she were a guest in his bed-and-breakfast. "Now's the time. The baby's sleeping. You know how it is." He settled back down on the bed and put on his shoes. He used a shoehorn—she hadn't seen anyone use one of those since she was a little girl and spent summers at her grandparents' house in Brooklyn. "Chop-chop," he said. "Time's a-wastin'."

As if on command, Jamie walked into the bathroom and shut the door. It was still steamy from Bailino's shower, and condensation covered the raised scrollwork of the ceramic tiles, which conjured up images of ornate bathhouses in Rome. Avoiding the mirror, Jamie disrobed and stepped into the deep, old-fashioned bathtub and pulled the shower curtain closed. She knew at any moment he could come in, so she moved fast. She turned on the water and grabbed the only shampoo that was there, one of those heavy-duty dandruff kinds, and poured the liquid onto her head. She lathered and then stood under the water, feeling the bubbles drift over her closed eyelids and down her body, imagining the suds carrying away the events of the day before and funneling them down the drain. She took scented soap and scrubbed her skin, when something dawned on her: Perhaps this was some kind of trick, a way to get the baby alone, to take her away. Then Jamie would really be alone; the thought terrified her. She washed off the lather and turned off the faucet.

Wrapping herself in the plush bathrobe, she leaned her ear against the bathroom door, but didn't hear anything. She opened it a crack and peered out. No movement. Jamie opened the door all the way and ran across the floor, drips marking her path, to the nursery. The baby was asleep, just as she'd left her. There was no one else in the bedroom, and the bedroom door was still closed. Bailino must have gone. She glanced at the bed: In the few minutes she had been in the shower, the bed had been pristinely made, the flat sheet over the fitted sheet with military corners, the floral print duvet rolled neatly on top, all the pillows picked up from the floor and tucked behind one another against the headboard. A pair of boot-cut jeans, a plain white T-shirt, and a pair of women's bikini underwear had been laid out on the bed, as well as the bra she'd left on the night table. The clothing looked as if it had never been worn. She held the tee and spied the label: 34/36. It was a man's shirt. But the jeans were women's. In her size.

The last thing Jamie wanted to do was indulge Bailino in this game, whatever it was, but there was no denying what she saw last night, and she knew that she was but one blow to the head between life and death, at the mercy of a man who was capable of quick and sudden violence on a whim. But she had somehow managed to stay alive for the past twelve hours. Wounded physically and emotionally, but alive. She knew it was better, smarter, to play along for now. Something told her that Bailino—the man who kidnapped and raped her—was her best bet for getting through this thing. She picked up her bra and tightened the straps. And as she slipped on the unfamiliar underwear, a memory formed: It was the morning following her wedding night, which she had spent in a tony hotel on Long Island's north shore overlooking the Sound, and Bob had gone out for coffee, which she didn't drink, so she had stayed behind. A wave of déjà vu swept through her—the sunlight streaming through the large windows, the barely used furnishings, the foreign detergent smells, the intense quiet, and that lingering sense of incongruity that reminded her of that childhood riddle, "Which of the following does not belong?" In both instances, the answer was the same.

20

Phillip's hands shook as he buttoned his cotton shirt, his large fingers fumbling to get the tiny plastic through the holes. He hadn't slept at all, and there were dark circles under his eyes. The voice on the cell phone played over and over in his mind. It had been years, but its cadence and tone were instantly recognizable.

"Where are you going?" Katherine turned over in bed. Her voice was raspy.

Phillip had been practicing his response all night in his head. He put on a weary expression, which wasn't difficult. "For a drive. I need air."

"A drive? To where?"

"I need to get out of the house, Katherine. I need to think."

"I'll go with you." She got out of bed.

"*No.*" The word came out brusquer than he had intended.

"Well, you can't go alone," she said.

"I'm not. Henry's driving me."

"Henry doesn't count."

"Why, Katherine? Because he's a driver and sits in the front seat?"

"Don't start, Phillip," Katherine said. "Did you clear this with Nurberg?"

"Katherine, I won't be long. Please. It's just a drive." He tucked his shirt into his slacks.

"Have you heard from Nurberg at all?"

"No, but Detective Matrick said he would be stopping by this morning."

Katherine reached for her cell phone. She pushed a few buttons as she walked toward her computer, turned it on, and then brushed aside the long, heavy drapes to gaze out the window where a few detectives were milling around. The drapes had always reminded Phillip of a funeral home. He would have given anything to replace them with something lightweight, like beige linen tab-top curtains, but the historical society wouldn't go for it.

"What do you think of that Nurberg?" Katherine asked.

"Oh, I don't know, seems conscientious . . . and bright . . . and determined. Why?"

Katherine wrinkled her nose. "I don't like him."

"You don't like anyone."

Katherine faced him and put her hands on her hips. In her flannel pajamas and her hair flopping in her face, she looked like a young co-ed rather than the most powerful woman in New York State. "Hey, I'm on your side, remember?" She stuck her hands in the pockets of her pajama pants, her rows of knuckles appearing as tiny ridges of red plaid.

"I'm sorry." Phillip wrapped his arms around his wife, hoping that she couldn't feel his heart racing. "I haven't slept, and I can't think straight. I just need to get out."

"Let me go with you."

"No, stay here. One of us should, in case the detectives need something. Remember, I'm just a phone call away." He held up his phone and put it into his pocket.

Katherine sat back on the bed. "Why haven't we heard anything?" she asked. "What does that mean, Phillip?"

"No news is good news, Katherine," he said. He planted a kiss on the top of his wife's head and walked out the bedroom door.

Katherine watched her husband disappear down the hall. He was usually the first one out of the bedroom on any given day, letting her sleep in or tending to Charlotte so that she could get work done if Rosalia had not yet arrived. In that respect, this morning was like any other. But Katherine felt very different, and the shame traveled up the skin of her arms as she realized that what she felt was relief.

This was the first morning in the past ten months that Katherine didn't feel the obligatory pull of Charlotte on her—that sensation, she imagined, experienced by mothers of young children whose time is suddenly no longer their own. Today, of all days, she should have felt that pull the most—her child had been taken from her—and she felt nothing. She thought of Nurberg and his suspicious eyes, and of the press who had given her a multimedia flogging this past year. Was it so wrong to grieve for the life she'd had when it was just her and Phillip? When she could unwind by watching television without being saddled with guilt?

She peered down the hall to be sure Phillip was gone, walked over to the bookshelves near her desk, and pulled out a small, wrinkled paper bag from behind a Spanish-English dictionary. All her life she'd had people depending on her, *thrived* on having people depend on her, but for the one person who really needed her, Katherine had failed. She stuffed the bag into her purse, checking one last time to see if the hallway was empty. Then she sat back at her computer and tried to focus on work, but it was fruitless. Right now, Katherine had only one thing on her mind. And that was Don Bailino.

21

"What the fuck are you doing?" Leo asked, pouring himself a cup of coffee. Tony was sitting in the dining room, his head tilted down and practically touching the screen of a laptop computer that was set up on the buffet. "You gonna marry that thing?"

"What?" Tony pulled back. "I'm comfortable like that. Stop busting my balls, Leo."

"What are you doing?"

"I'm updating my Facebook page."

"Are you fuckin' nuts?" Leo stood behind Tony, taking loud slurps of his coffee. "What the fuck you writing? 'Kidnapped a baby today'?" Leo slapped him in the head. Benny, who was reading the newspaper at the dining room table, let out a loud laugh and looked at Joey, who sat across from him reading a book while listening to his headphones.

"No," Tony said. "I just wrote 'feeling hungry.'"

"Oh, that's riveting stuff. You should write a novel." Leo sat on the sofa and stretched his legs onto the coffee table, rubbing his socked feet together. "I don't understand that shit. The photos . . . everyone's showing pictures of themselves from twenty years ago or pictures that are half-cropped out because they're so fuckin' fat. Look at your picture."

"What's wrong with it?"

"It's the side of your fuckin' face. Where are the rest of your chins?"

"Ha, ha."

"What's the point of writing all that shit down anyway? Waste of time." Leo took another swig of his coffee.

"So I take it you don't want to *friend* me," Tony asked.

Leo stared. "Do I look like I want to friend you? I don't even want to be in the same room with you." He looked at Benny. "Are you friends with him?"

Benny nodded.

"No shit? Another dummy."

Bailino walked in, followed by Jamie, who was wearing the outfit that had been placed on the bed for her and carrying the little girl, who had just downed another eight ounces of formula and had on a fresh onesie and white socks. The jeans were long, so Jamie had cuffed them a few times on the bottom, but the waist was a perfect fit. Her feet were bare, and she was conscious of her red toenail polish that she had so carefully painted on just two days before. The three of them looked like a family making their way into the kitchen on a sunny spring morning.

"Hey, maybe *she* wants to friend you," Leo said to Tony.

Jamie's eyes glanced at the computer and then looked away. From the colors and layout of the monitor, she could tell that there was a Facebook page showing. *That meant there was Internet access in the house.* She held the baby tighter in her arms.

"Finally!" Tony said. "I'm starving."

"Morning, Sunshine," Leo said, winking at Jamie. "Rough night?"

The sores on Jamie's face and head, which swelled slightly after her hot shower, seemed to sting from Leo's gaze. The little girl put her head down on Jamie's shoulder.

"What's for breakfast?" Tony asked.

"Make your own fucking breakfast," Bailino said. "Have a little respect. You're in my house." Bailino picked up a newspaper from the floor, put it on the kitchen counter, and poured himself a cup of coffee.

The men looked at one another.

"But Blondie made breakfast for us yesterday morning?" Tony said.

"It wasn't her idea." Leo said with a sneer.

"Yeah, well, she's not Blondie. How difficult is a fuckin' Pop-Tart?" Bailino turned to Jamie. "Go ahead, sweetheart. Sit down." He pulled out one of the barstools and then reached up on the top shelf of a nearby cabinet for a box of Cheerios. The little girl watched Bailino, her eyes on the cereal box. Bailino held the box out, and she recoiled at first, but then took it from his hands and fumbled with its top.

Jamie sat down and placed the little girl on her lap. She stuck her hand into the box, grabbed a handful of Cheerios, and placed them on a napkin in front of the baby, who grabbed at them, shoving them into her mouth. She put so many in that Jamie was afraid she was going to choke.

"Easy, easy," she said. "Slow down."

"Don't mess up my computer," Bailino said, unpeeling a banana and kicking Tony's chair.

"I'm not messing it up," Tony said, "I'm on Facebook. You said to do the things we normally do."

"Fine, just don't be like that nitwit in Louisiana they tracked down." He put a key into an electronic lock on the glass back doors, which, Jamie noticed, was the same as the lock on the upstairs bedroom door. There was a soft *click*, and Bailino slid the glass door open and stepped outside.

"I'm not a wanted man," Tony muttered under his breath.

"That's for sure," Leo said, which made Benny laugh again.

"You better quit laughing, you fuck," Tony said and then got up and went into the kitchen to grab a box of Pop-Tarts from the cabinet. "Anybody else want one?"

Benny and Leo's hands went up.

The little girl started to say something, but her mouth was full of crumbs. She clapped her hands with her fingertips pressing together.

"Yay," Jamie whispered and poured more Cheerios onto her napkin, stealing another glance at the computer. All she needed was thirty seconds to log onto her profile and get out a quick message, but she could feel Leo's eyes on her, and she averted her gaze and looked out the glass back doors.

"How do you spell *judgment*?" Benny asked Joey, who appeared lost in music, his head nodding up and down.

"Joey, I'm talkin' to you!" Benny pulled the book out of his hands.

Joey blinked and took off his headphones. "What?"

"*Judgment*. How do you spell it?"

"J-U-D-G-E-M-E-N-T, you moron," said Leo from the living room.

"There's no *e*," Joey said, putting his headphones back on.

"What do you mean there's no fuckin' *e*? You mean the one after the *g*? That can't be right," Leo said.

"I think he's right, Leo," Benny said, looking at the newspaper. "There's only eight boxes for the letters, so it fits without the *e*. "

"Would you look at that?" Leo stood up and wandered over to the dining room table. "Did you know that, Sunshine? That the word *judgment* only has one *e*?"

Jamie pretended to assist the baby by flattening and reflattening the creases of her onesie.

"Yo, I'm talkin' to you," Leo said, getting closer, when Bailino stepped back into the house.

"What a fuckin' day out there. Gorgeous. Gotta be 70 degrees."

"Now what the fuck you doin'?" Leo said, watching Tony unscrew a bottle of powdered cinnamon.

"Did you know that sniffing cinnamon actually boosts brainpower?" Tony said.

"Really? Maybe you should pour the whole thing on your head."

"Oh, you're in rare form today, Leo," Tony said, handing him a Pop-Tart, and then tossing one in front of Benny before sitting back at the computer.

"You eat?" Bailino asked Jamie.

Jamie shook her head no. "I'm not hungry."

"You should eat," Bailino said. "What do you want?"

"I'll just take an apple."

"Good." Bailino took an apple from a fruit basket and pulled out a stool next to her. "I have to leave here for a few hours to take care of some things." He rubbed the apple on his slacks until the sides developed a dull sheen and handed it to Jamie. "I expect you to watch this child, to keep her quiet and happy. Understand?"

Jamie nodded.

"I asked you if you understood."

"Yes," Jamie said.

"Good girl," Bailino said, squeezing her chin.

"You want to take her for a walk?" Joey had taken off his headphones and was speaking to Jamie.

"Outside?" Jamie asked with a hint of enthusiasm. She took a bite of the apple, while the child pushed Cheerios around the counter with her hands.

"Yeah, she could probably use the sunlight," Joey said.

Jamie looked at Bailino, who nodded his approval.

"Give me a second. I just want to log out," Tony said, typing at the keyboard.

"You don't have to log off," Joey said.

"And leave her with you?" Leo said. "You've gotta be kidding."

"They'll be fine," Bailino said, slipping on a jacket.

"Yeah, well, I'll be watching from the back," Leo said to Jamie. "So don't get any ideas. That would be bad *judgment*."

With the baby in her arms, Jamie followed Joey outside, and it was as if she'd entered Oz: Birds were singing, the colors seemed brighter, and there was a slight morning breeze. Even the baby let out a tiny coo as she blinked her eyes in the sunlight, and then she straightened her body in Jamie's arms.

"What's the matter?" Jamie asked and then realized the little girl wanted to be put down. She placed her on the ground, and her bent legs stood tentatively, wobbling. Jamie tried to hold her hands, but she pulled them away and tried to take a step on her own, then toppled over.

"I'll help you," Jamie said, grabbing both hands and pulling the child up to a stand. The little girl pushed her tiny socked feet forward while Jamie held her and started walking across the manicured lawn.

From inside, Bailino and Leo watched them.

"Stay away from her," Bailino said, his eyes on Jamie.

"What, only you can have all the fun?"

"You think I think this is fun?" Bailino took a sip of his coffee and set the cup down on the counter. "I have better things to do."

"Oh, really? Like what? Accept another award, maybe?"

Bailino ignored him. "I have to go. You think you can handle things while I'm gone."

"Oh, yes," Leo said with sarcasm. "Who took care of your mess last night?"

"That wasn't my mess."

"Oh, no? So is that your mess out there?" Leo pointed at Jamie.

"Listen, Leo, we have to put up with each other for a few days. Let's just do it and get it over with, and we can be on our way."

"Fine by me."

Bailino grabbed his keys and walked out the back door.

"I'll be back soon," Bailino called out to Jamie, who watched him hop into a white Ford Flex and pull out of the driveway. The little girl stopped to examine a ladybug, and Jamie stood up and stretched—her back was hurting from hunching over. Joey, who was a few steps ahead, took the headphones out of his ears.

"You all right?" he asked.

She nodded. "You're Joey, right?"

Joey looked back at the house. He kicked a small rock.

"Just keep your head down, do what they say, and you'll get out of this thing," he whispered.

His words surprised her. She glanced at Leo who was still watching them from the back door. "I don't think so." Jamie could feel her eyes water. "After what I saw?"

"You just have to keep quiet. Can you do that?"

Charlotte reached for Jamie's hands, and she picked up the little girl, who continued walking along the grass.

"I don't know," Jamie said. "I don't know if I can do that."

"You'd be surprised at what you can do."

Jamie studied the young man. He reminded her a little of Edward, tall and pale, with a long neck and sprinkling of freckles on his nose and cheeks. He kept blowing the hair out of his eyes, but his bangs would always fall back down. They walked for a few minutes in silence.

"Who are you listening to?" she asked.

"Switchfoot. Do you know them?"

"Sure, I've heard of them. Kind of like an alternative rock band, right?"

"Yep. They have this new sound ever since they broke with their record company." There was genuine enthusiasm in Joey's voice. "What do you listen to?"

"Oh, nothing special." Her thoughts turned to Bob, who liked to call her Ms. Top Forty, because her musical tastes were so cliché and uninteresting.

"No, serious. There's gotta be someone you really like."

Jamie shrugged her shoulders. "I don't know. . . Pink?"

"Pink's cool." Joey smiled. "Kind of a badass, but feminine too, you know?" He looked toward the cabin; they were about a city-street block's worth of distance from the glass doors. "We should turn back."

"It's nice around here," Jamie said, ignoring him. She wanted to stay as far away from the cabin as possible and keep surveying the area. The woods stretched as far as the eye could see—an openness lacking in her Long Island suburb where backyards resembled little fiefdoms, cordoned off with their six-foot-high PVC fences. She often dreamt of living in a place like this where she could stroll unwatched by neighbors and collect her thoughts, maybe write. But now the woods felt too open and clandestine, as if she were floating in space away from civilization, and no one could hear her scream.

"I prefer the city, actually." Joey shrugged his shoulders. "It's so . . . I don't know, boring here."

"Do you live here all the time?" Jamie asked.

"No, I don't live here. Uncle Don does."

They came upon a large vegetable garden with segmented square plots, each with a different handwritten sign: TOMATOES, BASIL, GREEN PEPPERS, OREGANO. Small white stones dotted the edges of the garden, which measured about eight feet around.

"This is nice," Jamie said.

"Yeah, it's Uncle Don's," Joey said without much enthusiasm. "He likes to grow things." He turned back toward the house again.

"He likes to garden?"

"Yeah, among other things," Joey said. "C'mon, we really have to go back."

Jamie got the urge to run, to grab the baby and just go and see what would happen. She knew south was straight ahead of her, but she feared that with the baby in tow, Joey would catch up to them in no time or worse, Leo and the others would. But maybe Joey would let them leave, she reasoned, maybe he'd just turn around and walk back. He seemed like a nice enough kid. She wanted to plead with him, to look into his eyes and tell him to have pity on her and to let her go. But Jamie knew he wouldn't. There was fear in his eyes too.

"C'mon, we need to go back," Joey said, trying to make his voice a little sterner, as if he were trying to be more like his Uncle Don.

Deflated, Jamie turned to go back when the little girl, who'd been walking along quietly the whole time, decided to drop Jamie's hands. She stood there before the vegetable garden like a queen before her court.

"C'mon, honey," Jamie said. She reached for her hand, but the little girl pulled away.

Joey crouched down. "C'mon, we have to go," he said in a quiet voice. "Be a good girl, Charlotte."

Charlotte.

Jamie didn't react. Joey didn't realize that he'd said the little girl's name. He was still trying to cajole her into going back, but Jamie's mind was racing. *Charlotte. Charlotte. Charlotte.* And then it hit her. Those blonde curls. About a year old. Upstate New York.

Charlotte Grand. The governor's daughter.

Suddenly all the press releases that had inundated her in-box for ten months flooded back into her memory. The pregnancy announcement. The "It's a Girl" ultrasound. Jamie could still picture the photo of the governor and Mrs. Grand on the balcony of Milton Hospital holding the newborn baby, all smiles and waving. *Saturday Night Live* had even done a parody of the press photo, likening it to the infamous Michael Jackson/Blanket video footage from Germany years before.

Without warning, Charlotte made a run for it. She ran a good five or six steps, but her little legs were moving too fast for the rest of her body, and her knees buckled outward as if she had just gotten off a horse. She fell face-first into a patch of unplanted dirt. The wailing started immediately, and the three men—Leo, Benny, and Tony—reached them in seconds. *I would have never made it,* Jamie thought.

The men stopped when they saw the reason for the cries and collectively caught their breath.

"Jesus, Joey," Tony said. "I was in the middle of a hand of online poker."

"All right, leave the kid alone," Leo said. "The baby fell. What do you want?"

"It was a good hand, too," Tony said as the three men headed back to the cabin.

"Let's play some real poker, not that fairy kind," Leo said.

"Sure, I'll take your money, Leo," Tony said. "Benny, you in?"

Benny nodded.

"No problem," said Leo. He called to Joey. "Let's go. Playtime's over. Back to the house."

The dirt was so loose where Charlotte had fallen that when she lifted her head, her face was covered—there was dirt in her mouth, in her hair, and in her eyelashes. Jamie stood the little girl up and bent down to brush her off.

"You're okay," Jamie soothed. "It's all right." Crouched down, Jamie could hear the sound of running water again, like when she had first arrived the day before. Charlotte must have heard it too, because her head turned. It was close by.

"She really likes you," Joey said, standing over them.

Charlotte crouched down and started pushing the loose dirt around with her hands. With her index finger, she drew swirls and patted down the earth. Then she was on all fours, using both hands.

"We have to go now," Joey said. He was giving Jamie a look that said they had no other choice. She picked Charlotte up when the little girl suddenly exclaimed, "MaBa! MaBa!" She fought to get down, stiffening her body, but Jamie held Charlotte firmly and followed her gaze: There was a small yellow shrub at the corner of the patch of dirt that had gotten the little girl's attention. Jamie reached down to pick it up.

"No," Joey said, "don't . . ."

But it was too late. In Jamie's hand was a knotted ball of blonde human hair.

22

Bailino parked the Ford Flex on the side of the road, across the street from Taryn's Diner. The diner, known for its homemade pies, was a favorite among locals and was busy twenty-four hours a day—even on Christmas. Especially on Christmas. Today, the large blackboard that hung in the front window read LEMON MERINGUE in brightly colored chalk, and patrons spilled in and out in a constant flow.

Bailino checked his watch—11:00 a.m. He scanned the large front windows of the diner, but the sun's reflection kept him from being able to see inside, so he clicked off the ignition, silencing the rumble of the engine, and opened the car door.

Dressed as inconspicuously as he'd allow in his gray khakis and a black T-shirt, Bailino blended in well with the other passersby, many of them upper middle-classers who'd escaped from New York City for better schools and friendlier neighbors even if it meant putting up with the harsh winters. And this past winter had been a doozy—it was only in the past few days that the remnants of the tallest bulldozed snow piles had finally melted—so it was no surprise to see people out and about on such a glorious day.

Bailino eyed the residents who were chatting amicably while they window-shopped along the strip mall facing the diner. A young couple made their way out of a used bookshop. The young man had longish hair that reminded him of Joey, and he thought about Jamie and young Charlotte Grand being put into Joey's care and how it had irked

Leo. He smiled. The couple were holding hands and stopping every few feet to embrace and cuddle. Bailino stuck his hand in his pocket, pulled out Jamie's cell phone, and turned it on. There were twenty-five missed calls and seven messages, all from the same person: Edward. Ignoring the prompt, he swiped the screen with his finger until he pulled up Jamie's photos. The first one quickly came into focus: a little boy and a girl, neither of whom had front teeth. They had their hands wrapped around each other and were mushing their faces together. Bailino pressed the right arrow, and a photo of a man appeared. The jealousy swelled within him, so much so that he had to look away for a moment. Then he examined the man's features: soft eyes, kind face. The man was posing with his arm resting on a wooden fence. Bailino hit the arrow again, and a photo of a little girl with a woman appeared, a beautiful brunette wearing patched bell-bottom jeans. The little girl was dressed in a navy-blue jumper and looked somewhat startled, as if the snapshot had been taken in midstep.

Bailino turned the phone off and replaced it back into his pocket. The front door of Taryn's opened, and two men wearing army fatigues emerged, one of them holding the door for a woman carrying a car seat. The two servicemen crossed the street, and as they passed him, he bowed his head. Their faces were hidden by their caps, but Bailino could make out the boyish innocence of their features. *They haven't seen any real action*, he thought. He could tell.

Bailino thought back to when his battalion landed in Iraq for the first time, after the initial invasion during the first Gulf War—his fellow soldiers looked a lot like those two young men. The touchdown was rocky, not at all what he'd expected for a military landing in the desert, and had shaken the windowless carrier violently, but Bailino had learned to veil his fear at an early age and was sure no one on board could tell that it had been his first time on a plane. At twenty-six, Bailino had been older than many of his comrades who were fresh out of high school or college, and during the open-desert tank battles, his leadership emerged as US tanks outclassed the Iraqi forces, who were poorly supplied and operating largely without command and control from Baghdad. Only one other man in his unit had enlisted at age twenty-six, a quiet silver spooner who had just graduated from Harvard Law and whose father had insisted he join the army, war or no war, as was the tradition of the men in his family.

At first, Bailino was suspicious of Ivy Leaguer Phillip Grand, but a mutual respect formed between them, perhaps because of their differences—Pfc. Bailino, dark skinned and tenacious, was as quick on his feet as he was in his decision making, while tall and lean Pfc. Grand, "the thinker," as he was known in the unit, was pensive and thorough. The unlikely friendship the two formed during boot camp lasted throughout their entire tour of duty. It was only after the men returned to civilian life, three years later, that their friendship was cut short abruptly by the election of Phillip Grand to the New York State Assembly.

A black town car pulled up in front of Taryn's. The back door opened, and Governor Grand emerged. The governor ran his hands through his hair, something Bailino had seen him do countless times in crisis, and motioned for the driver to find a spot in the parking lot. It was not an unusual sight to see Phillip Grand, considered "the People's Governor," roaming around near the vicinity of Taryn's Diner without his official entourage. Every week, he met his mother for brunch, an intimate affair that both the local residents and media respected, keeping their distance. As the governor ran toward the doors of the diner, both he and Don Bailino, who followed behind, knew that this time the governor's mother would not be inside.

23

Phillip sat on one of the stools at the counter.

"The usual, Governor?" A redheaded waitress, whose weathered countenance belied a light-spirited soul, brought him a stout glass of ice water, spilling it a little as she placed it onto his paper place mat. The governor watched the spilt water spread evenly into a quarter-sized circle and placed his napkin on top of it. The waitress reached under the counter and pulled out two dessert plates; she placed one in front of the governor and the other before the seat next to him on the right. The governor was about to tell Mitzy—he knew all the waitresses by name—that his mother would not be joining him today, but thought better of it. It might attract suspicion if it was thought that he was dining there alone.

"Yes, Mitzy, the usual." Phillip forced a smile.

"You all right, Guv?" Taryn herself had come out of the kitchen. Although she was over 250 pounds, Taryn had a buoyancy about her and a solid work ethic that was contagious among her employees. She had run the diner alone for the past five years since her husband, Jet, passed away, showing up for work every day at 6:00 a.m. and never leaving before 9:00 p.m. She usually got a quick heads-up when Phillip came in for a visit. "You're looking kinda pale, sir," she said with concern. "You all right?" Her white apron was caked with confectioner's sugar, which she spread to the bottom of her nose after she wiped it.

"Oh, just a little under the weather, I guess. I'm sure it'll pass."

"Maybe it's allergies," Don Bailino said, sitting on the seat to the governor's left. Bailino looked at a menu and then back at Phillip. "Hey, aren't you the governor of this fine state? I always wondered if I'd ever see you in here."

"Sure is," Taryn said, placing a drippy glass of ice water on top of Bailino's paper place mat. "Gotta admire a man who takes time to see his momma once a week. I don't know about you, but that's the kind of man I want fightin' for me in government. One who has his priorities straight, right, Don?"

"That's right," Bailino said with a smile.

"How's that book comin'?" Taryn asked.

"Oh, slow, very slow." Bailino answered.

"Well, now, you keep plugging along. You'll get it done."

Phillip listened to the light conversation as Taryn placed a slice of cherry pie on Phillip's plate and on the one beside it.

"A family man," Bailino said, taking a long sip of his ice water. "I do believe I agree with you, ma'am. The love between a parent and a child is one of the most sacred bonds. It's nice to see an elected official remember that." He inspected Phillip's plate. "*Hmmm*, that cherry pie looks good. I think I'll have that as well today."

"Comin' right up." Taryn placed the dish on Bailino's place mat. She poured them both a cup of coffee. "If you need anything else, I'll be right in the back."

"Thank you," Bailino said cheerily.

Phillip Grand watched as Bailino wolfed down the cherry pie with deliberate attentiveness—the way, Phillip remembered, he did everything. With the exception of the graying hair over his ears, Bailino looked virtually the same as he did nearly twenty years ago. He had gained some weight, but that only served to make his presence more powerful.

"I'm gonna make this fast," Bailino said, scraping up the last bits of pie from his plate with his finger and pulling a twenty-dollar bill out of his pocket. "If I'm not back in forty-five minutes, your daughter will be dead."

Knowing him as well as he did, Phillip believed Bailino meant what he said. He was honest and direct as much as he was ruthless. Having those qualities on his side during the days of war, and friendship, had been a blessing, but this was the first time he was viewing them from the other side, and it was more terrifying than he had imagined.

Bailino stood up. "Grant Gino Cataldi a thirty-day stay of execution," he said. "Make any excuse you want—DNA testing or whatever—and she won't get hurt."

"How do I know she's okay?" Phillip asked, staring at his plate, his voice a whisper.

"You don't. But I'm giving you my word, and you know the value of my word."

Bailino walked out of the diner, but not before giving a friendly wave to Taryn, who had returned and was cleaning up his dirty dishes.

"Such a handsome man," Taryn said, wiping the counter with a rag. "Always so friendly and courteous. He always comes alone. I don't think he's married." She looked at the governor's untouched piece of pie. "Want me to freshen your coffee, governor?"

Phillip shook his head.

"Is Mrs. Grand not joining us today, after all?"

Phillip forced a smile. "I'm afraid not."

"Oh, I'm sorry to hear that." Taryn looked genuinely disappointed. "Do you want me to box that for you?" she asked, motioning toward the pie slices. "I know how much Charlotte loves the taste of my cherry pie." She picked up the plates before Phillip could protest. "How is the little darlin' these days?"

"Fine, just fine," Phillip said, taking the small cardboard doggie bag from Taryn, who smiled and shuffled off to chat with old Lester Higgins, the owner of the downtown antique shop, who had just walked in and taken a seat at the counter. Phillip saw from the corner of his eye that Higgins was ready to say a cheerful hello, but the governor quickly turned away and headed toward the exit. He had just told his first willful lie to a constituent and was eager to avoid a second one.

24

Nurberg sat in his car scribbling notes into a small notepad. He looked up to see if Phillip Grand had left Taryn's, but there was no sign of him in the swirl of people near the diner entrance, and the town car was still in the parking lot. He had expected to have the governor all to himself for the day to go over the visitor lists, political opponents, allies. He expected to see Phillip Grand sitting in his office, his head characteristically in his hands, having called off all of the day's appointments. When Det. Matrick phoned his cell to tell him that the governor "was going for a drive," Nurberg thought it was odd—odd enough to follow him. And when the governor pulled into the Taryn's parking lot, Nurberg thought it odder still. He couldn't imagine Phillip Grand would keep his weekly lunch appointment with his mother or tell her about Charlotte's disappearance, especially this early on when everything was so speculative. News like that could put an eighty-year-old woman over the edge.

Nurberg leaned his head back on his seat's headrest. That was the part that was most difficult for him to swallow: There were no leads. None. The cleanness of Charlotte's disappearance was baffling, and common sense dictated that it must have been some kind of inside job. But the investigation so far had turned up nothing. The housekeeper had no reason to dislike the Grands or betray them; by virtually all accounts, she seemed happy and appeared to be treated rather well there. And, in his heart, he didn't think she'd ever hurt the little girl. It was Rosalia, after all, that Nurberg saw holding little Charlotte during press events, right up until the cameras rolled, which is when she'd hand the baby off to Mrs. Grand. And Rosalia had said the rest of the mansion staff seemed to feel the same way about the little girl; they adored her.

Mrs. Grand was another story. Disliked. Feared. Revered. Nurberg reached down to the side of his seat and flicked a switch, tilting his seat back. He'd seen his share of domestic disturbances, and, for the most part, the offenders were easy to detect—drunk, high, overly nice—but he knew that things were not always as they seemed and he suspected as much with the state's First Lady. It was quite possible that even her sudden blowup the previous day could have been carefully orchestrated.

Nurberg tapped the manila folder next to him, which contained lists of names of possible suspects. He had spent the entire morning combing through police arrests that were conducted in the past eighteen months and were related to the governor in any way. Most of them were college-aged pro-choice, anti-gun, and anti-capital-punishment protestors who, minor brushes with police officers aside, probably couldn't hurt a fly. Then there was the issue of the Grand fortune. That was sizable enough to lure any hoodlum, and, as the only child, Charlotte was the only heir. He looked again at the governor's file. Political opponents and gold diggers notwithstanding, Nurberg had nothing. The governor was a veritable boy scout.

"Hey, Nurberg."

Across the street, a man was waving at him. He was a tall, tanned fellow accompanied by a pretty brunette holding a little boy who was wearing a Yankee baseball cap. The couple walked toward him as he got out of the car.

"Hey, Mark Nurberg, right?"

"Yeah." Nurberg couldn't place him.

"John Callahan. From Schenectady High School?"

"John? My God, I didn't recognize you." The two men clasped hands.

"Yeah, not many people do since I lost all that weight."

"No, it's just . . . You look so . . . mature. You're a dad!"

"Yeah," Callahan beamed. "This is my wife, Debbie. Debbie, this is Mark Nurberg. We went to high school together."

Debbie rearranged the little boy in her arm and said, "Nice to meet you."

"And this is our little guy, Jack."

The boy stuck out his hand, and Nurberg shook it.

"Wow, a cop, huh?" Callahan said.

Nurberg looked at his plain clothes. "Is it that obvious?"

"Well, that, and I've googled you a few times and saw your name come up here and there." Callahan turned to his wife. "That's what Mark always wanted—to be a cop."

"You're living your dream then," Debbie said with a smile.

"Yeah, I guess so." Nurberg said.

"Listen, we gotta go. We're meeting Debbie's parents for an early lunch, but we should keep in touch." Callahan reached into his pocket and pulled out a business card. "Call me, sometime. I'd love to catch up. We'll go to lunch. I work right down the road."

"He's the manager of Dick's Sporting Goods," Debbie said proudly.

"Debbie . . ."

"Well, you didn't say . . ." Debbie said, and Callahan gave his wife a squeeze.

"Yeah, sure thing." Nurberg put the business card in his pocket. "It was good to see you, John."

"You too."

"Nice meeting you," Debbie said as the family crossed the street and the little boy waved.

Nurberg watched them go until he saw Governor Grand finally emerge from Taryn's. He was alone, no sign of his mother, who usually arrived with a cavalcade of her senior-citizen friends. The governor looked left and right and then hurried to his car in the parking lot as residents, the Callahan family among them, oohed and aahed, watching their elected official make his way to the parking lot.

When the sedan pulled out, Nurberg waited a few car lengths and then followed behind. Something was up; he could feel it. He made a mental note to check on the whereabouts of the governor's mother this morning. The sedan made a right and then a left and appeared to be heading back toward the Executive Mansion, and Nurberg's thoughts turned to John Callahan. How long had it been since he'd seen him last? Ten years? Fifteen? He couldn't remember, nor could he remember why the two had lost touch, considering they were practically best friends in high school. How many times had they lay on the floor of Callahan's basement, spending hours talking about what they wanted to do with their lives? John had wanted to be an artist, and was pretty good too, until his mother encouraged him to major in business—"something more practical"—and that was the end of that. Nurberg, on the other hand, wanted to become a police officer from the time he was a little boy.

"I want to use my powers for good," he remembered telling John one day over a half-eaten pizza and greasy video-game controls, in the way that a child talks dreamily about the future. Of course, like any other profession, there were times when police work wasn't all it was cracked up to be, when the bad guys were released on a technicality, or when his boss told him to "lose" the paperwork on an influential offender. But then a case comes along like the disappearance of Baby Grand, and that do-gooder feeling returns—the chance to make a difference.

Nurberg could sense his friend's admiration today at seeing him achieve his professional goals, and he felt a certain pride in that. But little did John Callahan know that Nurberg would trade it all—the respect, the commendations, the *powers*—for the chance to have a Debbie and a Jack.

25

Jamie rushed Charlotte back into the cabin. The thought of the clump of the blonde girl's hair in her palm was making it difficult for Jamie to breathe, as if it had gotten caught in her throat. Joey slid the glass door closed behind them, leaving it slightly ajar.

"Are you okay?" he asked her.

"Not really."

Somehow, they had gotten past Benny, Tony, and Leo, who were engaged in a game of poker on a small dining table in the yard, without many questions, despite all the shrieking and the crying. Jamie watched the men through the glass doors. Charlotte had calmed down and was sitting on the floor playing with the zipper of a throw pillow.

"I think she's hungry," Jamie said. "I should give her something to eat."

"Okay. I'll see what there is."

It was quiet in the house with just the three of them in there, and Jamie's eyes drifted to the computer sitting idly on the buffet. The screen was off, but it looked as though the unit was still running. Jamie could hear Joey opening and closing cabinets in the kitchen, but she could not see him—the wall of the breakfast nook was blocking her view. She leaned over and casually dragged her finger across the keypad of the laptop. The screen lit up. Charlotte had managed to stand, pushing her palms on the glass door, and was banging on it, drawing the attention of the men outside. Leo smiled and waved, and all the men laughed and went back to their game.

Charlotte steadied herself and then leaned away from the doors—one step, then another, each one carefully planted as if she were navigating a minefield. She got about six or seven steps into the room and turned back to look at Jamie, who smiled.

"She's really getting the hang of that," Joey said, returning from the kitchen. "Okay, we don't have all that much. There are Cheerios."

Jamie winced.

"I know, we're Cheerioed out," Joey said. "There's a banana?"

Jamie shook her head.

"Crackers?"

Jamie shrugged her shoulders.

"Grapes?"

Jamie thought quickly and said, "Yes, I think grapes would be great." She turned to Charlotte. "You want grapes, baby? Yes? Yes?" Her face became a contorted smile of overenthusiasm. Charlotte, who seemed overwhelmed by Jamie's eagerness, nodded her head yes.

"Well, grapes it is!" Joey said and returned to the kitchen.

The refrigerator was located to the right of the nook, which Jamie hoped would buy her some more time. The moment Joey was out of view, she nudged herself closer to the computer. At the bottom of the screen, she could see that the Facebook site was minimized, but then Joey returned with some grapes in a bowl and handed them to Charlotte.

"Wait, I have to wash those and cut them," Jamie said, reaching for the fruit. "It's a choking hazard. Where do you keep your big knives?"

Joey hesitated and took the bowl of grapes back.

"*I'll* cut them," he said, looking somewhat embarrassed.

"Oh, okay," Jamie said, as if it didn't matter one way or the other, and returned to the back doors where Charlotte had managed to walk back on her own and was pressing her tiny face into the glass pane.

Jamie crossed her fingers that Joey would cut the grapes on the table of the breakfast nook, which is where most of the kitchen mess seemed to accumulate, perhaps because the men were fearful of damaging Bailino's marble countertops. Once Joey ran the bowl of grapes under cold water, he stepped again out of sight, and at the first sound of a knife hitting the table, and with Charlotte leaning on her right leg, Jamie reached with her left hand to the computer keyboard and maximized the Facebook page. As she did, she glanced outside at the men, who were laughing and smoking. She didn't have much time.

Tony's profile was still open, and she dragged her finger across the keypad, bringing the cursor to the top right corner, and logged him out. Then, with the deftness of a seasoned freelance writer, she typed her email address and password to log into her account while keeping her eye on the poker game outside.

"Please make sure the large grapes still aren't too big as halves," she called out.

The chopping stopped. "All right," Joey said, and the chopping resumed.

Jamie's page appeared. With a quick sidelong glance, she scanned it and clicked in the *What's on your mind?* box. When she looked back out the window, Leo was staring at her with a piercing, probing look that seemed to suspend time. She froze. It was only when Charlotte began bouncing up and down on her leg that Jamie, with her gaze still on Leo, moved her left hand, which was out of his sight, across the QWERTY keyboard that she knew so well. She typed *H-E-L-P* and was about to log off, but then paused. Quickly, she typed *A-L-B-A-N-Y* and then *C-H-A-R-L-O-T-T-E*, but before she could type *Grand*, Leo stood up from the table and began walking toward the house. Frantically, Jamie's fingers jerked along the keypad, trying to move the cursor diagonally to log out, but with her eyes on Leo she couldn't be sure of where it was. He was only a few feet away when Jamie picked up Charlotte, blocking Leo's view, and glanced at the screen. *Damn, she was off target. Her Facebook profile was still there.* As she heard the soft swish of the glass door sliding, Jamie leaned Charlotte down next to the laptop, pretending to check her diaper with her right hand as her left moved the cursor and pressed the *X* in the top right corner of the screen just as Joey entered the room.

"Wow, that was fast," Jamie said, picking Charlotte up.

"Does she need a diaper?" Joey asked.

"I thought she did, but no."

Leo poked his head in. "Everything all right in here?" he asked.

"Yep," Joey said, proudly placing the bowl of grapes on a coffee table.

"Okay, just checking." Leo winked at Jamie and turned on his heel, leaving the glass door open.

Jamie placed Charlotte on the floor, watching as she ambled over to the coffee table, plucked one of the cut grapes out of the bowl, and shoved it into her mouth with her dirty hands.

"*Ewww*, gross." Jamie grabbed a paper towel from the kitchen and wet it under cold water. When she returned, Joey was staring at the computer screen. Her panic was instant.

"What's the matter?" she said.

"I don't know, something weird," Joey said. The glass doors opened and in walked Leo, Tony, and Benny. "The computer screen froze."

Shit! Jamie prayed she was able to log out of Facebook successfully before the computer crashed.

"What the fuck you doin', Joey?" Tony asked, taking one of the cut grapes and plopping it into his mouth, much to Charlotte's dismay. She covered the bowl with her hands.

"It crashed," Joey said. "I think we're going to have to restart."

"You better not have broken that thing, Tony," Benny said. "Bailino will fuckin' freak."

"I didn't break it," Tony said and then looked at Joey. "Did I?"

"I don't think so." Within a few minutes, Joey had the machine up and running and all new windows appeared, much to Jamie's relief.

"You'll have to log yourself back into Facebook, Ton," Joey said.

"Shit, I was playing Texas Hold 'em. I better not have fuckin' lost my chips."

"You lost more than that a long time ago," Leo said, sitting on the couch and cracking open a beer. He looked at Jamie and smiled. "So, Dimples, what should we do now?"

26

The general visitors' room at the Stanton correctional facility looked like a school lunchroom, with its long bench tables; windows inlaid with wire mesh; dirty, cracked tiled floors; and creaky fans lining the ceiling overhead, blowing back down little more than an odor of sweat. Gino's memory of that room, the memory of his mother's, and later his wife's, touch on his arm, of their earnest belief that Gino was, at heart, *a good boy*, faded as he entered the death-row visitors' room, a cramped four-by-four space with nothing but a bench situated below a narrow safety-glass window. With hands and feet shackled, Gino shuffled over and took his appointed seat.

On the other side of the glass, Don Bailino held up a piece of paper. On it was a drawing, colored with crayons, of a stick-figured man and a stick-figured little girl standing outside a house in a green field. In purple crayon, scrawled at the top was, "Me and Pop-Pop."

"From Gina," Bailino said with a smile. His voice was tinny coming from the small speaker in the corner of the room.

Gino nodded. He had never seen his great-granddaughter, who had been named for him. And, very probably, never would.

"You all right?" Bailino asked.

Gino nodded again, his eyes on the drawing on Bailino's lap.

"All is all right here too," Bailino said. It wasn't worth bothering Gino with the details of the second abduction and the fact that three-

and-a-half grown men couldn't take care of one infant. He looked at the security camera overhead.

Gino reached into his pocket to take out a cigarette he didn't have. He fumbled with the flap of his shirt fabric as he too eyed the camera focused on him.

"Fuckin' Potsy, what a goof," Gino said, the steely look returning to his eyes.

Bailino nodded.

Years ago, when he had first come to Stanton and was a relatively young man, Gino had been told by the medical staff that he was entering early-stage dementia because he was prone to sudden outbursts of gibberish. Although his brain scans were clean, the episodes appeared to become more frequent over the years, and soon Gino developed the reputation of a poor old man who was progressively losing his marbles. The prison psychologist had other ideas, of course. Because Gino's outbursts occurred particularly with visiting family and friends, she wrote in his report: *"Gino is unable to deal with the horrific nature of his crimes and face his loved ones. Therefore, his conscious self subverts, or hides, which most commonly manifests as disorganized speech or thinking with significant social dysfunction."* The psychologist requested a meeting with Bailino in 2004 to explain her diagnosis and ask that Bailino remain calm during these periods of disorientation. Bailino said he would do all that he could to make Gino comfortable.

Bailino smiled at the memory, at the way the psychologist, a kid barely out of school, spoke to him in that rehearsed maternal, calm voice that always got on his nerves. He even let her put her hand on his as a show of sympathy. As he watched her walk out the door in her tight navy-blue suit, he couldn't help but smile. With all her years of training and those expensive little pieces of paper hanging on her office wall, Ms. Psychologist failed to deduce that Gino Cataldi's mind was far from disorganized. Rather, it was icy sharp, and his ramblings a cover for a lifetime of covert operations taking place right under the nose of New York's finest.

As a young marine in World War II, Gino served in the Pacific

Theater with a group of young Navajo men who had been enlisted to help the United States strengthen military communications, since Japanese intelligence experts were breaking every code that US forces devised. These young men, many of them boys who had never been off their reservations before, would become known as the Navajo Code Talkers and create the only unbroken code in modern military history, saving thousands of lives and helping to end the Second World War. For many years after the war, their code was considered a military secret too important to divulge; however, it finally was declassified in 1968, about the same time Gino had been pinched for his first homicide.

Using the basic tenets of the Navajo code, Gino devised a way to communicate clandestinely with family and colleagues, while living in the fishbowl that was the New York State Department of Correctional Services. The secret language had baffled law enforcement, who had begun to suspect that Gino was using code to manage his illegal operations, particularly after several known enemies of his had turned up in the Hudson in 1975, but they could never be sure. And because Gino had gotten into the habit of talking nonsense in areas other than the visitors' room—in his cell, in the weight room, in the yard—he managed to throw police detectives off his scent.

As with the Navajo code, Gino's language wasn't complicated at all, but actually very simple: Gino used old neighborhood slang, or terms that were derivatives of neighborhood slang, for related words. For example, the word for *killed* was *upstate*, or any variation of the word, such as *up* or *state*, since the old gang, back in the Brooklyn days of Gino and Bailino's father, referred to anything north of the New York City border as *The Kills*—Fishkill, Peekskill, etc. *Cops* were *blue*, and *mothers* were *white*. Ex-cons were *striped*. Words that didn't have an associated term, such as people's names, were spelled out or abbreviated using slang words that represented letters of the alphabet, excluding curse words, articles, and pronouns. Therefore, if Gino said, "Fuckin' Potsie, what a goof," he was asking about Phillip Grand—*Potsie* and *goof* represented the initials in play, *P. G.* After many years, Gino and Bailino had developed a succinct and thorough shorthand.

"And the blue?" Gino asked.

Bailino shook his head no.

Gino nodded. "It's time."

Bailino nodded.

There was an awkward pause. Business was done. Under normal circumstances, these kinds of visitations were full of emotional outbursts, the kissing lips of family members or lovers separated by wire-mesh glass, but the two men simply sat and stared. Gino glanced at the guard behind him and returned his gaze to Bailino. "You're looking healthy today."

Bailino lifted his shoulders in uncertainty. "Am I?" he asked, looking down at his clothing and then at Gino's. At Stanton, death-row inmates were distinguished from other inmates by their orange T-shirts; their pants were the same blue-colored trousers.

"No, it's in your face," Gino said. "Something's different."

Bailino folded the drawing and put it in his pocket. "ToniAnne wants to come."

"No!" Gino said. "I told you this last week."

"I know, but she keeps asking. I told her that I would mention it again."

"I can't . . . see her now, Donny," Gino said, his eyes focusing on a speck of dirt on the corner of the glass window. He reached out and scraped it with his fingernail. "How's Joey?"

"Good, good. Picked him up in the City yesterday. Enjoying his spring break. You know he got accepted to MIT?" Bailino said with pride.

"No shit. Fucking $60,000 a year. And for what?"

"It's a good school, Jeen. The kid's bright."

"So are you, and you didn't go to some fancy-pants school. Kid should be going into the military. Knock some sense into him."

Bailino hesitated. This was a sore subject for him. Although he was the first to admit that most college-educated adults were no smarter or more successful than anyone else, especially nowadays when a witty Twitter profile could land someone a book deal, he had pressured ToniAnne to have Joey apply to MIT and a few Ivy-League schools.

The kid had an IQ of 150 and needed to be around people like himself, not the slobs he was hanging around with now.

"I respectfully disagree," Bailino said with a laugh.

"We're so polite today." Gino gave a slight chuckle himself. "Did you get the Earl?"

Bailino shook his head. Gino had slipped back into code and was asking about the name of the executioner. The state of New York used private citizens as its executioners, paying them a paltry $150 per execution, but their identities remained anonymous. Last week, Don had tried to find out who the state was using, but couldn't. He wasn't sure how much time it would buy them—if any—to knock off the guy, or girl, the morning of the execution. Still, it had never been tried and was an interesting alternate plan. He had to give Gino credit.

Gino tilted his head so that his left ear nearly met his left shoulder, and Bailino thought he could hear Gino's neck crack through the thick glass.

"Do you have everything you need?" Bailino said.

"Yes, everything I could ever want."

"Good. Then I need something done for me."

"Really? I'll have to check my calendar and get back to you."

"You know what I mean," Bailino said. He held up three fingers.

"Yeah, I know," Gino said, knowing Bailino was referring to the $3 million he was promised for organizing this little scheme.

"And, of course, there's the other thing."

Curiosity getting the better of him, the prison guard stationed behind Gino leaned in, waiting for the words, but they never came. They didn't have to. For Gino, the message was loud and clear. Don Bailino wanted what he'd always wanted. Out.

27

Although it made sense that he would be shaken up, given the events of the past twenty-four hours, Phillip Grand felt the need to appear calm before the mansion's front security guard, as if looking nervous would give away his meeting with Bailino.

"Hey, Barry," he said as nonchalantly as he could, as the gates opened for his limousine.

"You okay, Governor?" Barry asked.

"Yes, yes, fine, thank you." Phillip forced a smile, and as Henry pulled the car up the driveway, the governor eyed his security guard, who was eating a large sandwich inside the small gate booth, with suspicion. Arthur had been their day security guard for Phillip's first term, but had expressed interest in moving to the nightshift when the previous night guard decided to retire. Apparently, Arthur's wife had had enough of domesticity and decided to go back to work after their youngest went into full-day kindergarten, and Arthur felt strongly, as Phillip did, that at least one parent should be home when the kids stepped off the school bus. Phillip was happy to oblige the request, and Barry was hired not long afterward to take Arthur's shift. In the short time Barry had been with the Grands, he had been reprimanded twice for drinking on the job and once for sleeping. Phillip had wanted to let him go three months ago, but Katherine insisted he stay, not because she had any real affinity for him, but because she was carefully watching the number of minorities they had on staff in order to, as she said, "keep the NAACP and their ilk" off their backs. Barry satisfied two minority categories: He was black and he was gay. Plus, he walked with a slight limp that didn't affect his job performance, but was enough to classify him as disabled in the eyes of the government. In terms of appeasing the AFL-CIO, Barry was the holy grail.

Phillip's cell phone rang. He looked at the caller ID. It was his mother. *Crap.*

"Hi, Mother."

"Phillip, was I supposed to meet you at the diner today? Didn't you remember that I was taking a trip with the girls this week to Buffalo to see Aunt June?"

"Yes, I remembered."

"Then why were you there?"

In so many ways, Albany, the capital city of one of the biggest states in the union, was like a small town. "How did you know I was there?"

"Jason Seegert . . . you know, Edna's son, had stopped in to pick up a pie and saw you sitting alone at the counter."

"No, no, I did remember," Phillip said. "I just wanted to grab a bite to eat. How are you, Mother?"

"Oh, I'm fine. Picked up a pretty little sweater at the outlets here although the prices don't seem much lower than at a regular store."

"That's nice," Phillip said. He hated keeping anything from his mother, with whom, despite a few contentious years when he was a teenager, he had a relatively good relationship. But there was no reason to alarm her yet. "Listen, I've got to go, governor stuff . . . I love you."

"Love back, Phillip." That was the closest his mother came to saying *I love you.* "Aunt June says hello. And tell Charlotte that Grandma will see her this weekend."

"This weekend?"

"Yes, you haven't forgotten, have you?"

"No, no . . . I, um . . ."

His mother breathed a heavy sigh of annoyance. "For the tulip festival. Check your calendar, dear. I'm sure it's on there. And remember to give that housekeeper, nanny, whatever she is, the afternoon off. I don't need her hovering around."

"Her name is Rosalia, Mother."

"Whatever."

"Have a good day, Mother."

Phillip stuck his phone in his pocket and ran his fingers through his hair. The feeling that time was running out overcame him, and even after Henry opened his door, he stayed inside the car to gain his composure.

"Sir?" Henry's face looked concerned.

Henry Jackson, named after his great-grandfather, three kids, married for twenty-seven years, hired three days after the beginning of Phillip's second term. Everything Phillip knew about Henry filled his mind. But what didn't he know? *Someone* had to be Bailino's inside man. As good as Bailino was, he needed access, someone to guarantee that he could get in and out of the mansion undetected. Was it Henry? Or Barry?

"Yes, Henry, thank you." Phillip stepped out of the car and was instantly reminded of one of those horror films where all the villagers turn into zombies and stare. The groundskeepers, normally quite reticent no matter what time of day, instead were alert and chatty, but they all stopped what they were doing when Governor Grand walked toward the mansion. Mario, the gardener, who was tending the rose bushes along the main walkway, took off his cap and placed it by his heart.

Mario Lopez, twenty-seven years old, single, conscientious worker, helped Katherine into the house that day last fall when her briefcase flopped open and her paperwork spilled out.

Glen, the head groundskeeper, stopped mowing and bowed his head. *Glen Scheuer, thirty-two, majored in accounting at SUNY Albany, but fell in love with flowers while working part time at Gretchen's Greenhouse and switched his major to business. Opened up his own landscaping firm seven years ago.*

He eyed them all distrustfully.

"Governor." Det. Matrick was standing just outside the front door to the mansion. He nodded as Phillip came up the front steps. "Did you have a good drive?"

Phillip thought he could sense irony in the detective's voice, but he just nodded and walked inside. Katherine was sitting in the main dining room at the head of the long wooden table, a historic furnishing that still featured the parallel etchings at its head made by Franklin Roosevelt's wheelchair. Her laptop was open, and Phillip could see she was working on an Excel document.

"Why were you at the diner?" Katherine asked without looking up when Phillip walked in.

Phillip sighed. He didn't know why he even bothered trying to be so secretive. "I needed air."

"The air here isn't to your liking."

"Jesus, Katherine, after what's happened, is it that unusual I needed to get away from you? I mean . . . here?"

Katherine was quiet.

"Have you heard anything?" Phillip asked.

She shook her head. "Have you?"

The thought of lying to Katherine again within the span of a few hours made Phillip feel more than deceitful—it made him feel practically unfaithful. Eventually, he was going to have to tell her, but before he could say anything, Katherine's cell phone rang. She looked at the caller ID.

"Hello, Mara," she said into the phone, glaring at Phillip. "What? I can't understand . . . TMZ what?" Katherine frowned.

"What is it?" the governor asked.

Mrs. Grand threw the phone on the table and typed *TMZ.com* into her browser. A large photo of Charlotte Grand, credited to an anonymous source, appeared on the Web site's homepage. The photo looked like it had been taken at the Veterans Day parade in November: Charlotte, who was being held in Phillip's arms, was dressed in red, white, and blue and waving a small flag. Beside the photo, a screaming headline read: "Grand Larceny? NY Gov's Daughter Goes Missing."

"Son of a bitch!" Katherine said. She and Phillip inched closer to the computer screen.

"According to an Albany police report—obtained by TMZ—Charlotte Grand went missing on the afternoon of April 10, 2012. Police at this time have no leads, but have questioned the mansion family and staff."

"What the fuck!" Katherine said, bolting upright. "How did that asshole Harvey Levin get his hands on an Albany police report? Nurberg, that goddamn novice!"

"It could have been anyone," Phillip said. He turned the monitor toward him. Charlotte's soft, kind blue eyes stared back at him.

"Yes, you're right." Katherine was leaning on the table and running her fingernails up and down the wheelchair scratches. "People will sell nude photos of their mother for fifty dollars and virtual bragging rights."

"But this isn't even Los Angeles?"

"Oh, Phillip, please. You're a public figure, makes you fair game for any juicy story no matter the jurisdiction."

The cell phone rang again. The caller ID said CNN.

"Jesus, CNN is calling. Don't answer it. Where the hell is Maddox? Get him on the phone. Damn, now we need to get a statement together fast." Katherine was in the zone.

"I thought we were going to stay quiet, like the detective said."

"It's too late for that." The mansion phone rang. "Get Nurberg on the phone. We have a mole."

Phillip agreed, but, for no particular reason, other than an increasingly small well of denial, or perhaps hope, he decided to play devil's advocate. "You don't know that, Katherine."

"The hell I don't." Katherine was pacing up and down the length of the table and then stopped to survey the workers outside through the front window. Henry was chatting with Barry outside the guardhouse.

"You were with Henry the whole time?" she asked. "During your drive?"

Before Phillip could even think about a response, Katherine asked,

"Did you use the phone at all? Was it in Henry's presence? Did Henry talk to anyone? Did he use his phone?"

Phillip had seen Katherine like this many times before, her brain on overdrive, trying to connect the random dots of a giant puzzle. She wasn't particularly looking for answers to any of her questions, but liked having a witness to her mental checklist.

Katherine focused back on the room, then on Phillip, and then on her laptop computer, which still showed the photo of Charlotte. She pulled the screen toward her and away from her husband. Beneath the photo and the Excel document, in a separate browser there were no fewer than six tabs displaying various search results for the name "Don Bailino." She closed them all and deleted the browsing history.

"We have to remember that everything we do and say will be seen and heard by the people who have Charlotte," she said.

The people who have Charlotte . . .

Probably for the first time in his married life, Phillip Grand realized he was a step ahead of his wife. And he didn't like it. Not at all. Little did he know that, at that moment, his wife was thinking the very same thing.

28

Rosalia had outdone herself: a western omelet, stuffed with green peppers, onions, and ham—served with home fries and buttered toast. On a normal day, a cup of coffee and a cigarette was as close as Reynaldo got to the five major food groups, and as worried as he was about his aunt, who looked as though she hadn't slept a wink, he had to admit that it was nice to have a home-cooked meal for a change.

"*Gracias, Tía,*" he said, as she refilled his glass with orange juice.

"*De nada*, Reyito," she said, patting his head.

The small television sitting on the kitchen counter was playing a rerun of *Family Matters*, Rosalia's favorite program next to *The George Lopez Show*, but she ignored it and began putting the dirty pots and pans into the sink for washing. Watching his aunt scoot about the kitchen, Reynaldo again thought of his mother, and that familiar lump lodged in his throat. As the water fell from the faucet into Rosalia's soapy sponge, he thought of his mother filling the sink so that he, as a boy, could take a bath.

"*Ay*, Rey, that's yucky," his mother had told him once, when she caught him sucking the water out of the sponge. She had taken the sponge from his mouth and tapped him on the head with it. According to his mother, everything bad was *yucky*—her favorite American word. It would be twenty years in August that Reynaldo would never hear his mother utter that word again, twenty years since she had stood on the street corner across from Crain's Grocery, her hands filled with shopping bags, smiling, maybe even whistling, as witnesses later told police. She never saw the car that hit her. Reynaldo ran his fingers along his cheeks and chin and felt the prickliness of his uncut beard and the loose, sagging skin of his cheeks, which every day seemed to sag a little more.

"I should go to work," Rosalia said, inching Reynaldo's plate closer to him and sitting down.

"No, no, Aunt Ro." Reynaldo put his hand on hers. "They said to stay home. They will call you if they need you."

"What if she is in the house? I know her hiding spots."

"They searched the house. She isn't there."

"Then where could she be?" A tear welled in the corner of Rosalia's eye until it got so fat that it fell onto the table. She wiped it with her finger. "Who wants to hurt a little baby?"

"I don't know." Reynaldo squeezed his aunt's hand. He looked at the TV, his eyes squinting and then becoming very wide. "*Dios mío!*" he said.

"*Qué?*" Rosalia asked, following Reynaldo's gaze.

At the bottom of the television, in letters that raced across the screen, it read:

"Breaking news: TMZ.com reports that Charlotte Grand, daughter of New York Governor Phillip Grand, has been missing for nearly twenty-four hours. An investigation is underway. We will keep you up to date on the latest events as we get them."

The words kept running again and again, and Reynaldo clicked the remote to change the channel, when video footage of Charlotte eating a french fry appeared on screen. The image zoomed out, and Rosalia saw herself on television, standing behind Mrs. Grand, who was holding the little girl. Charlotte was smiling, exuberant, as the governor pinched her cheeks.

Overcome with grief, Rosalia left the room as Reynaldo turned off the TV.

The phone rang—an old-fashioned rotary phone that hung on

the wall—and Reynaldo had to cross the kitchen to answer. When he picked it up, its long cord, which hung partly in a trash can, untwisted.

"Rey?" Pedro's voice sounded scruffy and confused, as if he'd just woken up.

"*Sí*. I'm here with Aunt Ro."

"Did you see the TV? Is Aunt Ro all right?"

"*Sí*, she is all right."

"What happened?"

"I don't know. The police are looking for Charlotte. That's all I know. Pedro, I don't know if I'm going to be able to come in today. I need to stay with Aunt Ro. Is everything okay at the garage?"

"Uh . . ." There was muffled talking in the background.

"Pedro!" Reynaldo stamped his foot. "You are at the garage, yes?"

"Ricardo is there."

"Well, get there too, and please remember to make sure to start the coffee."

"That's Nada's job."

"Well, don't forget to tell her."

Pedro put his hand over the phone. "Nada, start the coffee when we get to the garage." The line opened again. "Okay."

Reynaldo sighed. "Nada is there with you?"

"*Sí*. I told you. Ricky doesn't mind." Then there was a pause. "Why, do you?"

"I don't care, if no one else cares."

"Oh, you lie, *hermano*."

"Please, just get to the garage," Reynaldo said, "and make sure Ricky is nice to Mr. Pena, who is coming in for an oil change."

"Oh, that prick," Pedro said. Reynaldo could hear Nada giggling in the background. "He accused us of using used oil for his oil change."

"Just let it go, Pedro."

"Not everyone's like you, Rey, eh? Let enough things go, and the whole world slips by."

29

The warehouse was buzzing with activity. Two young male workers wearing jeans and identical navy-blue polo shirts were standing on a platform before one of two semitrailer trucks that had been parked just inside the rear wall. They waved to Bailino, who entered the cavernous space from the back parking lot. He waved back.

Bailino beamed with pride whenever he walked through any Upackk warehouse. When he purchased the company back in 1997, it was a struggling family-owned operation on the brink of bankruptcy. Nearly fifteen years later, it was the leading distributor of shipping, industrial, and packaging materials in the nation, with seven warehouses across the United States, including this one just outside Albany that also served as the company's headquarters and factory. Upackk's claim to fame—publicized prominently on its "Why Us?" Web-site page—was that it dealt only in materials that were green and made domestically. The company's most popular product was a starch-based peanut, a loose-fill packing and cushioning material made partially from shredded paper and a patented vegetable-oil base that made it just as durable and inexpensive as the popular Styrofoam peanuts or air-filled plastic bags—only more environmentally sound. Company sales increased slowly every year, despite the recent economic downturn, and last year Bailino invested millions by installing a robotic picking system that aimed to increase Upackk's efficiency while reducing labor costs. Over the years, he had been approached many times to go public, but was never interested. He was told that without accessing a substantial source of corporate funding, the business could never survive, let alone thrive. Bailino loved exceeding expectations.

"I thought you weren't coming in this week?" George Smith raised his head when Bailino walked into the office, his small, round eyes showing just above the monitor.

"Yeah, well, I thought I'd stop in since I was nearby . . . I visited my Uncle Gino," Bailino said.

"Oh." George's right eye began to twitch. "That's right. I forgot. How is he related to you again?"

Bailino smiled. He knew that George, who served as the Albany warehouse supervisor, was working with the Feds to monitor his business operations. The government suspected, and perhaps rightly so, that the Bailino family's close ties to the Cataldis made them a perennial red flag for illegal activity. Over the years, Bailino's homes had been raided, his vacations interrupted, but nothing was ever found, and no criminal charges were ever filed against him. Bailino suspected that George had been approached a few years back, since that's when the interest in Bailino's personal life, and all the questions, had started. About a year and a half ago, Bailino followed him one night into Tanzer Park and spotted one of his secret meetings along a hiking trail.

George wasn't the greatest spy the Feds had ever enlisted, since he was sort of an uptight fellow whose right eye twitched whenever he was nervous, but he was competent. And despite the obvious, Bailino thought he was a decent guy—he did his work, seemed to take care of his family. Plus, Bailino wasn't worried. The warehouse was clean. After all, the shredded paper used to make his award-winning packing peanuts had to come from somewhere.

"Yeah, well, he's not *really* my uncle. He and my father were close back in the day. Grew up together. Served in the war."

"Oh, that's right." George said. "You look kinda tired for someone who's on vacation."

"Yeah, well my teenage . . . nephew is here staying with me

on spring break. A bunch of my cousins are in town—to pay their respects. I have a full house. Is this the last pickup?" Bailino pointed toward the warehouse.

"No, there's one more scheduled." He handed Bailino a clipboard with rows of data highlighted.

Bailino stepped over to his office, where a pile of boxes had been placed on his desk. "What's all this stuff?"

"I don't know. I signed for them yesterday. They had *personal* written on them, so I just left them on your desk."

Bailino looked at the return address on the top box. The package was from the Wounded Warrior Project. Bailino had worked with the organization, which raised awareness and funds for severely injured servicemen and women, for years. He opened the box—tsk, tsk, tsking at the use of Styrofoam—and pulled out a gleaming bronze award. He read the inscription: "To Don Bailino in appreciation of his generosity of support and ongoing commitment to the Wounded Warrior Project."

There was something else in the box. Bailino reached in and pulled out a framed photograph of a group of men standing in the desert. Bailino recognized the image from his trip last year to Iraq. To the left of Bailino were several Wounded Warrior executives, to his right was Kid Rock.

"Another one, huh?" George said, looking at the award over Bailino's shoulder and placing a file on Bailino's desk. George always seemed to have to stop in Bailino's office whenever he was opening a personal package. "They really love you over there." He pointed to Bailino's shelves of awards and trophies. "Looks like we may have to build another shelf." George busied himself over by the shelving units, stalling as he waited for Bailino to open the other box.

Bailino ripped it open and pulled out a gourmet chocolate gift basket containing cocoa, truffles, and cookies. He read the card: "Don, just a little something to thank you for helping to publicize our recent networking event. You're so SWEET. Love, Barbara."

"Nice, truffles," George said, returning to Bailino's side. "You want me to bring it out to the guys?" Cakes, cookies, just about anything that was edible, could be brought to the warehouse, any time of day, and be gone, crumbs and all, in less than ten minutes.

Bailino inspected the ingredient list for the truffles, which were flecked with bits of dried cherry and encased in white chocolate—"the perfect treat to give to that special someone," said the packaging.

"Nah, I'm going to take this one home," Bailino said.

30

"Bob, what's the status on Dover?"

Bob took another sip of his coffee. He could hardly keep his eyes open. "He wants to plea bargain, but I can convince him to take this to trial." He knew Turner liked headlines.

"Good," Hick Turner said. He looked at his agenda. "Jefferies, what's going on with . . ."

Bob tuned out once again. These late-morning meetings were such a bore. Since he'd made partner last year—the youngest man ever to perform such a feat at Worcester, Payne & Leach—he had somehow lost his verve for impressing the folks around the conference table. Been there. Done that. And done it well.

He sat back in his chair, satisfied with the way things were going in his life. It really was all coming together for him now, Bob thought. Divorced, finally, although it had taken years longer than he'd anticipated. Awesome new car. Hot, young, new girlfriend—with no issues about going downtown. $500K a year. Six weeks' vacation. He was the king of world.

The meeting adjourned, and, simultaneously, every lawyer reached for his or her smartphone and left the conference table talking to clients or colleagues. On his way out, Hick Turner detoured in Bob's direction. Bob pinched his upper thigh to increase his alertness.

"Bob, meant to ask . . . Heard from Edward lately?"

Bob winced. "Yeah, just yesterday."

"Still buds, huh? College friendships really are the ones that last."

"Yep," Bob said. "Buds."

"Well, I hope you mentioned my offer again. We'd love to have him back. He's got quite the legal eye. Clients are still asking about him. Just this morning, old Joe Sentril requested Edward take the lead on his son's drug case. I didn't have the heart to tell him Edward left years ago."

"Yes, I had mentioned your offer a while back," Bob lied, "but I think Edward's happy where he is with the Manhattan DA."

"Shame about his mother. She was such a lovely woman."

"Yeah."

"And how's Jamie?"

"Oh, she's fine, fine." Bob knew he was eventually going to have to tell Turner about the divorce, but the longer he could put it off, the better.

"Publishing is tough right now. She finding work all right? You both should really come back to the house. I know Paula would love to have you for dinner again."

"Oh, uh, that would be great," Bob said, thankful to feel his phone vibrate in his pocket. He pulled it out and was shocked to see Jamie's number. He put on a smile. "Speak of the devil."

"Oh, I'll let you take that." Hick patted him on the back and walked over to the large flat screen, which had been turned on at the far end of the conference room. Several lawyers were congregating around it.

Bob stepped into a corner of the room. "Yeah," he said curtly into the phone. "Hello? Hello?"

There was silence on the other end.

"James, are you there?"

Bob looked at his phone. The connection was still intact; seconds were clicking by.

"I can't hear you. Can you hear me?" Nothing. "Whatever. Listen, Jamie, Edward is looking for you. Shocker, right? What, did you not check in?" Bob chuckled. "No, seriously, Jamie, call your brother, all right, if you haven't already. I hope you heard this. Call me later to tell me whatever it was you wanted to tell me. I'm in a meeting right now."

He clicked off his phone and faced the conference room. Now everyone was watching the flat screen.

"Hey, Scott, that's some strange shit about the governor, huh?" Steve Andrews, one of the new paralegals, walked over and handed Bob a cup of coffee. Andrews had been lobbying to get onto the Dover case for weeks, asking Bob if he "needed anything"—coffee, lunch, a pack of gum—while he was "stepping out" of the office. Bob wasn't interested in food, or Andrews, but he liked the attention.

"What about the governor?" Bob asked, disinterested.

"His daughter's missing."

"Yeah, so? Not my problem."

"Yeah, you're right." Andrews nodded. "But I wonder if this is going to affect the Brightest Minds thing."

"The what?" Bob said. "You mean that legal internship?"

"No, Grand decided to make it a part-time paid position. A consulting thing. He's looking to lure seasoned lawyers—one from each county—who are at the top of their game. He wants to create a roundtable of the best legal minds to sort through some of the shit they got up there in Albany. Kind of like King Arthur and his court." Andrews leaned in. "You know, you should apply for it. Some people are saying it's the quickest way to the state attorney general post, and then who knows? Especially if Grand runs for president like they say he will."

Bob thought *Sir Robert Scott* had a nice ring to it.

Andrews added, "That is, if you ever get sick of this place. And why would you?" He nudged Bob with his elbow.

Bob had made quite the name for himself in legal circles, but this wasn't the first time the idea of national credentials entered his mind. The book deals, speaking engagements. Too bad Larry King already retired; Piers Morgan just didn't have the same cred.

"Didn't Edward Carter work with Grand a few years back?" Andrews asked.

"Nah," Bob said, annoyed that Edward's name had come up in

conversation, not once, but twice in the past five minutes. "A liberal like Edward wouldn't be seen anywhere near Phillip Grand's employ." He thought a moment. "Although he did do a paper on Phillip Grand in law school that was published in some national journal. I can't remember which one." *American Lawyer.* August 2001.

"Why would he want to do a paper on Phillip Grand?"

"Oh, Edward's about seeing things from all sides, what makes people tick. He's probably more interested in people whose views are diametrically opposed to his than those who share his beliefs."

"Sounds like an interesting guy. Some of the guys here were saying that Carter'd be a shoo-in for Grand's legal roundtable."

Not if I can help it, Bob thought. Any interest that Bob had in joining the governor's little consortium had quadrupled at the thought of vying for a position against the incomparable Edward Carter and beating him.

"You never know," Bob said. "May the best man win."

31

It had been twenty-four hours since he'd heard from Jamie, and Edward was in complete panic mode. After calling in sick this morning, he contacted everyone she knew—even those he wasn't sure she knew—but she hadn't turned up. Trish said he was overreacting, that Jamie was a grown woman who may have decided to change her plans, take a trip, go off on an adventure—and maybe she had. But she would have called. Edward knew that. She always called. Every day. College. Marriage. Divorce. Not a day had gone by in the past who-knows-how-long that he hadn't spoken to his sister on the phone, most of the time just to say hi. Still, he had listened to Trish, as he usually did, and held off on filing a missing-persons report, hoping that Jamie would call or come home, and now he was regretting that decision. Who knows what could have happened by now? He picked up the phone and dialed 911.

"I need to file a missing-persons report," Edward said when he heard a voice on the line.

"Who is the missing person?" a female voice asked.

"My sister."

"What is her name?"

"Jamie. Jamie Scott. No, no . . . it's Jamie Carter. That's her name. Her maiden name. She just got divorced. But she actually used it when she was married—she's a writer—so I guess it doesn't really matter that she's no longer married. Does it?" Edward was gasping for breath.

"The more information you can provide me, sir, the better. And what is your name?"

"Edward. It's Edward."

"Carter?"

"Yes."

"How old is she?"

"Thirty-two."

"How long has she been missing?"

"Twenty-four hours." Edward paced the kitchen floor. "I last heard from her yesterday afternoon."

"Where was she?"

"She was . . ." Edward stopped pacing. "I don't . . . know where she was. She had just come from a job interview. In Manhattan. She texted me. Said she was coming over for dinner."

"And that's the last you heard from her?"

"Yes."

"Did she get it?"

"Get what?"

"The job, sir."

"I don't know," Edward said, annoyed. "But it didn't sound like it went well. Does that matter?"

There was a pause on the line.

"Listen, I know what it sounds like," Edward said. "Just got divorced. Bad interview. Been out of a job for nearly a year . . ."

"A year?"

"It's a tough job market, okay?" Edward opened the kitchen window. "Jesus."

"Okay, sir, calm down."

But Edward wasn't calm. He realized how this all sounded.

"Wait, wait. . . You need to know," he continued. "I'm not calling because I think she . . . you know . . . she, um . . . she would never . . ."

"Sir, let's take this one step at a time, all right?"

"Okay."

"All right, what does your sister look like?"

"What?"

"Your sister, sir. What does she look like?"

Edward flashed back thirty years to a muggy summer's day on Long Beach Island on the Jersey shore. His mother—tall, beautiful—was packing up the plastic pails and shovels that had been left scattered along the sand and bringing them to the water to rinse out. He and Jamie were removing the pairs of shoes they had placed on the corners of their blanket so that they could fold it. A sudden storm was approaching from the south, causing a mass exodus from the beach, and Edward had turned to marvel at the speed with which the dark clouds were advancing. When he turned back around, Jamie was gone.

"Where's Jamie?" his mother asked, her chapped lips creasing as she smiled. She dropped a stack of pails onto a beach chair.

"I . . . I . . ." Edward stammered. "She was . . . just here."

His mother's freshly sun-kissed face went white. She turned her head from side to side. "Jamie!" she yelled. "Jamie!"

But there was no answer. No giggling of "Peekaboo!" His mother ran up to the large woman who had been sitting on a lounge chair next to them all afternoon. "Have you seen my daughter?" The woman shook her head. She stopped an old man who was heading toward the boardwalk. "Have you seen my daughter?" No. "Have you seen a little girl about this big, two years old?" No. No. No.

The sky grew darker. A slight breeze blew. *This is my fault,* Edward thought. At the tender age of five, he felt an intense protectiveness for his little sister, particularly since his father had left them the year before, making him the "man of the house," as his mother used to say. Wracked with guilt, he started to run. He heard his mother calling, "Edward! Edward!" But he just kept going. *Where was she? Had someone taken her?* The thought of something happening to his sister made his belly hurt. He spotted a policeman stationed on a horse on the boardwalk and ran to him.

"Sir," Edward called out in his tiny voice. "My sister is missing."

"What did you say, son?" The officer got off his horse and bent down to hear him. Edward imagined how his scared but determined little self must have looked trying to be brave.

"My sister. She's missing," young Edward repeated.

"What does she look like?"

What does she look like?

Edward remembered being put off by this question; he had never really *looked* at Jamie before. "She's two," he answered. "She's wearing a white T-shirt. She has brown hair. Green eyes. Smiles a lot."

Even at such a young age, Edward could feel an encroaching sense of dread as he gave the policeman what he knew was not a very vivid description. He had seen dozens of children on the beach that day who looked like that. As the seconds passed, there was also the horrible feeling that life as he knew it was over, that he would never be the same. His mother would never be the same.

The officer pulled his walkie-talkie from its holster, when Edward saw his mother running toward him, waving her arm frantically. "Edward! Edward! I found her!" she yelled, pointing to the bundle she was carrying in her other arm.

"Is that your mother, son?" the police officer asked, but Edward was already running back down the beach and into his mother's free arm.

"Sir, are you there?" the voice on the phone grew concerned.

"I'm here," Edward said, wiping his brow.

"Can you tell me what your sister looks like?"

"Yes," Edward said. "She's about five foot five, about 140 pounds, maybe. Brown hair. Green eyes." He paused. "Smiles a lot."

"All right, I need you to fill out a complete missing-persons report. We have a form online that you can use, or you can come to Pier Ninety-Four, which is at Fifty-Fourth and Twelfth Avenue. Although we do have a Long Island office . . ."

"No, no, Fifty-Fourth and Twelfth. She was in Manhattan. I'm sure of it."

"Please be sure to bring photographs, dental records, personal articles, and any other identifying information about your sister."

"All right. Thank you."

Edward tossed the phone onto the couch. The mad rush of adrenaline he'd felt earlier had been replaced by an abrupt malaise, triggered by the memory of the beach. Edward had never recovered from the incident—even though his mother had told him, again and again, that it wasn't his fault, that he was only a baby himself, that Jamie had simply walked away, watching her feet in the sand under the cover of the exiting crowd. But Edward felt that he'd let his mother down, and he had spent the rest of his life trying to make up for it.

And now his sister was missing again.

Where in the hell am I going to find dental records, Edward wondered. He couldn't recall seeing anything like that. Then he remembered that when Jamie was in the third grade, the local precinct had visited her elementary school to talk about stranger danger and had fingerprinted all the kids. Edward knew he had those somewhere packed up in the garage.

And photos. He needed photos. The most recent ones he had were online, posted like everybody else's on Facebook, particularly so that Aunt Clara in Arizona could see them. He ran upstairs to his home office and logged on to his laptop computer. Out of habit, he first checked his email. Tons of garbage, but nothing from Jamie. He opened Facebook and saw on his news feed that Bob and six of his friends had changed their profile photo. From the thumbnail, it looked as though it were a photo of Bob standing next to a red car.

"Asshole," Edward muttered.

He scrolled down the page and stopped. Jamie's name appeared. Written next to it was "Help Albany Charlotte."

He looked at the time stamp: 10:23 a.m.

Edward leaned back in his swivel chair and exhaled. *She was alive.* And then without giving himself more than a moment of relief, he hunched over his keyboard, clicked open a comment box just below a person named Ralph Beckman who had written, "Help Buffalo Raleigh," and he typed, "Where r u??"

He pressed *share* and folded his arms across his chest, watching the computer, half-expecting Jamie to reply immediately, his fear now mixed with anger. *Why hadn't she called? She knew he'd be anxious to know where she was.* While he was waiting, Edward also checked Twitter, Google+, LinkedIn, and any other social networking site he could think of, but there was nothing.

Tricia's words rang in his ears. "She's a grown woman, Edward!"—Tricia's go-to mantra whenever they argued about Jamie—"You're so goddamned overprotective. She can do what she wants. She doesn't have to report to *you*."

Edward felt a bit embarrassed at the thought that Trish had been right, that Jamie was fine, and that he had jumped the gun.

He looked at her post again. "Help Albany Charlotte."

What did that mean?

Edward refreshed the page to see if she had answered, but he already could see that she wasn't logged on to her profile. He picked up his phone to call her again, but he'd already sent dozens of texts and voicemails. He put the phone down, clicked out of the news feed and onto his profile, and scanned through his photos. He stopped at one that was taken last Christmas of him and Jamie holding up the matching wool sweaters that they'd received from Aunt Clara. There she was. Smiling. Happy.

Help Albany Charlotte.

Help . . .

Albany . . .

Charlotte . . .

Edward studied Jamie's face, the way her arm was draped over his shoulder.

Help . . .

Help . . .

Help . . .

"Overprotective, my ass," he griped.

He printed the photo and another, and then he ran downstairs and out into the garage to find those tiny fingerprints.

32

Jamie looked down the meadow at the stream of rushing water. *So this was the source of the noise,* she thought. The river wasn't a wide crossing, perhaps about fifty feet across, and she wondered how deep it was and how quickly it would take her to swim its width with a baby in tow. She wasn't the strongest swimmer, but she did have practice in carrying small children across pools until she thought her legs were going to fall off. *How different could this be?*

It distressed her that she was relieved to see Bailino return to the log cabin, but it was getting difficult to keep ducking Leo, which she'd been doing all morning and afternoon. He followed her from room to room, asking if she were hungry, wanted to lie down, needed a massage. She must have changed Charlotte's diaper fifteen times for no reason other than to have something to keep her busy and away from him.

The gurgling of the water had drawn the attention of Charlotte, who was walking beside her, and the little girl pulled Jamie's hand in the direction of the river.

"No, no, honey, we can't go there." Jamie picked Charlotte up so that she wouldn't fall on the smooth pebbles that had replaced the firm terrain of grass and dirt.

"Why not?"

Even though she knew he was directly behind her, the sound of Bailino's voice startled Jamie anyway. "There's no one around for miles," he continued, as if reading her mind. "Let her get wet. Have some fun. You know, after what she's been through."

When Bailino had suggested that she and Charlotte go for a walk with him, she immediately thought he had discovered her Facebook post and that this was it. She hesitated by the back doors, remembering the ball of blonde hair by the vegetable garden, the swing of the shovel, the steely look in his eyes at Bryant Park. But they had been walking for fifteen minutes, and he had pretty much stayed a few feet behind them the whole time. The others were playing cards again on the backyard table, with the exception of Leo, who said he was going for a drive, and Joey, who was watching SpongeBob SquarePants.

Walking there in the woods, with Bailino's presence looming behind her, Jamie remembered a freelance article she'd written years before about a forest ranger, Joe Buck, who had saved a pair of teenagers from a wolf attack in Oregon. Buck had visited Long Island during the tail end of his promotional tour for his book: *The Teens Who Cried Wolf.* He had told the bookstore crowds—none of whom, Jamie ventured, would ever come into contact with the animal—that when confronted by a wolf, it was unwise to stare directly into his eyes for he considered that a challenge. Jamie imagined Buck's wolf didn't have the habit of saying, "Please look at me when I talk to you."

Charlotte grabbed the side of Jamie's face and tried to worm her way out of her arms, pointing toward the water.

"No, honey."

Charlotte pointed again, this time with more emphasis.

"I think the decision's been made," Bailino said.

"I just don't think it's a good idea," Jamie said. "She's still not that steady on her feet. She's been falling all morning."

Bailino stepped over a large rock so that he was standing between her and the river. He reached out for Charlotte with two hands, palm-side up, like a well-meaning relative at a family reunion. Charlotte recoiled.

Bailino stared out into the water. "You know, loyalties are an interesting thing," he said. "They tend to shift depending upon what you want. Don't you think?"

Jamie, who was focusing on a piece of dirt on Charlotte's shirt, was silent.

This was it.

"I asked you a question. Please look at me when I talk to you."

"No." She looked into Bailino's eyes. "I don't think that's true."

Bailino smirked and shifted his feet. The sides of his loafers were wet and darker than the rest of the shoes. He looked amused.

"Really. Why?"

"I . . . just . . ." Bailino's eyes were boring into her, and she was struggling for the words.

"You're free to say whatever you like," he said.

"I just think that . . ." She thought about what Joey had said, about keeping quiet, and about whether these would be her last words.

"You think . . . what?"

"I think true loyalty isn't something that can be bought or . . . frightened into someone. Or changed on a whim. I think it's something that develops over time." She lifted Charlotte higher in her arms. "I think it's something that runs deep. When you're loyal, nothing can break it." Suddenly, she couldn't stop talking. "I think when someone has been a loyal friend or person, you know that you should always give them the benefit of the doubt even if you suspect disloyalty." Would that be enough to save her if Bailino discovered the Facebook comment? She didn't know.

"*Hmmm* . . . So you're saying that loyalty is something you learn?"

"It's something you earn," Jamie said.

Bailino looked out at the water. His heavy breathing, which she had become used to hearing, was inaudible so close to the river.

"So we both agree that loyalty is not something you're born with," Bailino said.

"No . . . Well . . ." Jamie stammered. The thought of finding common philosophical ground with Bailino repulsed her. "I guess what I'm saying is that I think loyalty is steadfast." She squeezed a small mosquito that landed on Charlotte's cheek; she could feel them biting her legs. "I think that if you're committed to something, then the right thing is to go through with it. If it's real loyalty, then there's nothing . . . nothing that can break that bond, even if you have misgivings."

Charlotte grabbed Jamie's face and pointed again to the water.

Bailino was quiet, which made Jamie anxious. She wanted to show that she was smart and capable, but now wondered if she had made any sense at all. Maybe she should have stayed quiet—she had a tendency to ramble, particularly when she was nervous, her point getting lost in a string of non sequiturs, or so Bob, the debate king, liked to tell her. She flinched when Bailino held out his hands again.

"Don't you want to go to the water?" he asked Charlotte. His voice was gentle, in a way Jamie had never heard it before. His eyes had softened, the deep creases on his forehead relaxed.

Confused, Charlotte looked at Jamie and then back at Bailino. She didn't know what to do. Then, slowly, Charlotte took her arms from around Jamie's neck and just let them flop down. She leaned away from Jamie in Bailino's direction.

"That-a-girl," Bailino said, scooping her up. He held Charlotte in his right arm capably, in a way in which she was both comfortable and secure, as if he'd been holding children his whole life, and headed straight for the water, his feet now submerged. As the pair walked away, Charlotte turned in Jamie's direction and extended her hand to signal that she wanted Jamie to follow along.

Jamie was stunned. She felt betrayed and a bit humiliated. But she was still alive.

Bailino placed Charlotte on the ground, and the little girl squealed with delight as the cold water covered her toes. She bent down and touched the water with the tips of her fingers. Jamie looked around. *What was stopping her from just running?* She could make a break for it. Was there really no one around for miles, as Bailino had said? Bailino had his back toward her and was pointing out a fish jumping out of the water to Charlotte, who wasn't looking for Jamie anymore.

But something wasn't right. Was this a trap? Or a test? With his back turned, was he pulling a *Charlotte* on her—standing there with outstretched hands, testing her loyalties?

Then something dawned on Jamie. Could it be possible that Charlotte had not abandoned her at all, had not switched loyalties at random, but had a sense, the same sense that Jamie had, that Bailino was her ticket out of there and that it was better to keep him happy? She watched Bailino splash Charlotte with water. In the little girl's eyes, if Jamie trusted the big scary man, or so it seemed, and Charlotte trusted Jamie, then wouldn't it make sense that Charlotte should trust him too?

Charlotte was pressing both hands onto a pair of moss-covered rocks, watching the waves ripple around them, as Jamie walked beside her.

"Waa, waa, waa," Charlotte said, smiling.

"Yes, water," Jamie said.

"The kid loves the water," Bailino said, sitting on a tall rock. Charlotte picked up a small stone and threw it into the stream and giggled. She lifted up another one and was startled by a small frog and fell backward. She started to cry and crawled toward Jamie on all fours.

"It's all right." Jamie wiped the mud from Charlotte's knees. "Just a frog." They watched the tiny creature hop away into the weeds. "You see? He's going home to his mommy and . . ."

Jamie caught herself. She'd said *mommy*. She didn't mean to. It was a habit, something she used to say to Peter and Sara when they'd have run-ins with mice and frogs in the backyard. Charlotte seemed to look at her for a moment, as if the word conjured up a distant memory, but then she kicked her feet to get back down on the ground. This time, Charlotte held onto Jamie's pant leg for steadiness while she picked up nearby rocks to toss into the water.

"Are you happy?" Bailino asked her. She could feel he had been studying her as he sat leisurely on the rock, as if he hadn't a care in the world.

"Happy?" Jamie asked.

"Yeah, you know, in your life." He paused. "Your *real* life."

It was odd to hear Bailino categorize what exactly was going on here, intimating that her being at the cabin with Charlotte and him was some sort of fantastical extension of life, rather than the real thing, and it dawned on her for the first time that perhaps he was not only speaking about her, but himself as well.

"Yes," she said. "I am." She paused and then felt the urge to keep going. "I wasn't happy for a long time, though."

"You mean, in your marriage?"

Jamie didn't answer. A canoe had come into her line of sight. There were two rowers, and both of them picked their oars out of the water to wave. Bailino waved back, and although she couldn't see his face, she heard him say, "Wave." She obeyed and waved, and, following Jamie's lead, Charlotte did too. The rowers put their oars back in the water and continued on their way.

"So," Bailino asked, readjusting himself on the rock. "Why weren't you happy for a long time?"

"I was married to a guy I didn't love—didn't even like—for eight years."

"Why would you marry someone you didn't love?"

Jamie picked up a rock and threw it far into the water. Charlotte giggled.

"Nice arm," Bailino said, impressed.

"My brother taught me how not to throw like a girl."

"So why would you marry someone you didn't love? You told me this morning you got caught up in something. What?"

Jamie picked up another rock.

"I know," Bailino smirked. "I'm very persistent."

"It's a long story, why I married Bob."

"I'm not going anywhere."

Jamie hesitated. She thought about her mother lying in bed, frail, her eyes sunken, long strands of hair laying on her pillow and sheets, her lips so chapped that they went through a tube of Chap Stick every day.

Sensing her struggle, Bailino stood up. "All right," he said. "Let's head back."

Relieved, Jamie picked up Charlotte, who was filthy and reluctant to go and was doing the body-as-a-board thing again, but

Jamie held her firmly until the little girl settled down in her arms. As they followed Bailino back up the hill toward the log cabin, Jamie was aware of how comfortable she felt having him in front of her this time, where she could see him, rather than having him follow behind, as he had on the way to the river. *It was always easier to know what was in front of you, what's ahead, wasn't it?* she thought. If only her mother had thought the same way, had given her and Edward and everyone enough time to prepare.

Jamie watched Bailino stride past the trees and the rocky terrain with ease, like he owned the place, which he did. She knew he was going to ask her questions again and again until he got the answers he wanted—that satisfied him—of that she was sure, but that was the least of her concerns. In a few hours, it would be dark, and she would have to spend another night with him. Her stomach tightened as she remembered Bailino on top of her, grunting, sweating, unrelenting. She was going to have to brace herself for the inevitable and face the fact that Edward was not going to rescue her, that no one was. She was on her own.

But not alone. Jamie ran her hand over Charlotte Grand's head, which rested on her shoulder. She would have to be strong, and smart, for the both of them, but what that meant Jamie wasn't sure. She thought of Bailino's hot, piercing eyes in the dark of the bedroom. She was going to have to look the wolf right in the eyes and challenge him—not with threats or violence, Lord knows that didn't work, but in a way that would gain his respect and confidence, and maybe, just maybe, she'd get her chance.

"You all right?" Bailino asked, turning around, but without slowing down.

"Yes," Jamie nodded.

And the time to start was now.

Jamie juggled Charlotte higher in her arms and picked up her pace until she was walking side by side with Bailino. She looked straight ahead at the log cabin, which had just come into view, but from the corner of her eye, she could see Bailino was looking at her. And smiling.

33

Pandemonium erupted at the Executive Mansion as news of Charlotte's disappearance hit the major news outlets, all of which had reps camped just outside the black iron gates, rendering the narrow sidewalk, as well as Eagle Street, unnavigable.

Detective Nurberg watched the commotion from the mansion entrance. This was exactly what he was trying to avoid. In the last hour alone, the department had gotten fifteen calls from individuals claiming to have spotted ten-month-old Charlotte Grand from places as far away as Tucson and San Francisco. His small staff, already taxed, was spending its time mired in paperwork and chasing down dead-end leads. And to top things off, Nurberg left his folder and notepad in his car, which he had to park in the museum lot around the block. He had no desire to trudge through that mayhem again to get them.

"Detective Nurberg?"

Nurberg was greeted by the governor's press secretary, Leonard Maddox, who had been sent to escort him into the mansion. He was told that the governor and his wife were trying their best to remain out of public sight.

Not so much this morning, huh, governor, Nurberg thought about Phillip Grand's midmorning jaunt to Taryn's Diner. He followed the press secretary inside.

Maddox, a small, stout man with a pointy nose, looked exhausted. He had been with the Grands since the governor was first inaugurated six years ago and served as Katherine Grand's right-hand man. Nurberg spotted him on the news about an hour ago making a brief statement about Charlotte's disappearance, after which he avoided all of the press' inquiries, but promised regular updates, pretty much defying Nurberg's instructions about keeping things quiet.

"I saw you on TV," Nurberg said as they walked.

"Detective, no offense, but I don't answer to you. I answer to the First Lady."

He stopped just before the Drawing Room and prompted Nurberg to enter. The Drawing Room, historically, was a place for after-dinner socializing at the mansion, although the mood this evening was somber, in spite of the ruckus outside. The room was also where the governor was officially inaugurated every four years—the day before the public swearing-in. Phillip and Katherine Grand were sitting on a pair of facing velvet red sofas that flanked a large fireplace, over which hung a portrait of Nelson Rockefeller.

"Detective Nurberg." Governor Grand pushed himself up, using the sofa's armrest. He too looked quite tired. "Please, come and sit down."

Nurberg shook the governor's hand, and as he sat down he caught the eye of Mrs. Grand, who was glowering at him.

"Mrs. Grand." Nurberg said, with a nod of his head.

"How did this happen?" Katherine Grand looked as if she had eaten something horribly bitter and was looking for a plate—or a face—to spit it into.

"Ma'am?"

"This, this . . . media circus," she said, pointing outside. "What kind of operation are you running here, Nurberg? The *Titanic* had fewer fucking leaks."

"Katherine . . ." Phillip Grand shook his head apologetically.

Nurberg was defensive. "The leak didn't come from my end, Ma'am."

"Detective, you have scores of people working at the station. Any one of them could have called that freak Harvey Levin."

"Mrs. Grand, I could say the very same thing about your staff, but pointing fingers isn't going to help matters and isn't going to help find your daughter."

Mrs. Grand folded her arms across her chest and let out an irritated sigh.

"What's the status on the investigation, Detective?" the governor asked.

"I wish I had better news," Nurberg said. "But, at this point, I'm afraid we haven't come up with anything concrete."

"Jesus!" Katherine threw her hands up in the air.

"Mrs. Grand," Nurberg said, trying to remain calm and reminding himself that it was Mrs. Grand's daughter who was missing and that she had every right to be perturbed. "I have interviewed every mansion staff member, chased down every lead personally. I assure you that we have done everything we can."

"Well, it looks like it's not enough." Katherine stood up. Nurberg could tell she was gearing up for another tongue-lashing. "You mean to tell me that with every news station and Web site now broadcasting the disappearance of my daughter, there's nothing new for you to report?"

"Tons of calls are coming in, Mrs. Grand, but none so far have panned out."

"Tons of calls?" Phillip asked. "From where?"

"From everywhere," Nurberg said. "California. Arizona. Louisiana. South Carolina. It's keeping my office quite busy." He glared at Mrs. Grand. "*This*"—Nurberg pointed toward the front window, where even through the heavy red drapes, the bright lights of the news cameras were visible—"was not part of the plan. At least, not yet." Nurberg was standing now. "I wasn't the one on the news today making a statement."

"You're right. Somebody had to do something, Detective," Katherine said. She smoothed the velvet down on the top of the sofa with her hand. "What should I have expected? After all, your track record isn't all that remarkable."

"Excuse me?" Nurberg could feel the skin on his cheeks reddening.

"I mean, this case was a huge step up for you, wasn't it, Detective

Nurberg?" Katherine stepped out from behind the sofa. "Kidnapping is a far cry from public disturbance."

Nurberg was furious. "Ma'am, I have an exemplary record and several commendations, not that I need to defend myself."

"Apparently, you do."

"All right . . . all right . . ." Phillip stood in between Katherine and the detective. "This isn't getting us anywhere. Katherine, please, would you leave the detective and me alone for a moment?"

Katherine fluffed the back of her hair and pulled at the string of beads wound tightly around her neck. Against the backdrop of the historical room, she resembled—although Nurberg hated to admit it—a slender Eleanor Roosevelt. A small sprinkler head, installed in 1961 after an electrical fire tore through the entire first floor of the mansion, hung above her and was the only clue that this was a modern-day scene. Nurberg wished something would set it off right now.

"All right," Katherine said. She gazed at Detective Nurberg as if to say something—or perhaps waiting for him to—and then marched off for the second time in two days.

As Mrs. Grand left, so did the hostility, and Nurberg felt somewhat embarrassed. "Governor, I'm . . ."

Phillip shook his head. "No need to apologize. This is a difficult time for everyone. We all seem to be losing our heads."

"But please know, sir, that we are doing everything we can to find your daughter."

But Phillip Grand wasn't listening. He picked up a photo, which was displayed on a circular wooden table, of him and Mrs. Grand with President and Mrs. Obama from the presidential inauguration three years ago. There were several sterling-silver photo frames there featuring a variety of dignitaries, all facing toward the main hall so that the tourists, who were roped off from entering the Drawing Room, could see them.

"You know, he called this afternoon," Phillip said. "The president."

"Oh?"

"Yes, he'd seen the story on the news and took a moment to call. Nice fellow."

"Governor, there *is* something I'd like to talk with you about."

Phillip returned to his spot on the sofa. "Yes, Detective. What is it?"

"This morning, you visited Taryn's Diner downtown."

The governor pushed himself back on the sofa and rolled up the sleeve on his right arm, then his left. "Yes."

"Why?"

"He needed air," Katherine said, returning to the room and bending down on the far side of the sofa closest to her to pick up her pocketbook, which had been placed on the floor. "Sorry, forgot my bag." She put it over her shoulder.

As she left the room, Phillip said, "I had to get out of the house."

"Away from me, supposedly," Katherine yelled as she stepped up the nearby staircase that led to the mansion's private quarters.

Phillip sighed and put his head back, resting it on the sofa back. "That woman . . ."

"Sir? Taryn's?"

"Detective, I just . . . needed to go."

"Were you hungry?"

"Yes," Phillip said. "I was hungry."

Detective Nurberg sat on the facing sofa, where Katherine Grand had been seated when he first arrived. "But witnesses say that you had nothing to eat while you were there, sir."

"Witnesses?" The governor sat up straight. "Detective, am I under police surveillance?"

"No, sir." Nurberg hesitated. He was about to piss off his only ally. "I just thought it strange that you would go out for a bite in the middle of an investigation, particularly when I had asked you to stick around."

"Strange enough to start asking questions about me, I see. Didn't you think soliciting residents would arouse suspicion? Or get people talking?"

"Governor Grand," Nurberg leaned forward. "We are on the same side here, aren't we?"

"Why wouldn't we be?" Phillip said.

"What I mean is . . ." Nurberg cleared his throat. "We *are* on the same side. You do know that, right?"

"Yes, Detective, yes." Phillip rubbed his temple. "I'm sorry. I think this is all getting to me."

"I understand, sir, and, again, I'm sorry I don't have better news."

"You are doing all you can, I know."

"It's just that I really thought we would have heard something by now," Nurberg said. "In most kidnapping cases, where there is a ransom or any other kind of demand, the abductors make contact within the first twenty-four hours."

"Is that right?" Phillip shifted in his seat. "Well, what does that mean then?"

"I wish I knew," Nurberg said. "As much as my gut tells me I'm wrong, I keep going back to your nanny, Rosalia. She was the last one to see Charlotte."

"No, no . . . Rosalia. She can't be involved," Phillip said. "Can't be."

"How confident are you?" Nurberg asked.

"I'm sure of it."

Nurberg shook his head. "Well, please call me if you think of anything. And don't—DON'T—talk to *them*." Nurberg pointed toward the front mansion window.

"Good. I thought you were going to tell me to make a statement or something—or some kind of plea."

"A plea? To whom?"

"Oh," Phillip shrugged. "I don't know."

"No, I'll just keep going over what we do know, look again at the security tapes. Maybe we missed something."

"Thank you for all your hard work, Detective Nurberg."

The two men rose from the sofas and walked out of the Drawing Room. Phillip escorted Nurberg as far as the main corridor and then stopped.

"I'll be in touch," Nurberg said.

As Nurberg left the mansion, Phillip could hear the immediate rush of entreaties calling "Detective! Detective!" Peeking through a front window, he watched Nurberg bully his way through the crowd of media as if he were digging a tunnel, which kept collapsing behind him. When the detective was out of sight, the governor stepped into the adjoining room, a gold-hued sitting room that housed several of Franklin Roosevelt's personal items, including a wheelchair and an ashtray. He opened the door that led to the first-floor bathroom, the one used by mansion visitors, and immediately threw up in the forty-year-old porcelain pedestal sink installed by Governor Nelson Rockefeller.

34

Gino's last meal arrived at 4:30 p.m. with less pomp and circumstance than even he could imagine. The gate to his cell opened, Hank placed the food tray in Gino's hands, relocked the gate, and was on his way all within a matter of seconds.

It's a common misconception that last meals are something of a lavish endowment for condemned inmates. The truth was that the federal government only allowed an expenditure of twenty dollars on a last meal, not quite enough for the lobster tails Gino had been counting on. And no tobacco or alcohol products were allowed. Gino could have had his food purchased at a local restaurant—it was rumored that the last guy to be put to death at Stanton ordered from the McDonald's Dollar Menu—or had it prepared by the Institution Food Services Supervisor at the prison.

Gino, whose expensive tastes had been humbled in recent years, went with the latter. He looked at his plate: tuna fish on white toast with lettuce and extra mayo, a one-liter plastic bottle of Coke with a tall plastic cup of ice, a side order of Tater Tots, and a Bavarian cream donut. Simple. His only extravagant demand had been ten packets of ketchup, since the prison tended to be stingy with those. The whole thing probably cost five bucks, if that.

No one seemed to question why Gino had asked for his last meal a day early. They probably figured he was being his usual batty self, but it had been a long time since Gino had had a Bavarian cream donut, and nothing, not even a stay of execution, was going to stop him from having one. He put the tray on his knees and was taking a bite of his sandwich when Hank returned to his cell.

"Got a visitor, Gino."

"Now?" he asked, a glob of mayonnaise in the corner of his mouth. "You fuckin' with me?"

"Nope, let's go. You know the drill."

Gino put the tray on his cot and stuck his hands through the opening in the cell door. Hank cuffed them. As the cell door opened, Gino turned around, and Hank shackled his ankles as well. The two slowly made their way toward the visitors' room. Phillip Grand broke rank with the other governors when it came to death-row visitation. In addition to legal visits—and media interviews, of course—Grand allowed family members to visit condemned inmates up until twenty-four hours before an execution. What a guy.

"What time is it, Hank?" Gino asked.

"Time to get a new watch," Hank said with a chuckle.

Gino rolled his eyes.

"All right, all right, it's . . ." Hank looked at his watch. "6:03 p.m."

"Thanks."

Whoever was visiting got in just under the wire.

As Gino shuffled into the visitors' room, he let out a groan. Sitting across the wired glass was Leo, his right leg shaking up and down. The fact that his son was here to see him when he was explicitly told not to was *a)* not a good sign and *b)* immediately validated Gino's decision to let Bailino take the lead on this little operation. Gino shot a glance at the video cameras and sat down.

"Hi, Pop," Leo said.

Gino stared through the glass.

"I know you're not happy to see me. But I had to come and see you and talk to you about somethin'."

Talk, oh great, Gino thought. Leo had never really mastered the code.

Gino arched his eyebrows. "Boss?"

Leo nodded.

It was about Bailino. "What's . . . the . . . matter?" Gino said, like a child, in an attempt to remind Leo to speak wisely.

Leo hesitated and appeared to be thinking hard, but it didn't last long. "The fuckin' guy is playing house," Leo said. "With the girl and the kid."

"Are you out of your fuckin' mind?" Gino yelled into the glass, the outburst reverberating in the small room. He glanced at Hank who was standing behind him, but the guard wasn't the least bit rattled. Gino looked back at Leo. "Shut. The. Fuck. Up." He thought quickly. "What he does with ToniAnne and Joey doesn't concern you."

Confused, Leo looked as though he wanted to make himself clearer. "I'm just sayin' . . ."

"No, you say nothing. I'm going to talk, and you're going to say *nothing*." Gino felt a fluttering in his chest and thought how damn ironic it would be if he keeled over right there. Even though he was looking at his son through a thick piece of glass, there was no denying the red glassiness of his eyes. He had been drinking again.

"Good, now first of all, you don't think I have enough shit on my mind that you have to come to me with this garbage? Think, Leo. *Think.*"

"I don't know, Pop. Now that you mention Joey, he's putting crazy ideas in that kid's head."

"Yeah, I know," Gino said. "I'm not so crazy about the college thing either."

"Pop, but that's not what I'm talking about. It's Joey . . . and Don. Since Mikey died, it's like Don thinks he's running the show, acting like . . . It's bad enough the kid goes upstate every summer to intern in that stupid factory."

Gino had had enough. "Leo, I don't have time for this. I'm getting up and I'm going to eat my meal. I love you, kid, but you're killing me. Literally. Go home. Be nice to your sister." Gino turned to leave the room.

"Pop, I'm sorry," Leo called. "I shouldn't have come."

Gino waved his hand, and, with Hank behind him, shuffled his way back toward his cell.

"Kids, huh?" Hank said. "Can't live with them, can't die with them."

"Yeah. Kids."

A wave of despair filled Gino as he sat back down on his cot. He returned his tray to his lap and took another bite of his tuna sandwich. There was a scene every time ToniAnne or Leo visited him. *Every time.* Yelling, crying, bickering. Even in the early days, when Gino greeted them in the general visitors' room, with arms outstretched, he'd want to choke them within minutes. The other prisoners would stop their hand-holding and hugs to stare. For that reason, he had asked ToniAnne to stop visiting him three years ago—her visits depressed the shit out of him. And as the years passed, his kids had gotten older and fatter. And stupider. He much preferred contact by phone. Even Skype was too much to bear.

Gino picked up the newspaper that he'd left on the cot and flipped through it, stopping to look at the small headline on page twenty-three: "Cataldi Death Imminent." The story placement was a slap in the face. To make matters worse, the article had called him "the last of a dying breed." The accompanying photo showed a crumpled-up old man.

Where did I go wrong, he wondered, picking at his Tater Tots. He used to dream of a robust network of Cataldis, the linchpins of major corporate and governmental enterprises, but these kids were too damn spoiled and vain and distracted. Patsy Bailino, that son of a bitch, managed to raise a son who was competent and levelheaded and fearless. Gino's jealousy was palpable. In his early years, Donny Bailino was a bit of a weird, awkward kid, a loner type who liked to read—a lot like Joey, for sure—but he had grown into a formidable man. He had the brains and stomach for anything that Gino proposed, and he was a fountain of bold initiatives. After all, it had been Bailino's idea to contact *reliable* workers at his warehouses across the country and have them call in sightings of Charlotte Grand in order to throw off the local scent. Gino thought it would never work—one of those people was bound to squeal—and told him so, but so far, so good. And it was Bailino's plan to have all this take place at his log cabin, which happened to be isolated and soundproof, right under the nose of the local police. "It's not unusual for a family to come together in anticipation of the death of a patriarch," he'd told Gino. "The Feds'll have their hands full with the disappearance. This won't even be on their radar." And he was right. It wasn't. It was genius. Gino had to admit that without Don Bailino's support over the years, and savvy business sense, he would not have been able to maintain the few business ties he still had from behind bars.

Gino scratched his ass and took another bite of his sandwich, thinking about Joey and Don and what Leo had said. Leo was starting to connect the dots, and it was only a matter of time until he knew the truth about the relationship between Joey and Don—Gino was embarrassed that it had taken even this long for his son to figure it out. The resemblance, the identical mannerisms, the brains. *What a tool.*

But what Leo would never know—*could* never know—is that this had all been part of Gino's master plan. And for all of Don Bailino's savvy and brilliance, Gino had played him too—sending him to check in on ToniAnne all those times while Mikey was in prison, knowing full well what would happen. Mikey was a putz and probably had used his one sperm cell to father his granddaughter Anna, who, as much as Gino loved her, was a putz too and ugly as a motherfucker. And when ToniAnne announced her second pregnancy, Gino kept his fingers crossed that when that kid popped out it was anything but a conjugal-visit baby. And his wish had come true. He knew it. Donny knew it. ToniAnne probably knew too, although she never let on.

And Don Bailino's fate had been sealed. For the past seventeen years. Forever.

Bailino wanted out, sure. He'd been saying that for as long as Gino could remember. But as long as Joey was around, Gino had the leverage he needed to make the Great Bailino his errand boy—a feeling of satisfaction filled him.

But if Leo figured it out . . .

I'm getting too old for this shit, he thought. The ice cubes in his glass were nearly melted; Gino poured in some Coke and took a bite of his Bavarian cream donut.

35

Rey drove up the ramp onto the sidewalk and parked in front of the service station.

"Aunt Ro, I just have to stop in for a moment, and then we'll go, okay?" Rosalia sat quietly in the passenger seat. "You want to come in?"

"No, no. I'll stay here."

Reynaldo hesitated, but then he opened the front car windows an inch or two on each side, took his keys, and ran toward the station entrance. *This had better be important.*

Pedro was sitting on the leather bench, panting and looking guilty. Reynaldo spotted Nada bending down by the coffee machine looking for the plug.

"Why you leave Aunt Ro in the car, eh?" Pedro asked, looking out the window.

"She didn't want to come in. I asked her." Reynaldo looked around the office. "So? What's the big emergency?"

"No 'big emergency,' Rey. I told you . . ." Pedro walked behind the counter.

"Pedro, you said 'a big, scary, tall man' came in asking questions. What man?"

"I'm looking for the paper I wrote his name on, *hermano*. And his phone number."

Reynaldo waited while Pedro shuffled through papers. He stopped when he got to a magazine that had come in the day's mail and flipped through it.

"Pedro, Pedro . . . I don't have time. I have to take Aunt Ro to the police station."

"What did she do?" Nada asked, pouring coffee into the filter.

"Nothing, you twit," Pedro said. "The governor's daughter is missing, remember?"

"Oh." Nada shot Pedro a look before taking the coffeepot and leaving the room.

"Do you think they found the guy?" Pedro asked excitedly. "Do you think Aunt Ro has to identify him in a lineup? Can I come?"

"Pedro, I don't know anything. But what about the man who came into the station?"

"He was asking for you."

"Okay. . ." That was not unusual since Reynaldo ran the station. "What else?"

"He was scary looking." Pedro raised his eyebrows.

"Yeah, you said that."

"No, but I don't mean, like, you know, Hulk scary. He had shifty eyes. I didn't trust him. He looked kind of upset that you weren't here. Was snooping around too. Oh . . ." Pedro pulled a slip of paper out from under a pile. "Here's his card. Told you I had it," he said, handing it to Reynaldo proudly.

Nada returned with the pot of water as Reynaldo read the business card:
Philip Goldberg, Tax Advisor

"Jesus, Pedro, you know him. What is wrong with you? He's our tax guy, Phil. He's been coming here for years."

"Twit," Nada said with a sneer.

"Shut up, Nada." Pedro came out from behind the counter, and Reynaldo clotheslined him and put him in a headlock.

"Get off me, Rey."

"You've got to pay more attention, *hermano*," he whispered into his ear. Reynaldo let him go, picked up the cordless phone handset on the wall, and dialed.

"What does he want, Rey?"

Rey held up his finger while he kept the phone by his ear. He looked through the open blinds of the front window. He could see Rosalia waiting in the car.

"Yes, hello." Reynaldo spoke into the handset. "This is Reynaldo Rodriguez. My apologies for not being here when you came into the station today. I had completely forgotten about our appointment. We've had some family issues. Would it be possible to reschedule for Friday? Please call me on my cell phone at 323-3493. Thank you."

"Very nice, Rey," Pedro said. "Very professional."

"Pedro, I need you to come to Aunt Ro's tomorrow night. Rikki and Terry can't get up here from Queens until Friday morning."

"Tomorrow? Night? Um . . . I don't know if I'm available." Pedro looked at Nada, who was pushing buttons on the coffee machine.

"*Basta*, Pedro! You are going to Aunt Ro's. She can't be alone. And I need to be here going through tax papers or else we'll all be going to prison."

The door from the garage opened, and Ricardo walked in. His blue overalls and his face were covered in grease.

"Goddamn oil tank sprung a leak. What are you doing here?" he asked Reynaldo. "And why is Aunt Ro sitting in the car outside, crying?" Ricardo spotted Nada by the coffee machine. "Where have *you* been?"

"She's crying? I have to go." Reynaldo looked at Pedro. "You are coming tomorrow night, yes?"

"Coming where?" Ricardo asked.

"Yes, yes, I will be there," Pedro said.

"*Alone . . .*"

"Yes, alone." Pedro looked at the floor and put his hands in his pockets.

"Why does he have to go alone?" Ricardo grabbed a dirty washcloth that was hanging on a hook near the garage door and wiped his face, creating dark streak marks that made him look as if he had been crying giant black tears. "Why doesn't anyone ever tell me what's going on, eh?"

"Oh, *basta*, Ricky, or else I will tell Rey how you made that girl in the tight skirt walk all the way through the garage, past everyone, instead of letting her exit right here."

"*Shush, hermano.*" Ricardo put his finger to his lips.

"Is that right?" Nada asked.

Reynaldo wasn't listening. "Pedro, put those papers away, so I can go through them tomorrow night, eh? Use one of the big envelopes in the drawer." Reynaldo swung the front door open. "And when you lock up, don't forget to make sure the garage door closes all the way this time. I don't need any more little visitors sneaking in during the middle of the night."

"Yeah, yeah . . . go, go," Pedro said.

"Don't you have anything for me to do?" Ricardo asked.

"Yeah, go jump into a lake," Pedro said. "You could use the bath."

"Ricky, you just stay out of trouble, okay?" Reynaldo said.

Ricardo looked dejected.

"And take out the garbage."

He perked up instantly. "¡Aye, aye, *capitán*!"

Reynaldo hurried back toward his aunt, who remained slumped in the passenger seat.

"*Tía*, I'm sorry I took so long." Reynaldo started the car and pulled into the street.

Rosalia smiled weakly. "Reyito, if the *policía* arrest me . . ."

"Arrest you? For what?"

"Will you water my plants for me?"

"Yes, but . . . I mean, you are not going to jail. You didn't do anything."

Rosalia looked at the road and rubbed her rosary beads, which she had cupped in her hands. "How are your brothers?"

"Fine. The same."

She patted his hand on the steering wheel. "They are lucky to have you."

Some people are meant to care for others, Reyito.

Yes, Reynaldo thought as he sped down the road, *whether they want to or not.*

36

Charlotte cackled in the bath as Jamie poured another cup of water over her head. Bailino was right. This kid loved water. The stream slid like silk over the smoothness of Charlotte's forehead, washing away the grime of the riverbank and leaving behind glowing skin—the kind that belonged in a home with loved ones, not complete strangers.

Jamie kept her left hand securely behind Charlotte so that she didn't flop backward as Jamie put down the cup and picked up a bar of soap and washed around the little girl's shoulders. Charlotte's hands were probably the dirtiest part of her, but Charlotte was taking care of those herself, splashing them down in the water, soaking Jamie's shirt and hair. Seeing the cup float, Charlotte grabbed it with both hands and shook it up and down, then held it in one hand and slapped it with the other.

"Mo, Mo, Mo," she said, creating her own little rhythmic beat.

The unadulterated glee in Charlotte's voice was almost enough to wash away the events of the past two days. *Almost.*

"Mo, Mo, Mo?" Jamie smiled, squeezing a bit of that yucky dandruff shampoo, the only kind on hand, into Charlotte's hair and working up a lather with her free hand. "Are you trying to say *Jamie*?"

"Mo, Mo, Mo," Charlotte said again.

"Ja-mie," Jamie said, pinching her chin.

Charlotte's sweet smile turned into a scowl. She shook her head and threw the cup into the water.

"Hey, that's not very nice," Jamie said in a voice that was surprisingly firm.

"Mo, Mo, Mo . . ." Charlotte said sternly, as stern as a little girl whose hair has been fashioned into a sudsy pyramid can look. She brought the fingertips of her hands together and touched them several times. It was the same motion she'd made during breakfast.

Suddenly, Jamie realized that Charlotte wasn't trying to say her name at all. And she wasn't clapping. She was *signing*. She remembered when her nephew had had a severe speech delay as a toddler and had qualified for free therapy services provided by New York State; the therapist would bring Peter's bunched fingertips together—the sign for *more*—and say slowly "More. More." Before that, Peter had just been banging his fists on the table to get more of whatever it was he wanted.

"Why teach him sign language?" Jamie had asked the therapist, a young, enthusiastic brunette with a bright smile. "It seems like the opposite direction we want to go. Isn't the idea to get him to talk?"

"It's interesting," the therapist had answered, as she continued moving Peter's fingertips apart and then together. "You would think that teaching sign language would make the child *not* want to talk. I mean, why should he, if he is able to communicate in other ways, right? But what we've found is that sign language helps ease a child's frustration and actually promotes verbal language."

Jamie looked at Charlotte, who now had the empty cup by her mouth and was trying to drink from it. *Somebody taught this little girl sign language.*

"Are you saying *more*, sweetie?"

"Mo, mo, mo!" Charlotte squealed, bringing the fingertips of her hands together once again. She held the cup out to Jamie, who took it and scooped more water into it. When she poured it over Charlotte's head, the little girl clapped wildly, chanting, "Mo, mo, mo!"

From the bedroom, Bailino watched, hidden behind the half-closed door. He was impressed by the confidence with which Jamie handled the little girl, the way she reprimanded her when she thought she was being impolite, the way one hand held her firmly while the other washed, shampooed, and poured like a machine. Or a mother. It was obvious that Jamie had had practice with small children. He imagined she had teaching experience or perhaps her brother Edward had kids—he had seen children in the photos on her phone. Something had told him when he first saw her walking around, looking for a place to sit, at Bryant Park that she was the one. It was the honesty of her face, her smile, her politeness; there was a refreshing unsophistication about her, a naiveté, a purity that he was drawn to. He thought about their conversation in the woods, the utter disbelief on Jamie's face when Charlotte had come to him willingly, and the first time they made love, and he smiled.

Jamie's T-shirt had gotten wet, and Bailino could see the outline of her nipples poking through her bra and shirt, which roused him; he stepped away from the door and into the bedroom.

Charlotte was now pouring cupfuls of water down the wall tiles and watching the drops make their way back into the tub as Jamie held her with two hands. She tried to stand up.

"No, no," Jamie said. "Not in the tub. You'll get hurt."

Undeterred, the little girl poured another cupful of water, and as it weaved its way down the grout lines of the tile, Jamie's thoughts turned to escape. It was going to be difficult. She was rarely left alone, unless she was in the upstairs bedroom or bathroom. It was true that when she was outdoors, although they watched, they gave her a long leash, but not enough to give her a good head start, particularly if she were carrying twenty pounds of baby.

Charlotte threw her head back in laughter. She poured more water down the wall until she stopped and let out a big yawn. Jamie knew how quickly children could decelerate and, sure enough, Charlotte dropped the cup into the bathwater, blinking her eyes lazily.

Jamie released her hand a little from Charlotte's back and reclined her until the little girl was lying straight back and resting on her right hand. She lifted Charlotte up and down in the water, causing tiny waves to ripple along the sides of the bathtub, marveling at how pliant she was, how restful and trusting, and how easy she was to hold in the water. Jamie submerged her more until everything except her head was underwater and with her left hand, Jamie smoothed down the wet curls from Charlotte's face, her hair floating out in all directions. She looked like a pudgy little mermaid. Charlotte's eyelids drooped as the water caressed her cheeks.

The water. Jamie thought about the river. They had seen those people in canoes, but there was no relying on when the next one would paddle by. She had to get across. It was the only way. But with a baby?

Jamie took a deep breath and lowered her hand further down into the bathwater until its surface crept up over Charlotte's ears. She held her there, and Charlotte opened her eyes wide, perhaps confused by the change of sound and sensation, but then closed them again.

"It's all right, sweetie," Jamie soothed.

Charlotte's lids opened at the sound of her voice, and their eyes met. Then they closed again. Jamie had the little girl's complete and total trust. She glanced at the bathroom doorway. No one was there.

Then she lowered her hand to the bottom of the tub, and the child's head went with it, submerging completely.

37

Before Jamie could lift Charlotte up out of the water, the little girl's survival instincts kicked in, and she pushed herself forward with a jolt. Gasping for air, eyes closed, Charlotte reached in Jamie's direction to get out of the bathtub at once. She coughed up tiny drops of water, her pale, wet face blotched red from the strain, her confused wails bouncing off the ceramic tiles.

"It's okay, it's okay, I'm sorry." Jamie only wanted to dip her quickly, just to see. She pulled Charlotte out and onto her lap and was patting her back when Bailino stormed inside the bathroom.

"What the hell happened?" he roared.

"She swallowed some water, but she's okay. She's crying. That means she's okay, she's breathing."

"She doesn't look okay!" Bailino's yells were making Charlotte cry even more. He was bending down, towering over them as Jamie wrapped Charlotte in a towel.

"Please stop yelling," Jamie said. It had become claustrophobic in the small bathroom. "You're scaring her."

"*I'm* scaring her? Get her dressed now!"

With her arms wrapped around Charlotte, Jamie ran out of the bathroom while Bailino sat down on the lid of the toilet bowl, gripping the top edges of the bathtub and sink, suddenly feeling all of his forty-seven years. His heart was thumping in his chest, and he pressed back against the cool of the toilet tank as the steam in the air filled his lungs with soothing vapor. The sight of the little girl struggling to breathe had knocked the wind out of him—her clenched face, the sucking of air. It wasn't until that moment that he realized how much Charlotte Grand resembled her father.

****

Phillip Grand's head was being yanked out of the small bucket of water, probably the only water around for miles in the Iraqi desert; he was gasping, begging for them to stop. The Republican Guardsmen, dressed in their four-color desert uniforms, were laughing, having a good old time. No sooner had they pulled Phillip's head out, and he had gotten oxygen into his deflated lungs, did they put him back in and hold him there. It took both men to hold Phillip Grand—although he was skinny and soft-spoken, he had considerable strength.

Bailino was lying facedown in the hot sand searing his face and palms as he held onto his M16, but he lay still. Like a gray wolf, Bailino relied on his stamina, rather than his speed, for hunting. As far as he could see, the two men were alone, and they hadn't seen him. His walkie-talkie rattled, but Bailino ignored it, inching closer. He was going to do this alone. When he thought he was close enough, he readied his weapon, and just as they forced Phillip Grand's head down again, Bailino fired two times, shooting both men once in the head. As the bodies collapsed to the ground, Phillip came thrashing out of the water, his tall, lanky body recoiling into a fetal position as he coughed up sprays of inhaled water that pooled in the hot sand and immediately evaporated. Phillip looked up, his dirty-blond eyebrows and lashes wet and full of sand, and saw Bailino.

"Thanks, brother," Phillip wheezed. Bailino slammed him on the back with the palm of his hand several times until his breathing sounded clear.

"Where . . . where is everyone?" Phillip asked.

"I was just going to ask you that."

"They left," Phillip said. "About a half hour ago. I couldn't understand them. But there was one other . . ."

A shot fired, and Bailino went down.

"Fuck," Bailino said, grabbing his shoulder.

Phillip grabbed Bailino's gun. He fired back, hitting the Iraqi soldier in his thigh, causing him to fall. The man was writhing in the sand when Phillip reached him. The Iraqi turned his weapon on him, and Phillip shot him in the head. Without wasting time, he ran back to Bailino, who was using whatever water was left in the bucket to clean his wound.

"C'mon, we have to get out of here."

"This is the thanks I get for saving your ass," Bailino said, trying to stand.

Phillip secured his arm under Bailino's armpit, and the pair ran south toward the border.

****

Charlotte was still heaving by the time Jamie got to the nursery. It was dark inside, and she fumbled for the light switch. She bounced the little girl up and down, hoping the vertical movement would quiet Charlotte's screams—it had worked for Peter when he was colicky. It didn't. She laid Charlotte on the crib mattress, and as the child rolled around kicking her strong legs, Jamie diapered her and then reached for a clean onesie and snapped it shut. The little girl had reached that state of delirium where the bawling had taken on a life of its own, and there was nothing to be done but let her cry it out. Jamie watched, surprised by how little guilt she felt for what she had done. She just had to know.

Charlotte was standing now and grasping the bars of the crib, shaking them. Jamie picked her up and paced back and forth in the little room, hesitant to leave, not wanting to see Bailino's outraged face again. She peeked into the bedroom, but he wasn't there.

She couldn't let Charlotte cry for much longer, but she also knew kids could find the strength to cry for hours if they wanted to. She had to get Charlotte to relax. Across the bedroom, the black wood of the baby grand piano gleamed. There was a quiet majesty about the instrument that was in sharp contrast to the anarchic events playing out all around her. She had never seen anyone play it and wondered if it was even in working order. Jamie brought the exhausted child out of the nursery and peeked into the bathroom. It was empty. *Where had Bailino gone,* she wondered. She stepped over to the piano, sat on the small bench, and flipped up the little door that exposed the smooth black and white keys. She placed Charlotte on her lap, opened one of her clenched fists and placed her pointer on middle C, pressing several times and eliciting a melodic *ding ding ding*.

Within seconds, Charlotte's crying waned and then disappeared. As her little body hiccupped, she pressed her tiny fingers, all of which fit on a single key, down—but so softly that the noise emitted was imperceptible. Jamie placed her finger over the child's and pressed until a *ding* sounded once again.

Charlotte smiled. "Mo?" she said with weak enthusiasm.

"You do." Jamie placed her hands on the keys, and Charlotte pressed one and then two keys at a time, making a symphony of loud, disjointed notes—a welcome change from the crying.

As Charlotte played, Jamie looked outside the window and saw Bailino and Joey standing near a large pine tree. Joey appeared upset, and Bailino had his hand on the teen's shoulders.

"Mo, mo, mo!" Charlotte banged on the piano with both fists, one after the other, the chords rattling the bedroom like a preschool orchestra. But neither Bailino nor Joey seemed to be able to hear the music; Jamie imagined the entire log cabin had been soundproofed.

As the little girl played, Jamie's gaze lifted to the trees and beyond, the music carrying her into the clouds. She could see a divide, below which, she assumed, was the river and all the way to the hills on the other side, which were in full bloom. The array of greens created a natural complexity of shade that was made dazzling by the setting sun. Her life was somewhere out there waiting to be reclaimed. Or perhaps, she thought, it was in this pristine bedroom waiting to begin.

When Jamie turned her attention back to Charlotte, she realized the noise had stopped. The little girl had passed out, her head atop the black piano keys and her hands spread out like wings across the rest. She lifted her up and carried her to the crib. When she got back to the window, the two men were gone, but Jamie knew that although Bailino had disappeared, it wouldn't be for long.

38

Nurberg returned to the station still steamed from his showdown with Mrs. Grand. He'd heard plenty of stories among the officers about run-ins with the First Lady and got a taste of what it felt like to be in her crosshairs—and he didn't like it. What bothered him the most, though, was that he had let her get under his skin. For years, he dealt with scum-of-the-earth types, men who slapped around their women, mothers who ran prostitution rings from their children's bedrooms, and he always managed to remain cool—cool enough to earn the nickname "Ice"—a moniker that belied his boyish face and friendly demeanor. Professionally, Nurberg was unflappable. Until today.

He tossed his notebook and folders onto his desk and threw himself into his swivel chair, which rolled back toward the wall. It had been a long day. Katherine Grand attacked him. Why? Yes, he understood her anger, but was there more? And the governor's late morning stroll to "get air." What was that about? Nurberg remembered Phillip Grand's face as he was leaving Taryn's—distraught, but was he hiding something? After all, wasn't the First Lady right—doesn't it always turn out to be the parents in these things?

Nurberg leaned his swivel chair so far back that the front wheels came off the floor. Both Phillip and Katherine Grand had been at Kliger Nursing Home from 11:00 a.m. till 2:00 p.m. for the ribbon cutting and luncheon yesterday. Their appearance was witnessed by hundreds of people, recorded for the evening news. They were clean. *But couldn't they have had help?*

Nurberg imagined Katherine Grand barking out orders to a roomful of degenerates, her beady little eyes piercing the dark like laser beams. There was no motive, but did she need one? Was there a reason why anyone did anything? Because they can? Because they "needed air"?

He regretted asking Rosalia Garcia to stop by the station this evening for a few more questions—a spur-of-the-moment decision he'd made after leaving the Executive Mansion. In his heart, he thought that the governor was right, that the nanny was not involved in the disappearance of Charlotte Grand, but Mrs. Grand had gotten him all out of whack, and he thought maybe another interview might turn up something new. In other words, he was grasping at straws.

Nurberg looked at his watch. Five thirty. *Mrs. Garcia should be here any minute*, he thought. He emptied his pockets onto his desk— his house keys, three breath mints, two quarters, his change from a two-dollar pretzel, and a thin wallet containing two credit cards, his driver's license, twenty bucks, and an expired library card. *Yep, that about summed things up.* He was feeling moody and frustrated, as if he was trying to swim across an ocean, but could only tread water. Underneath his wallet, a slim piece of white cardboard peeked out, and Nurberg picked up John Callahan's business card. There was nothing extraordinary about it, just your run-of-the-mill card with points of contact and Callahan's photo in the top right corner. Once upon a time, real-estate agents were the only ones with enough chutzpah to put their pictures on their business cards and billboards, but nowadays vanity had become a commodity. He thought of his police badge and how skeptical people were when he showed it to them—they studied it suspiciously to be sure he was a real cop, as if they'd know. Nurberg imagined nobody bothered doing that when handed the business card of John Callahan—why would anyone pretend to be the manager of Dick's Sporting Goods? But for a moment, Nurberg imagined his name on the card, of leaving all his work at the office at 6:00 p.m. and going home to a house full of noise. He imagined carrying a wallet that was fat, overflowing with family photos.

"Hey." Missy Giles peeked her head into Nurberg's office.

"Hey," Nurberg replied. Missy had her hair in a ponytail now, rather than the freshly blow-dried bob she wore early this morning, a telltale sign that it was the end of the workday. She wore a gray pantsuit with flared legs that made her look taller and thinner than she really was. Missy always wore a suit. She told him once that it was because she had a youthful face and when working in a place made up mostly of men—who tended to pat her on the head to show she had done a job well—a *uniform* made her seem like one of them. Looking at the curves of her hips under the polyester blend, Nurberg couldn't help but think otherwise.

"Not going well?" she asked, concerned. "Need to talk?"

Missy was always asking people if they needed to talk. It was one of the hazards of being a domestic violence advocate. "No, I'm fine."

Missy nodded in disbelief. "Can you sign off on this? It's my report on the Kramer case."

"Sure." Nurberg took the forms, gave them a perfunctory glance, and then signed the bottom of the last one. He returned them to Missy, who lingered behind his chair admiring the commendations on his wall.

"These are so great," she said.

"You think?" He stood next to her. "I guess they're all right."

"Don't worry. You'll find out who did this, Mark." Missy smiled.

"At this point, I don't think I'd be able to find a drunk at a bar . . ."

She laughed politely.

"Do you want to go out for a drink Saturday night?" he asked.

The department had strict codes on interoffice dating, which had kept Nurberg from asking Missy out before, but his altercation with the First Lady made him suddenly want to break some rules. "I mean, actually, I really should be working . . ."

"I'd love to," Missy said.

"Really, you mean it won't be a problem with, you know, us working together and you, like, being one of my . . . associates?" *So much for "Ice,"*? Nurberg thought.

"If it becomes a problem, I'll just have to find another job," Missy said with a smile.

Nurberg laughed. "Okay, then."

"Okay, then."

She walked toward the office door and, turning to wave, slammed into Det. McDonnell, who was walking in.

"Oh, I'm sorry. Excuse me," Missy said.

"The pleasure is all mine." McDonnell was a lascivious sort, made all the worse because he was also a slob. There were ketchup stains on his tie that had been there for months. It hadn't occurred to him, after three years of manning the station's front desk, that maybe if he'd show a little bit more discretion or conscientiousness he would no longer be manning the front desk. Missy ignored his remark and left.

"Is there something I can help you with, McDonnell?" Nurberg said.

"Yeah, someone here to see you—a Mrs. Garcia," he said. "I tried to buzz you, but your line was busy."

Nurberg glanced at his phone. The handset had been displaced when he tossed his keys there. "Oh, sorry about that. Thank you, send her in."

The Grands' housekeeper approached his office accompanied by a tall, dark man with curly hair. She looked nervous and tired.

"Mrs. Garcia, thank you for coming this evening," Nurberg said when they had reached his office.

Rosalia nodded. "This is Reynaldo Rodriguez, my nephew."

Nurberg and Reynaldo shook hands.

"Nice to meet you," Nurberg said. "Please, sit."

Rosalia and Reynaldo looked around the small office before taking the seats in front of Nurberg's desk.

"Can I get you some coffee?" Nurberg asked.

"No, thank you," Rosalia said. Reynaldo was busy looking over Nurberg's head at the commendations.

Nurberg hadn't prepared anything for this follow-up interview since he'd called for it on a whim and was about to open his file folder to buy himself some time to think, when Rosalia spoke.

"Detective, I know why you called me down here." Rosalia cast her eyes downward.

"You do?" Nurberg and Reynaldo asked in unison.

Rosalia nodded. She reached into her large pocketbook and pulled out Miss Beatrice, Charlotte's cherished toy. She held it out for the detective.

"I don't understand," Nurberg said, taking the doll.

"I took it from the house. Yesterday. You said not to take anything. But I . . . took it. I needed . . . to have something."

"Mrs. Garcia . . ."

"I'm so sorry. I hope I didn't ruin your DNA."

"Mrs. Garcia," Nurberg handed the doll back to the housekeeper. "You can hold onto the doll. It's all right. Remember, you had her with you when you went upstairs. You were bringing her to Charlotte when you noticed the crib was empty. As far as I'm concerned, the doll is not a suspect." Nurberg smiled.

The memory of the empty crib caused Rosalia to shudder.

"Do you have any specific questions you'd like to ask my aunt?" Reynaldo asked, studying Nurberg's face. The detective looked vaguely familiar. Reynaldo was no stranger to the police station and had been there many times to bail out his brothers for one thing or another, but he didn't recall ever seeing Nurberg there. "She did not sleep very much last night, and I'd really like her to go home and rest."

"I'm okay, Rey." Rosalia patted Reynaldo's arm.

"Oh, yes." Nurberg opened his file. "Actually, I was hoping we could talk a little bit about Mrs. Grand."

"Why? Is she a suspect?" Reynaldo asked.

"Oh, *Dios mío*!" Rosalia said.

"No, no," Nurbeg said, "but I was hoping to just . . . well . . . what time did she leave yesterday morning for Kliger?"

Rosalia thought. "It's hard to say. Mrs. Grand doesn't usually check in with me. I see her in the mornings when I come to get Charlotte. But I would say, probably about eight o'clock."

"And was there anything unusual about her or the governor that morning?"

Rosalia shook her head. "No, nothing. It was just a regular day."

"Have you been contacted at all today by either the governor or Mrs. Grand?"

"No, no one," Rosalia answered. "Just you."

Nurberg took a deep breath. He had nothing, and there was no use keeping them there longer than they were needed. "Well, thank you anyway, Mrs. Garcia, Mr. Rodriguez," Nurberg said, standing up. "I appreciate you both coming down."

"That's it?" Reynaldo asked.

"Yes, I'm afraid so," Nurberg said, embarrassed. "I'm sorry if I troubled you in any way."

"It's all right, Rey." Rosalia squeezed Reynaldo's arm.

"No, *Tía*, it's not okay. We could have taken care of this by phone, or he could have come to the house."

"Rey . . ."

"No, he's right, Mrs. Garcia," Nurberg said, and then he had a thought. He reached into a box on his desk, pulled out Rosalia's cell phone and handed it to her.

"You could have dropped that off at the house," Reynaldo said.

"Mr. Rodriguez, again I apologize for the inconvenience. I hope you understand that I'm just trying to figure out what happened to that little girl. And sometimes the right way of doing things gets lost in trying to do the right thing." He stuck out his hand.

Reynaldo shook it, the feel of the detective's small hand conjuring up a memory. "*Sí*," he said. "Have we met before?"

Nurberg shook his head. "I don't think so."

"You look very familiar," Reynaldo said, as the circumstances surrounding Nurberg's face pieced together in his mind—the early morning breeze blowing the tall weeds, the tiny body lying awkwardly on the riverbank, the soft handshake of the detective. "Yes, I met you about two years ago, when the body of little Tyler Jackson was found."

Nurberg felt as if he were slapped in the face. "You were there?" he asked. "By the river?" Nurberg's eyes took on a hazy look as details of the case came back to him. "That was awful. Tyler's mother had called

911 to report her boyfriend had taken her son only an hour before we got the call that someone had found him on the riverbank."

"I know," Reynaldo said. "That was me. I called."

Nurberg's eyes grew wide. "That's right," he said, remembering. "You were riding your bike and saw the body. And we spoke, right?"

"Yes, you asked me a few questions, and that was it," Reynaldo said. "I wasn't much of a help. I didn't see anything."

"Yes, but you found the boy," Nurberg smiled. "And he was able to have a proper burial."

"Did you ever catch the guy? *El novio?*" Rosalia asked.

Nurberg's smile faded. "No," he said, shaking his head. "We didn't. He took off. We think he's in Mexico somewhere."

"*Qué horror,*" Rosalia said.

"Indeed." Nurberg had been haunted by the image of the little boy's contorted arms and legs for months, although surprisingly, or perhaps not so surprisingly, the crime had gotten little attention in the press— most of the crimes Nurberg dealt with flew under the radar of what was considered newsworthy. *Unless, of course,* he thought, *your last name was Grand.* "I'm sorry to have met again under somber circumstances." He turned his attention to Rosalia. "Please let me know if there's anything else you can think of. It doesn't matter how small it is or how irrelevant you think it is. It might be able to help."

Reynaldo was helping his aunt up from her chair when Rosalia said, "Well, there is something. I thought it was stupid, so I didn't say anything."

"Yes?" A glimmer of hope ignited within Nurberg. "Remember, nothing is stupid, Mrs. Garcia. What do you remember?"

"Well, it was the carpet," Rosalia said. "Mrs. Grand had it cleaned last week, so that it would be fresh for Easter Sunday, and when I went into Charlotte's room to tuck her in, I noticed the smell. It was stronger than I'd remembered."

"*Hmmm . . .*" Nurberg said, hiding his disappointment.

"It reminded me of your uncle's cologne," Rosalia said to Reynaldo. "Old Spice. Your uncle's favorite. May he rest in peace."

Nurberg jotted the information down in a folder.

"See, *Tía*," Reynaldo said. "You helped."

Rosalia smiled.

"Yes, thank you, Mrs. Garcia . . . McDonnell?" Nurberg called. "Can you see Mrs. Garcia and Mr. Rodriquez out, please?"

McDonnell, who had been eating from a small bag of pretzels and reading a newspaper, got off his stool to open the small swinging gate for Rosalia and Reynaldo as they left the main area of the station.

"Who was that, the nanny?" Det. Grohl popped his head into Nurberg's office.

"Yeah."

"Why did you bring her down?"

"Just a shot in the dark."

"And?"

Nurberg shook his head. "Nothing."

"Got a minute?" Grohl asked, already walking into Nurberg's office.

"What is it?"

"I just got a call. The Feds are going to be taking over the Grand case."

"What? Why?"

"It's just gotten out of control with the press coverage, and, let's face it, Nurberg, we've got no leads. And, to be honest, I'll be glad to get this thing off my shoulders. The last thing I want is anyone snooping around and looking at things with a magnifying glass. Who knows what they'll find."

"Can I assist in the federal investigation?" Nurberg asked. "I'm sure they'll need someone local to work with."

"I'm afraid not." Det. Grohl drummed his fingers on Nurberg's desk. "I've been asked to have you, specifically, taken off the case."

"Are you kidding?" Nurberg said. "Let me guess . . . Mrs. Grand."

"Well, you're half right."

Nurberg raised his eyebrows. "The governor too?"

"I'm afraid so." Grohl picked up the folder and box on Nurberg's desk. "Is this all the stuff for the Grand case?"

Nurberg nodded.

"You don't mind if I take this, do you?" Grohl said. "I'll need to give them everything we have tomorrow." He patted Nurberg on the back. "Sorry about this, Ice. But you know what? It's a good thing. Go home. Relax. Get some sleep."

"Yeah, sure."

Nurberg watched Grohl leave, his thoughts fixated on the missing little girl he was unable to find and the little boy whose murderer was living it up somewhere in Mexico.

39

Traffic was unbearable on the Joe DiMaggio Highway. Edward was nearing Seventy-Second Street, the point at which the highway turned into the Henry Hudson Parkway—although for many New Yorkers and a few ill-informed media traffic reporters, it was all still the West Side Highway—and the vast conglomeration of ensuing metal looked like one of his son's Matchbox car carrying cases, with all the vehicles neatly stowed in parallel rows of four.

This was a bad idea. He should have tried his luck with midtown.

Edward's left arm, tanned from the elbow down, hung out the driver's-side window as exhaust fumes from his engine blurred his view of the license plate in front of him. It was one of those newer *Empire Gold* plates, a throwback to the license plates of his youth, the kind that he and Jamie and their friends would read as they piled into his mother's old Bonneville for road trips to Rockaway Beach.

Jamie.

It had taken him two hours to get into Manhattan by car, one hour to find a legal parking spot, and a mere fifteen minutes to file a missing-persons report. By the looks of things, he'd probably make it back across the Queens/Nassau border by 9:00 p.m., just in time to say good night to the kids before they went to bed.

He checked his cell phone again, but there had been no missed calls. And in the past five minutes, he didn't think he took his foot off the brake pedal once. He dialed home.

"Hi," Tricia said.

"Hey."

"Did you file it?"

"Yeah, and I know, I know . . . You think it's premature."

"I'm too tired to think anything right now. Fleisher had me completely redo the plans for the Vallers' dining room. Apparently, they changed their mind, and now instead of a neutral palette, they want something flashier."

"I just know something is wrong. This isn't like her . . ."

"Did you even hear what I said?"

"What? About the palette? My sister is missing, Trish."

"How about the time last year when Jamie didn't call you by afternoon on Mother's Day, and you drove all the way to her house only to find out that she'd fallen asleep on the couch because she'd been up all night on deadline. You wound up missing dinner with my parents."

"That was understandable. She always calls on Mother's Day."

"Or the time when . . ."

"Trish, please. I get it." Edward changed the subject. "The kids all right?"

"Yeah. Peter wants you to see his spelling test. He got a hundred. You coming home now?"

Edward could hear the increasing irritation in Tricia's voice and was half-thankful that he wouldn't be home until late, when traffic started to let up, and the needle on the speedometer read twenty miles per hour. He tried his best to imagine how absurd this all seemed to everyone else—Tricia, Bob, the 911 operator, the nice clerk at the police precinct who had patiently gone over the missing-persons report with him and filed his fingerprints and photos. Edward even mentioned his working for the Manhattan DA, thinking that might help pull a few strings, but it didn't seem to light a fire under her to move any faster. The precinct was in a frenzy since just hours before an AMBER Alert had come through regarding Governor Grand's missing daughter, and there was chatter among the desk officers, who were surmising what could have happened to the little girl. By comparison, a missing, down-on-her-luck thirty-two-year-old woman was boring.

Edward saw the approaching signs for the George Washington Bridge and the Robert F. Kennedy Memorial Bridge, formerly—and still affectionately—known by locals as the Triboro Bridge. The latter was the way home to Long Island. To his house. Edward thought about Jamie's cryptic Facebook post: "Help Albany Charlotte."

"Edward? I asked if you were coming home." Tricia's voice crackled on Edward's cell phone, which he had on speaker and was balancing on his right thigh. "Or have you decided to organize a search party and troll the streets of midtown Manhattan with pitchforks?"

"I don't think so. Kiss the kids for me. Tell them I love them. I'll call you later."

"What?"

Edward clicked off the call. There was no explaining it. Trish, an only child with two parents still living, would never understand, and to try to make her would just exasperate them both. Edward got into the exit lane for the George Washington Bridge, which would get him across the Hudson River and eventually put him onto the thruway and into upstate New York.

40

The front door of the log cabin was open, but the screen door was locked. Annoyed, Leo rang the doorbell.

"Who is it?" Tony called, although from the dining room, he could see Leo standing there.

"Just open the fuckin' door, would you?" Leo said through the mesh screen.

"Sheesh, what a grouch." Tony opened the door and stepped back so Leo could enter.

"It would be nice if someone gave me a key around here." Leo took off his jacket and flopped it on the couch, emitting a pungent smell of alcohol and cigarettes into the room.

Bailino was standing in the kitchen in front of the oven and wearing oven mitts on his hands. He eyed Leo's jacket, but let it go.

"Look at you. The happy homemaker, huh?" Leo said. "Smells like chocolate in here. Good, I'm starving."

"Yeah, brownies," Bailino said, pulling a tray out of the oven. "But they're not for you."

"Oh, really? Guests don't get brownies."

"Nope, and they don't get keys either."

"They do at hotels," Benny said.

"This isn't a hotel." Bailino placed the brownies on the counter. "It's my home."

"Yeah, so you've told us." Leo sat down at the dining room table.

"What do you need a key for?" Bailino asked.

"Forget about it," Leo waved his hand. "I wouldn't be able to figure out those cockamamie locks anyway."

"They're electronic," Joey said. He had been sitting on the couch when Leo walked in, but had gone into the kitchen and was standing next to Bailino. "Inserting the key unarms the circuit and . . ."

"Yeah, whatever, kid." Leo said. "I didn't ask for an episode of *How Stuff Works*." Leo put his feet up on one of the dining-room-table chairs. "So what's the word? Is Grand gonna go for it?"

"I think so." Bailino took a tub of chocolate frosting from the top shelf of a cabinet.

"You think? My father's life is in your hands, and you think he's gonna go for it."

"Yeah, that's right." Bailino stuck a butter knife in the frosting and carefully coated the top of a brownie. "I think. Therefore, I am sure."

"Where ya been, Leo?" Tony was sitting at the computer again.

"Stanton."

Bailino stopped frosting. "Are you a fucking idiot?"

"Here we go . . ." Leo got up and grabbed a beer out of the refrigerator.

"What did I specifically tell you not to do? What did your father specifically tell you not to do?"

"I know, I know . . . I already got a tongue-lashing from my old man. I don't need another one." Leo looked around. "Where's the girl?"

"Didn't you bother her enough today?" Bailino asked.

Leo shot Joey a look. "You're a fucking tattletale, you know that."

"Don't yell at him." Bailino was holding the knife in the air, and the chocolate frosting oozed down onto his finger. He licked it.

Leo muttered something under his breath and sat back down at the dining-room table. "Back to virtual poker, huh?" Leo downed the beer and threw the can at Tony. "The real thing too much for you?"

"Why, you want to play again? Give me a chance to get even?"

"Sure, why not, I'll take more of your money, you putz." Leo turned to Benny. "You in?"

"Yeah, sure."

"Hey, Martha Stewart, you wanna play, or are you gonna crochet a blanket next?"

Bailino placed the brownies on a glass cake plate and washed his hands. "Yeah, I'll play a couple of hands."

"That's all you'll have money for, buddy, when I get through with you. Ton, tell him how much you're down from this afternoon."

"Three hundred," Tony said, reaching for the deck of cards on the buffet.

"No shit." Bailino sat down. "You must be real good."

"I am," Leo said, taking his feet off the seat next to him. "Joe, here, take this seat." He tapped the chair.

Joey hesitated.

"He's not playing." Bailino said.

"Why the hell not?"

"With what money?" Tony asked.

"He can play with his college fund, since he ain't gonna need it," Leo chuckled. He took the cards from Tony and started shuffling.

"Is that right?" Bailino put his hand on Joey's shoulder. "You want to play, Joe?"

"No, thanks."

"Sit the fuck down already. Just one hand. See how much of a genius you really are. Get me another beer before you do, though."

"I thought we agreed to dry out for a few days." Bailino reached into his pants pocket and pulled out a roll of hundred dollar bills.

"You agreed. I didn't agree." Leo took the beer from Joey. "Better say good-bye to that wad," Leo said, tilting his chin at Bailino's cash.

"What's the ante?" Benny asked.

"Five hundred." Leo tossed five hundred-dollar bills into the center of the table.

Joey looked concerned.

"I'll spot you," Bailino assured him.

"C'mon, cough it up, fellas." Leo said, as Benny and Tony each put their money in the pot and he dealt the cards.

"So where's the girl?" Leo asked.

"Didn't we cover this already?" Bailino picked up his cards.

"You didn't say where she was."

"Upstairs."

"I'll bet she is."

Leo kicked Benny under the table. "So? Did you forget how to play?"

"Check," Benny said.

"Check," Tony said, scratching behind his ear.

"I open," Bailino said, tossing in a hundred-dollar bill.

"Woo hoo! I call," Leo said. He, Tony, and Benny threw in their bills. "What about you, brainiac?"

Joey showed Bailino his cards.

"Don't show him your fucking hand."

"You should fold, Joe."

"I fold," Joey said.

"When did you get a job as a ventriloquist's dummy, Joey?" Leo laughed, one of those loud, irritating guffaws. "How many cards you want, Ben?"

"Three."

"Ton?"

"Three."

"I'll take one," Bailino said.

Leo gave him a card. "Just one, huh?"

"Yep."

"Okay, then."

"I call," said Benny.

"Me too," Tony said.

"I call too," Bailino said.

"Really, well, I raise five hundred," Leo said, making a big show of reaching into his pocket and tossing crisp bills into the pot.

"I fold," Benny and Tony said in unison, tossing their cards facedown onto the table.

Bailino studied his hand. "I'll see that," he said. "And I'll raise you another hundred."

"Oh, now we're raising, huh?" Leo placed another hundred-dollar bill in the pot. "This'll be interesting."

"Oh, yeah. Why?"

"Because I know you're full of shit."

"Really?" Bailino said. "So raise me again."

"I have an idea." Leo tilted his chair back. "I'll raise you the girl."

"Excuse me?"

"I win this, and the girl, Jamie, spends the night with me tonight."

"I don't think so." Bailino shook his head and sat back in his seat.

"Does that mean you fold?" Leo reached out his hands to pull the pot toward him.

"Wait." Bailino looked again at his hand. "All right . . ."

"Uncle Don . . ." Joey said.

"Shut up, Joe," Leo said. "You folded, remember?"

"Okay, big man," Bailino said, "if your hand beats mine, you can have her for the night." He raised his eyebrows. "But . . . if *mine* beats *yours*, then you pay the first year's tuition for Joey to go to MIT."

"What? I'm not paying no fucking tuition . . ."

"Uh, does that mean you fold?"

"No fucking chance," Leo said, "but that's not a fair bet."

"Why not?" Bailino smirked.

"That's fucking tens of thousands of dollars."

"That's my raise," he said. "If you don't like it, or your hand isn't good enough, then you can fold."

Leo shoved Joey in the shoulder. "Why the fuck you want to go to college anyway?"

"To get the fuck away from you," Bailino said. "And don't fucking touch him."

"I'm not talking to you. What is it with the two of you? You're like two peas in a pod."

"Play the fucking game, Leo," Tony said.

"Stay the fuck out of it, Tony. It's not about the game."

Leo stood up, staggering a little and holding on to the table for support. He scowled at Joey. "You're a little big shot here, aren't you? Let's see how tough you are when I get you home."

"He's not going home." Bailino said flatly.

"Oh, no?" Leo asked.

"When the school year is out, he's moving up here. I already spoke to ToniAnne this afternoon. Then in the fall, he'll stay on campus at MIT."

"What the . . . ? Does my father know anything about this? Who decided all of this?"

"He did," Bailino said, motioning to Joey, whose eyes were cast downward.

"Is that right?" Leo asked Joey. "Do you speak at all?"

Joey looked up. "I want to live with Uncle Don."

"After all your mother has done for you, you little shit."

"This has nothing to do with his mother, you fucking small-minded bastard," Bailino said, his eyes narrowing, his rage bubbling under the surface. "Kids all over the world go to college. This has to do with him, for him to lead his own fucking life, away from all this shit. Can't you see that?"

"All I see is a kid trying to be something he's not. You don't got it, kid. You're a fucking freak. Learn that now." Leo kicked the sofa. "What? You gonna be a businessman like him? Hang around with Kid Rock and the secretary of defense?"

"No, I'm fucking stuck here, but I won't let that happen to him. With any luck, he'll move somewhere far away."

"Oh, you won't let that happen. Who died and made you boss? Or is that the plan?"

"You got something you want to ask me, Leo? Go ahead. Ask me." Bailino held his cards on his lap. "If not, let me see your fucking hand, so I know whether I'll be making a big withdrawal this month from my bank account."

Leo's expression changed. "The things I'm gonna do to that girl . . ."

"Show your fucking hand."

Leo slapped his cards on the table. "Two fuckin' pair, kings and jacks. Now, go ahead," Leo said, "show your flush that didn't happen. Or was it a straight?"

"How about the full house that did happen?" Bailino fanned out his cards on the table, three nines and two sixes.

"FUCK!" Leo ran his arm across the table and knocked all the money and the cards onto the floor. "You think I'm paying that fucking tuition, you're out of your fucking mind." He stormed toward the back doors and tried to open them, but they were locked. "How do you open this fucking thing?"

Bailino, as if in slow motion, took his electronic key out of his pocket and undid the lock, and Leo slammed open the glass door and stomped out.

"Well, that was entertaining," Tony said.

"Ben, Tony, take the money." He reached into his pocket. "Here are my car keys. Take the hothead with you. Go get something to eat."

"You sure?" Tony asked.

"Don't worry about it," Bailino said. "But don't let him smoke in the car."

"Cool," Benny said. "Thanks, Don."

Benny and Tony picked up the money that Leo had knocked onto the floor and left, while Bailino and Joey began scooping up the playing cards.

"Would you have really let him spend the night with Jamie, Uncle Don?" Joey asked, stacking his cards on the table in a neat pile.

"Not in a million years."

"What if you would have lost the hand?"

"But I didn't." Bailino smiled. He put his arm around Joey. "You want to rent a movie? I saw you had your eye on that Angelia Jolie one."

Joey blushed.

"Go ahead, Joe, watch whatever you want." He handed Joey the cards that he had picked up from the floor. "It's gonna be okay, you know."

Joey nodded, his eyes welling with tears. As he started to cry, he leaned on Bailino's shoulder. "Thank you, Uncle Don . . . I love you."

"I love you too, kid. Always have."

41

Bob sat at his large mahogany desk. The hours ticked by as if he were watching the world through a series of time-lapse photos: coworkers passed, back and forth, by his office door, stuck their heads in, waved hello, good-bye, all while the sunlight rose and fell through his office window.

It was like college all over again, Bob thought. Edward Carter loomed over him like a storm cloud forever stealing his sunshine. It didn't matter that Edward had left the firm and had become a public defender. It didn't matter whether Edward quit law altogether and opened his own online coupon business. Edward would always be one of the greatest legal minds anyone who knew him ever met no matter how long he was out of the picture.

Eight years ago, when Edward announced his leave of absence to care for his ailing mother, Bob knew that a window of opportunity had opened. Bob had gotten the brunt of Edward's caseload—he actually volunteered to take on as much as possible—and had worked day and night to impress the powers-that-be at his firm. And when that leave of absence turned into a resignation, Bob knew that his future at Worcester, Payne & Leach had been sealed. Over time, he became the go-to guy—the lawyer who was first choice when an important client was taken on and the voice of the firm when it came to media relations. And, he was sure of it, he was this close to being the token lawyer in *People* magazine's "Sexiest Man Alive" issue for 2010.

Bob knew the idea of Edward sitting on Governor Grand's roundtable of the state's best legal minds shouldn't have fazed him—considering he was raking it in on Easy Street while Edward was sweating it out on Main Street, paying his perpetual dues in the DA's office—but it did. Just when he had finally gotten rid of the Carter siblings altogether, they kept popping back into his life when he least expected, or wanted, them. *Sir Edward Carter*—it just didn't have the same ring to it, that was for sure.

To cheer himself up, he checked his Twitter profile. He had just over 26,000 followers, up about thirty since this morning. He typed something witty and retweeted a few inspirational quotes from several influential people he followed and then logged out.

Maybe he was wrong. What he had told Andrews was true—the politics of Edward Carter were at the opposite end of the spectrum from those of Phillip Grand. And although Edward may have welcomed the prospect of being part of a group with a wide diversity of opinion, he preferred keeping a low profile. Bob decided this kind of thing wasn't even on Edward's radar.

Still, he just had to know. He picked up his office phone and dialed, trying in his mind to formulate a reason for the call. But he didn't need one when Edward picked up on the first ring.

"Is she with you?" Edward said, without saying hello.

"Who?" Bob asked, startled.

"Jamie."

"What? You *still* can't find her? How long has it been?"

"Listen, I don't have time."

"She called me earlier today."

"She did?! What did she say?"

"I couldn't hear her. There was a bad connection."

"But you heard her voice?"

Bob thought back to the phone call this morning. "No, I don't think I did, but does that matter?"

"Listen, I can't talk. I'm on my way to Albany. Call me if she calls again and you actually hear her voice. Thanks." Edward ended the call.

Albany?

So it was true, Bob thought. Edward was answering the governor's call for the state's brightest legal minds, and he was driving all the way upstate to make his case in person. He imagined Edward ringing the doorbell of the Executive Mansion with his *American Lawyer* article on Grand in one hand and his reference-filled resume in the other. He was probably determined to get his liberal mind on that panel and keep Phillip Grand's conservative agenda at bay. Hell, Bob thought, he might even try to stop the execution of Gino Cataldi tomorrow night while he's up there.

Bob shut down his computer, grabbed his keys, and ran out his office door.

"Leaving for the day, Mr. Scott?" Patsy, his secretary, asked as he ran past her desk.

"Yes," he called back. "Oh, and tell Mr. Turner I won't be in tomorrow, Patsy. I need to travel upstate and take care of a few things. I'll touch base with him in the morning."

Sir Robert Scott, Bob thought, jamming his finger into the elevator's down button. He had to get home, craft a quick resume and clips, pick up his briefcase, pack an overnight bag, and get himself upstate to dazzle Phillip Grand. Although the thought occurred to him that the governor might have his hands full with the current crisis involving his daughter, this was the perfect opportunity to make a name for himself and jump ahead of the line, he reasoned. The elevator door opened. *And I'll help find the governor's daughter*, Bob thought, crossing the threshold. And save the day. All in a knight's work.

42

Jamie lay in the corner of Bailino's bed, although she didn't start off there. In the hours after Charlotte had fallen asleep, she kept herself busy by pacing the nursery, looking out the window and washing her hands—all while trying to formulate a good plan for escape, but nothing seemed feasible. She hadn't seen Bailino since the bathroom incident earlier that evening when he wasn't too happy with her, and she had decided that the best plan was just to get through whatever was going to happen and live to see another day. She thought about her mother who taught her to be, as she liked to say, "a lady," and was probably looking down on her and wondering, *How could you just lay there and let him do whatever he wanted*? Truth be told, Jamie felt like she had been doing that for years, long before Bailino kidnapped her life, and she wondered whether it was naïve to think that, given the chance, Bailino would not hurt her, even after she witnessed the brutality of which she knew he was capable.

For now, though, she thought it best to perform the duties of her *job* and crawled into her side of the bed. She still had her clothing on and wondered if that would infuriate him. She had to keep him calm, yet stand her ground—he seemed to admire that. She remembered what Bailino had said about the bra that morning, so she slipped it off through her sleeve and placed it on the nightstand and pulled the blankets up to her neck. In the quiet of the dark, she could hear her stomach rumble and realized how hungry she was. She had had a few of Charlotte's

Cheerios that morning and a handful of Joey's cut grapes, but couldn't remember eating anything else.

The electronic lock of the bedroom door clicked, and the creakiness of the door's swing was as quiet as it was ear piercing; Jamie braced herself. The familiar smell of Bailino's cologne reached her nose, but it was fainter this time. Muddled. A lamp turned on as another smell became more pungent and recognizable.

Brownies.

On a serving tray were twelve frosted brownies carefully cut into twelve equal squares. Next to them was a basket of gourmet chocolate.

"There was a box of brownie mix in the closet, so I just made them," Bailino said, as if it were no trouble at all. "Want one?"

Jamie reached for a brownie and was about to take a bite, then hesitated.

"If I wanted to kill you, I would have done it already," Bailino said, as if that were supposed to make her feel better. "And not like that."

Jamie took a bite, careful to catch any crumbs with her free hand and then toss them into her mouth.

Bailino opened a few drawers, taking out a pair of flannel pajama bottoms and a T-shirt, and excused himself into the bathroom. He seemed to have calmed down. When he returned, he sat down on the bed, his knee bent forward so he was partially facing Jamie. "Actually," he rubbed his temples. "I just wanted to apologize for my behavior in the bathroom earlier. I overreacted. Do you want another one?" he asked, holding out the tray. "Do you like chocolate? The truffles have cherry flecks."

Jamie took another brownie and stuck the whole thing in her mouth to keep from having to worry about the crumbs.

"Well, what do you know . . . a woman who eats." Bailino put the tray on the nightstand.

Jamie smiled weakly to mask the quiver in her cheek and then lay down and pulled the blanket up, her cheeks puffy with cake.

"You must be tired," Bailino said, reaching for the lamp switch. "There's probably nothing more exhausting than following a toddler around all day. Do you want me to leave the light on?"

Jamie shrugged her shoulders. "It doesn't matter." She felt as though she were in a haunted house and waiting for something to jump out at her from an unseen corner.

Bailino turned off the light and lay down on his side of the bed. She'd thought about turning over to the side and pretending to sleep, but she didn't think that she would fool anyone or that it mattered much if Bailino were going to go at her again. She decided to just lie there and wait, but Bailino appeared to be doing the same. It was quiet for a long time.

"You're very good with children," Bailino said finally. His voice was softer, the way it had been down by the river with Charlotte. *Was this another test?*

"Thank you," Jamie said.

It was quiet again. Jamie's heart began to race.

"You're welcome," Bailino said finally.

"Are you going to kill me?" Jamie blurted out suddenly. The room was completely dark since the sun had set, and Jamie was feeling courageous under the cover of night, although part of her felt as if she were alone on a desert island and her question merely a message in a bottle being thrown out to sea.

"Again?" Bailino asked.

"You never answered me this morning."

Jamie heard the ticking of Bailino's wristwatch. "No," he said.

"But you killed that other girl."

"She was a whore."

"How do you know?"

"She was a stripper, a dime-a-lap-dance whore who took care of Leo and everyone else in the private room of the Exotica Strip Club downtown. For some godforsaken reason, he thought she'd make a good nanny. Stupid, stupid." Bailino sounded like a parent who had sent his child out to buy milk and was disappointed when he came home with candy.

"But even so, if she was, that didn't mean she deserved to die. She was somebody's daughter. I'm sure she had friends, a life somewhere."

"You're feeling suddenly brave," Bailino said. Jamie turned her head to look in Bailino's direction, but she couldn't see him at all. She wondered if he could see her in the dark—wolves had keen eyesight and could detect the slightest movement in front of them.

"You said I was free to talk," Jamie said. "By the river."

"Yeah, but I didn't say anything about the house."

"Oh," Jamie said.

"That was a joke."

Jamie paused. "Why are you being nice to me now?" she asked.

"Would you rather I weren't?"

"No, I mean . . . You tell me that you're not going to kill me, but you're telling me things I shouldn't know, and I've seen your face."

"So you think I'm lying?"

Jamie thought she felt Bailino inching closer in the dark.

"I just don't know . . . anything." She crept toward her end of the mattress.

"Especially about loyalty."

There was a playfulness in Bailino's voice, and it emboldened her. "Another joke, right?" she said.

He chuckled. "Okay, now, it's my turn for questions." Jamie could sense Bailino propping himself on his pillow. "Is one of the reasons why your husband left because you wanted children and he didn't?"

Wham.

The question caught Jamie off guard. Without knowing it, Bailino had hurt her very core, and she let out a reluctant sniffle.

He turned on the light and looked at her. "That rat bastard," he said.

"No." Jamie inhaled and exhaled slowly, trying to keep her composure. "It was the opposite."

"The opposite?" he asked incredulously. "You didn't want children?"

"He . . . we both wanted children," Jamie said, "and I couldn't have them."

There was a long pause. "Oh," he said finally, turning the light off again, as if he were trying to give her a little privacy. Jamie felt him worm his way back under the blanket, but then the questions started again. "Did you think about adoption?"

All the time. "He wouldn't," she said, shaking her head, as if the movement itself would repel Bailino's questions.

"What exactly was wrong?"

"The doctor said it was an unexplained fertility issue."

"Did you get a second opinion?"

"Yes, but the second doctor said the same thing. My bro . . ." Jamie hesitated.

"Your brother?" Bailino finished. "Edward?"

"Yeah. He said that I should get another opinion, but after two, I just didn't have it in me."

"Maybe it was his fault, your husband's."

"Ha!" The sound came out louder than Jamie had meant it to. She remembered the look on Bob's face when Jamie had suggested that very same thing. "He said that was impossible. He claims he had a girlfriend in high school who he'd gotten pregnant."

"Is that so?"

"Yeah. She had an abortion."

"Do we have confirmation of that?"

Jamie didn't answer. She was thinking about Bob's face as he described the story of the conception. In his basement. How uninhibited she was, the girl—a crack, Jamie knew, at her—and how it had been the most exciting sexual time of his life. When recalling his past sexual exploits, Jamie half-expected Bob to rip open his shirt and beat his chest like a gorilla.

"Sweetheart?"

Jamie was startled. "I'm sorry?"

"Did you ask her?"

"Ask her?" Jamie repeated. "Who? Bob's girlfriend? I don't even know her."

"Maybe someone else knocked her up."

Jamie smiled thinking about the insinuation. Even suggesting something like that would be viewed by Bob as an attempt to take away his mojo. "It doesn't matter anyway." Jamie didn't want to talk anymore and closed her eyes. "It's for the best."

Bailino rustled a little under the blankets and then his hand was on her shoulder.

"Why did you marry someone you didn't love?" he asked.

Jamie's eyes opened wide. One way or another, it was going to be a long night.

****

Under normal circumstances, college senior Robert Scott never would have given sophomore Jamie Carter the time of day. With his sights set on a legal career and having just been accepted to New York University's School of Law, he was plotting his impending takeover of the world—one case, and woman, at a time. Who among him could boast a 3.96 GPA—a ranking that had landed him the number two spot in his graduating class of 1,200 students—while never, once, having missed a happy hour in four years? Being interviewed for the school newspaper, *The Chronicle*, for being one of only two students in the state to be named a Bankman Charles fellow, the recipient of a prestigious public service fellowship, was only the beginning of what Bob knew would be a long line of media accolades.

Jamie, student affairs reporter for *The Chronicle*, despised Bob the moment she'd met him. He was arrogant and boorish, commenting on what great legs she had the moment they'd shaken hands, followed by the requisite wink and nudge of the elbow that Jamie would learn was a Bob Scott trademark. Noticing the camera hanging around her neck, Bob had somehow finagled her to take five photos of him at various angles, including one with Jamie herself: "You can say, 'I knew him when . . .,'" he said with a wink and a nudge.

Afterwards, they were sitting at the student center for an interview that Jamie had surmised would take about ten minutes; they were there for nearly forty-five. After a half hour of detailing his "working class" upbringing in upscale Dix Hills and ignoring Jamie's questions, he finally wrapped things up with his life philosophies. "It's all about the people," he'd said. "Devoting my life to those who can't understand the legal system, providing a voice for those who can't fight for themselves . . ." Jamie had stopped listening after Bob had said "intensive purposes" instead of "intents and purposes."

Jamie hadn't taken her tape recorder with her—something that had disappointed Bob immensely—because not much space was being given to the story, which was running on the Student Stars page with five similar articles. In fact, the article was considered pretty cursory—the editor sent Jamie out on these assignments as a feel-good effort to flatter the high-achieving students, but after meeting Bob, Jamie realized that such a token was unnecessary. There wasn't much more hot air a human head could tolerate.

"You know, my brother is studying prelaw here too," she said, putting her notebook into her backpack.

"Really?" Bob said, uninterested, chewing the rest of his Hostess cupcake. "Maybe I know him. What's his name?"

"Edward. Edward Carter."

Bob stopped chewing. "Edward Carter . . ." he said, half to himself. "Hmmm . . . the name rings a bell. I think we might have a few classes together."

"Oh, yeah. Well, nice meeting you," Jamie said, sticking out her hand.

Bob took it, but instead of shaking it, he bent down and kissed it.

"The pleasure was all mine," he said. "Perhaps we'll run into each other again."

"Perhaps." Jamie pulled her hand away and left the student center.

As Bob watched her go, the name *Edward Carter* hung over him like a shroud. He knew the name very well. Edward Carter, who had interned at Weng Felter in DC last summer and had turned down a full scholarship to Georgetown so he could continue his studies locally and care for his sick mother. Edward Carter, who'd Heimliched Mrs. Phelps, the old legal secretary in Compton Hall, two semesters ago and prevented her from choking on a chicken bone. His picture still hung on the admissions-office wall. Edward Carter, GPA 3.98. Edward Carter, class valedictorian.

****

"He pursued me like he did those fellowships," Jamie said. "He and Edward both went to NYU and somehow he started hanging around more. And he . . ."

"Won you over?" Bailino asked.

"No, not really. It's just that my mother was sick . . . She'd had a round of chemo while Edward and I were at Hofstra, and then she seemed to get better, or maybe we just wanted her to get better, but for a few years things were pretty good. That was at the time Bob was hanging around."

"Your mother wanted you to marry him?"

"No, the ironic thing is my mom didn't even like Bob. But as she began to get sick again a year or two later, Bob asked me to marry him. Why he asked, I'm not even sure. We had become, you know, friendly, but marriage? I wasn't doing much socializing at the time, and he was just . . . there." Jamie adjusted herself under the blanket. "I hadn't really given it much thought, but when I mentioned it to my mother, I saw a gleam in her eye. She loved weddings. Always had. I thought a wedding would get her mind off things and help her to be happy, and I could worry about the divorce later. I don't really care much about weddings and all that."

"I thought it was every girl's dream to have a big wedding."

"Not mine." Jamie remembered standing there on the altar feeling miserable and like a fraud before her friends and family and how when the priest had asked if there was "anyone here who had any reason why these two should not wed," she had caught Edward's eye for just the briefest of moments, but neither one of them made a peep.

"Truth is, I'd be happy getting married in Vegas with an Elvis impersonator as my witness. But I knew that my mom would love the planning of a big wedding and getting all pretty and dressed up. And it worked for a while. She was getting better . . ."

Jamie let out a tiny sniffle. After eight years, the wounds associated with her mother's death had never healed.

"It's okay. You don't have to say anymore."

But the words seemed to be pouring out in a rush. "She died of lung cancer," Jamie said. "She never smoked a day in her life. Underwent chemo. Lost her hair. Underwent it again. Radiation. The whole thing. Dragging her into Sloan-Kettering when all she wanted to do was sleep. And when she died, I couldn't breathe. Edward and I had to clean out her apartment. Her bedroom closet had tons of dresses in it that she had bought over the years for *a special day*. They still had the tags on them. She died three weeks before the wedding. Bob was there, and I latched onto him, onto something . . . someone familiar. I still married him, why? I don't know. To do something. To finish what I'd started. To prove that I was okay. To make my mother happy, because she was always worried about me. To move forward, even if it was in the wrong direction. It really was . . . never about Bob. Or maybe it was never about me."

Jamie took a deep breath. "We tried hard to have kids, but it just didn't happen. I blamed myself, the fact that I didn't love him. And the more it didn't happen, the angrier and more distant Bob got until our marriage became a . . . Not that it ever was . . ." She wiped a tear. "I became a fixture at my brother's house. Trish was just popping out kids, one after the other. With ease. They weren't even trying. Then I lost my job, and he left, and I went back to live with my brother. In the apartment downstairs, where my mom . . . Well, I'm starting over again. Or at least I'm trying to."

"Why didn't you leave him? Bob? If that had been the plan?"

"I don't know." Jamie had the sensation that she had been floating underwater and was suddenly coming up for air. It was as if Bailino had opened a dam that had been holding back years of repressed memories, and she had gotten swept up in the flood. She felt embarrassed, and disoriented.

"You really don't know?" Bailino asked. Jamie felt him inching closer in the darkness.

She thought of Bob in those weeks after her mother had died, of how he had enjoyed being the knight in shining armor, comforting Jamie in her hour of need, how he relished his role as Jamie's protector, her hero. Jamie breathed deeply and turned toward Bailino.

"Because I'm weak. Because I was scared. Because I felt old and used up. Maybe because, after all those years," she paused, "I didn't think anyone else would want me."

"Because you're loyal."

Bailino stroked her cheek and pulled Jamie toward him as his hand slipped under her shirt.

"You're not wearing a bra," he said. "Good girl."

43

Reynaldo's small iron mailbox was crammed with mail, and it took several minutes to worm his finger inside and yank out a thick, plastic-wrapped magazine that had been jammed in by the mail carrier. He looked at the glossy—it was the May issue of *Penthouse* addressed to Pedro Rodriguez—and then pulled out the rest of the mail and went into his house.

The worn, musty smell overpowered him as he entered the living room and tossed his keys on the hall table. Had he had more time, he would run the house fan for a while to circulate the stale air, but he promised his Aunt Ro that he would hurry back. He had wanted to take her with him, but she preferred to stay home and rest. He hated leaving her alone, but he needed to get some clothing and personal items so he could stay with her until Friday when his cousins would arrive. He surveyed the room. It looked as weathered and old looking as Aunt Ro's place. *I live like an old woman*, he thought. A light film of dust covered all the high shelves and knickknacks, and there was a long pull in the brown carpeting, over by the television, that seemed to get longer every time he vacuumed. The faded brown wall paneling near the light switch was still cracked where Ricardo had jammed it with his fist after a fight with his father ten years ago. Reynaldo had meant to fix it over the years—he had meant to take care of a lot of things—but forgot to or lost interest. The truth was, he hardly noticed them anymore—as each day passed, they blended more and more into the background of his life. And Reynaldo often felt like he was disappearing along with them.

A quiet *tap, tap, tap* that sounded like a small rodent came from the kitchen. Reynaldo peeked in the direction of the noise coming from the ceiling. An orange latex balloon was floating across the room near the window, blown ever so gently by what must have been a soft draft coming in through a crack in the window seal. Written on the balloon in Sharpie was "Happy Birthday, Rey."

Reynaldo had brought the balloon home last Friday from the garage following a small party his brothers had thrown for him to celebrate his forty-second birthday. He had hoped the day would just pass by without any fanfare, as he did all his birthdays, but Pedro told him that Aunt Ro would not allow it. The balloon bobbed up and down along the corner of the ceiling as if it were trying to escape through a vent. Reynaldo was surprised that there was enough helium to keep it afloat all this time. He had meant to pop it or release it to the clouds, but couldn't bring himself to do it. It was nice to have movement in the house other than his own. On Monday, he had awoken to a string dangling above his nose. Monday night, when he got home from work, the balloon had been in the bathroom, near the showerhead. Now it was in the kitchen. Reynaldo thought of his mother, floating around the house, watching over him.

There was a knock at the door. When Reynaldo opened it, Mrs. Lapinski was standing there, although it took Reynaldo a moment to place her. She was wearing tight spandex bike shorts and a cotton tank top, the loose kind that exposes a woman's bra straps on the side, and she held a water bottle in her hand. A bicycle was leaning against the wooden fence.

"Hi," she said.

"Hi." Reynaldo looked at the bicycle. "Is there something wrong with your car?"

"No, the car's fine," she said. "You did a great job with it, as always. I was looking for you this evening at the garage, but your brothers said you hadn't been there all day. I just wanted to stop by and . . . see if you wanted to join me for a bike ride. May I come in?"

"Actually, I . . ."

Mrs. Lapinski walked into the house. She looked around the living room and waved her hand in front of her face. "Gee, Rey, it's so stuffy in here." She stepped into the kitchen and turned on the sink faucet, placing her hand under the water stream and then picking up the back of her hair to wet her neck. The orange balloon floated over her, and its string grazed her ear—she swatted at it without looking up, thinking it was an insect.

"I haven't been home . . . Listen, how did you know where I live?"

"C'mon, Rey. We talked about it last year when I brought the car in for the flat. Remember? We both know Connie who lives around the block."

"Oh, that's right," he said. "But I don't remember giving you the house number."

"Yeah, well, that Connie . . ." Mrs. Lapinski dried her wet hands on her shirt, leaving handprint marks on the fabric over her breasts.

"Listen, I don't mean to be rude, but you can't stay," Reynaldo said. "I have to go. There's a family emergency."

"What's the emergency?" Mrs. Lapinski reached up and pulled a loose thread from Reynaldo's shirt.

"My aunt is waiting for me . . ."

"Is she sick?"

"No."

"Dying."

"No."

"Has she fallen on the floor and can't get up?"

"No," Reynaldo said and then, from Mrs. Lapinski's expression, realized he had missed some kind of joke.

"C'mon, Rey, let's not play games. We're not kids. We're both in our early forties. You're single. I'm divorced. What's wrong with having a little fun?" She slipped her hand under Rey's shirt. "Oh . . . I love a man who's man enough not to shave his chest."

Reynaldo pulled her hand out and held it there.

"So strong . . ." She said, leaning in.

"Enough. I don't know how else to say this." Reynaldo walked back toward the front door, pulling her along. "I think you should start taking your car to another service station."

"You gotta be kidding me?" Mrs. Lapinski ripped her hand from Reynaldo's hold.

"I'm not," he said.

"What? What's the problem, Rey? Am I too much woman for you?"

As Reynaldo opened the door, Pedro came walking up the front porch steps.

"Maybe you are," Reynaldo said.

Reynaldo didn't know if her face was flushed because of embarrassment, anger, or because it really *was* stuffy, but Mrs. Lapinski looked as if she were about to burst into flames. She picked up her water bottle and headed toward the door, stopping in front of Reynaldo. "You really *are* gay, aren't you, Rey?"

"Please leave," he said.

Reynaldo and Pedro watched Mrs. Lapinski hop on her bike, the tires bubbling beneath her weight, and disappear down the block. Reynaldo went inside.

"Rey, what are you doing?" Pedro followed his brother into the house.

"What am I doing, Pedro?" Reynaldo picked up the mail and flipped through it.

"You know what I mean, *hermano*. C'mon. You don't want Nada, you don't want her." He pointed down the block in the direction of Mrs. Lapinski. "You are a man. Act like one."

Reynaldo picked up the issue of *Penthouse* and threw it at Pedro. "Here's your mail, *hermano*. Why don't you be *man* enough to have it delivered to *your* house?" Rey walked into the bedroom and pulled a suitcase out from the closet and placed it on his bed. Pedro followed behind.

"That woman is really into you. *¿Qué es tu problema?*"

Rey threw a pair of blue briefs into the suitcase. "That's just it, Pedro. There's no problem."

"Bullshit."

"Why don't you go for Mrs. Lapinski, if you're so interested?"

"*Ewwww*. Old." Pedro contorted his face as if he'd just eaten a lemon.

"Oh, so, she's good for me, eh?"

"Rey . . . listen . . . Rey?" Reynaldo was opening drawers and pulling out pairs of jeans and T-shirts. Pedro sat on Reynaldo's suitcase to get his attention. "Why don't you take a vacation? I will stay with Aunt Ro."

"A vacation?"

"Yeah, you know, go someplace that you want to go. When was the last time you had a vacation. Or had fun, real fun?"

Reynaldo shrugged. The last vacation he had taken was more than twenty years ago when he was a teenager and his twelfth-grade class spent the weekend in New York City for its senior trip. Even then his father was reluctant to release him from his garage responsibilities for four whole days, but his mother had insisted that "it was good for him to be with kids his own age." Reynaldo could still remember sitting on the bus and watching the New York City skyline come into view, the small, glinting buildings growing larger with every mile driven south. Without any obligations other than checking in with his chaperone twice a day for meals, he spent the entire weekend canvassing the city's museums, eating hot dogs, and lying on park benches until his face sunburned. It wasn't until he had climbed the bouncy steps of the coach bus to head back upstate that he would again be around kids his own age.

"I wouldn't even know where to go," Reynaldo said, holding a gnarled pair of socks.

"Rey." Pedro took the clothing from his brother's hands and placed it in the suitcase. "No joke. I love you. You've been like a father to us since mama died and papa moved south to chase wrinkled *panocha*. But, Rey, you are not our father. We are grown men."

"Well . . ."

Pedro punched Reynaldo in the arm. "You know what I mean. I can watch the garage for a few days. What's the worst that could happen? Don't answer that."

Reynaldo smiled. "But the taxes . . ."

"Leave after that. Rikki and Terry are coming and will stay with Aunt Ro. You can meet with the scary tax guy on Friday, and then go away for the weekend. Just go. Drive until you don't want to drive anymore."

"I don't know," Reynaldo said, closing his suitcase and dragging the zipper all the way around its perimeter. "I may never come back."

44

When Jamie opened her eyes it was still dark although the outline of the clouds through the windows were visible, which meant sunrise wasn't far behind. She could feel Bailino's hand on her stomach. He was sleeping right behind her, up against her. Spooning.

It was difficult for Jamie to think about what had happened during the night without feeling partly responsible this time. Bailino had been gentler, that was for sure, but she had put up less of a struggle. That had been intentional, and not. Everything was so blurry—for what was probably the first time in her life, she was coloring outside the lines of what she had been taught was appropriate and right, and she found it disorienting and scary, but strangely liberating. She worried that if she ever got out of this, she would never be the same, but at the same time it was that very thought that was driving her.

Charlotte stirred in her crib, and, as if on cue, Bailino lifted his hand from Jamie's stomach, running it over the outline of her hips before taking his hand away. Jamie got up from the bed and put on the T-shirt and jeans that she had on the day before, which had been tossed onto the floor. By the time she got to the crib, the sun was creeping up over the horizon, illuminating Charlotte's wrinkled face as she peered over the top rung of the crib. Her eyes twinkled when she saw Jamie, and she put her hands in the air.

"Up," she said, clear as day.

"Wow," Jamie lifted Charlotte high into the air. "Did you say 'up'?" she said in a low, cheerful voice. It was difficult not to smile back at that happy little face. "Did you just say 'Upppp'? Jamie lifted the little girl higher, and Charlotte cooed.

When Jamie brought her back down, Charlotte pointed out the nursery door. "What do you want, sweetie?" Charlotte leaned her body as far away from Jamie as she could and pointed toward the far end of the bedroom, in the direction of the baby grand piano, which was barely visible in the low light. It never ceased to amaze Jamie the memory children had for the things they wanted.

"Oh, I don't think we can do that right now, honey. It's too early."

Charlotte put her fingers together. "Mo," she said.

"*Shhh . . .*"

"Mo," Charlotte repeated, whispering.

"Not right now . . ."

"No, go ahead," Bailino said, sitting up on the bed. "I have to get up anyway." He clicked the lamp on. When the piano came into clearer view, Charlotte stiffened her body like a board so that Jamie would put her down, and she toddled over to the piano. Jamie went to follow her, when Bailino grabbed her arm.

"I'm going in the shower." He planted a firm kiss on Jamie's lips.

"Okay," Jamie said, her body tensing as Bailino released her and went into the bathroom and shut the door. She glanced at the bedroom door, as was her habit, but it was closed, the small red light aglow.

"Mo, mo!" Charlotte was putting her hands on the piano key cover.

Jamie pulled out the piano bench and sat down. She placed Charlotte on her lap and folded back the cover, revealing the smooth black and white keys. Charlotte started banging, and the noise rocked the bedroom. Jamie had no idea where the other men were or where they slept, or if they slept, but she couldn't imagine anyone being able to rest through this racket, soundproofed or not.

Charlotte grabbed Jamie's hands and put them on the piano keys.

"Mo!" she said, pressing them down.

"You want me to play? *Me?*"

Charlotte clapped with glee.

Jamie knew one song. That was it. The theme from *Hill Street Blues*—and only the first few bars. She'd taught herself how to play it when she was eight years old for her mother, who was a big fan of the show. She put her hands on the keys and as the first chord played, Charlotte clapped along. It took lots of coordination to balance the excited child on her thighs and use both hands to work the piano keys. Jamie smiled and kissed the top of Charlotte's head as she finished off with a dramatic, slowed-for-emphasis ending. After the final keystroke, an abrupt sound came from behind them.

Someone was clapping.

Leo stood in the doorway of the bedroom.

Clap. Clap. Clap.

"Bravo," he said, one of the electronic keys dangling from his right middle finger. He jiggled it in the air. "Lookee what I found," he said, gently pushing the door closed.

Charlotte lurched toward Jamie and buried her head into her neck. Jamie held her firm and stood up.

"Your talents continue to amaze me," Leo said. There was a wildness in his red, glassy eyes. She looked toward the bathroom.

"Who you lookin' for?" Leo sneered. He reached into his jacket and took out a small handgun, the sight of which made Jamie's heart thunder in her chest. He held it out casually, as if he were showing it off, and then aimed it toward Jamie as he walked over to the small table near the piano, pulled out a chair and put it under the knob of the bathroom door.

"Put the kid down." Leo came toward her, pointing the gun at her head.

Hesitating, Jamie said, "I . . . She's . . . scared."

"Put the fuckin' kid down now, or I will." He pointed the gun at Charlotte.

Jamie unclasped the small arms of Charlotte Grand from her neck and placed her on the floor near the piano bench. Charlotte was crying now. She tried to stand, but Jamie looked at her firmly and said, "No," which caused Charlotte to wail and wrap her arms around Jamie's legs.

"You're a fuckin' beauty, aren't you?" Leo said. He was standing so close that Jamie could smell the liquor on his breath. "You got anything to say to me?"

She glanced at the bathroom door.

"Stop looking at the fuckin' bathroom door," Leo yelled.

Jamie reached deep down and pulled her own voice out from its hiding place. "Let me bring the baby to the nursery," she said.

"Nursery? You think that's a fuckin' nursery. It's a fuckin' closet. I don't care what you do in there. I don't care if you fuckin' paint a fuckin' purple dinosaur on the walls and sprinkle rose petals across the floor. It's still a fuckin' closet." Unsteady, Leo began to rock from side to side and then looked at her quizzically as if she were the one making him dizzy.

Jamie eyed the bathroom door again, compelled to look despite Leo's warnings, as she had been in Bryant Park to see if Bailino had been following her. She tried not to think about how baffling it was to want the protection of the very person who had inflicted the most harm on her. She almost yelped with glee when she thought she saw the doorknob turn.

"Who you lookin' for?" Leo taunted. "Your knight in shining armor?"

Jamie said nothing.

"You're not going fuckin' anywhere." Now there was banging on the bathroom door, a pulling so that the door was being ripped off its hinges, and Jamie could hear Bailino's muffled yells.

Charlotte stood up again, her cries intensifying. "Shut the fuck up," Leo told her.

"Leave her alone, you son of a bitch," Jamie yelled.

Leo slapped Jamie hard. Her face hit the wall, and blood sprayed from her nose. Leo grabbed her shirt and banged her head against the wall again as the baby screamed.

"Fuck you," Jamie managed, pushing against his bulky frame, but Leo's strength, to Jamie's surprise, surpassed his tallness.

"Fuck me?" Leo pushed Jamie down on the floor. "Fuck me?"

Jamie kicked at Leo, who was unbuttoning her jeans and trying to pull them down. He punched her in the left leg, which instantly buckled, a sharp pain shooting up through her thigh. He continued fussing with the zipper of the jeans, but she arched her body, making it difficult to remove them. "Fuckin' whore," he said, unzipping his own jeans. "Fuckin' *Hill Street Blues*," he laughed. "Be careful out there . . ."

Jamie slapped at Leo, forcing him to stop fiddling with her jeans and to deal with her hands. There were intense, intermittent bangs coming from both the bathroom and bedroom doors now. Leo managed to pin Jamie's arms above her, the gun crushing the fingers of her right hand, and out of the corner of her eye, Jamie saw Charlotte's blotchy face crawling over to them, and terror seized her as Leo shoved the little girl back—hard—making her fall onto her head.

"You son of a bitch," Jamie said, landing a punch under Leo's left eye. "She's only a baby. Big fuckin' man, right? You fuckin' bastard."

Leo slapped Jamie across the face again, and she lost her bearings. When the pain subsided, she realized that Leo had gotten her jeans down around her knees and that his were down as well.

"Noooo," she cried and tried to crawl away on her stomach, but Leo pounced on top of her, knocking the wind out of her. She gasped for air.

"You want it in the ass? Is that it?" he asked, pulling Jamie's body toward his with one hand and pulling down her underwear with the other.

Jamie was lightheaded and her chest burned, but she thought she could manage an elbow in the groin when suddenly Leo was off her.

She turned over onto her back, her breathing now a painful wheeze, and saw Bailino pressing Leo against the wall. He was soaking wet, in a bathrobe, and Leo's pant legs had fallen around his ankles showing his hairy, white legs. They were struggling over the gun, which Leo held straight in the air.

"I'll fucking kill you," Leo said, spit flying from the corners of his mouth.

Bailino forced Leo's hands back and as he held them there, he turned, with an eerie calm, to Jamie. "You all right?" He banged Leo's arm against the wall, and the gun fired, causing flakes of plaster to shoot across the room, coating them all with a white dust. The gunshot had so shocked Charlotte that she stopped crying and crawled like lightning over to Jamie, who was scrambling to get dressed. "No," Jamie screamed. "I'm not."

The two men, pressed up against each other, fell onto the baby grand piano.

"Take the kid, and bring her into the nursery," Bailino yelled as he banged Leo's arm on the piano again to release the gun from his grip. "Go!"

"You fuckin' shit," Leo yelled. "I know what you did to my sister, you fuckin' bastard."

Jamie struggled to her feet and, with Charlotte in hand, limped toward the nursery and shut the door. In the sudden darkness, she felt around until she reached the back corner of the room, slunk down onto the floor and plopped the shaking baby onto her lap. A small thread of light shone from the opening at the bottom of the nursery door, when another shot was fired.

Her eyes were fixed on that light, praying for it not to widen, for the door *never* to open, as she heard Leo's voice piercing the air. She ran her hand along Charlotte's curls, but the little girl had stopped shaking and had become very still. Then there was a solid *thud*, followed by another gunshot, and everything was quiet, except for Jamie's heart, which was pounding so hard that she thought blood was going to spill out of her ears.

She tilted her head back against the wall, her fingers pinching her nose to stem the bleeding while her other hand continued to caress Charlotte's head. The pounding had morphed into an incessant ringing in her ears, and she thought she heard new voices coming from the bedroom. She took her hand from Charlotte, her curls sticking to the blood and sweat on Jamie's palms, and felt around in the dark on the floor until she found the container of baby wipes. She pulled one out and stuck it into her left nostril. The little girl's breathing was steady. Incredibly, she'd fallen asleep again.

The closet door opened, throwing sudden light into the room. Jamie braced herself, shielding Charlotte's eyes, when a familiar shadow appeared in the doorframe.

"Are you all right?" Bailino asked. He had changed from his bathrobe into a pair of jeans and a white T-shirt.

"No." The tears were free-flowing now.

"Is she sleeping?"

Jamie nodded.

Bailino reached down and put his arms on Charlotte's small body.

"No." Jamie was speaking softly, but firmly. "Don't."

"*Shhh* . . . It's all right." Bailino crept his hands around Charlotte's body to lift her.

"No," Jamie whispered, putting her hand on his. "Let me do it."

Bailino stood back as Jamie struggled to stand, pressing her back against the wall and sliding up, keeping a hold onto Charlotte. The bloody baby wipe fell out of her nostril and onto the floor. She was dizzy, but she walked across the small room and placed Charlotte in the crib and covered her with a blanket and then stood there swaying. She wanted to crawl in there with her.

"C'mon," he said gently and extended his hand.

Too tired to think about why or what it meant, Jamie took Bailino's hand and followed him into the bedroom. It was empty. The baby grand piano had fallen onto its side, and there was plaster and dust everywhere, colored white and red. Leo was gone.

Bailino walked Jamie into the bathroom and pulled down the toilet seat. "Sit down," he said. Jamie obeyed, her compliance no longer out of terror but from, she feared, a growing hopelessness. He reached over her head and grabbed a washcloth, which he ran under warm water from the faucet. The bathroom air still had remnants of steam from when Bailino had showered, and it felt good in her nostrils and on her skin. Carefully, Bailino wiped Jamie's face.

"Does that hurt?" he asked.

She shook her head, which made her dizzier. She leaned her back against the toilet tank.

Bailino touched around the bridge of her nose. "Your eyes are swollen," he said and opened the medicine cabinet.

"They have been for days," Jamie said with a sniffle.

"Have they?" Bailino asked.

Jamie had always marveled at how people saw only what they wanted to see, particularly when it came to their own destruction, the undeniable pile of rubble left in their wake that was visible to everyone else, except them.

"Where is he?" she asked.

Bailino applied something to her forehead. The burn made Jamie recoil.

"He's not gonna bother you anymore." Bailino leaned down and kissed Jamie's forehead. "Okay?"

"Okay," Jamie nodded, looking into Bailino's once menacing eyes that had turned softer, as they had been the night before. But in the crisp daylight, suddenly another fear took hold of her. Whatever strategy she had employed, whatever game she had been trying to play to get herself and Charlotte out of there, had relied on building a trust with Bailino, on earning his respect and perhaps his confidence. But looking into his eyes right now, Jamie realized that she had been wrong. Very, very wrong. No matter what he said or what she hoped, she knew now that in the end he would never let her go.

45

There was an aching stiffness in Edward's neck as he opened his eyes and tried to remember where he was. A crumpled McDonald's bag lay on the passenger seat of his car, and there was a lingering wetness on the inner thighs of his jeans from the condensation of his Coke, which sat between his legs still full. He took a sip of the warm, watered down soda and reached for his phone. There were three missed calls from Tricia, none from Jamie. Outside, he saw a trailer truck parked in front of him. The highway cars to his left were whizzing north, a far cry from the virtual standstill of the Thruway the night before because of construction that closed all but one lane. Edward remembered pulling off to get something to eat and then parking at a rest stop at around 10:00 p.m. He must have fallen asleep. He looked at his phone. It was 6:10 a.m.

"*Damn,*" Edward muttered, turning the key in the ignition. He drove onto the highway and within seconds saw a sign: He was only about fifteen minutes from downtown Albany.

Edward called his office and told them he wouldn't be in. He held off on calling Tricia even though he knew she would be worried. He didn't know what to tell her—he didn't know himself what he was doing, so he just texted a quick "I'm fine. Call you later."

Dark storm clouds were rolling in from the west, and Edward was reminded of that day at the beach long ago. He saw a sign for the Albany police station and took the exit. The station was only a few blocks down, and he parked in one of the visitors' spots in front of the building—he was surprised to see quite a few cars there so early in the morning, but then remembered about the kidnapping of Charlotte Grand.

Edward walked into the police station, his legs still wobbly from the long ride, and approached a big, burly man behind the front desk. "Hi, can you help me?" he huffed, his voice groggy. "I'm looking for a woman."

"Aren't we all?" the officer said, with a smirk.

Edward looked at the officer's badge: Det. McDonnell.

"Does she work here?" McDonnell asked.

"No, no," Edward said. "She's missing."

"Jesus, another one?"

"I'm sorry?"

"I just filled out a report. Does she work at the Exotica Strip Club?"

"What? No, no . . ."

"Oh." The officer pulled out another sheet of paper. "For how long?" he asked, less interested than before.

"Since Tuesday. But I already filled out one of these things."

The policeman raised his eyebrows. "You did? Where?"

"In Manhattan."

"Manhattan? Do you live in Albany County?"

"No," Edward said.

"What county do you live in?"

"Nassau County."

The policeman stared. "Nassau County? As in Long Island?"

"Yes," Edward said. "I know . . . But I think she might be here. There was a post on her . . ."

"Does your sister live here, sir?" the man interrupted.

"No, she lives with me. I mean, in my house."

"On Long Island?"

"Yes."

"So she went missing on Long Island?"

"Yes, I mean . . . no, no, actually New York City. Manhattan."

"So your sister who lives on Long Island went missing two days ago in Manhattan, and you want to fill out a missing person's report in Albany?"

"Well, I guess," Edward said. "You see . . ."

"Hold on a minute." The policeman went to the back of the room and leaned his head inside a small office door. "Hey, Nurberg, can you take care of this?" He tossed the missing-persons file onto Nurberg's desk. "I gotta pee."

Edward saw the file sitting on the desk untouched until a pair of hands picked it up and a young, tired-looking plainclothes officer approached the front desk.

"I'm Detective Mark Nurberg." Nurberg stuck out his hand.

"Edward. Carter." Edward shook the detective's hand.

"Come into my office," Nurberg said politely, waving him inside the swinging gate.

"Thank you, Detective."

Once inside, Nurberg returned to his swivel chair as Edward sat in one of the chairs before his desk. "What can I do for you, Mr. Carter?" He looked at the form. "You want to report a missing person?"

"My sister is missing." Edward glanced at all the newspapers scattered on the desk and floor and the clippings that hung on a corkboard with tacks. There was a blanket and pillow strewn on the floor behind Nurberg's chair. "She's been missing for two days. I last heard from her when she was in Manhattan on Tuesday. She lives on Long Island. With me. Well, not with me, but downstairs from me. She's recently divorced, was married to a shit, but I don't think he has anything to do with it, but who the hell knows. She had seen him the day before at the lawyer's." Edward took a breath. "I've already filled out a missing-persons report downstate, and I've contacted everyone she knows, but no one has seen or heard from her."

"I'm sorry to hear that," Nurberg said, jotting down notes.

"Listen, I know how this looks, but I'm not a crackpot. I'm a levelheaded guy. I work in the Manhattan DA's office. Here, here's my business card." Edward reached into his pocket.

Nurberg shook his head. "No, that's not necessary," but Edward put his card on the desk anyway. Nurberg picked it up and studied it. "The Manhattan DA?"

Edward nodded.

"Do you know Sandra Conlon?"

"Sandy? Yeah, why, you know her?"

"She's my second cousin. On my mother's side. She's getting married next month."

"Yeah, I know. I'm going to the wedding."

"Really?"

"Yeah, why, are you?"

"I don't know. I haven't RSVP'd yet. If my mother has her wish, I will be there wearing a big, flashing neon sign that says, *Single*."

Edward smiled politely. "Wow, that's weird," he said. "If I hadn't met you today, I may have met you there."

"Yeah," Nurberg said. "How old is she? Your sister?"

"Thirty-two."

"And you're from Long Island?"

"Yes," Edward said, "but I saw something on her Facebook page, and I couldn't stay in the house anymore and do nothing. Before I knew it, I was driving upstate."

"Does she have relatives or friends living up here?"

"No," Edward shook his head. "Not that I know of."

Nurberg continued writing. "Did you say 'Facebook page'?" he asked.

"Yes," Edward said. "I don't know if it's her or what. So many scammers on that thing, or if it's a friend, but yesterday, under her profile, the word *Albany* was typed."

"And you thought that meant she was here?"

"I don't know what it means, but I just couldn't sit home."

"Mr. Carter, perhaps your sister decided to leave and not tell anyone . . ."

"She wouldn't do that, Detective," Edward interrupted.

"Mr. Carter, you'd be surprised at the things I've been told that people never do that they end up doing."

Edward was quiet.

"But if your sister, who just got a divorce, wanted to get away from it all and not tell anyone, it's a bit odd that she'd write where she was on her Facebook page. Unless it was a code for someone else?"

Edward shook his head. "I don't think so," he said, relieved that someone else besides him was finding all this strange. "Who? She knows I'd see it."

"Or maybe *from* someone else," Nurberg said. "Did anyone else know the password to her Facebook profile?"

"Not likely." Edward slumped back in his chair. "Bob, her ex-husband, maybe? I doubt it, though."

"Mr. Carter, a sizable percentage of reported missing persons end up not being missing persons at all." Nurberg sucked on the pen cap at the end of his ballpoint pen. "There is a very strong possibility that your sister doesn't want to be found."

The ceiling lights dimmed across the police station, and Nurberg's computer screen blinked. "Here we go," Nurberg said. "We're supposed to get a whopper of a storm this afternoon. Looks like it's rolling in early."

Edward put his head in his hands. "Detective, I don't know what to do. It was either drive here or drive to North Carolina."

"North Carolina?"

"Yes, the Facebook post said, 'Help Albany Charlotte.'"

Nurberg's pen fell out of his mouth. "What did you say?"

"I said Charlotte."

Nurberg swung his computer monitor toward Edward. "Do you mind logging into your Facebook profile for me?"

"Sure. What's the matter?"

"I just want to see for myself."

Edward brought up his news feed, and Nurberg studied the screen.

"What is it?" Edward asked.

"I'm just wondering if it's a coincidence."

"If what's a coincidence?"

"Well, what does your sister do for a living?"

"She's a writer," Edward said. "Why? What are you thinking?"

"Has she had any dealings with Governor Grand?"

"Governor Grand? I don't understand. What does he . . .?" Just behind Nurberg's head, tacked to the corkboard, was the early edition of the *Albany Times* featuring a large photo of Charlotte Grand. The headline read: "Day 3: Charlotte Grand Still Missing."

"Oh my God . . ."

"Mr. Carter, does your sister have any dealings with the governor?"

Edward sat forward in his seat. "Are you implying that my sister has anything to do with the disappearance of the governor's daughter?"

Nurberg checked the missing-persons report. "They've both been missing for the same amount of time, correct?"

"My sister was in Manhattan on Tuesday for a job interview. How could she be involved?"

"Do you know that for sure?"

"Why is everyone asking me that?" Edward stood up. "Why would she lie to me?"

"Where was the interview? What company?"

"I don't know." For someone who was accused of being on top of his sister's every move, Edward seemed to be missing a lot of important information.

"Does your sister have any children?"

The question forced Edward to sit back down. "No," he said quietly. Nurberg saw something dark come over Edward Carter. "What is it?"

Edward shook his head. "This can't be."

"Mr. Carter . . ."

"My sister can't have children, Detective." Edward paused. "But I'm telling you that she would never, ever, have anything to do with hurting a child in any way."

"Mr. Carter, I'd love to believe you, but my experience tells me otherwise."

Nurberg pulled out the Executive Mansion visitors' list from Tuesday and scanned it. No Jamie Carter. But she surely would have used an alias.

"How would she even get up here?" Edward said, mostly to himself. "Her car is parked in front of my house."

"By train, plane, who knows?" Nurberg was feeling an adrenaline rush. Could this be the break he was looking for? But this wasn't his case anymore. The Feds had taken over, and all new information had to be given to Grohl to pass over.

"But if she wanted to abduct Charlotte Grand, why would see put clues on Facebook?"

"A cry for help, maybe?" Nurberg asked. He was about to ask Edward for his sister's cell phone number so that he could track it, but then hesitated. He had gotten reprimanded last year for using a cell phone number to track a man whose wife accused him of abducting their daughter. Turned out the woman lied to get back at her husband for cheating on her with her sister, which meant that Nurberg had invaded the privacy of an innocent man. Since then, the cell phone industry and privacy advocates were calling for clear, standardized rules to stem the widespread police practice of using cell phones to track suspects without probable cause. Did this constitute probable cause? Probably not.

"C'mon, you're reaching, Detective."

Nurberg knew Carter was right. This was a shot in the dark, and he couldn't risk another blemish on his record. Still, this was the only shot he had. He picked up his phone.

"Who are you calling?"

Nurberg shook his head and spoke into the phone. "Yeah, hey, Chris, it's Mark . . . No, nothing yet . . . But I need a favor . . . A location on a Facebook IP address." Nurberg gave Jamie's information, including the date and time of her post. "When you get it, call me on my cell. I'll be in the car. Thanks." Nurberg grabbed his coat from the back of his chair. He wasn't sure where he was going—for all he knew, Jamie Carter's Facebook post was made from Timbuktu, but in his mind this was still his case, and this was the closest he had to anything resembling a lead, and he was going to investigate it himself.

"Where are you going?" Edward said, standing up.

"Mr. Carter, maybe it's better if you let me check this one out. Give me your cell number, and I'll call you as soon as I hear anything."

"Call me Edward, and I'm coming with you."

46

The rain pounded the windows, streaking the glass and blurring the only view of the world Jamie had had for three days. A never-ending parade of storm clouds, billows of thick, gray cotton, sped eastward as the trees flapped frantically. A bolt of lightning lit up the bedroom like a flash of a camera, followed by loud claps of thunder, the kind that Jamie hadn't heard since she was a little girl.

The storm had awoken Charlotte, who snuggled next to Jamie on the bed. The two of them stared out the window as Bailino sat on the other side, putting on his shoes. The light of the lamp blinked with each streak of lightning.

Pressed against Jamie's chest, Charlotte was still, her tiny hand holding onto Jamie's. *What a strong little girl*, Jamie thought. How proud the governor and Mrs. Grand must be of this beautiful child. She thought of her own mother and of Edward, who seemed so far away.

There was a knock on the bedroom door. Tony and Joey stood in the doorway.

"Don, we need to talk," Tony said.

"There's nothing to talk about." Bailino stood up. "Nothing changes. We continue on as planned."

"But what about Gino? Shouldn't he know?"

"Know what? That his sick fuck of a son tried to kill me? He's got enough on his mind. I'll tell him tomorrow. Let's just get through tonight." Bailino looked at Joey. "Give us a minute, Ton." Tony nodded and left the room.

"You, okay, Joe?"

"Yeah."

"Do you have anything you need to talk to me about? Anything you want to know? About Leo?"

Joey shook his head.

"Okay." Bailino took a breath. "There's something I need to tell you. Can you sit down?"

"I know already," Joey said. "Ma told me a long time ago."

Bailino was surprised. "She did? Why didn't you ever say anything?"

"She told me not to."

"Why?"

"She said when the time was right you'd come to me."

Bailino rubbed his chin. "I didn't mean for it to happen this way."

"I know."

"So . . . what do you think about that?" Bailino asked. It was the first time he could remember feeling nervous in a very long time.

"You know how I feel about you, Uncle D . . . I mean . . ."

"You can call me whatever you like, son." Joey's eyes crinkled with tears. "What's the matter?"

"I feel responsible for what happened this morning."

"You? Why?"

Joey took a breath. "Uncle Leo was asking me questions yesterday about you when he got back from dinner. When you were . . . up here."

"What'd he say?"

"He'd say things like 'Don't you think you guys look a lot alike?' or 'You think that's a coincidence.' I told him that I couldn't ask for a better father figure than you. And I think that got him mad."

"Don't worry about it. It's not your fault. What do I always tell you?"

"That the people who die are supposed to die," Joey said.

"That's right." Bailino put his arm around Joey. "I'm going to get you out of here. You're going to MIT, you hear me? You're a smart kid, and you've got great things ahead of you."

Joey smiled. "You think so?"

"Yeah."

Joey glanced at Jamie. "Is she okay?"

"I don't know," Bailino said.

"Do you want anything, Jamie?"

Without turning around, Jamie shook her head no.

"Okay, I'll see you later then," Joey said and left the bedroom.

Bailino sat down on the bed and put his hand on Jamie's side. "You sure you don't want anything, hon?"

"I want to go home," Jamie said into Charlotte's hair.

Bailino pursed his lips. "To what?"

"To my life."

"No offense, sweetie, but your life doesn't seem all that great. Can you please . . ."

Jamie turned around before he could finish asking her to. Charlotte was still on her side facing the window.

"Thank you."

The swelling around Jamie's eyes had gone down, but the skin on her face felt tight, like a drum. Bailino leaned over and brushed the hair out of her eyes.

"You just got divorced, from an asshole, I might add. You have no job. You're living in the downstairs apartment of your dead mother. Did you ever think that maybe things could be different for you? Someplace else?" Bailino paused. "With someone else? A change?"

Jamie was quiet.

"When this is over, and it'll be over very soon, I'll leave the kid somewhere safe for them to find. That's a promise, understand?"

Jamie watched Bailino's face closely, as lightning lit up the room once more.

"You stay here with me. We can start again." Bailino leaned down. "I know how this sounds . . . but it's really not all that crazy. People start again all the time . . . Think about it. Okay?"

Jamie nodded. "Okay," she said.

"I have to run out, but I'm going to be stopping at the supermarket to pick up a few things. Do you want anything?"

Jamie thought for a moment. "Maybe some chocolate milk?" she said. There were still crease marks on the side of her face from the pillowcase as it pressed against her skin overnight, and they made her look like a little girl.

"Chocolate milk, it is." He bent down, and Jamie braced herself for another firm kiss. Instead, Bailino whispered in her ear: "I'll take care of you."

47

To Katherine's delight, federal agents coursed through the mansion like a factory assembly line. There were at least three agents in every room of the main level, and groups scattered throughout the grounds—on the porch, at the security gate, and in the parking lot.

"Now, this is what I'm talking about," she said to Phillip, who was facing her, seated in one of the visitor chairs in the main hall. Empty folding chairs surrounded him on all sides, making him look like the sole patron in a movie theater. He was holding a stack of papers. "That schlub Nurberg is back where he belongs, getting cats out of trees," Katherine said. "Maybe now we'll see some results. For Christ's sake, it's been more than two days."

Phillip lifted his head up and gave a cursory look around. "Well, it certainly is busier around here," he said distantly.

Katherine was worried about her husband. She had spent the better part of the morning getting the agents—who had arrived at 6:30 a.m.—up to speed on what had transpired since Tuesday and going over Nurberg's reports, which, she had to admit, had been pretty thorough. Phillip had been little help, keeping to himself. She looked at him, slumped on his chair, and was about to sit with him when Marla, the mansion's tour guide, took one of the empty seats next to him.

"How are you, Governor Grand?" Marla said, with an air of concern.

In the last forty-eight hours, not one person—even from the press—had asked Katherine how *she* was coping.

Phillip nodded, but said nothing.

"I'm sure they'll find her." Marla stood up, but not before Katherine detected a slight squeeze on Phillip's arm. She nodded at Katherine as she left.

Katherine sat down next to Phillip, who didn't seem to notice she was even there. She leaned over and looked at his paperwork. Phillip shook his head. "I made the mistake of trying to keep my early afternoon meeting with the Division of the Budget," he said. "I scheduled it last Thursday, before, you know . . . to discuss the revenue and expenditure plan for the state, but I think I'm going to cancel it." Phillip looked up at the clock. Thirteen hours and three minutes to go until the execution of Gino Cataldi.

Anti–capital-punishment picketers, undeterred by the rain, had already started congregating outside the Executive Mansion, jockeying for position with the media, who, disillusioned with the governor's lack of face time, had turned their cameras on the protesters in order to have *something* to report. Phillip and Katherine listened to the muffled cacophony of voices outside. She wasn't sure what to say and reached out and held Phillip's hand. He squeezed hers in return.

"Phillip, I want to talk with you about something. I was going to wait, but . . ."

The front door to the mansion opened and closed, making the outside noise grow in intensity, but then die down again quickly. Maddox unfolded his umbrella and walked into the room.

"Governor? Hello, Katherine . . . I'm sorry to interrupt."

"That's all right," Phillip said. "How is it out there?"

"Insanity," Maddox said. "Between the rain and the picketers . . . And the news continues to report sightings of Charlotte all over the country. I just don't understand it."

"It happens all the time," the governor said. "People want to help, feel like they're a part of the solution."

Katherine shook her head. "They end up being part of the problem."

"They mean well," Phillip said.

"That's true," Maddox said. "You just never know when the right lead is going to come along."

Maddox had been a trouper through all this, working round the clock since TMZ.com broke the story. He'd come as a package deal with Katherine on her first day of work back when Phillip was running for the assemblyman spot—"a bonus," as she referred to Maddox, who had worked with her as an independent PR consultant. Phillip had no problem with Katherine bringing her own people as long as they did the job, and in the years since, Maddox had proved to be a deft public relations specialist with an uncanny ability to feed the voracity of the media with no qualms about being the bad guy, whether it was telling out-of-line reporters to take a hike or limiting press access on a whim. Maddox took the brunt of the heat, leaving Phillip virtually unscathed by public opinion. "You won't regret this," Katherine had told him on that very first day. And Phillip never did.

"Sir, are you familiar with a Robert Scott?" Maddox asked.

"Who?" Katherine asked, letting go of Phillip's hand.

"Robert Scott."

The governor shook his head.

"Well, he called this morning to speak with you and was told repeatedly that you were not available for obvious reasons and that he should make a request in writing and that we would get back to him. Apparently, he's being persistent."

"Really?" Katherine asked. "What do you mean?"

"He's at the security gate."

"He's *here*?"

"Yeah. Here's his business card." Maddox handed the card to Katherine. "He's a lawyer with Worcester, Payne & Leach in Manhattan."

Katherine thought for a moment. "Wait a minute. I know that firm. Phillip, don't we know that firm?"

"Katherine, we deal with a lot of lawyers."

"I know, but it sounds so damn familiar." Katherine peeked out the window, but with so many people and umbrellas, it was difficult to see anyone in particular. "Which one is he, Lenny?"

Maddox stood next to Katherine. "*Hmmm* . . . Oh, that's him, at the right side of the door to the security office. You see him? Tall, brown hair, he's got his foot on the gate?"

"Oh yes, I see him now. He's a young guy."

"I'd say midthirties."

"Really?" Katherine turned to Phillip, who was again staring at the clock. "Phillip, don't you find this unusual? This Scott person from Manhattan driving all the way up here without an appointment? I mean, doesn't he read the paper or watch the news? All he has to do is open his eyes to know something is going on right now." She looked again out the window. "He seems so . . . unfazed."

"He's a bit of a freak, if you ask me," Maddox said as his cell phone rang. He put it to his ear. "Yeah? . . .You're kidding? . . . All right, I'll call you back."

"What is it?" Katherine asked.

"Mr. Scott apparently just mentioned that he has an idea that might help us find Charlotte." Three federal agents, who had been standing nearby, approached the window and peeked outside.

"What?" Katherine looked at Phillip, whose attention was finally secured. "Is he for real? What do we do?"

"I say we just say, 'thanks, but no thanks' and send him on his way," Maddox said.

The governor got up and stood with Katherine and Maddox near the window.

"What do you think, Phillip?" she asked.

Phillip stared through the small slit in the drapes. "I'm inclined to agree with Len."

"So there you have it," Maddox dialed his phone.

"I'm curious though," Phillip said.

"Barry? Wait, hold on a minute," Maddox said into his phone.

"Do we know exactly what kind of ideas Mr. Scott has about the disappearance?"

"You're joking, right, governor?" Maddox said. "I can't believe you're really going to entertain this. If you want opinions, you can go turn on Fox News."

"What is it you said just before, Len?" Phillip said. "That you never know when the right lead is going to come along?"

"Ugh, I hate it when I'm right," Maddox said and spoke into his cell phone. "Hi, Barry, can I talk to Special Agent Wilcox? Thanks . . . Hi, it's Leonard Maddox. The governor would like to know if you have taken a statement from Mr. Scott . . . Yes . . . All right . . . Hold on."

"So what is it?" Katherine asked.

"According to Wilcox, Mr. Scott seems to think that Charlotte's disappearance might have to do with Gino Cataldi's execution tonight."

The words came as a sucker punch for Phillip Grand, who very well could have fallen over had he not been leaning against the wall. He was so stunned by the suggestion, and its implications, that he didn't notice that Katherine appeared to have had the same reaction. "The Cataldi execution? Did he say what the connection could be?"

"I told you, governor," Maddox said. "He may as well have said that Charlotte's disappearance is linked to the death of Elvis Presley. Can we send this kook on his way now?"

That was the last thing Phillip wanted to do. Somehow this Scott fellow had put two and two together, and Phillip wondered if anyone else out there had done the same. He needed to know for sure what he knew, or thought he knew, and put the kibosh on his theories before they made their way into the press, all of whom right now were within earshot of Robert Scott and could jeopardize his daughter's safety.

"Send him in," Phillip said and returned to the main lobby.

"What?" Maddox said.

"I'd like to hear what this man has to say."

Maddox looked at the First Lady. "Katherine . . ."

Katherine stared out the window at Robert Scott, who had uttered the very thing that had been on her mind for the past two days. "Phillip, are you sure?" she asked.

"Yes, I am."

Katherine shrugged her shoulders. "I guess we have nothing to lose."

Maddox relayed the governor's request into his phone and stood by the front door. "They said it will take a few moments while they search him and run his credentials."

"All right," said Phillip, who was hoping to bide some time in order to come up with something credible to say.

Katherine stood next to her husband. "Who do you think this guy is? Do you think he really knows something?" Inside, she was a mix of strong, contradicting emotions—validation, humiliation—that her hunch may have been right.

The front door opened. "Well, we're about to find out," Phillip said.

Bob, his face and collar tinged with rain, strode into the mansion with the bravado of a man who had been inaugurated there himself and as if he weren't being escorted by six federal agents. Special Agent Wilcox led him straight to the governor, who, Bob thought, looked taller and much thinner in person.

"Mr. Scott? I'm Governor Grand."

Bob stepped forward. He was wearing a dark-blue suit he had bought off the rack at Brooks Brothers the night before, and he was carrying his briefcase, which he set down on the floor—a few papers were left sticking out after the security guard had ransacked it.

"Governor, what a pleasure to meet you," he said, shaking his hand. "I'm sorry it's under these inauspicious circumstances."

"Thank you. I appreciate that," Phillip said. "This is my wife, Katherine."

Bob nodded. "Ma'am." Katherine nodded in return.

"So what is this I hear?" Phillip said. "That you know something that can help us find my daughter?"

"Governor Grand, I must be frank," Bob said. "My primary reason for wanting to see you was with regard to the legal roundtable you are currently assembling. I think I would be a tremendous asset."

"Oh, Lord," Maddox said, sitting on one of the lobby's folding chairs.

"But," Bob added quickly, "that's not the reason I came. I drove up here to offer my services to help in the investigation in any way I can. I have an exemplary record at Worcester, Payne & Leach, and . . ."

"We have our own lawyers and investigators, Mr. Scott," Phillip said.

"Wait a minute, now I remember why that law firm is so familiar," said Mrs. Grand, who had been standing beside Phillip. "You worked with the NAACP last year as part of Tay Jackson's defense team. The papers said that it was because of your firm that Jackson didn't get the death penalty."

"Yes, that's right, Mrs. Grand. We're very good at what we do."

"You realize I was on the opposing side," Phillip said. "That man murdered an innocent girl in cold blood."

"Yes, I know, but we were hired to do a job, and we did it," Bob said. "Actually, speaking of capital-punishment cases, that's why I wanted to speak with you in person."

"You think Tay Jackson has something to do with Charlotte," Phillip said.

"No," Bob said. "But I'm thinking Gino Cataldi does."

Phillip kept his eyes steady on Bob. "Yes, that's what I was told."

"The timing of the disappearance seems very coincidental . . ."

"I think the Albany police department considered this," Phillip said, "and thought there was nothing there."

"Actually, that's not true, Phillip," said Katherine, who was eager to hear Robert Scott out. "There was nothing in Nurberg's report about Gino Cataldi, other than a notation of the execution tonight along with dozens of other items on your agenda this week."

"It is certainly a possibility," Bob said. "I did a little reading last night on the Cataldi crime family, and there seems to be a history of witness tampering that . . ."

"Mr. Scott, I sure hope this isn't some left-wing attempt to save another man—one who has killed at least two people and has a long, long history of crime in this state, I might add. If you are here for a stay of execution . . ."

"Who? Me?" Bob's smile faded. "Are you kidding? I say, 'Kill the son of a bitch.'" The profanity slipped out, but Bob hoped it would be seen as proof of his fervor for capital punishment or his conservative allegiance. "You know, it's no skin off my nose. I'm just trying to help."

"I don't know, Phillip," Katherine said. "That's an interesting idea."

"Katherine, please . . . If this was in any way related to Gino Cataldi, don't you think we would have heard something by now?"

Katherine nodded. "That's true," she said. "We haven't gotten any demands of any kind."

"Mr. Scott, you think capital punishment is the only hot-button issue in this state?" Phillip said. "Last week, my office was threatened when word got out that I was vetoing the No-Divorce Bill, which, as I see it, is really a Pro-Divorce Bill, since New York has one of the lower divorce rates in the country. And the week before that, I riled up the wrong people in the legislature by vetoing a stack of spending bills two feet high. Now, I hope you'll forgive me for not seeing this connection between a condemned eighty-plus-year-old man who hasn't tasted freedom in more than thirty years and the disappearance of my daughter."

"Governor Grand, my apologies if I spoke out of place," Bob said. For the first time since he arrived, he felt the weight of the air in the room.

"I know you mean well, Mr. Scott, but things are very tense, and this is just more complicated than you can know." Phillip held up Bob's business card. "I will hold onto your card and certainly keep you in mind for the legal roundtable. I do appreciate your initiative and concern. Please know that it hasn't gone unnoticed." Phillip stuck out his hand.

Bob brightened as he shook it. "I appreciate that, Governor."

Special Agent Wilcox stepped forward. "Governor, if it's all right, I'd like to speak with Mr. Scott and get a more detailed statement and get his contact information."

"Whatever you think is necessary, Agent Wilcox," Phillip said.

"Thank you, sir. Mr. Scott, would you come with me?"

As Phillip watched Bob trail Wilcox, Maddox and a cluster of dark suits into the dining room, he hoped that he had spooked him enough to keep him quiet, but massaged his ego enough to keep him loyal. Still, it worried Phillip that Wilcox was giving him some additional attention.

"Something tells me that won't be the last we hear of Robert Scott," Katherine said.

"Yeah, I get the same feeling," said Phillip.

Katherine's cell phone dinged, indicating she had a text message. It had been dinging regularly for the past twenty-four hours with inquiries from the media, political colleagues, and well-wishers. She glanced at the caller ID and froze: The text was from Don Bailino.

Shielding the screen with her hand, she opened it.

CAN WE TALK?

She typed quickly:

IT'S NOT A GOOD TIME.

The phone dinged again.

ARE YOU OK?

I WILL CALL U LATER, Katherine wrote and then erased the message thread and put her phone into her jacket pocket as Phillip put his arm around her.

"What was it you wanted to discuss?" Phillip asked. "Before?"

"Oh, it's not important," Katherine said. "It can wait."

48

The heavy rain started up again as Jamie sat on the main floor of the log cabin looking out the glass back doors. Large puddles had formed all over the pebbled driveway, making it look like a minefield. Charlotte sat next to her, ripping pages out of a magazine that had been on the recycling pile. Other than the intermittent shredding, it was quiet, and, true to Bailino's word, Jamie hadn't seen Leo all day.

Benny was sleeping on the sofa behind her, and Tony was on Facebook again—he had been sitting there for half an hour and commented on at least twenty posts, as far as she could tell.

"Are you hungry?" Joey stood in the kitchen.

Jamie shook her head.

"What about her?" Joey pointed to Charlotte, who was arranging all of the scrunched up pages around her into groups.

"She had her bottle about an hour ago," Jamie said, looking at the little girl. "She seems fine right now."

"Crap, where's the sound on this thing?" Tony said to no one in particular. A Yahoo news page was coming up on the screen. "Oh, here it is." As Tony turned up the volume, a news reporter was speaking. ". . . identified as Robert Scott of Worcester, Payne & Leach, a Manhattan law firm that specializes in high-profile criminal cases. Why Scott had been called to the . . ."

"That's too loud," Joey said, stepping over to lower the volume.

Jamie sat still, her face toward the back doors, but her eyes watched the footage of Bob walking into the Executive Mansion in Albany, which was being shown on a loop. *What was he doing here*, Jamie wondered. *Had he seen her post? Would he be coming for her?* There was a flutter of excitement in her belly when she had a frightening thought: What if Bailino had seen this news report as well?

A bolt of lightning shot through the trees, and the log cabin lights went out.

"Fuck," Tony said. The computer screen dimmed as the machine switched to battery power. "Where's the fuse box?"

"It's downstairs," Joey said. "I'll go. I know where it is." He opened a cabinet and grabbed a flashlight.

"Son of a bitch," Tony muttered, looking over at Benny, who remained asleep on the couch. "Fuckin' guy can sleep through anything." He stood up and stretched his arms. "Joe, what if it's not just the house, but the whole area? I'm supposed to play in a poker tournament this afternoon. This battery won't last forever."

"Power down now, and save your battery," Joey suggested. "I'll be right back."

"This fuckin' sucks." Tony pushed the laptop across the buffet. "What are you looking at?" he asked Jamie, who averted her eyes.

Joey was yelling something from the basement.

"What? I can't hear you?" Tony yelled back.

"Shut the fuck up, already," Benny said, turning over on the sofa.

Tony kicked one of Charlotte's piles of paper on the floor and walked into the kitchen. "What?" He leaned his head inside the basement stairwell.

Nobody else saw it, except for Jamie, because she was sitting so close to the glass doors. When the power blew, the small red indicator light on the electronic lock turned green—probably as a safety precaution. Her mother's words came to her again in a whisper: *Driving is easy. Go when it's green, stop when it's red. The real trick is learning to live your life that way.*

Without wasting any time, she stood, picked up Charlotte, pulled on the glass doors, and was half-surprised when they opened with ease, but not before making a heavy dragging sound.

"What the . . . ?" she heard Tony say as she darted out the door and into the rain.

The grass was wet and furry under her bare feet, and Jamie ran as fast as she could across the manicured lawn and into the brush and trees, toward the river. The raindrops felt like pellets against her forehead and Charlotte felt like a sack of potatoes in her arms, but she wasn't crying—the little girl hid her head in the crook of Jamie's neck and was holding on tightly. There were yells coming from behind her now and rustling. *Don't turn back*, she thought. *Just go.* She ran around trees, hoping they'd shield her from detection as lightning lit up the sky, followed by a quick clap of thunder, and Charlotte held Jamie tighter.

The river appeared through the brush. It seemed wider and rougher than it had the day before as Jamie ran across the riverbank, ignoring the pain under her feet, trying to keep from slipping. Her steps stomped through the mud and then splashed into the shockingly cold water. More splashes came from behind her as she waded into the river.

SINK OR SWIM: THE TIME IS NOW TO LIVE THE LIFE YOU DESERVE.

Random images flashed across Jamie's mind with every push through the water: The swing of the rake . . . Leo tearing at her clothing . . . The footage of Bob at the Executive Mansion . . . Her mother's closet filled with clothes with the tags still on them . . . *I'll take care of you* . . . Charlotte's screaming face as she came up from under the bathtub water. Jamie looked at the little girl: *You can do this, I know it.* She strengthened her grip on Charlotte and, just as the river was waist high, dove in.

49

Bailino put his three items on the supermarket checkout belt: a box of Cheerios, a gallon of chocolate milk, and a bouquet of roses.

"That'll be six dollars and ninety-seven cents, ma'am," the trainee in pinstripes said to the customer in front of him.

"This isn't mine," the old woman said, waving a box of tampons in the air.

The cashier sighed. "I need a void!" she yelled.

Bailino looked over at the self-checkouts, but there was a line five people long, so he decided to stay where he was. He unclipped his phone from his belt and quickly waded through a series of emails and texts from George, who needed his authorization on a few things. He sent a quick text, placed the phone back in its holder, reached into his pocket, and took out Jamie's phone again, clicking to the photo of the little girl and her mother. He looked closely at the girl in the navy-blue jumper. Jamie hadn't changed much from the time she was a child—she had the same innocent eyes and cherubic face. She looked very much like her mother.

The food on the checkout belt sputtered forward, and Bailino took a step with it.

"Do you have a store card?" the cashier asked him.

Bailino shook his head.

"No worries. I can swipe one for you." She placed a small

plastic card over the scanner. "This way, you can get the store specials." She smiled.

"Thank you," he said. As the young lady rang up his items, Bailino pressed the menu button on Jamie's phone, and several applications popped up: Maps, Browser, Camera, Facebook, Twitter, Evernote, Sudoku. He grazed his finger along the Evernote app, which opened into a series of folders titled "Things to Remember," "2012 Goals," and "Story Ideas." Bailino was impressed by the receptiveness of this particular smartphone model—sometimes he'd literally had to jab his into compliance—and made a mental note to upgrade. He closed Evernote and touched on the Facebook icon and was brought to Jamie's profile page, where the words "Help Albany Charlotte," posted with the timestamp *yesterday, 10:21 a.m.*, leapt off the screen. By the time Bailino read the comment "Where r u??" left by Edward, he was already in his car.

50

Nurberg parked the police car in the driveway of the log cabin, behind a black limousine. The rain streaked the foggy driver's-side window, and he couldn't see the address on the mailbox. He rolled the window down as rain spilled into the car.

"This is it," he said to Edward, who was sitting next to him.

Tracing Jamie Carter's Facebook IP address was the first deviation Nurberg had ever taken from police procedure. Having Edward Carter in the car was the second, but that certainly wasn't his idea. Edward sensed that Nurberg was going rogue in taking this little road trip, especially since he had to duck past Grohl on his way out of the station. The son of a bitch threatened to go to his "superiors" if he didn't let him tag along; Nurberg's hands were tied.

"Well, let's go," Edward said, putting his hand on the door lever.

"Wait, I think you should stay in the car."

"You're kidding, right?"

"No, Mr. Carter . . ."

"Please call me Edward."

"Edward, this isn't . . ."

"I'm not staying." Edward opened the passenger door, and the wet air rushed inside the car.

"Wait," Nurberg said. "We can both get into a lot of trouble."

"For what? Ringing a doorbell?" Edward closed the car door, leaving it slightly ajar to keep the rain from coming in.

"At least, I don't know . . . Let's have some kind of plan. If she's here, fine. But what if she's not? Why are we here?" Nurberg thought quickly. "Okay, you came to the police station, and there was something wrong with your car, and I'm driving you to your relatives' house, but you wrote down the wrong address, and . . ."

Edward was out the door and walking toward the house.

"Fuck," Nurberg muttered as he followed him toward the cabin.

By the time the two men reached the front door, they were soaked. Nurberg pushed the doorbell and undid the safety on his weapon, but left it in its holster. Edward shot him a look.

"Just in case," Nurberg said.

A bolt of lightning lit up the woods, the bellowing thunder seeming like it would crack the sky. "Jesus," Nurberg said, looking around at the trees. "This is probably the worst place to be in a lightning storm."

"Yeah, or in that river we just passed," Edward said.

Nurberg pushed the wet hair out of his eyes and rang the bell again as Edward knocked on the door.

"Hello?" Edward called. "Is anyone here? Jamie?"

Nurberg opened the screen door and peered through the small window in the front door. "It doesn't look like anyone's home."

"But there's a car in the driveway," Edward said. "Let's go around to the back."

Nurberg hesitated. "Wait . . ."

"Detective, please, we've come this far," Edward said.

With his wet hair plastered to his head like a helmet, Edward Carter looked pitiful, like a little boy who'd lost his best friend. "All right," Nurberg sighed.

The two men, shielding their eyes from the driving rain, reached the back of the cabin and stood before the open glass doors.

"Hello?" Nurberg said, stepping inside; his clothing dripped onto the small throw rug by the door.

"Where is everybody?" Edward asked.

"I don't know." Nurberg eyed the clumps of papers scattered on the floor, the lit-up screen of the laptop and the bowl of chips on the kitchen counter. "*Somebody* was just here," he said.

A series of loud pops came from the trees behind the cabin. Instinctively, Nurberg pulled out his weapon.

"What are you doing?" Edward said.

"That didn't sound like thunder."

Another one was heard, and then another.

Nurberg picked his phone out of his pocket. "Damn, the cell service is out. Edward, go in the car. Call this in. And stay in the car."

"Where are you going?"

"Back there." Nurberg hunched down and, with gun drawn, ran out the back door as Edward stumbled across the main floor of the cabin. He pulled open the front door and nearly slammed into the body of Don Bailino.

"Who are you?" Bailino asked, stepping into the cabin, his handgun pointed in the center of Edward's face.

Edward put his hands in the air. "Please, this is a mistake," he said. "I'm in the wrong house."

"Who are you, I asked." Bailino steadied the revolver.

"I'm . . ." Shots fired from behind the log cabin, and Edward backed against the wall.

Bailino's eyes narrowed on the face of the intruder—the crystal blue eyes, the freckles on the nose, the pale skin. He arched his eyebrows. "Edward?" he asked.

Edward's eyes opened wide.

"Is your name Edward?" Bailino asked.

"Yes. But how do you know my name?"

"Edward Carter," Bailino said to himself, a smile appearing across his lips. "Come with me."

51

The intense rain flooded the grass and driveway, making it difficult to follow any footprint trail. Bailino, holding his pistol close to his side, headed toward the woods behind the cabin. He stood behind a tree and just watched, waiting for something to move. About twenty yards ahead, a husky body limped along the ground. He ran toward it.

"Where is she?" Bailino said. Tony was lying in a puddle of mud, his arm around a fallen tree trunk, the other clutching his chest.

"Where is she, I asked." Bailino opened Tony's shirt; blood poured from a small hole behind his fingers.

"The girl . . . took the kid . . . into the river." Tony coughed.

"How long ago?"

"About fifteen or twenty minutes."

"How did she get out of the house?"

"Don, I can't catch my breath."

"How did she get out of the fucking house?"

"Lightning knocked the power out." Tony's voice came in quick, shallow mouthfuls. "Locks must've opened."

"Who did this?" Bailino asked, gesturing toward Tony's chest wound.

"I don't know . . . I . . . got him . . . in the leg . . ." Tony pointed toward the house.

"One guy?"

Tony nodded.

"Where's Joey?" Bailino asked.

Tony pointed toward the river, and then his arm fell to the ground. His breathing was coming in short puffs now, the raindrops making his eyelids flutter until they stopped and water pooled around them.

Bailino continued walking toward the river. About ten yards down, a body lay motionless in a small ravine. Diluted blood streaked down Benny's face, the driving rain cleaning a gunshot wound above his right eye. The river ahead roared, dotted by raindrops, but Bailino saw no one else.

He stood very still, listening, and then walked in measured steps back to the cabin, his trained eyes exploring every inch of the terrain. The glass doors were still open. Off to the side, he glimpsed a man limping over the pebbled driveway toward the front of the house.

Bailino grabbed Nurberg's shoulder and flipped him onto his back. Nurberg went down hard onto the gravel as Bailino kicked the gun out of his hands.

"You a cop?" Bailino pointed his gun.

Nurberg nodded. He was clutching his inside upper thigh, which was bleeding heavily.

"Albany police?"

Nurberg nodded again.

"How did you find this place?"

Nurberg hesitated. Bailino cocked the hammer of his pistol and held it in the center of his forehead.

"I got a lead." Nurberg's voice was hoarse. He looked toward the driveway, where his car was now blocked by a white Ford Flex. There was no sign of Edward.

"Look at me, please," Bailino said. "So you got a lead?"

"Yeah, and when I got here, I heard gunshots, and . . . I thought somebody was in trouble, and . . . I called it into the station right away."

"I see," Bailino said. "So the police are on their way?"

Nurberg nodded. He kept his eyes steady on Bailino, whose hulk was sheltering him from the rain with the exception of a stream of water that was dripping off the handle of the gun, right near his mouth.

Bailino looked at his wristwatch. "They're taking their sweet time to get here, no?"

Nurberg glanced toward the empty country road, which, on a good day, probably saw one or two cars pass by. He looked back at Bailino, the gold cross around his neck glistening.

Bailino stared at the young officer lying on the ground trying to be brave and to remain calm in the face of his lie. "Son, I'm afraid you picked the wrong day to be a hero," Bailino said and shot Nurberg in the head.

52

Charlotte was shivering.

The extended time in the frigid river had brought the little girl's body temperature down, and, with the rain-dampened air, there was no escaping the chill. Jamie tried lifting Charlotte's sopping wet T-shirt, thinking the skin-to-skin contact would help the little girl retain heat, but that only seemed to make her tremble more, so she just held her little wrinkled body close.

The roar of the river had quieted as the rain stopped, and Jamie, from behind the cover of a large rock, peeked out, her hand slipping on the moss. She couldn't fathom how far the rapids had dropped her from the cabin. Miles, maybe? It had taken her longer than she expected to cross the water, having underestimated the difficulty of swimming with a screaming child. It had been an arduous trip trying to make sure the little girl was able to get enough air into her lungs—Jamie had to lift Charlotte in and out of the water in order to attain any kind of speed stroke. As they made their way across, the only way Jamie could lift her own body up enough to fill her own lungs with air was by dunking Charlotte at the same time, and the sound of the little girl's choking sobs, while distressing, told Jamie that Charlotte was at least breathing. They alternated like that for some time, and it became harder to lift the little girl as Jamie's muscles became fatigued. At some point, she just let the current take them until she regained some strength and managed to bob her way to the other side.

Jamie searched the small waves for the subtlest splash, but all was still—the eerie calm after a vicious rainstorm. There was no sign of Joey, who dove into the river behind them just after Tony opened fire with his revolver. For what felt like hours, but Jamie was sure was only a matter of minutes, the splash of Joey's strokes followed hers, stroke for stroke, one after the other. He had gotten so close to them at one point that their fingertips grazed, but Joey wasn't a confident swimmer, and when he made a move to grab her, she was able to kick off him and use his body as a launching pad to propel her and Charlotte farther ahead. It was only as Jamie sat there on the cold, muddy riverbank that she realized that it was because Joey jumped into the river that the gunfire had stopped. By diving in after them, Joey probably had saved them.

It was getting dark. Jamie thought it better to travel by night, but the reality of nightfall in a place without streetlights and street traffic hit her, and she realized that she wouldn't be able to see a thing. She picked up Charlotte and started to walk; the cuts along the soles of her feet stung as they scraped against the underbrush. It would be slow going without proper shoes, and the mosquitoes were having a field day with her bare arms and feet. Plus, there wasn't much time—she could no longer make out the tree trunks and branches that had sheltered her for the past few hours, and everything was turning black as clouds continued to cover the sky, leaving no signs of a helpful moon. Jamie walked faster, holding one hand in front of her to keep from bumping into things, and felt the flutter of bugs brushing past her palm. The sounds of cracking branches were everywhere, as if she were being followed, but she convinced herself otherwise and kept going. The trill chant of crickets and the screaming of mating frogs, who called to one another from all parts of the woods, created an unsettling soundtrack to the dark, blank screen before her.

Just take it one step at a time, she told herself.

Soon Jamie stumbled upon a clearing and solid ground. It was a road. She picked a direction and just started walking, carefully navigating her steps to make sure she stayed on the pavement. She walked for about ten minutes, when headlights appeared from behind, and she ran off the road to hide, terrified that it would be *them*. It dawned on her that by doing so she was letting potential help get away, but she couldn't take the chance. Bailino would kill them both this time if he found them, she was sure of it. Or at least kill her. The car came and went without seeing her, and Jamie returned to the road and kept walking.

Charlotte was unresponsive and limp, her arms dangling down, her head remaining in the crook of Jamie's neck. Jamie worried that she was dehydrated.

"Charlotte," Jamie whispered, her small voice breaking the silence. "Charlotte, honey, are you okay?"

The little girl said nothing, although Jamie thought she may have felt her head move. She needed to get her to a doctor. Up ahead, a car was coming. The headlights were picked up by small reflectors positioned along the sides of the road, and Jamie realized she was at an intersection. She crouched down just off the pavement, and as the car came closer, its blinker, signaling a right-hand turn, acted as a slow strobe light illuminating the area. She watched the small red taillights go on their way and stood in the center of the intersection box, trying to remember what she had just seen: To the left, there appeared to be nothing but barren fields; to the right, in the direction the car was heading, the road cut through the brush back toward the river, probably over a bridge—Jamie had floated underneath two on her way downriver. There was no way she was going that way. She decided to keep walking straight ahead.

The curved outline of a parked automobile came into focus, and as she walked toward it, she noticed several vehicles parked on the side of the road, illuminated by a light source coming from a one-story building. She walked up to the first car and pulled on the door handle. Locked. She tried the next. Also locked. The building itself looked a little run-down, but Jamie saw a lantern hanging from the ceiling inside, appearing as a beacon in this darkened, empty place, and, with Charlotte wrapped in her arms, she ran toward it.

53

It will be a miracle if the garage doesn't get audited, Reynaldo thought as he placed another receipt on top of a pile on the counter. He reached his hand into the manila folder labeled "tax stuff," his sophisticated system of keeping track of the year's tax-deductible expenditures, and pulled out a small, crumpled piece of paper. He smoothed it out and saw that it was a Sunglass Hut receipt from the previous summer. There was a note scribbled in red ink in the margins:

Rey, I REALLY need these to see when the sun is out, or else I cannot work. —Pedro.

He threw the receipt into the garbage.

Doing the taxes each year reminded Reynaldo of his papa, who, although an honest man, was deathly afraid of the IRS—just signing his name on the tax forms would yield a forehead full of sweat. When Reynaldo was about eight or nine years old, his father had walked into his bedroom one day and asked him if he'd be interested in assisting him with his yearly tax prep.

"Why, Papa?" Reynaldo had asked.

"Because you're good in school," he'd said.

Being good in school was the ultimate compliment that his father, who dropped out in the sixth grade, could bestow, and Reynaldo basked in the opportunity to make his father proud. And he'd been doing the taxes ever since.

Reynaldo looked at his watch. He had gotten to the garage later than he'd hoped because Pedro had decided to take Nada to McDonald's before dropping her off at home to get ready for her date with Ricardo. Reynaldo didn't understand either one of his brothers. Neither one seemed to have developed any kind of respect for each other, or for women, or for the business that financed them and enabled them to carouse around town for years. And as much as he complained about them, he worried too. When he got back from his vacation, he was going to sit down with both of them and discuss some changes that he wanted to make, including the implementation of a new work schedule that would better equalize the business responsibilities between them. They'll love *that*, Reynaldo thought with a smile as the front door to the office swung open.

Jamie practically fell into the small room and shut the door behind her, pressing her back against it. It was warm inside; she was grateful for it and almost didn't notice Reynaldo standing stunned behind the counter.

"Can you help us?" she asked.

In her arms, to Reynaldo's immense surprise, was Charlotte Grand.

"Do you know this little girl?" she asked.

Reynaldo nodded, looking at the wet, filthy, bruised woman standing in his office. "What happened to you?"

"I need to call the police," Jamie said.

A pair of headlights flashed across the front windows. "Don't move," she said, adjusting her body so that she was unnoticeable from the outside. "Pretend I'm not here. Look at your papers."

Reynaldo did as Jamie told him. He moved his head down until the headlights were gone.

"Can I use your phone?" Jamie asked.

"The power is out," Reynaldo said, motioning to the lantern hanging above them. "It's running on battery."

"Do you have a cell?"

"Yes, but the service has been touch and go for the last couple of hours," Reynaldo said. "I can drive you to the police station."

Jamie had an overwhelming desire not to leave, to stay in this warm, dingy office in the middle of nowhere with this tall man with the long, curly hair and the kind eyes until the power came back on, but she knew Bailino would be looking for her, and she had to keep going.

Reynaldo sensed her indecision. "You're safe here," he said, coming out from behind the counter.

"Please, wait . . ." Jamie held out her hand.

"Okay, okay. I'm staying here." Reynaldo put his hands in the air. "I'm not going to hurt you. I'm not."

The tears poured from Jamie's eyes, the kind of powerful tears that a child who has been trying to be brave cries after an ordeal is over. She held up Charlotte. "I don't think she's okay anymore. I think she's sick." Jamie sucked in air. "She hasn't been moving. I don't know what to do."

"I'm coming over, okay?"

Jamie nodded.

Reynaldo slowly approached and put his hand on the little girl's chest. "She's breathing all right," he said, "but you're not. Let me take her."

"I'm not letting her go."

"But I know her."

"But I don't know you," Jamie said. "Please, if you're going to drive us, we need to go now. Where's your car?"

"It's right outside. By the curb. I'll get it and bring it to the door . . ."

"No," Jamie said. "Please don't leave me."

"I won't," Reynaldo said. And he meant it. "We'll go out together."

"Wait, I'm not ready." The thought of going back outside frightened her, and she began to choke.

"Are you all right? Do you want something to drink?"

"Yes, if you have . . ."

"What would you like?"

"Anything."

Reynaldo ran to the back of the room and stooped down to open the small fridge he kept stowed under the counter. It was Nada's job to keep it stocked for the customers, and, against his better judgment, he hoped that it would be. He swung the door open and found a half-used quart of milk, a leftover cheese sandwich, and an unopened can of Yoo-Hoo.

"Does this work?" he asked, holding up the Yoo-Hoo.

"That's fine."

Reynaldo jumped up on top of the counter and grabbed the lantern.

"Can you turn that off?" Jamie asked, peering outside the front window.

"Sure." Reynaldo turned off the lantern, the room went black, and Jamie felt as if she were again in the woods, alone, running.

"Take my hand," Reynaldo said.

Reynaldo waited in the dark, hand outstretched, but he didn't feel anything.

"It's okay," he said. "I'm going to help you."

He felt her hand press into his palm, and he tightened his fingers over it and opened the front door.

There were no approaching headlights. Everything was still, quiet. Reynaldo locked the shop door and pulled Jamie behind him toward his car. He clicked open the locks, which caused the car's interior light to go on, and he opened the passenger's-side door for Jamie, tossing his aunt's pocketbook, which she had forgotten, into the backseat. By the time Reynaldo got around to the other side, Jamie had turned Charlotte around so that she was sitting with her back toward Jamie's chest.

"Can I have the Yoo-Hoo, please?" she asked.

Reynaldo shook it and handed it to Jamie, who opened it and put it near Charlotte's mouth. She maneuvered the can opening so that it was against the girl's lips, which were unresponsive, and began to pour. Chocolate liquid spilled over Charlotte's mouth and clothes, but a few drops had gone in, because Charlotte coughed and pushed the can away.

"Please, honey, drink," Jamie said, bringing the Yoo-Hoo again to her mouth. Her hand was shaking, and Reynaldo reached over to help steady the can.

"*Carlota,*" Reynaldo said, gently. "*Carlota . . .*"

Charlotte's eyes opened, tiny slits of recognition, and she turned toward Reynaldo's face. Jamie put the can to her mouth. "Drink, baby, drink." But when Jamie poured, the liquid spilled again.

"Oh my God," Jamie said.

"*Espera!*" Reynaldo reached into the back seat and pulled Miss Beatrice out of his aunt's bag. "*Carlota . . . Mira!*"

The little girl's eyes opened and then grew wide at the sight of Miss Beatrice.

"MaBa . . ." the little girl said softly. "MaBa, MaBa . . ." Charlotte patted the doll's hair and rested it across her belly.

Jamie stared at Reynaldo in disbelief. "Who are you?" she asked.

"A friend," Reynaldo said and pulled into the street.

54

Phillip looked at the clock on his nightstand: 11:00 p.m. Time was running out. He had been lying in bed for the past few hours with the telephone in his hand, trying to decide what he'd say when they picked up the phone at Stanton. He'd never stayed an execution before, so this was going to be big news, and he envisioned the rampant speculation on the next day's news hours when Charlotte turned up unharmed hours later. Nothing he could say seemed believable or convincing enough, especially for a vocal, stalwart, card-carrying conservative like Phillip Grand.

The Executive Mansion was running on auxiliary power, and for a brief moment that afternoon, when the lights blinked off and then on again, Phillip thought the execution would have to be postponed and was terrified at the prospect of not knowing what that meant for his daughter's safety. But he realized that Stanton prison, even if on the same power grid as Albany County, also had supplementary electrical systems in place. The court-sanctioned killing of Gino Cataldi would go on as scheduled.

All afternoon, Lieutenant Governor Waxman Tanner had issued hourly press statements about the blackout and when power would be restored, as Phillip lay under his blankets, like a little boy who had been told to go to his room and think about what he'd done to deserve what was happening to him. Katherine had stopped in once or twice to check on him, carrying a sandwich both times, but he was standoffish and curt, and she took the hint, putting the meal trays on the table and leaving. They were still there untouched, the bread hard, the mayo soured, as Phillip had only one thing on his mind: Don Bailino.

Over the years, Phillip had watched Don rise up the ranks of the local business scene, but always from a distance. Following their discharge from the army in 1992, he and Don, having grown very close during their time in the service, had tossed around the idea of getting an apartment together downstate in one of the outlying boroughs of New York City. The idea had intrigued Phillip, who'd yearned for an adventure, a life away from the Grand legacy, but his father wouldn't hear of it.

"Do you know who that fellow's family is?" he had said. "Who they associate with?"

Phillip did know. Don had told him. They had talked about lots of things in the extreme heat of the constant desert sun when they thought that they would drop from fatigue, when they thought that they may not live to see another day. Still, feeling the pressure of being an only heir, Phillip obeyed his father. He and Don had that in common—they felt that overpowering need to make their fathers happy, two capable men trapped within a course that had been predetermined, including their enlistment in the military.

From that point on, the relationship had strayed. Years passed, and the contact dwindled. On the night Phillip was elected to the state assembly, his assistant had tapped him on the shoulder to tell him he had a call. "Who is it?" Phillip asked, champagne glass in hand. "Don Bailino," she said. A wave of nervousness overcame him. "Take his number, and tell him I'll call him back," he told her. But he never did. He'd kept that telephone number, scribbled on a piece of paper, in his desk drawer for years until he finally threw it away; he hadn't seen it again until it popped up on his caller ID two nights ago.

Although their paths hadn't crossed until Wednesday, it would be a lie to say that Phillip didn't think of Don often—he'd been an important influence on Phillip during the years they served together. It was Don who had counseled him when he'd hesitate during a shooting exercise at boot camp. "The people who die are supposed to die," he'd say. It was Don who pushed him to make a decision based on instinct rather than knowledge, a concept foreign to Phillip. Ever since, Don Bailino remained, hovering in the background of his life, silently influencing his political decision making, until Gino Cataldi decided to kill a fellow inmate while in prison, making him eligible for the death penalty—a core issue of Phillip's ascendance to the governorship. Phillip had pushed hard for capital punishment in the Cataldi case—harder than he ever had—and most political pundits assumed it had been to make good on the campaign promises that had gotten him elected. But Philip always wondered if part of the reason he doggedly pursued Gino's case was to banish the ghost of the man who, while once his friend and confidant, always made him feel like the lesser man in the room. On paper, Don Bailino had nothing on Phillip Grand—he dropped out of high school, lived a life on the streets in a forgotten section of Brooklyn, had a police record with a string of minor offenses—but in reality he was quite an extraordinary man. After all, it was Don Bailino who had saved his life in Iraq, a feat for which he earned the Army Medal of Honor, and as he lay in bed, Phillip also wondered if his taking on the Cataldi case was, at heart, some kind of perverse desire to see his old friend again. Although Bailino had visited Cataldi countless times at Stanton according to the prison logs, he never showed up in the courtroom or tried to contact Phillip after that phone call he made to his state assembly headquarters that first election night.

Since then, Phillip went out of his way to avoid crossing paths with his old friend, and he wasn't sure if it was out of embarrassment or fear. When Don's new Upackk factory opened last year and had gotten accolades not only from the trade but from Leadership in Energy & Environmental Design—a big to-do in today's eco-friendly world—Phillip had feigned a conflict and sent Tanner in his place for the recognition ceremony. Don was doing very well for himself, and although there was a part of Phillip that was competitive and jealous, for the most part he was glad. In the absence of a true relationship, with his only knowledge of Don Bailino coming from local or trade-press clippings or what he could glean online, Phillip found himself conjuring a new life for Don in his mind, one of the self-made businessman who was free from the constraints of his childhood and familial obligations. Phillip fantasized that Don had managed to do what he couldn't— escape the leash of his father. He imagined Don visiting old Gino Cataldi in prison more as an act of paying homage to his father than a harbinger of illegal activity, as the Feds would have him believe. Phillip was well aware that the government was keeping a close eye on Upackk and all of Don Bailino's business dealings, but until this point they had found nothing, and Phillip took that as a good sign that Don had left the bad behind. He probably would have lived the rest of his life under that delusion if he had not received that phone call Tuesday night.

Phillip got out of bed and walked toward Charlotte's nursery. The entrance had been cordoned off with crime-scene tape. He stuck his arm through, flicked the wall light switch, and peered into the empty room. The stuffed animals of the mobile over the crib, usually rocking in a gentle breeze, were still, the window closed. The familiar smell of baby powder and Desitin was faint.

He pulled the tape off the wall, each strand floating down and hanging along the doorframe, and stepped into the room. Out the window, he saw that the rain had stopped, and the picketers had grown in numbers as the clock ticked closer to midnight. Phillip watched the to-and-fro of the throng of people, thought of how small everyone looked from this high up, and wondered how Don had managed to pull this off. Had someone in the mansion betrayed him? He still didn't know.

A scuffle broke out among the picketers, resulting in a shoving match between two young women, one of whom was holding a sign that read, GOVERNOR GRAND: CAN YOU LIVE WITH THIS?

Could he?

Phillip picked up a framed picture that was sitting on a small table next to the crib. It was a photo he had taken of his wife and daughter immediately after the birth, at the moment the doctor had placed Charlotte on Katherine's belly for the first time. Katherine hated the photo—"Look at me," she'd said, "I look so fat"—and only kept it there because of Phillip's insistence.

"Katherine," Phillip muttered to himself, as he placed the frame back down. He thought about what his wife would say about the last-minute stay of execution. She'd know if he placed the call that something was wrong, and she wouldn't let it go until she knew what. And he could never tell her, because she wouldn't be quiet, she wouldn't sit on the sidelines and watch Don Bailino go unprosecuted for the kidnapping of her daughter. It would be a wedge between them for the rest of their lives, and that's assuming they would be lucky enough to live them.

"Phillip?"

Katherine was standing in the doorway to Charlotte's room. She held up her hand, which held the baby-monitor receiver; the transmitter was located near the crib, next to the photo he'd picked up.

"I thought I heard you call me," she said to her husband who, standing there in her daughter's room, looked sadder than Katherine had ever seen him.

Phillip opened his arms, that familiar, welcoming gesture he always made toward her, and Katherine ran into his arms.

"I'm sorry," Katherine whispered into her husband's ear.

"I told you. Nothing to be sorry about," Phillip said.

"It doesn't look good, does it, Phillip?" She held him tightly.

"Have hope, honey."

Katherine pulled away. "I do need to tell you something," she said.

Phillip looked at his watch: forty-five more minutes.

"Can it wait?"

Katherine shook her head.

"What is it?" Phillip sat down on the rocking chair.

Katherine held onto the crib. "This is difficult to say . . ." She took a deep breath. "A few months ago, I attended the opening of the Lystretta Gallery downtown. I'm not sure if you remember . . . You were committed to a dinner of some kind, and I'm not even sure I put it on your agenda. The place is so tiny, and it wasn't even that impressive of an exhibit, actually, but the owner of the gallery, Jim Lystretta, is a board member of the New York State Council of the Arts, and you're not the biggest arts supporter, so I thought I should make an appearance and dragged Maddox with me. Anyway, I had had a bad day, the teachers' union had been on my back, and I was in a foul mood, and . . ." She took another breath. "I was standing there looking at a digital painting, and . . . this man came over, and we started talking."

"Who?"

The vivid image of Don Bailino flashed through Katherine's memory, but she shook her head; she just couldn't tell him that part yet. "It doesn't matter. He just came up to me and introduced himself politely and started talking about that detestable artwork. We talked for about thirty minutes that night, far longer than I ever expected to stay there. And when we parted, he said that he enjoyed chatting with me and hoped he'd see me again sometime." Katherine frowned. "It seems so silly now."

Phillip shuffled his feet. "What are you saying, Katherine?"

"I'm saying that . . ." She paused. "I'm . . . saying . . . that . . ."

"Are you telling me you had an affair?"

"No, I did not." She looked Phillip in the eye. "I. Did. Not."

"Then what are you saying?"

"I'm saying that it was . . . unexpectedly . . . nice."

"All right," Phillip said. "So you had a conversation with a man in an art gallery, and you liked it." He smiled. "Katherine, that's okay."

"But that's not all."

"It's not?" Phillip's smile faded.

"A few days later, he called the switchboard and asked for me and left his number. I called him back from my cell phone, and we talked a bit. Although I wasn't doing anything wrong, I knew it was wrong. It *felt* wrong. He asked if I'd like to meet him for lunch. Apparently, there was another gallery opening somewhere."

"What did you say?"

"I told him no."

"Did you want to go?" Phillip fumbled with the phone in his hands. Katherine shook her head.

"But you liked him?"

Katherine shrugged her shoulders. "I think I liked the attention." She crouched down in front of her husband. "You know, most men are afraid of me . . . I can't imagine why."

Phillip laughed.

"I love you, Phillip. I just need you to know that. You do know that, don't you?"

Phillip nodded. "Yes, and I've loved you from the moment you stormed into my life." He kissed his wife on the mouth. "Maybe it's my fault. Since Charlotte came . . ."

"It doesn't matter," she said. Under normal circumstances, Phillip volunteering to shoulder the blame for another person's indiscretions would infuriate Katherine, but this time, when those indiscretions had been her own, she felt comforted and protected. "As long as we can get past this."

"I think so." He smiled. "Baby steps."

There was a loud cheer from the crowd outside, a collection of diverse faces lit up by the line of street lamps along Eagle Street.

"Looks like the power's back on," Phillip said.

"There's actually something else I have to tell you . . ."

"Katherine . . ."

"I mean, no, this is something different entirely. But come with me downstairs." Katherine held his face in her hands and ran her thumbs over his graying eyebrows. "You've been up here all night and haven't eaten a thing." She smiled. "I found a box of Oreos hidden in the pantry. You can dunk while I talk."

"I will." Phillip looked at his watch: 11:30 p.m. "But just give me a few minutes first."

"Okay," she said. "I'll wait for you in the kitchen."

As Katherine went downstairs, Phillip hurried to his private office across the hall and shut the door. *Just stay the execution*, Phillip told himself. *Don't give a reason. Just do it, and worry about the rest later.* He dialed the Stanton death house.

"Hello, this is Governor Grand," he said into the telephone, just as his cell phone vibrated in his pants pocket.

55

The appeals process in the United States was not only expensive, but time-consuming. The procedure took so long that nearly a quarter of deaths on death row in the United States occurred from natural causes. Gino remembered when triple-murderer Joe Stock had arrived on death row at Stanton in the late 1980s, far earlier than Gino had; Stock awaited execution for more than twenty years—He finally died of heart failure at age ninety-four.

Gino stood shackled before the execution chamber, four Department of Corrections officers, including Hank, around him. Three years earlier, New York had implemented lethal injection as its primary method of execution after protestors sought to rid the state of its electric chair, citing "cruel and unusual punishment." Gino was surprised to learn there were still states, like Utah and Oklahoma, which, not very long ago, used firing squads as their form of execution. Although lethal injection was now the primary method, inmates who were sentenced to death in those states before the new law was enacted had the option of dying at the hand of a row of gun-toting do-gooders. *Now there was a way to go,* Gino thought.

Like virtually all capital punishment states, New York used three drugs in its lethal injection executions: sodium thiopental, a fast-acting sedative; pancuronium bromide, which caused paralysis; and potassium chloride, which caused cardiac arrest. When it was reported recently that the lone US manufacturer of sodium thiopental had decided to halt production—and the European company asked to step in as supplier would not sell the drug to the US if it was to be used in executions— Gino thought perhaps the firing-squad option would be on the table. But that smarty-pants Phillip Grand, in anticipation of a possible shortage, had stockpiled sodium thiopental and apparently had enough to carry New York State's capital-punishment program into the next decade, maintaining lethal injection as the quickest, cleanest method of ridding the world of its undesirables; the whole process was said to take less than ten minutes.

For the last twenty-four hours, security had been so tight that Gino couldn't piss without an audience, making him feel like some inadvertent performer, and he longed for the virtual solitude of his six-by-six death-row cell. Gino knew that Grand, even with his daughter in jeopardy, would wait until the very last minute to make a decision—the governor was a master of debating issues not only in the courtroom but in his own mind, and Gino had no doubt that the phone call would come in the execution room.

The officers led Gino to a sterile gurney in the center of the small room, where a thick, heavy curtain had been drawn across a panel of four long windows, behind which were seated, Gino assumed, the witnesses— an assortment of people that most likely included family members, his and his victims'; law-enforcement officials; and curiosity freaks who just signed up to watch this sort of thing. Inside the room, in addition to the prison staff and his assigned priest, there were several people he didn't recognize, and Gino wondered who among them was the civilian executioner whose name Bailino had been unable to determine. *You don't know how lucky you are, buddy,* he thought to himself.

"Lie back, please," the prison warden said.

Gino complied, and the guards began fastening the thick leather straps to his body. The guards moved in step, and as they circled the gurney to check one another's work, he caught the eye of Hank, who nodded. They swabbed his arms with alcohol and inserted two IVs, one in each arm. Gino knew only one was needed; the other was a backup—no reason to let an air bubble hold up an execution. He found it humorous that such precautions against infection were being taken while putting a man to death, although the routine was probably done more to protect the prison personnel. When the guards were done, there was an annoying squeak as the curtain was opened, revealing rows of solemn faces, both men and women, sitting on tiered seats as if at the opera. Gino scanned the crowd and thought he recognized a few individuals from the trials, but was thankful that Leo and ToniAnne had stayed away.

The warden stepped forward. "Gino Cataldi, you have been sentenced to death by lethal injection. Do you have any last words?" he asked.

As if on cue, the red phone—direct line to the governor of New York—rang.

A man, who had been standing next to the red phone for the very purpose of answering it, looked for a moment as if he didn't know what to do. He picked up the receiver.

"Yes, Governor," he said and listened. His eyebrows furrowed.

A smile crept over Gino Cataldi, as he thought of how they'd write about him in the history books—the first stay of execution of Republican governor Phillip Grand's tenure. He thought of Grand's tea-party constituents going nuts, considering all the time and taxpayers' money he'd spent to put Gino there, and of the conflicted man on the other side of the telephone who had to choose between the death of a man he detested and the death of the daughter he loved.

The man hung up the phone and took a step forward.

"The governor said he sees no reason for this execution to not take place as planned," he said and returned to his place next to the red phone.

The men in the room looked at one another. The phone call had created an odd twist to an otherwise routine procedure and had caused mild confusion among the usually unflustered prison personnel. But they continued as if nothing had occurred.

The warden repeated: "Any last words, Mr. Cataldi? . . . Mr. Cataldi?"

The tautness of the leather straps tore into his wrists and ankles. The room lost its air. Gino looked through the thick windows of the execution room and, for the first time, wished he could see a familiar face on the other side of the glass.

"Gino?" the warden asked again. Then, with a slight nod, he stepped away from the gurney.

"Son of a bitch," Gino muttered to himself as the first plunger, filled with sodium thiopental, fell.

56

"Where are you?" Phillip asked, dialing Detective Nurberg on his other line.

"We are on our way to the police station," Reynaldo said into Rosalia's phone, which he'd found at the bottom of her pocketbook underneath Miss Beatrice. "Phillip Grand's private line" was listed fourth on her contact list.

"No!" Phillip shouted into the phone. The governor stood up, his face red. "I don't know if that's the safest course of action. That's what he'd expect."

"Who?" Reynaldo asked.

"I'm dialing Detective Nurberg. He'll tell us what to do. Stay on the line, please. Is my daughter all right?"

"She seems fine. Jamie has her."

"Who has her?"

"She's okay," Reynaldo stressed, looking over at Jamie, whose eyes were glued on him. "Please, governor, the police station is only a few miles away. We need to know if you want us to go in another direction."

"Hold on, it's ringing, but no one is answering. Damn, the call went to voice mail." Phillip ended the call and redialed. The ringing was distorted, and Phillip stood closer to the window, hoping that would give him better reception. The phone rang and rang on the other end, and just as Phillip feared he'd get voice mail again, the ringing stopped.

"Hello? Hello?" Phillip said into the phone, but he couldn't hear anything. "Nurberg? Can you hear me? If you can hear me, my daughter is safe and in a red Escort on its way to the police station on . . . hold on . . ."

Phillip spoke into his cell phone. "Reynaldo, where are you? . . . Going south? Okay, hold on . . ." He switched back to the cordless and gave the car's location. "Should I have them keep going? . . . Hello? Nurberg?" The line was dead. He picked up his cell phone.

"Reynaldo, I lost Nurberg . . . Reynaldo?"

But the cell-phone screen showed that the call had ended.

57

"Hello? Hello?" Reynaldo yelled into the phone.

"What happened?" Jamie asked, adjusting the seat belt across Charlotte's chest.

"I don't know. Reception's still iffy. Might have hit a dead zone." He put the phone down on the console between them.

"What did the governor say? Can we go to the station?"

"I don't know. He didn't get a chance to say."

"Shouldn't we call him back?"

Reynaldo was looking into the rearview mirror, scrutinizing it in a way that looked as if it were a riddle that needed unraveling.

"What's the matter?" Jamie asked.

"I think somebody's following us."

The words floated to Jamie as if in slow motion, their meaning coating her in a thick blanket of alarm. She held Charlotte tighter to keep her own body from shaking and turned around slightly to peek behind them. "I don't see anyone," she said.

"The headlights are off."

Jamie watched Reynaldo's eyes jump from the mirror to the road and back to the mirror. "What kind of car is it?" she asked.

"I don't know. It's hard to tell."

She took a breath. "Is it a Ford Flex? A truck? Is it white?"

Reynaldo looked into the mirror and then at Jamie. "Yes, it might be."

Jamie's eyes grew wide, and that was all the confirmation Reynaldo needed. He slammed his foot onto the accelerator, the wheels sliding on the slippery pavement, but within seconds the Ford Flex was right behind them, crossing the double yellow line and coming up on the left-hand side.

"Go faster!" Jamie yelled. "Please!"

"Hold on," Reynaldo said, jamming on the brakes and forcing the Escort into a vicious skid. The Ford Flex also came to a screeching halt, but not before Reynaldo was able to turn left onto an unpaved side road. An avid bike rider, Reynaldo knew these streets, most of them not even found on maps of the area, like the back of his hand, but it didn't take long for the white truck to recover and follow behind.

The narrow lane rocked the Escort, which was no match for its jagged, rocky terrain, over which the Ford Flex seemed to glide with ease, coming steadily toward them. Reynaldo glanced at Jamie who, despite the hard bounce of the car, had Charlotte tucked under her arms, her legs planted on the dashboard, her head bent down so that her hair fell around the little girl as if it were a protective seal.

Up ahead, the Albany County Bridge came into view behind the racing trees, and Reynaldo made a quick right onto an even narrower bike path hoping to use the smallness of his car as an advantage against the goliath following behind. Branches slapped and scraped against the windows as Reynaldo careened through the thicket of trees, jumping from one path to another, hoping to slow down the truck or perhaps force it into a ravine, but the Ford Flex seemed undeterred, following like a hungry predator intent on reaching its prey, the beams of its headlights framing the Escort's every move. Reynaldo made a hard left, turning toward the paved road once again, and sputtered his way around a short guardrail and up onto the wide street. He started for the bridge just as the Ford Flex crashed through the rails behind him, its brakes screeching with anger.

"C'mon, c'mon," Reynaldo said, the accelerator pedal pushed to the floor as the Escort spit and choked before again picking up speed.

The crisscrossing metal grid of the bridge reflected the pairs of headlights in every direction as both cars barreled onto it, Reynaldo desperately trying to keep the car from hydroplaning, realizing that his tires were now caked with mud. He stayed in the center, riding the double yellow line, so that the white car couldn't come up beside him, but the Ford Flex slammed into the Escort from behind, causing Reynaldo to lose control of the car, which crashed into the bridge on its right side, sparks flying as it bounced against the rails. Instinctively, Reynaldo threw his arm across the front seats over Jamie and Charlotte, bracing for another impact, but instead the truck spun and swerved across the double line, colliding with the guard rail on the other side about twenty feet behind.

"Are you all right?" Reynaldo asked Jamie as the Escort thudded to a stop.

"Where is he?" is all Jamie could muster, unlocking her arms from Charlotte, and for the first time Reynaldo heard the wails of the terrified little girl who sat shaking in the space between Jamie's knees.

Reynaldo turned around and saw that the Ford Flex was facing backward, its driver's side smashed in, the bulb of the left taillight exposed. There wasn't much time.

"Get out, Jamie, go. Run. *Run!*"

Jamie tried her door, but it was crushed by the impact with the bridge. "It's jammed. It won't open."

Reynaldo undid the passenger's-side seat belt. "You have to let go of Charlotte," he said.

"Why?"

"Please. You have to trust me."

Jamie released the screaming little girl, and Reynaldo pulled Jamie across his chest and pushed her out the driver's-side window headfirst. He reached for Charlotte, who was crawling on the floor trying to get Miss Beatrice, but Reynaldo grabbed her by the legs and placed her into Jamie's waiting arms.

"Go! Now!"

Jamie ran, and Reynaldo turned off his headlights and switched his interior light on, hoping to distract the man—the "he," Reynaldo surmised, that Governor Grand had been alluding to—in the Ford Flex, hoping he had not seen them leave the car. He watched the idling white truck in his side-view mirror until gunshots shattered the Escort's back window, and Reynaldo threw himself down across the front seat as the truck slammed into the driver's side of the Escort, pushing it further against the edge of the bridge, before speeding past toward Jamie and Charlotte.

"Son of a bitch," Reynaldo said. He tried to get up, but his left leg was pinned under the dashboard. With a quick jerk, he got it loose and, ignoring the pain, tried to open his car door, but it was completely disfigured by the crash, metal jutting up in all directions. Reynaldo wiped the large pieces of broken glass from his clothing, crawled across the seats to the other side, and shimmied out the passenger's-side window, balancing himself on the wet rail—the same one he had stood on only two days before. As he pulled his sore leg out, his foot caught on the passenger's-seat headrest, and Reynaldo fell forward, pain piercing his leg as he dangled off the side of the bridge.

Jamie heard Reynaldo scream, but was afraid to look behind her and, squeezing Charlotte tighter in her arms, kept running as fast as she could, the toes of her bloodied feet getting caught inside the grooves of the metallic grate of the roadway. The headlights of the Ford Flex were bearing down on her like the piercing eyes of a wild animal, her silhouette lengthening in their bright glow, the roar of the engine ricocheting along the metal bridge. Just as it felt as if the truck were going to mow her down, Jamie reached the end and ran off the road as the car screeched to a halt.

Without the headlights lighting her path, Jamie stumbled into the weeds and fell, bending her knees to keep from crushing Charlotte beneath her. The low hum of sirens filled the air. She picked up the little girl and kept running, ignoring the strong ache in her right knee, ignoring the cuts and bruises that seemed to be everywhere. The ground squished under her bare feet, and Jamie was afraid she was going to run out of land and have to dive into the cold water once again—she didn't know if Charlotte could manage another arduous swim.

A flashlight was searching the dark, heading in the direction of Charlotte's screams.

"*Shhh . . .*" Jamie said and fell with Charlotte again into the mud.

She scrambled to get up, pulling at the muddy little girl who kept slipping out of her arms, but her foot tripped on a patch of twigs, and she fell again, this time on her side. She and Charlotte landed in a puddle when the flashlight shone on her face.

"Ma'am, are you all right?"

"Leave me alone," Jamie said, grabbing Charlotte.

"Ma'am, my name is Detective Matrick. I'm with the Albany Police Department. Are you okay?"

Jamie shielded her eyes from the bright beam. "This is Charlotte Grand," Jamie said breathlessly, holding the little girl up. There were more flashing lights in the distance, swarming like a bunch of large fireflies.

"Yes, we know," the detective said. "The governor called and told us you had contacted him. He also alerted the Feds, and we were able to track the GPS of the phone number belonging to the cell phone you were using."

"It wasn't my phone." Jamie looked back toward the bridge.

"Mr. Rodriguez is all right. He's very lucky. His leg got caught inside his car, which probably kept him from falling over the guardrail. He's being taken to the hospital." The officer crouched down. "Stay put, we have a gurney coming for you and Charlotte. It'll be here momentarily. Ma'am . . . what's the matter?"

Jamie was looking toward the road, filled now with police cars, fire trucks, ambulances, and other vehicles, except the one she expected to see, a white Ford Flex. It was gone.

58

"**M**a'am?"

Katherine opened her eyes. Special Agent Wilcox was tapping her shoulder.

"Ma'am, we found your daughter. She's okay."

"What?" Katherine bolted upright, and a sharp crick throbbed at the base of her head. She must have fallen asleep at the kitchen table waiting for Phillip to come down, but he never had—the box of unopened Oreos was still on the table.

"Where's the governor?" she asked, rubbing her eyes.

"He's on his way to the hospital. He asked me to bring you there to meet him."

Katherine stopped rubbing. "Why didn't he wait for me?" she asked.

"I don't know, Ma'am. He was very excited, and agitated, upon hearing the news and said he needed to get there right away. He made it clear that I escort you there myself immediately. If I may?"

Wilcox helped Katherine up from the seat.

"But . . ."

"Please, we'll talk on the way." Wilcox led Katherine toward the main hallway where dozens of agents were congregating. Maddox was talking into his cell phone near the front entrance. When he saw her, he waved and rushed over.

"Lenny, did you hear?" Katherine asked.

"Yes, yes, I know," Maddox said. "They say she's all right.

Some cuts and bruises, but all right." He took Katherine's hand and squeezed it.

Outside the Executive Mansion, the media was in a frenzy, buzzing outside the gates like agitated bees in a hive. At the sight of Katherine Grand within the narrow front door opening, they looked as though they were ready to attack. Katherine thought there was something different about the crowd, and she realized that virtually all of the picketers were gone.

"What time is it?" she asked. "Did the execution . . . ?"

"Please, talk and walk, talk and walk," Wilcox said, ushering Katherine out the front door. When she stepped onto the front porch, there was an immediate roar:

"Mrs. Grand?"

"How do you feel now that they've found your daughter?"

"Where do you think she was all this time?"

"Are you going to see her now?"

"Can you give us a statement?"

Katherine felt a hand on her shoulder.

"I got this," Maddox said. "Go to the hospital."

"Mrs. Grand, please, quickly, we need to go." Wilcox hurried down the pathway toward a waiting sedan and several agents.

"I'm coming," she said. She turned to Maddox. "Lenny, the execution, Cataldi . . ."

Maddox nodded. "Done."

"Oh." She had missed it. For the first time since she and Phillip had been together, she was not by his side when a capital-punishment case had come to a close.

"Katherine, are you all right?"

"Yes, I'm . . . I'm fine."

"Are you going to the hospital, First Lady?"

"Is the governor there?"

The crowd surged against the iron gates, outstretched arms holding microphones waving through the bars.

"Jesus," Maddox said. "Bunch 'a animals."

"Mrs. Grand," Wilcox called. He was holding open the passenger's-side door to his sedan.

"Yes, I'm coming," she yelled. She turned toward Maddox and instead banged into Henry, who seemed to have appeared from out of nowhere.

"Henry!" Katherine was confused. With the blaring lights of the news media, it was easy to forget what time it was. Henry normally didn't work at night. "Why aren't you with Phillip, I mean, Governor Grand?"

"One of the men, down over yonder," Henry pointed to Wilcox, "that one there, he said one of his men was going to drive the governor to the hospital." Henry had a very slow way of talking, and Katherine felt her anxiety ratchet up a few notches. She had no idea how Phillip put up with it. Maddox was rolling his eyes.

"Then what are you doing here?" Katherine said.

"Well, I had been hanging around to see if Governor Grand needed me, you know, just in case. But seein' as he's got a ride, I figured I'd go home and come back tomorrow morning." Henry shuffled his feet. "I also wanted to tell you that I heard the news about Charlotte and how very happy I am that she is okay."

"Thank you," Katherine said.

"No, I mean, I am really, really happy." Henry looked as if he was going to lean in for a hug until Maddox put a hand on his shoulder.

"Yes, she heard you," Maddox said. "That's awfully nice of you."

Katherine thanked Maddox with her eyes, as Henry nodded and shuffled off down the path toward the parking lot.

"What the hell is he doing here, anyway?" Maddox said. "Isn't Big Bird looking for him somewhere on Sesame Street?"

"I don't know. I can't think right now, Len."

Katherine was dizzy. The camera lights. The yelling of the press. The guilt over Don Bailino and of not having told Phillip the entire truth. The news that he had left without her. She held onto Maddox's arm to steady herself.

"Are you sure you're all right?" Maddox asked. "Maybe I should meet you at the hospital. It might be a madhouse there."

Katherine knew she should have told Maddox to go home and get some sleep—he was as tired as anyone. But for the second time in a few hours, another person had volunteered to help shoulder some of her burden, and she was relieved once more. "Would you mind?"

"Not at all."

"Lenny . . ."

"I know . . . What would you do without me? Now go."

"Thank you," Katherine called, as she ran down the path and stepped into the waiting sedan. She watched Maddox stride toward the hungry crowd as a cacophony of flashbulbs lit up the night and followed their car halfway down Eagle Street until it sped away.

59

When Phillip arrived at Albany Memorial Hospital, a horde of press people already had assembled outside the main doors under the large overhang, the television camera lights illuminating the building's stately marquee.

"Drive around back," he told the federal agent.

It had taken them more than forty-five minutes to reach the hospital for a ride that was normally less than half the time. Between the flooding and the blackout, there were accidents all along the main roads, holding up traffic for miles and forcing them to take side roads, which weren't much better. Originally, Phillip had wanted to drive himself, but Special Agent Wilcox wouldn't hear of it. "This isn't over, Governor," he'd said—a grim reminder of what Phillip knew to be true. His daughter had been saved, but Don Bailino was still at large. What that meant, Phillip wasn't quite sure, but for now he knew he needed to get to his daughter.

The agent parked next to a pair of ambulances, and Phillip got out and rushed through the automatic doors.

The bustling emergency ward was crowded with strange, foreign faces, and the thought that Bailino could be inside the hospital suddenly crossed Phillip's mind. He looked behind to see if the federal agent was in tow. He was.

"Governor!" a nurse said, snapping to attention. A hush fell over the room.

"My daughter, I'm looking for my daughter."

"Yes," the nurse said, placing a handful of files onto a desk. "I'll bring you to her. Come this way."

The nurse pushed a large button, automatically opening two swinging doors that led into an empty side corridor, which spilled into a large room filled with hospital workers as well as uniformed police and other plainclothes officers. Phillip recognized many of the men and women as agents from the mansion, which put his mind a little more at ease, until from the corner of his eye he saw a dark-headed figure start toward him.

"Governor Grand!"

Rosalia came running with outstretched arms, but was stopped by one of the officers.

"It's all right," Phillip said.

"Is it true?" Rosalia asked, her angelic, worn face fervent with anticipation. "On the news, they say Charlotte is okay."

"Yes, she is. I'm going to see her now."

"*Ay! Dios mío!*" Rosalia said. Her children, Rikki and Terry, appeared behind her, along with Pedro and Ricardo; all four were drinking sodas and were looking frantically around the room until they spotted Rosalia.

"Mama, I told you not to leave the chair," Rikki said, but then noticed Phillip and her demeanor softened. "Oh, I'm sorry, Governor," she said and curtsied.

"*¡Ella está aquí!*" she told them. "*Carlota.*"

"*Sí?*" Pedro asked.

"Your nephew is a hero, Rosalia." Phillip put his hand on her shoulder. "Where is he?"

"What do you mean?" she asked. "Rey?"

"They said there was a car accident," Pedro said. "He's in the emergency room, but they won't let us in yet."

"Sir?" the nurse interrupted. "Right this way."

Phillip nodded. "I have to go, Rosalia. I will be in soon to see Reynaldo." He started toward the nurse, but on the other side of the room Katherine appeared in a doorway escorted by Special Agent Wilcox.

The animated buzz died down slightly at her entrance, and

Katherine nodded at no one in particular, as if to give the illusion that someone had gone out of his or her way to greet her. She scanned the large room until she saw the tall frame of her husband sticking out among the swarm of people.

"Katherine!" Phillip called. "Here!"

Katherine made her way through the crowd. She was still wobbly from the ride over when Wilcox had filled her in on the details of what had happened, that Charlotte had been found in the hands of a woman from Long Island as well as the nephew of her housekeeper. Katherine was about to pronounce a hearty "I knew it" when she was told that the pair had saved Charlotte, not snatched her, and that as far as they could tell the kindly, sweet old housekeeper was just a kindly, sweet old housekeeper, and that the man they were looking for, the one who had masterminded the entire kidnapping, had been identified as Don Bailino.

The name was still ringing in her ears when Phillip reached for her hand. "Are you okay?" he asked.

She nodded, wanting the first words out of her mouth to be "why didn't you wait for me?" but instead only asked, "Have you seen her?"

"No, not yet."

"Oh, Mrs. Grand . . ." Rosalia pounced on Katherine, throwing her large arms around her with glee. "Our little girl is safe!"

"Yes, yes," Katherine said, standing stiff while the housekeeper slobbered all over her. Rosalia bounced around the hospital room, her joy palpable, believable, causing smiles everywhere she turned, even among the usually grim federal agents. Katherine could already feel the conflict building up inside from the moment Wilcox said in his sedan, "You must be so happy to know that Charlotte is safe." And there it was, the expectation of a big, emotional reunion between grieving mother and lost child, the coming together of the most natural pair in the history of the world. For a woman who could turn any situation into a public-relations event, and probably had, Katherine didn't know how to be, what to do, and being face-to-face with the woman who made her feel most inferior as a mother was not helping bolster her confidence. She was relieved to see Maddox walk into the room.

"Lenny!" she waved.

"Where the hell is hospital security, that's what I want to know," Maddox said in a huff. "I could barely turn into the ambulatory lot, and are those reporters supposed to be so close to hospital grounds like that? Where's Charlotte?"

"Come, we're going now," Phillip said.

Phillip, Katherine, and Maddox followed the nurse away from the busyness of the main room to a private examination suite guarded by two officers. Jamie was sitting at the far back on a cot with Charlotte on her lap, and she was stroking her hair as a doctor pumped up a blood pressure band around the little girl's arm. Charlotte had a bag of potato chips hanging from one hand and Miss Beatrice from the other. When Jamie saw the governor and Mrs. Grand approach, she stood up.

"Hi," Jamie said, and for the first time in several days, she felt awkward holding the little girl. "She's okay, I think . . . I wouldn't give her to anyone else."

Charlotte's eyes grew wide upon seeing the governor.

"Da Da Da Da," she said, dropping the potato chips onto the floor and reaching out her arms, Miss Beatrice dangling by a single strand of yarn from between two of Charlotte's grubby fingers.

"My girl . . ." Phillip swooped down and swung Charlotte in the air and then brought her down into a giant hug. She felt wonderful in his arms, like a radiating ball of love. "Look at you." He kissed her forehead, her cheeks, her neck. "You look so big. Doesn't she, Katherine?"

And filthy, Katherine thought, nodding. A half-hearted sense of relief settled upon her, seeing her daughter once again in her husband's arms and knowing that Charlotte was, indeed, safe and seemingly unharmed, but Katherine still felt as if she were atop a rocky precipice. One false step . . .

Sensing her ambivalence, Phillip took Katherine's hand, placed it over the little girl's hand and cupped his on top, reminding her of a huddled football team strategizing before a big play.

"It's going to be okay," he whispered, taking Charlotte's hand and slapping it lightly against Katherine's cheek. "Ma Ma Ma Ma," he said, making Charlotte laugh.

"Phillip, stop," Katherine said quietly, embarrassed. "Not here."

"Mo Mo Mo," Charlotte said, bringing the fingertips of her hands together.

Phillip leaned in so that Charlotte could tap Katherine's cheeks and then wrapped his arms around his wife as the others in the examination room smiled.

"Hello, I'm Leonard Maddox, Governor Grand's press secretary." Maddox said, walking over to Jamie and breaking the silence.

"Jamie Carter." Jamie shook his hand.

"Jamie Carter, you saved my daughter's life," Phillip said.

"I don't know. I'm starting to think she saved mine."

Looking at the little girl happy in the governor's hands, Jamie felt a pang of bereavement. She wondered how Charlotte would remember her one day, if at all: Jamie had gone from being a protector in an awful circumstance to being a reminder of it now that it was over, and while she felt sad at the prospect of never seeing Charlotte again, she could understand if that was what the governor decided was best for his daughter. Bailino had been right: loyalty wasn't as clearly defined as she once thought.

The doctor stepped forward. "Governor, my name is Doctor Tucker."

"Yes, doctor, how is she?" Phillip extended his hand.

"Well, I did a preliminary exam of Charlotte, and, frankly, she seems fine. It's quite remarkable, actually, after all she's been through. A little dehydrated and undernourished, but other than that, I'd say she's perfectly healthy."

"That's wonderful news!" Phillip said, lifting Charlotte into the air and eliciting a string of tired giggles from the little girl. "We can take her home then?"

"You sure can."

"What about Ms. Carter?" Katherine asked.

"Yes, I'm okay. Thank you." Jamie touched the bruises on her face. "They look worse than they are."

"The man who . . . had Charlotte . . ." Phillip started.

Jamie shook her head. "I don't know what happened to him. He's gone." She tried not to think about that and just revel in the happiness of the moment, a reunited family, a safe place, but there was something hidden in the governor's gaze that brought to the surface what she had spent the last few hours trying to suppress—the prospect of a future where Don Bailino could jump out from any corner.

"Have you spoken to the police?"

Jamie had. She told them everything she knew. She thought about what Joey had asked her, if she could keep quiet, and decided that she couldn't. "They want me to come down to the station for more questioning and, well, because they're worried about my safety . . . You know, since they can't seem to find him, Don Bailino."

Katherine flinched again at the mention of his name, when Special Agent Wilcox came into the room.

"Any news, Agent Wilcox?" Phillip asked.

"We sent agents to his house, Don Bailino, the log cabin. He wasn't there, which really wasn't a surprise." Wilcox shook his head. "But we found the body of Detective Mark Nurberg at the side of the house, in front of his car. He had been shot in the forehead."

Small gasps filled the room as the governor bowed his head, his thoughts turning to the boyish face of the detective. He wished he could take back the hostility he had felt, and inadvertently showed, toward Nurberg, who had only been trying to do his job when it was Phillip himself who had been the one with something to hide.

"Why would he be there?" Katherine asked.

"I don't know," Wilcox said. "There were two other men found at the scene as well. Also killed. Based on Ms. Carter's story, we've been able to identify them as Tony Seti and Benjamin Bracco."

"But I don't understand. I had just spoken to . . ." Phillip remembered the phone call to Nurberg, the silence on the other end. His heart sank.

"Sir?" Wilcox said.

"When Reynaldo called me, I called Detective Nurberg to ask him what to do, where I should have Reynaldo take Charlotte."

"You called him before me?" Wilcox asked. "Nurberg had been taken off the case."

"I know, I know . . . I guess I wasn't thinking clearly. And I thought we had a bad connection, and I gave him the location of Reynaldo's car."

"Do you think Nurberg could have been working with . . . Don Bailino?" Katherine asked. It was the first time she had uttered his name; it felt sour on her tongue. "And perhaps they had a falling out?"

Phillip again thought about the earnestness of Nurberg's face in the Drawing Room when he had questioned Phillip about his little trip to Taryn's Diner. He found it hard to believe that Nurberg had been involved.

"We just don't know yet," Wilcox said.

"Bailino left every day," Jamie said. "But I can't say for sure who he was meeting with."

"His nephew—or whoever he is—Joey Santelli, Gino Cataldi's grandson, is here at the hospital." Wilcox said. "He's being guarded on the off chance Bailino tries to visit him."

"What happened to him?" Jamie asked. During the police officers' questioning, she had faltered somewhat when they had asked about Joey, not knowing exactly how to explain his involvement. Children, of course, couldn't help the families they were born into, but did that excuse his complicity? And while she knew that it was, at least in part, because of Joey that she had made it out of the river alive, was that enough for her to keep quiet?

"He was found by the river, a few miles down from the log cabin by some vacationers who got stuck out in the water when the rainstorm started. The doctors said he was in bad shape when he got here, but he's in stable condition now."

Det. Grohl of the Albany Police came into the room. There was a sadness in his eyes that hadn't been there when he had questioned Jamie earlier that morning; she imagined it was a result of hearing the news about the detective in his department. "Excuse me, Governor, Mrs. Grand, I need to take Ms. Carter to the station for additional questioning."

"Like hell you are," Katherine said, stepping in front of Jamie. Her voice, in the somber room, came across as an irritated meow, as if she were an idle cat who just had a shoe thrown at her. If Jamie had detected any sadness in the detective, it quickly dissipated. "Mrs. Grand, it's procedure."

"Don't you think she's been through enough?" She turned to Jamie. "Where is your family, dear?"

"I've been trying to reach my brother Edward but . . ."

Jamie stopped talking at the sight of Bob, who walked into the examination room escorted by an officer. He wore plaid pajama pants and a T-shirt, with an overcoat wrapped around him, as if he had just woken up. "Bob?"

"Jamie, what's going on?" Bob looked around the room, his eyes landing on Phillip and Charlotte Grand. "Governor?"

"Mr. Scott," Phillip said, surprised. "This is a bit of an odd coincidence meeting you for the first time and then seeing you again the same day."

"This is my wife." Bob pointed to Jamie.

"You're kidding," Maddox said.

"Ex-wife," Jamie corrected.

"Well, your ex-wife helped save the governor's daughter," Maddox said.

"Serious?" Bob wondered how he'd pegged the wrong Carter as the knight in shining armor. "How did . . . ?"

"What are you doing here, Bob?" Jamie asked. She felt as if she had aged six years since the last time she had seen him, which was only four days before.

"The police called my cell phone and told me you were here. I guess I'm still listed as your husband."

"No, I mean, what are you doing in Albany?"

Bob had been asking himself the very same thing all night. "It's a long story," he said. "Where's Edward?"

"What do you mean?"

"Isn't he here? He told me he was driving to Albany."

"When was this?" Agent Wilcox asked.

"Um, Wednesday night was the last time I spoke with him," Bob said. "Why?"

"He's not picking up his cell." Jamie said. "Maybe he went home?"

"We contacted Edward's home address," Wilcox said, "and spoke to a woman named Tricia."

"That's my sister-in-law."

"She said Edward is here, in Albany, looking for you, and she hasn't spoken to him in over twenty-four hours."

Bob looked confused. "I thought he had a meeting with the governor."

"Why would he meet with me?" Phillip asked.

All eyes were on Bob, the consummate litigator and orator, who decided the only appropriate thing to do was to shrug his shoulders and be quiet.

Jamie broke the silence. "Why isn't he picking up his phone then?" She sat on the hospital bed.

"Don't worry, Ms. Carter, cell phone service has been very haphazard with the storms," Maddox said. "It's quite possible that he hasn't been receiving any messages."

"But he must have seen the news," Jamie said.

"That settles it," Katherine said. "Ms. Carter, you're staying with us. At the mansion."

"That's not a bad idea," Phillip said.

Det. Grohl stepped forward. "I'm afraid I don't like that idea at all."

"Pardon me," Katherine said, "Detective . . ."

"Grohl, ma'am."

"Grohl . . . Pardon me if the idea of the watchful eye of the Albany Police Department doesn't give me a warm, fuzzy feeling inside. Personally, I don't think your department is capable of keeping a hamster safe, let alone this young woman."

"Katherine . . ." Phillip said.

"Especially when Detective Nurberg was apparently working with the other side."

"Now, wait just a minute." Grohl, a short man, raised himself off his heels so that he was an inch or two taller than the First Lady.

"That's impossible. And, Mrs. Grand, no disrespect, but this Don Bailino somehow managed to get into the mansion before. Who says he wouldn't be able to do it again?"

"Not with my men there, Detective," Wilcox said.

"The mansion has been checked and rechecked and has a gazillion agents patrolling the rooms," Katherine said. "That's the safest place for Ms. Carter to be."

"Thank you, Mrs. Grand," Jamie said. "That's a kind offer, but I really just want to go home."

"I can take you home," Bob said. At this point, he was more than happy to leave.

"Ma'am, that's not a good idea," Wilcox said. "Do you think Don Bailino knows where you live?"

Jamie panicked, remembering her resume and her portfolio. Don Bailino knew more than where she lived. Much, much more. "Oh, God, he knows everything. What about Tricia? The kids?"

"I've already sent someone to the house from our downstate bureau," Wilcox said.

"Come home with us, dear," Phillip said. "You can try to get a few hours of rest while the Albany police and Agent Wilcox's men look for your brother. It really is the least we can do."

Jamie looked at the little girl in the governor's arms who was leaning her head on her father's shoulder, comforted by her father's hold, his smell, his voice. She had to admit, she felt rather safe with him too. "All right," she said. "Thank you."

"Good," Phillip said. "That's settled."

"I'll have one of my men take you to the mansion, Ms. Carter," Wilcox said.

"She can ride with me," Maddox said.

"Lenny, you look exhausted," Katherine said. "You really should just go home."

"And do what?" he said with a smile.

"That's fine," Wilcox said. "I'll have one of my men ride with you."

"All right," Maddox said.

"Perhaps I should stay at the mansion as well," Bob offered.

"I don't think that'll be necessary, Mr. Scott." Wilcox patted Bob on the back. "I know how to reach you if we need you."

"Remember, I have your card," Phillip said.

"Yes, apparently, you were right, Mr. Scott," Katherine said. "I have to give you credit. The abduction of Charlotte *did* have something to do with Gino Cataldi."

A feeling of pride swept over Bob, who forgot he was standing in a room with the governor of New York while wearing a newly bought pair of pajamas that still had the squares of fold marks on the legs and a bathrobe with the insignia of his hotel. He had unraveled the mystery after all. *Sir Robert Scott*, he thought and walked a little taller in his slippers.

Maddox buttoned his overcoat. "Do you want to give the press a photo op before we go, Katherine?"

Orchestrating a photo op would be vintage Katherine Grand, the happy family reunited, but for the first time in her professional career, perhaps in her entire life, she just didn't have it in her. She slipped her hand around Phillip's arm. "Not tonight, Lenny. Can you take care of it?"

Maddox nodded. "I'll be right back."

There was applause when the Grands left the examination room. Phillip held up his hand to quiet the crowd. "Thank you, everyone. Thank you for all of your help during this time. We really do appreciate . . ."

"*Carlota!*" Rosalia came running upon seeing the little girl in the governor's arms.

Charlotte instantly brightened. She put her hand to her forehead and then pushed it outward as if she were saluting, and Jamie recognized the American Sign Language gesture for *hello*. Rosalia responded in kind.

"Oh! Look at you! You're so beautiful." Rosalia fussed over the little girl, who clapped her hands and then straightened her little body so that she could be put down. The governor placed her on the floor and held out his hands of support for her, but Charlotte pushed them away and took one, and then another, wobbly step toward Rosalia on her own.

"*Dios mío! Mira!* Reynaldo! She's walking!" Rosalia squeezed the little girl's cheeks. "Oh, I've missed you."

Reynaldo was sitting in a wheelchair that looked too small for him, his gawky body spilling out of it, his left leg elevated and extended. His eyes twinkled as he watched the little girl dance before his aunt, who had begged to stay after he was discharged so that she might get a glimpse of Charlotte. Reynaldo was happy to oblige, as he was hoping to get a glimpse of someone as well.

"Are you all right?" Jamie said, walking over to his wheelchair.

"Broke his leg," Pedro said, sitting on Reynaldo's lap. "Very painful." He stuck out his hand. "Hi, I'm Pedro."

"And I'm Ricardo." Ricardo barreled into Pedro, nearly tipping over the wheelchair. "But you can call me 'Ricky.'"

"*Basta.* Enough." Reynaldo gave his brothers a light shove until they both tumbled onto the floor. "It's just a sprain, they said. And a muscle tear. It's not broken. I'm going to be all right."

"Oh, I'm so glad," Jamie said. "I just wanted to . . . thank you . . . for everything." She took Reynaldo's hand and shook it. "I don't know what I would have done without you."

"You're welcome," he said, squeezing her hand.

"*Ay*, does your face hurt?" Pedro asked.

"It's not as bad as it looks," Jamie said.

"That's good, because it doesn't look bad," Reynaldo said with a wink. His smile tightened. "Did they find him?"

"No," Jamie said, as Phillip, with Charlotte again in his arms, came up from behind.

"Reynaldo Rodriguez, you are a hero."

"Not me. Jamie's the hero." Reynaldo shook the governor's hand. "Governor Grand, you need to find that man. He's dangerous."

"I know," Phillip said. "They're looking for him. And they'll find him."

Again, Jamie thought she could see doubt within the governor's calm assurance.

Maddox returned from outside.

"How did it go?" Katherine asked.

"Did the standard," he said. "Said Mom, Dad, and Baby Grand are all doing fine. Said they will get police updates when they become available. Blah blah."

Wilcox stepped forward. "Governor Grand, whenever you're ready. You and Mrs. Grand are riding with me."

"Ms. Carter?" Maddox said.

"Yes, I'm ready," although Jamie realized that she was still holding Reynaldo's hand; it was calloused, but felt big and warm.

"Are you going home?" Reynaldo asked.

"No, I'm staying here for a little while at the Executive Mansion."

"Good," Reynaldo said. "You will be safe there."

"Get some rest," Jamie said with a smile.

"You too," he said and reluctantly let go of her hand.

"Ba Ba Ba Ba," Charlotte said, waving her hand.

Reynaldo waved back. "Good-bye, sweetie."

"*Adios, Carlota.*" Rosalia blew kisses at the little girl as the governor carried her away. "I see you soon."

"*Hermano, hermano . . .*" Pedro said, sitting back down on Reynaldo's lap, as they watched the Grands and their contingent leave. "Ooh, you like her, eh?" He punched him on the shoulder. "She's cute, eh? At least I think she's cute under those boo-boos."

"She is a beautiful, strong young woman," Rosalia said and grabbed Reynaldo's cheeks. "And you, *you*, are a hero and saved my little girl." She kissed him on his forehead.

"What about me?" Ricardo asked.

"What *about* you?" Pedro said. "Aunt Ro said *hero* not *zero*."

"Shut up," Ricardo said and threw a light punch at Pedro, who ran behind Reynaldo's wheelchair. They began circling it like dogs chasing their tails until Rosalia took Ricardo's arm.

"*Ah, sobrino.*" Rosalia pinched Ricardo's cheek. "You are brave too," she said, slipping her arm under Ricardo's and grabbing Terry's hand. "My family is here. My family is together. Come, Rikki. Pedro, help your brother."

"I am, *Tía*, I am." Pedro began pushing Reynaldo's wheelchair. He bent down next to Reynaldo's ear. "Geez, Rey, you gotta lose a few pounds, no?"

Reynaldo was still watching the hospital exit where Jamie had left.

"Rey, what's the matter?"

"I don't know," Reynaldo said. "I have a bad feeling."

60

The streets were slick, but clear and well lit as the sedan made its way along the main roads toward the Executive Mansion. Katherine and Phillip were seated in the backseat behind Wilcox and another agent, who were talking animatedly among themselves, going over the details regarding the search for Don Bailino. Charlotte had fallen asleep on Phillip with Miss Beatrice in her arms. Maddox's car followed behind with Jamie in the front seat and an agent in the rear. She waved. Phillip waved back.

"We got very lucky that it was Ms. Carter who had our daughter," Phillip said to his wife. "She's a very brave woman. What she did was very courageous. There are not many people who double-cross Don Bailino and get away with it."

Katherine was staring out the window. She had heard all the stories of Don Bailino told by Phillip over the years, of the war, of his family's relationship to the Cataldis, of Phillip's hope that Bailino had freed himself from all the bad to become a pioneer of industry. And when Bailino approached her in the Lystretta Gallery that night, he was the epitome of the American Dream—there was no sign of the down-on-his-luck kid from the streets, only an amiable, smart, successful, and highly respected businessman. How foolish she felt to have been swept away by his confidence and presence, the ever-suspicious Katherine Grand bamboozled by a charming smile and a handsome face. She wondered if part of the reason was that she too believed that people could change given aspiration, hard work, and a moment of opportunity, that they could erase past mistakes and rise above their station. As she had.

"Katherine?"

What would have happened if she had met Bailino that second time when he had asked her to attend the gallery opening, Katherine wondered—would *she* have been the one with the cuts and bruises on her face and who knows where else? As savvy and clever as she was, would she have been able to save herself, let alone an infant? She would never know. But she knew that if she told Phillip all of this, he would still look at her the way he looked at her now, like she was the most amazing woman he'd ever met. And she planned to tell him. One day.

"I have something to tell you," she whispered.

"Okay," Phillip whispered back.

Katherine opened her pocketbook and took out the wrinkled paper bag. She reached inside and pulled out the pregnancy test. "It's positive," she said, showing it to him.

Phillip stared incredulously at the small device.

"What can I say?" Katherine shrugged her shoulders. "You married an overachiever."

"Katherine . . ." Phillip leaned over, and the two embraced as Charlotte stretched her arms between them. As Phillip kissed his wife's forehead, he caught Wilcox looking in the rearview mirror. The agent pulled the car over onto the side of the road.

"It's all right," Phillip said, wiping a tear from his eye. "Everything is all right."

"No, it's not." Wilcox said. "Maddox's car is gone."

61

"What's the matter?" Jamie asked.

"I don't know, there's something wrong with the acceleration," Maddox said as the car came to a slow stop. He reached under his seat and, in an instant, pulled out a handgun and shot the agent in the backseat three times. The shots, muted by a silencer, sounded like firecrackers popping under a tin coffee can, and Jamie screamed as blood spattered throughout the car.

"Shut up," Maddox said, holding the gun on her. He turned off his headlights and made a quick left down a side road as the car carrying the governor and Mrs. Grand disappeared from view.

Jamie pulled on the door handle, but it was locked.

"Where are we going?" she asked.

"Shut up, I said," Maddox said. "Where do you think we're going?"

He sped down the road for several miles and then pulled off into a small clearing in a wooded area behind a deserted playground, one of those old-fashioned ones with metal swings and monkey bars and concrete grounds. Behind the picnic area, the parking lot was vacant except for one vehicle: a white Ford Flex.

"No!" Jamie screamed. She kicked Maddox's gun out of his hands and jumped into the backseat, but Maddox recovered and held the gun on her.

"You bitch," he barked. "Show your hands. Now!"

"Why are you doing this?" she asked, raising her arms in the air.

"None of your goddamn business," he said.

The slumped agent's walkie-talkie crackled.

"Don't touch it," Maddox said. "Keep those hands high."

"They're going to be looking for us," she said. "You're not going to be able to get away."

"I don't see what you mean," Maddox said, with a smile. "Don Bailino hijacked the car along the way, shot the federal agent and told me to drive here. Then he dragged you into the car and drove off. Of course, then I called the police immediately."

"That seems a bit farfetched."

"For a man who was able to sneak an infant out of the heavily guarded Executive Mansion and then pick up his nephew in midtown Manhattan the same day?" Maddox snickered. "I don't think so."

"You helped him kidnap Charlotte? A baby? What kind of person are you?" *Keep him talking,* Jamie thought, as if the words would slow down time.

"He was never going to hurt the girl. Until you came along. You became quite the plan spoiler. You and that ex-husband of yours. I almost choked when he showed up at the mansion with his bright ideas. If you hadn't managed your little getaway, I do believe next on Don's agenda was to do away with the confident Mr. Scott." Maddox smiled. "I can still see the governor's face when I told him that Scott thought the kidnapping had to do with Gino's execution. Priceless. But he held it together. And Katherine . . . Don was right. She was clueless."

Through the misty car window, Jamie saw the door of the Ford Flex open, and Bailino's unmistakable figure stepped out, lit by Maddox' headlights. As he approached the car, a familiar terror seized her, and she began pulling fruitlessly on the door handles.

"You know he's going to kill you," she said. "Don't be stupid."

Maddox laughed. "My dear, he's going to kill *you.*"

Without taking his eyes off Jamie, Maddox rolled down the driver's-side window. "As promised, Mr. B . . ."

Maddox never saw the bullet coming.

Jamie shrieked and threw herself onto the car floor, slapping off the pieces of flesh that had flown into her hair.

Bailino leaned down so that his face was visible through the car window. He rapped on the glass. *Knock, knock, knock.* "Did you really think I wouldn't find you?" he asked, his breath fogging the window in a small circle.

Jamie lay still at the bottom of the car.

"Open the door."

Jamie didn't move.

"*Open the fucking door!*" Bailino thundered.

"I can't," Jamie cried. "It's locked."

Bailino reached into the front window, pressed a knob that unlocked all the doors and took a step back.

"Open . . . the . . . door," he said again calmly.

Jamie reached up and pulled on the handle and pushed the door. It opened slightly, but because Maddox' car had been parked on a slight incline closed again.

"Jesus Christ." Bailino pulled the door open. "Get out."

Jamie struggled to her feet, her legs refusing to budge, but Bailino reached in, grabbed her by the hair and pulled.

"Please, I'm coming!" Jamie's scalp felt as if it were on fire. "Don't!"

"It's too late for that." Bailino dragged her to the wet ground. "Let's go. Get up! Get . . . UP!"

Jamie got on her knees and pushed herself up off the ground using her hands. It took all the strength she could muster to look Bailino in his eyes, which were ablaze in a way she had never seen before, not when he killed the blonde girl or wrestled with Leo, or when he raped her. There was a wildness that had replaced the methodical fury.

"Let's go," he said, pushing her toward the Ford Flex, the end of the gun in the small of her back.

Jamie looked around, but there was nothing and no one to help her. "I had to save that little girl," she said. "Can't you understand that?"

"I told you I wasn't going to hurt her."

"I couldn't take that chance." She tried to turn around, but Bailino pushed her forward and said, "Don't. Keep moving."

"Are you going to kill me?" she asked.

Bailino smirked. "That's a funny question to ask a man who was just told that he couldn't keep his word."

"You just killed Leonard Maddox, the man who helped you."

"Leonard Maddox was a second-rate spin doctor who sold out the only friends he had in the world for money, and not a lot of it. There's another little lesson in loyalty for you." Bailino turned Jamie around. "What about the man who helped *you*? Who's the Hispanic guy in the Escort?"

"Just some guy who found us."

"What's his name?"

"I don't know."

"Wrong answer." Bailino shoved Jamie hard in the chest with the tip of the gun, and she stumbled backward onto the wet, rocky ground. "His name is Reynaldo Rodriguez, the nephew of Rosalia Garcia, housekeeper and nanny to Charlotte Grand. Does that joggle your memory?" Bailino asked, the anger returning to his voice. "Or should I say, the soon-to-be-former Reynaldo Rodriguez."

"He was just trying to help us." Jamie stood back up and tried to regain her footing, but it was difficult. Although one of the nurses at the hospital had treated the bottoms of her feet and given her a pair of flip-flops to wear, some of the bandages had unraveled, exposing her sores. Still, she turned and faced Bailino with as much strength as she could muster.

"Keep walking," he said.

"Are you going to kill me?" she asked again, without moving.

"No, no . . . Now's not the time to be brave."

"Am I supposed to die?" She felt a sort of wildness overtake her as well. "You told Joey the people who die are supposed to die. Am I supposed to die?" Jamie thought she saw a glimmer of tenderness in Bailino's eyes, but then it was gone.

"Move" was all he said, motioning to his car, which was a few feet behind her. "Get in."

Jamie hesitated.

"Don't be stupid. Get into the fucking car."

"I can't . . ."

In a flash, Bailino grabbed and twisted Jamie's arm behind her back until the pain caused her to drop again to her knees. He held her there and opened the trunk, the small corner light revealing a black tarp. Bailino ripped it off, and lying there at the bottom, hog-tied and gagged, was Edward.

"Edward!" Jamie cried. Edward's face was badly bruised, and he was red and sweating and having difficulty breathing.

"Get in the car," Bailino said. "*Now.*"

Edward shook his head vehemently and muttered underneath his gag, when Bailino shot him in the shoulder, and he screamed a horrible, muffled sound, writhing in pain.

"Nooo!" Jamie said. "I'll go. Please, please, don't. Leave him alone."

Bailino let go of Jamie's arm, and she ran to the passenger door of the Ford Flex and climbed in. As Bailino slammed the trunk closed and walked around to the driver's seat, she reached under her shirt, into the front of her jeans, and plucked out the federal agent's handgun. She had never fired a gun before and prayed that the safety, whatever that was, wasn't on, and as Bailino opened his door she planted her feet against the dashboard, braced herself, and fired.

The bullet hit Bailino's shoulder, and he fell back, buffered by the car door, and Jamie shot again, this time into his chest, and he dropped to the ground. She held the gun steady in front of her, watching Bailino's legs, making sure he was down for good, and climbed into the driver's seat and stepped out of the car.

Bailino was clutching his chest, where Jamie had shot him right in the center; the other wound was gushing blood in short spurts. Jamie kicked away his gun, which had fallen out of his hands, and held hers on him as headlights passed over them, the roar of car engines and sirens replacing the damp quiet.

Bailino's eyes remained fixed on Jamie's as he coughed and tried to speak, but his words were gurgling. He spit out a mouthful of blood.

"Am I supposed to die?" he asked her. A small smile formed in the corners of his mouth and he started to laugh, and then choke.

Jamie's arms shook, but she held the gun steady.

Then Bailino turned serious, as his eyelids began to flutter. "I . . . I . . ." His breath came in staccato bursts. "I love you," he said as a series of shadows blocked his face from the glare of Maddox's headlights.

62

The beeping of the heart monitor was competing with Edward's snoring for hospital-room domination, the latter winning by a landslide. The familiar drone was comforting to Jamie as she stood in the bright room, in a newly bought pair of jeans and black T-shirt, looking out the window. The glass, speckled with the remains of past rainstorms, had an unexciting view of the parking lot, but it didn't matter—Jamie had gained a late appreciation for the mundane.

She had been told by hospital personnel that the camera crews had been camped out in front of the hospital since the night they'd first brought her in three weeks ago, and she imagined that's where they'd stay until Don Bailino was well enough to be transferred to a federal prison facility. After undergoing immediate surgery to remove the bullets and repair one of his lungs, which had collapsed, Bailino was admitted to Albany Memorial among widespread speculation that he wouldn't make it through the night. Medical experts had predicted pneumonia as well as other complications that were common among patients who had initially survived gunshot wounds to the chest, but Bailino had confounded doctors with a steady recovery. The surgeon's words had stayed with her: "The bullet caused severe tissue damage, but the integrity of Mr. Bailino's heart is intact." Now estimations were that he could be out in as little time as a month if his respiratory therapy continued to be as successful as it had been.

Bailino's room was located on the far side of the hospital, in the west wing, under twenty-four-hour surveillance, and Special Agent Wilcox stopped by Edward's room nearly every day to give Jamie an update on Bailino's status and also to reassure her that, should Bailino survive—and all indications pointed to his doing so—she and her family would have ongoing federal protection until his trial, when, he said, Bailino was sure to go "straight to prison, no question." With her testimony, of course, Jamie thought, as she watched a pigeon try to perch on a ledge that had metal prongs. Based on Jamie's information, the police were able to find the body of Inga Tyler, the blonde girl who worked at the Exotica Strip Club, and they also took Joey into custody once he was discharged from the hospital. About a week after his arrival, Edward had been cleared to talk to the police about what happened and managed to clear Nurberg's name in time for the young detective's funeral—a solemn ceremony attended by hundreds of law enforcement in full uniform from across the state.

Edward's snoring stopped as he changed positions, his bandaged shoulder protruding upward as he rested on his side. Jamie adjusted the blankets over him before she sat in what had become "her chair." Like Bailino, Edward had been rushed into surgery when he arrived at the hospital; Bailino's bullet had fractured both his shoulder blade and collar bone, requiring two surgeries—for which first Governor Grand and then Jamie donated blood—and he too would be receiving intensive rehabilitative therapy once he returned downstate. Today, fingers crossed, Edward would finally be able to go home.

Jamie checked her cell phone to see if Tricia had texted her—she had gone downstairs to get some drinks for the ride home and to call her mother to check on the kids—but there was only one text message, and it was from Bob, who was "just checking on things." Jamie had become far more interesting to Bob these days than she had been in a long time—perhaps than she'd ever been—since her photo and life story had become fodder for the morning news shows. She noticed the time on her phone and turned on the small television hanging from the ceiling, a high-pitched whirr filling the air. She flipped the stations until she saw the familiar front porch, rosebushes, and lush grounds of the Executive Mansion, her home away from home these past three weeks.

Governor Grand, who had taken a self-proclaimed *staycation* following the return of Charlotte, stepped forward on the television screen to a podium positioned a few feet in front of the towering, historic sugar maple tree. He had announced to Katherine and Jamie at breakfast that morning, in the disjointed silence between bangs of Charlotte's spoon on her high-chair tray, that he was ready to resume his gubernatorial duties and had scheduled this short press conference on the mansion grounds, allowing only a handful of news media inside the gates to operate the news feed. Two days later, he and Katherine planned to announce the news of the pregnancy. They never spoke a word publicly about the kidnapping.

"Good morning," said the governor, who was wearing a polo shirt, unbuttoned at the top, and khakis. *"I will make this brief. It is with great pride that I announce the following names to the inaugural Brightest Minds Legal Roundtable of New York State, an idea first proposed nearly a year ago—and was snickered at in a way that has become commonplace in the very unilateral political climate across the nation. But since our announcement, we have received thousands of applications from lawyers and all varieties of legal authorities throughout all sixty-two counties. I've always envisioned my tenure as governor as one of inclusion, not exclusion, no matter how diametrically opposed our political stances. To you who have been selected, I hope to have many lively debates and do great things together. Congratulations to the following . . ."* The governor pulled out a set of index cards. *"From Albany County, Doug Pritcher of Mann, Thomas & Webber; from Alleghany County, Dale Berner of Aster, Walker & O'Connell . . ."*

Jamie lowered the volume so that it didn't wake up Edward. She picked up her phone again and thumbed through her applications, clicking onto her photo gallery. A bunch of saved photos popped into view, and she clicked on them one by one: Peter and Sara at Jones Beach; Edward barbecuing spare ribs in his backyard . . .

"From Hamilton County," the governor read, *"Susan Keener . . ."*

. . . Jamie and Edward wearing matching bowling shirts; Edward sticking his tongue out; Jamie and Sara showing off red, white, and blue pedicures; a sunset at Eisenhower Park; a photo of her and her mother, her favorite one from when she was a little girl; and then there was a photo that Jamie had never seen before: a close-up of her sleeping on her side, with Charlotte Grand, also asleep, tucked under her chin, a blanket pulled neatly over them.

"From Nassau County, Tim . . ."

A text came in from Tricia: "Coming back up."

"From New York County, Robert Scott of Worcester, Payne & Leach . . ."

Jamie was sure Bob had set his DVR to record this morning's press announcement, even though he had no idea he'd been selected; the governor suggested they "let him sweat it out." She imagined he would spend the rest of the day eating in and playing the recorded segment over and over.

"Knock, knock," said a friendly voice.

Reynaldo, carrying a bouquet of flowers, limped in, favoring his left leg. He was told repeatedly that his leg injuries sustained during the car crash on the bridge would heal faster if he would remain on bed rest; however, Reynaldo balked, telling the doctors that he had done enough lying down to last a lifetime. In the past several days, he had even begun leaving his cane at home.

"Hi," Jamie said, sitting up, her lips meeting his. Without either of them thinking much about it, she and Reynaldo had fallen into an easy and comfortable courtship, one that filled Jamie with warmth, as if she had drunk a hot cup of cocoa at the sight of him. She had forgotten she could feel this way with a man. The relationship was just in the budding stages and felt almost like a middle-school romance—hand-holding, flowers, a kiss on the mouth here, a hand on the hip there. It was like starting over again. Although she knew what people said about the doomed nature of relationships formed during duress—she had even written a freelance article about it once for a psychology trade publication—and on a rational level she knew she should probably just be alone for a while, considering all that had happened, she felt herself drawn to Reynaldo and decided that she was tired of feeling empty inside. She decided to let herself indulge her emotions to see where they led her.

Reynaldo rubbed her face. "The bruises are just about gone."

Jamie felt her cheeks turning red as Reynaldo placed the flowers on her lap. "A going-away present," he said, frowning.

"When are you coming down?"

Reynaldo ran his hand through Jamie's hair, curling several strands around his finger. "I'll be down in a couple of weeks, as soon as I get Pedro up to speed." He looked at Edward. "How is he today?"

"A sleepyhead," said Jamie, mussing up Reynaldo's lush curls. He had a habit of wetting down and taming his luxurious hair when he came to see her—she could still see the wavy tracks of comb's teeth. Jamie much preferred it wild and erratic, and she made a mental note to tell him one day.

Doctor Tucker knocked on the door. "Good morning."

"Good morning," Jamie and Reynaldo said in unison.

Doctor Tucker was in his civilian clothes today—a pair of khakis and a white polo shirt. He hadn't bothered with the white lab coat. He had the day off but insisted on coming in, in hopes of seeing Edward, his favorite patient, get discharged. Edward had that effect on people, even as a boy. More than one schoolteacher had pulled Jamie's mother aside during parent/teacher conferences and back to school nights to wax poetic about the young man who not only scored straight A's, but was always kind to and supportive of his fellow students.

"Good news, Jamie," Doctor Tucker said, flipping through a series of papers on his clipboard. "As I had anticipated, your brother is stable enough to be transferred to a facility downstate, and very soon, he'll be going home."

"That's great," Tricia said, walking in. She looked refreshed, and Jamie could tell she had applied some makeup and brushed her hair, which was now pulled back in a neat ponytail. Tricia arrived immediately after Edward had been admitted and stayed for about a week until Edward insisted that she go home for a few days, get some rest, and be with the kids. She drove back and forth three or four times since, each time escorted by one of Special Agent Wilcox's men, who would be a familiar sight in the weeks, perhaps years, to come. Tricia had arrived yesterday, spending the night on the other side of Edward's hospital bed in what had become "her chair" right opposite Jamie's. "The kids can't wait to see him."

"Well, they won't have to wait much longer," Doctor Tucker said.

As if on cue, two orderlies arrived, amiable men whom Jamie had seen chatting up the nurses in the cafeteria.

"Please take Mr. Carter to Ambulatory," Doctor Tucker instructed. It was odd for Jamie to hear him refer to Edward by his last name; he had dispensed with the formalities not long after they arrived at the hospital.

"Right now?" Jamie asked.

"Yep, you're going home." Doctor Tucker looked as if he were about to break into his customary wide smile, but Jamie thought she saw something cut it short when he looked at her.

The team of men wasted no time and lifted Edward, using his bedsheet, which they unhooked from its hospital corners, and placed him, like a baby swathed in a sling, onto the gurney. It looked as if Edward might sleep through the entire transfer—like a child who has fallen asleep in his car seat and wakes up in his crib—when he opened his eyes.

"What's going on?" Edward asked, unsettled.

"Easy, easy," Doctor Tucker said. "You're fine. You're going home."

His eyes gaining their focus, Edward looked around the room. "Where's Jamie?" he asked.

Every time Edward awoke from a nap over the past three weeks, he asked for his sister.

"Right behind you," Jamie said, winking at Tricia.

"I'd better go," Reynaldo said. He leaned down and kissed Jamie's cheek. "I'll call you later, okay. Have a safe trip."

"Okay." Jamie gave him a hug. "See you soon."

"That's right, with me laid up, I'll need you to take care of her," said Edward, smiling. He reached out and shook Reynaldo's hand. Edward seemed to have accepted Reynaldo immediately. Jamie imagined that Edward saw the same goodness in him that she had seen. Or maybe Edward was just happy that Bob was finally gone.

She playfully rolled her eyes. "I can take care of myself."

"It's useless, Jamie," Tricia said. "You thought he was overprotective *before* . . ."

"Nah, I know you can, James," Edward said. "Maybe that's what I'm afraid of."

Doctor Tucker handed Jamie some of Edward's discharge paperwork. She had been Edward's power of attorney since the day her mother died. And vice versa.

"I'm perfectly capable of signing my own paperwork," Edward said, raising his arm, but then stiffened.

"No, that's all right," Doctor Tucker said. "You go. We'll take care of things here. And I expect a full recovery, young man."

"Thank you, Doctor Tucker."

"You're welcome."

"And don't take too long," Edward said to Jamie as the orderlies maneuvered the gurney out the door.

"I'll be right there," Jamie said.

Tricia threw her handbag strap over her shoulder and took the drawings and cards that Peter and Sara had made for Edward down from the wall. Jamie surveyed the room, which had been filled with flowers when Edward first arrived—gifts from the Grands; the Garcias; the Manhattan DA's office; Worcester, Payne & Leach; her aunt in Arizona; and all sorts of well-wishers. Weeks later, nothing was left but a white-bloomed gardenia, which arrived accompanied by a plush monkey wearing a "get well" T-shirt. Tricia picked it up.

"I'll see you downstairs," she said. No sooner had she rounded the corner of the doorway did Jamie hear Edward bellow, "Where is she?" from the corridor.

"She's coming, *Big Brother*," Tricia's voice echoed in response. "Here, hold your monkey."

Jamie smiled at Doctor Tucker. "I guess some things never change," she said with a shrug. "Where do you need me to sign?"

"Oh." Doctor Tucker appeared lost in thought. He indicated the signature lines. Using the flat surface of Edward's tray table, Jamie signed and dated the forms as Doctor Tucker gave her some instructions regarding Edward's care. She handed him the paperwork.

"Jamie, there's actually another matter I'd like to discuss with you."

"Sure, what is it?"

The doctor seemed troubled, at a loss for words, unlike the self-assured, good-natured man who had gotten them through these last few weeks. "It's rather difficult to say . . ."

"About Edward?"

"No, no, Edward is recovering nicely. There will be lots of rehabilitative therapy, of course, and hopefully he will regain much of his flexibility and strength. This actually has to do with you."

"Me? How do you mean?"

"Well, you understand that for your brother's transfusion that all donated blood had to be subjected to a series of tests so that we could check for a variety of infections," he faltered, "you know . . . so we could keep your brother safe."

"Yes, I understand." The gravity of what the doctor was trying to say began to weigh on her. "Did you find a problem with my blood?"

"Not a problem, exactly . . ."

He put his hand on her arm. It was the first time that Jamie could remember that Doctor Tucker, for all his kindness, had made physical contact with her; she flinched at its unexpectedness, and a memory came to her: When her nephew Peter was three years old, she and he had been walking in Eisenhower Park on Long Island after a game of miniature golf. A small sparrow came to perch on top of a nearby bench, and Peter had screamed, terrified, at the sight of the tiny thing; the startled bird flew away immediately, but Peter was inconsolable. "There's nothing to be afraid of," Jamie said. "It's only a bird. It can't hurt you. Look around. They're everywhere. No one else is afraid." But Peter shook his head and said, "No one else sees the danger. Only me."

Jamie looked past Doctor Tucker through the rain-speckled glass window. Across the parking lot stood the towering west wing of Albany Memorial Hospital where, somewhere, up on the third floor, healing on a hospital bed, was Don Bailino. She had spent many nights, in the relative quiet of the hospital, looking out that window and wondering if the fear and the anxiety would ever go away. Since Bailino's arrest, everyone—Wilcox, Governor Grand, Mrs. Grand, Reynaldo, and Edward among them—had been assuring Jamie that Don Bailino would no longer be able to hurt her, that she would be safe, have protection. Years later, her nephew, who has learned that birds cannot hurt him, still flinches when a sparrow flies too close. And for the first time, Jamie felt as if she knew why. *No one else sees the danger.*

But if she had learned anything during this time, it was to take things day by day, to trust herself and hope for the best, to learn from mistakes and try again. She imagined that trauma did that for people, reminded them of all that they had instead of the things that they lost. She remembered her mother's words: "You don't always need a doctor, or people, to tell you what's going to happen, sweetie. Some things you just know." Jamie knew that despite all the assurances there was still a real danger out there, but she hoped that by concentrating on the good, the bad could one day fall away. And she hoped that she could one day live a life free from fear. In the meantime, she would keep trying.

Jamie put her hand over Doctor Tucker's, which was still on her arm. "It'll be all right. Whatever it is," she said. And she meant it.

Then Doctor Tucker said the unexpected words, and everything changed.

"You're pregnant."

THE END